Praise for *The Wilding*

"At the core of this powerfully written first novel about a father-son-grandson hunting and fishing expedition into the mountains of central Oregon stands an old theme in American fiction: the test of ordinary folks against the wilderness. . . . Percy writes a clean, clear, muscular sentence. . . . And he delineates his characters with a knife-sharp psychological edge." —Alan Cheuse, *All Things Considered,* NPR

"An urgent and haunting look at the darker side of our nature and at our often futile attempts to control and manage the natural world. . . . Percy's vivid, direct prose style gives *The Wilding* a sense of immediacy that builds from the first sentence to the last." —*The Kansas City Star*

"Percy tells his adventure story in prose that doesn't pound its consumption themes into your brain; instead, his writing is as natural, dark, and deep as the woods he writes about. At 31, Percy is as promising a writer as anyone on a certain New York magazine's list of promising writers under 40." —*The Boston Globe*

"*The Wilding* exhibits the broad range of ambition expected of the debut writer: a keen and almost preening attention to language, a careful consideration of character, a nod towards the political and worldly and an attempt to tackle issues of the greatest moral importance. . . . *The Wilding* emerges as a creative, unique and deeply thought-provoking. More so, it speaks of an author with many more tricks up his sleeve." —*BookPage*

"Vested with the darkness of Percy's previous work, *The Wilding* is a conglomeration of almost clashing juxtapositions: A failing marriage. Big land deals. A bizarre fetish. A miscarriage. A marauding grizzly bear. . . . Percy gathers up the threads of these cheerless, fearful lives, dissatisfied with themselves and their families, angered by the sense their existence is meaningless, and spurs them to destiny." —*The Oregonian*

"Percy excels in placing his characters at their limits, and in describing their internal thoughts and external actions in his prose. . . . The story of a man going into the woods and coming out changed is a classic narrative that has persisted from the time of ancient myth. . . . *The Wilding* follows this tradition and updates it with great skill."

—*The Dallas Morning News*

"Equal parts grit, subtlety and a silver-tongued bravura. . . . Few writers under forty are doing what Percy is doing stylistically, which is producing a silky prosaic style blended seeming effortlessly with the rugged and savage ways of the wild. . . . Percy is the only author today giving [Wells] Tower a run for his money as *the* contemporary American short story writer." —*The Rumpus*

"Percy's excellent debut novel . . . digs into the ambiguous American attitude toward nature as it oscillates between Thoreau's romantic appreciation and sheer gothic horror. . . . A taut plot and cast of deeply flawed characters—Justin is a masterwork of pitiable wretchedness—will keep readers rapt as peril descends and split-second decisions come to have lifelong repercussions. It's as close as you can get to a contemporary *Deliverance*." —*Publishers Weekly*, starred review

"*The Wilding* is tense and compelling, described as a possible 'eco-novel,' yet never didactic. It is, rather, a persuasive and terrifying peek into the nature of violence, well worth the risk of a sleepless night."

—*The Literary Review*

"Percy's writing is filled with astonishingly precise images. . . . A rich and beautifully brutal book." —*Time Out Chicago*

"Percy skillfully limns the psychic wildernesses of his characters even as he paints a vivid image of central Oregon's high desert, the impact of development, and the divide between capitalism and conservation. . . . [*The Wilding*] draws readers in and holds them in its grasp." —*Booklist*

"[Percy's] sentences have the simplicity and beauty of Shaker furniture, but he also writes meaty action scenes that never feel like they depart from the book's emotional core."

—David Abrams, *Barnes & Noble Review*

"A powerful book packed with tension, unease, and life at the edge of the forest. . . . What Benjamin Percy does in *The Wilding* is remind us of ourselves, who we really are, intelligent beasts, and with that comes a certain responsibility, and a grace, a reverence for how we got here."

—*The Nervous Breakdown*

"Percy's novel perfectly captures our ambiguous attitudes toward the natural world, the tensions between rural and urban, the way untamed wilderness carries both grace and terror." —*High Country News*

"There are a hundred ways to feel frightened and lost in a forest, and the excellent, savvy Benjamin Percy can evoke them all. *The Wilding,* a brilliant literary novel that feels at times almost like Geoffrey Household's classic *Rogue Male,* seems to have been written on his vibrating nerve endings. This book is filled with dread, sadness, tension, and a tireless vision of mankind's thoughtless devastation of an ancient and more authentic way of life. It is almost impossible to put down. James Dickey must have been whispering to Ben Percy in his sleep." —Peter Straub

"Benjamin Percy's *The Wilding* is a tour de force meditation and treatise on the nature of violence, the violence of nature, man in the wild, and the wild in man—cleverly disguised as a page-turning adventure. Not just a 'must' read, but a *need* read, this book is timely, terrifying, terrific."

—Antonya Nelson

"Not your father's eco-novel. In compelling, image-driven prose, Benjamin Percy confounds the old polarities about wilderness and development by sending three generations of men into a doomed canyon, and letting so much hell break loose we can't tell the heroes from the villains—which feels exactly right. This is a dark, sly, honest, pleasing, slip-under-your-skin-and-stay-there kind of a book." —Pam Houston

"*The Wilding* is a compelling action narrative, universal in its dimensions while utterly grounded in specific particulars. Benjamin Percy is a stunning storyteller. His fearful wildernesses, both physical and psychic, kept me up through the night."

—William Kittredge, author of *Hole in the Sky* and *The Willow Field*

"*The Wilding* is a virtuoso blend of beauty and violence, hope and despair, tough and touching, lust and terror, literary craft and genre plotting. Like James Dickey, Benjamin Percy drags his characters into the wilderness—into a canyon as black as a gaping mouth, where they struggle to stay alive and in control of what makes them human—but for a new generation of readers concerned with the vanishing West."

—Danielle Trussoni, author of *Angelology* and *Falling Through the Earth*

"Benjamin Percy's descriptive powers are so potent and evocative in this impressive debut, that they sweep the reader out of his or her figurative armchair and into the Oregon wilderness, ready to fight to the death to preserve it."

—Helen Schulman, author of *A Day At The Beach* and *P.S.*

THE WILDING

Also by Benjamin Percy

Refresh, Refresh (graphic novel),
with Danica Novgorodoff and James Ponsoldt

Refresh, Refresh

The Language of Elk

THE WILDING

A Novel

Benjamin Percy

GRAYWOLF PRESS

This publication is made possible by funding provided in part by a grant from the Minnesota State Arts Board, through an appropriation by the Minnesota State Legislature, a grant from the National Endowment for the Arts, and private funders. Significant support has also been provided by Target; the McKnight Foundation; and other generous contributions from foundations, corporations, and individuals. To these organizations and individuals we offer our heartfelt thanks.

NATIONAL ENDOWMENT FOR THE ARTS
MINNESOTA STATE ARTS BOARD
WELLS FARGO
TARGET

Published by Graywolf Press
250 Third Avenue North, Suite 600
Minneapolis, MN 55401

www.graywolfpress.org

Published in the United States of America

ISBN 978-1-55597-569-2 (cloth)
ISBN 978-1-55597-596-8 (paper)

2 4 6 8 9 7 5 3 1

Library of Congress Control Number: 2011930484

Cover design: Scott Sorenson

Cover photo: Paul Nichols / Getty Images

For Lisa

I felt as though I had dipped into some supernatural source of primal energy.

—James Dickey, *Deliverance*

My father, I thought, could have told me things to know, actual as a stone with a code engraved on it, a thing you could put in your pocket and carry around, cool and hard and smooth, that you could touch when you were worried. But such a thing was not in our contract.

—William Kittredge, *Who Owns the West?*

Instead of adapting, as we began to do, we have tried to make country and climate over to fit our existing habits and desires. Instead of listening to the silence, we have shouted into the void. We have tried to make the arid West into what it was never meant to be and cannot remain, the Garden of the World and the home of the multiple millions.

—Wallace Stegner, "Striking the Rock"

PROLOGUE

His father came toward him with the rifle. From where Justin sat at his desk—his homework spread before him—both his father and the gun appeared to be growing, so that when handed the weapon, he wasn't sure he was strong enough to carry it. Around his father, Justin had always felt that way, as if everything were bigger than he was.

His father said he wanted to show him something, but he wouldn't say what. He only said for Justin to follow him. This happened outside of Bend, Oregon, where they lived in a cabin surrounded by ten acres of woods.

The moment they stepped off the porch, as if on cue, a sound rose from the forest, as slow as smoke. It sounded like a woman crying. Justin—who was twelve at the time—felt his veins constrict with alarm. "What's that?" he said. "What the hell *is* that?"

"Don't be a pantywaist," his father said over his shoulder. By now he was several steps ahead of Justin and moving across the lawn, a browned patch of grass choked with pine needles. "And don't say hell." When he reached the place where the grass met the trees, he perceived Justin had not followed him, and turned. "Come on," he said.

There followed a moment of silence where he motioned Justin forward with his hand and Justin clutched his rifle a little closer to his chest. Then the noise began again, sharper and louder now than before, reminding Justin of metal rasping across a file. Even his father—who was a big man with a mossy beard and a keg-of-beer belly—cringed.

This was that in-between time of day, not quite afternoon and not quite night, when the air begins to purple and thicken. Once they entered the forest the pines put a black color on things, and through their branches dropped a wet wind that carried with it the smell of the nearby mountains, the Cascades.

They walked for some time along a well-worn path, one of many that coiled through the property like snakes without end. The screaming sound continued, sometimes loud and sometimes soft, like some siren signaling the end of the world. It overwhelmed Justin's every thought and sensation so that he felt he was stuck in some box with only this horrible noise to keep him company. Everything seemed to tremble as it dragged its way through the air.

They hurried along as fast as they could, less out of wonder or sympathy than the urgent need to silence. They hated the noise—its mournful mixed-up music—as much as they feared it.

Then, between the trees, Justin saw it. The inky gleam of its eyes, and its huge ears drawn flat against its triangular skull, and then its bulky body. Blood trails oozed along it, dampening its black fur and the soil beneath it.

"Man alive," his father said.

It was a bear—maybe a year old, no longer a cub, big enough to do some damage—and it was tangled in a barbed-wire fence, the barbed wire crisscrossing its body. To this day Justin remembers the blood so clearly. It was *the* perfect shade of red. To this day he wants an old-time car—say a Mustang or one of those James Bond Aston Martins—the color of it.

The bear, bewildered, now let its head droop and took short nervous breaths before letting loose another wail, a high-pitched sound that lowered into a baritone moan, like pulling in a trombone. A tongue hung from its mouth. Its muscles jerked and rolled beneath its pelt.

Justin stood behind a clump of rabbitbrush as if to guard himself from the animal. The bush smelled great. It smelled sugary. It smelled like the color yellow ought to smell. By concentrating on it so deeply, he removed himself from the forest and was thereby able to contain the tears crowding his eyes.

Then his father said, "I want you to kill it."

Just like that. Like killing was throwing a knuckleball or fixing a carburetor.

That happened a long time ago. Thirty years ago. And still, Justin feels weighed down with the memory of it. When he lectures his students or when he feels the baby moving around in his wife's belly or when he lies in bed in a half dream, the bear sometimes emerges from the shadows, snapping its teeth, retreating back into shadow as quickly as it appeared.

Thirty years—and during this time little changed between Justin and his father, even as Oregon changed all around them.

JUSTIN

His wife, Karen, works as a dietitian for the school districts scattered throughout central Oregon. She spends her days designing new lunch programs for the cafeterias, sitting down with obese diabetics to ask them about their eating habits, and giving PowerPoint presentations to auditoriums full of bored children, telling them about the food pyramid and how they might incorporate it into their lives. At this time she is pregnant with their second child. She drinks orange juice every morning and what seems like gallons of water every day, but no soda or alcohol, not even to sneak a sip from Justin. She stays away from fish and red meat and spends the extra dollar on organic free-range chicken. And so on. Every precaution in the world—and none of it stops from happening what happens next.

Justin comes home from work to find a design of bloody footprints on the floor. He stares at them a long time as if to decipher their message. Only then does he pull out his cell phone. He shut it off earlier in the day so that it wouldn't go off when he was teaching. It reveals three new voice mails—one from the hospital, the next from his in-laws, the last from his wife.

He finds her in her hospital bed and she seems to have shrunk. Really, she has, her belly caved in, suddenly empty.

She is, she was, five months pregnant. The doctors tell her she has preeclampsia. Essentially her body came to recognize the baby as an allergen and expelled it from her. When she tells Justin this, her voice slurring from the Vicodin, she seems to be looking inward and outward at the same time, lost in dark thoughts in a too-bright room.

When the nurse comes to check Karen's vitals, she asks if Justin wants to see the baby, a baby girl. He does and doesn't. When his son, Graham, was born, he had looked so shiny, as if polished by Karen's insides, a precious gem they clutched to their chests and passed back and forth with the greatest care. That's how this baby looks, too, only smaller, bluer.

In the weeks that follow, Karen walks around as if bruised. She shrinks from Justin's touch—his, but lost to him. He finds her often in the office, the office they converted into a nursery. On one side of the room sits a rolltop desk stacked with ungraded papers—and on the other, the varnished pine crib, decorated with Winnie-the-Pooh bumpers and a mobile that plays "Twinkle, Twinkle, Little Star," the song sounding so eerie now, when Karen turns the knob, filling the empty crib and seeping through its slats to echo through the house.

When they finally make love again, five months later, she starts crying and when he asks if he should stop, she says, "What do you think?" A line comes to run down the middle of their bed. Neither of them crosses it.

He can't remember if they were having problems before. He tries to remember the last time they went on a date—a real date, without their son—white linen, lit candles, wine in goblets, their feet touching beneath the table—and can't. He tries to remember the last time he bought her jewelry or flowers. He tries to remember the last time she took him in her mouth. He tries to remember the last time they read novels on the couch, their legs intertwined, sharing favorite passages. Years. It's been years, hasn't it? So much of his memory is hazy, chunked up by memories of work. He can recall her frequent headaches—her full-throated sighing—her desire to be alone. He remembers putting away laundry, finding an enormous pink dildo shoved to the back of her underwear drawer, and feeling somehow betrayed. Maybe these are only the warts that naturally grow out of a marriage moving forward. Or maybe he and Karen have been in trouble for some time and only now does he notice it. He wants to blame the baby, but maybe the baby has only turned up the volume on what was there all along.

She takes up running. Every morning she pulls on pink shorts and a white tank top and laces her Nike cross-trainers and runs five miles. All the fat she accumulated during her pregnancy melts off to reveal hard-plated muscle that looks like the exoskeleton of something that lives at the bottom of the ocean. Her feet develop thick calluses. Her calves jump when she walks. Her forearms are a lacework of veins. Even her ears look skinny.

Sometimes Justin sees her on his drive to Mountain View High School, where he teaches. Her hair will be pulled back in a ponytail to reveal a red and compacted face. Her teeth, bared in a snarl. She pumps her legs and swings her arms wildly. She looks like a madwoman. He always beeps his horn and waves at her, but she never sees him, lost in the heat and rhythm of her run.

Normally she is gone by the time he showers and dresses and comes down to the kitchen for breakfast. But sometimes they run into each other, as they do this morning, when he finds her standing in front of the sink, looking out the window and drinking a short glass of orange juice. He says, "Hi," and she says, "Hey." He asks her if she heard the news, and when she says, "What news?" he tells her.

Last night—on Z-21, the NBC affiliate—the ten o'clock news reported a bear attack at Cline Falls. These girls, two teenage girls from Prineville, left their food and cooking supplies out, rather than washing them and bagging them and hanging them from the highest branch of a juniper tree. In the springtime bears possess a terrible hunger, having slept through the long winter, and this one was no exception. One slash of its claws parted the nylon like a zipper. Their screams didn't scare it away, only encouraged it, as it fit its jaws around the head of one girl, chewing her, her scalp finally sliding off her skull. The other, in trying to save her friend, was hurled against the canyon wall, then mauled. They played dead or fainted in their pain and after so many minutes the bear abandoned them. Now both are in critical condition at St. Charles Memorial in Bend. "They say they think it's a grizzly."

"There are no grizzlies in Oregon."

"That's what the Forest Service guy said, but then this other guy said—"

"I gotta run." She sets her glass down on the counter with a click. Yellow bits of pulp cling to its inside.

"Okay," he says and opens the cabinet and pulls a box of Cheerios from the shelf to rattle into a bowl and splash with milk. "Have fun. Watch out for bears."

"Don't worry about me," she says, already running, on her way out the door.

He teaches English. Several years ago a sophomore named Jimmy Westmoreland, after downing a twelve-pack of Budweiser, flipped his Camaro and died. Everyone gathered in the gym the next day. The principal—a leathery-looking man who dyed his hair jet black and kept it styled in an "Elvis"—stood before them all and muttered a few kind words about Jimmy. There was a chair next to him and it had a boom box resting on it. "This one's for Jimmy," he said and hit the play button. From the speakers came the drawling voices and disorderly guitar licks of Lynyrd Skynyrd. They sat and listened to "Free Bird." Eight minutes and twenty-three seconds had never seemed like such a long time.

This is the kind of school they are. Wranglers and Levi's. F-10s and Firebirds. All of old Bend send their kids here—while the Portland and California refugees, in their tight designer jeans and brightly polished SUVs, end up at the new high school across town. Justin prefers Billy Joel to Skynyrd—and Starbucks to Folgers—and finds himself identifying more with what Bend is becoming than what it once was. He often thinks about applying for a transfer, or maybe even going back to graduate school, maybe teaching at the college level or doing something else entirely.

There was a time when he enjoyed his job greatly. And then something happened. The same thing that happens to many teachers, he expects. The work begins to rub away at your heart. The exhaustion doesn't come all at once, but steadily, incessantly, like waves wearing away at rock. You get married. You buy a house. You have a kid. And then one day you realize ten, twenty years have passed, and during this time you have grown tired of the low pay, the endless piles of paper, the football players who sit in the back row and cross their arms and seem perpetually amused by everything, a smug smile never leaving their lips.

Sometimes, during the middle of a lecture, he feels strangely distant, separate from himself, as if he is hovering above the classroom, carried there by the drone of his voice. And when from above he looks down on everyone, when he see in their eyes—as he saw in his eyes—a dreamily veiled boredom, it gives him a general feeling of inconsequence, as if nothing he says or does matters.

This morning, during an exam, he glances out the window and sees a gaunt animal, what could be a dog or a coyote, slinking along the edge of the football field. It stays low to the ground, as if it has caught a scent, as if it is stalking something. And then it vanishes into the shadows between the trees. He leans forward and tries to follow it farther, but it is gone, so suddenly he wonders if he imagined it.

The door opens and startles him from his half dream.

The secretary stands there. She is a leggy blonde who spends all day forwarding calls while paging through the latest copy of *People* or *Us Weekly*. Today she wears too bright a shade of lipstick that makes her mouth appear like a bleeding gash. "Mr. Caves?" she says. "Your wife is on the phone. She needs to talk to you."

He looks at his students and his students look at him for a long twenty seconds. Then he says, "I'm in the middle of class. What's this about?"

She examines her nails as if they were a point of curiosity. "How should I know? I only know it's an emergency."

He looks about the room, his stomach like a stone, while digesting this. Dust rises in the sunbeams coming through the windows. The clock clicks its way toward three. Someone in the back row snaps their gum, the noise like a broken branch. "You have five more minutes," he tells them. "When you finish, lay the test on my desk. Don't cheat. And remember, for homework tonight, *Heart of Darkness,* pages fifty through one hundred."

He makes his way down the hall, to the lounge, certain something has happened to his father. Perhaps a stroke. He feels oddly calm, as if he has been waiting for this phone call all day. But this soon gives way to panic when he brings the phone to his ear and listens to his wife tell him about their son.

"It's Graham," she says. "He's missing."

She drove to Amity Creek Elementary, where Graham is a sixth grader, to pick him up. But he never emerged from the swarms of backpack-toting children, never met her at the top of the roundabout where she always waited, engine idling. Fifteen minutes passed—then twenty. She cut the ignition and got out of the car and tried to keep her walk steady in its pace as she approached the school, certain there must be a perfectly logical reason for his absence. Probably Graham had misbehaved and was now serving detention, clapping clouds of chalk from erasers or writing "I will not fire spitballs" again and again on a lined tablet of paper.

Though she knew better. He had never received a detention and likely never would. He was one of those children who took great pleasure in doing exactly as he was told, always saying *please* and *thank you*, never speaking out of turn. He favored chinos to jeans and wore his collared shirts tucked into them. Justin wasn't sure how this had happened, how Graham had become this self-possessed little man, and in fact Justin encouraged him to live a little more adventurously. When Justin was that age, he used to collect frogs along the riverbanks and carry them to the nearest road so that he might throw them high into the air, enjoying the sound and sight of them splatting against pavement. It was horrible, but boys are supposed to do horrible things. It's in their nature.

But Graham is different. He is the type of boy who prefers books to BB guns, who makes his bed every morning and plays computer games after he finishes his homework and never begs for the candy stacked next to the cash register. Exactly the type of boy, Karen was thinking, who might climb into a car with a stranger if told a convincing lie, not wanting to offend.

She found his teacher, Mrs. Glover, in her classroom, working her way through a stack of math quizzes. And no, she hadn't seen him, not since the final bell. Together they searched the school grounds and found no trace of him. With every room Karen peered into and found empty, a wind grew stronger inside her, until it felt as though there were a cyclone tearing loose everything she thought was securely nailed down.

She tells Justin this as they drive around Bend, poking their heads into the video arcade, the pizza parlor, the cinema, the library, all the places Graham knows. They have called the police. They have called everyone in his class. Now there is nothing to do but look and wait. They randomly zip up and down the streets of Bend, their heads swinging back and forth as the world flies past the bug-speckled windshield. Karen has her cell phone cradled in her palm. Her mouth incessantly quivers as if only just holding on to a scream. At one point she grabs Justin's arm and squeezes it, *once*. He can't remember the last time she touched him—really intentionally touched him. Her warmth lingers there after she pulls her hand away. "I can't do this again," she says.

"Don't worry," he says. "Everything is going to be fine."

Justin is a man with neat hair, parted clean on the right side, cut tight above the ears and along the neck. He brings a hand to it now, tidying it, part of him thinking that as long as every hair stays in its place, everything *will* be fine.

It is. Someone spots Graham at Lava River Lanes, bowling with a strange old man in a leather-fringe jacket. Within minutes, two squad cars pull up with their lights flashing. The deputies race into the building, past the pool tables and arcade games, through the clouds of cigarette smoke, to lane nine, where they find Justin's father, who decided on a whim to pick Graham up from school and teach him a thing or two about how to throw a hook ball.

When Justin arrives, his father is waiting for them in the parking lot, leaning against a squad car with his hands in his pockets. "Can't a man spend an afternoon with his grandson?" he says.

"Of course, Dad. It's just—"

"Just what?"

He goes on. Talking about how Justin needs to let the boy have some fun this, and how he ought to cut an old man some slack that—and so on—while his hands, big brown things, busily rake through his beard like paws through rotten wood, seeking grubs, worms to eat. Lately he has grown wilder and Justin has become more fearful and hesitant to challenge him.

Karen holds Graham to her chest, pressing him into her with a pained look on her face, as if he were a lost organ she wants to force back inside her.

Through the window comes a rectangle of moonlight, brightening the floor and the bottom of the bed. In the distance he can hear elk calling to each other. Their big booming voices spiral through the air, as if blown from a conch shell. He goes to the window. A cool juniper-scented breeze blows, making the curtains billow around him. In the distance he can see the Cascades. They glow in the moonlight, white-shouldered with snow and bearded with forests that look more black than green against them. In their foothills a small light flares, catching his eye. It vanishes a moment later and he is left to wonder about its origin, so far from the city—with no streetlamps or neon signs anywhere near it—a speck of glass caught in the folds of a vast black cloth.

His wife is awake as well. He can tell from her breathing. She showered before bed, scrubbed her skin pink, and shampooed her hair into a silky blackness. These past few hours, every time she readjusts her body, trying to find a comfortable position, a puff of air carries the smell of her cleanness.

He crawls into bed with her again. She has the sheet tucked over her chest and under her arms. She sighs in a way that means she is about to say something. And then she says it: "That man needs to be put in his place."

She is referring not only to today but to other days as well. Last week, for instance, when they went out to the cabin for lunch, his father took Graham into the backyard and Karen later found them hunched over a shallow hole, cheering for a scorpion they had pitted against a black widow spider.

"My heart was going a mile a minute," Karen says and puts her hand there, between her breasts.

"I know."

"I swear, I almost hit him. I almost slapped him. That man is as careless with other people as he is with his own body."

"I know, I know."

"I don't think you do, Justin. Everything went through my mind then. Everything you can imagine. I was certain he was dead. Our son. Do you know how that made me feel? Like *it* was happening all over again." He doesn't have to ask what she means by *it*. *It* has come to define her. She lifts her head off her pillow and then lets it fall again. "I don't ever want to feel like that again."

"I'm sorry."

"Don't apologize. Quit apologizing. That's how you talk to your father."

"Sorry."

She rolls on her side to fully face him and he says, "Kidding." He kisses her on the forehead and keeps his lips there when he says, "I'll talk to him."

"Will you really?"

"I will."

His hand goes to the lip of the sheet and fingers it. Slowly he pulls it down, taking it from her chest, revealing the swell of her breasts, their paleness exaggerated in the moonlight—and her lips pinch a little tighter for every inch he moves it. He wants to roll on top of her and make love with the abandon that sometimes grows out of small moments of anger.

Instead she says, "Please don't," and pulls the sheet around her and turns from him.

He thinks of the light off in the woods—flaring and then going dark, like a dying star—and it calls to mind a poem. He and Karen used to have this game they would play. One would speak a line of poetry—and the other would follow it up. The game was born out of their time together in college, when they seemed most in love, constantly hungry for each other. In his apartment, after they made love on his creaky futon, he used to read her poetry as she drifted off to sleep.

Now the game was more a thing of idleness, just two people calling back and forth to each other like birds in a forest. They might be in the kitchen, one of them chopping celery, the other peeling potatoes—or they might be hiking, one turning to observe the other behind on the trail. He took a moment to find the words, how they arranged themselves in a row, and then there they were: "My thoughts are crabbed and sallow / My tears like vinegar / Or the bitter blinking yellow / Of an acetic star." And if he said them aloud, would she call back to him about the wry-faced pucker of the sour lemon moon—or would she deepen her breathing and feign sleep?

Bobby Fremont is one of those men with money and enthusiasm, which allows him to do with his life whatever he wants. He is always coming or going, never standing still, traveling somewhere Justin has never been, doing something Justin never realized possible. He tells stories, often loudly and with many jabbing hand gestures, about hunting bighorn sheep in Wyoming or summiting Mount Cook in New Zealand or eating some twelve-course French meal that very nearly gave his mouth an orgasm. He is always smiling and has a big laugh that distracts your attention away from his close-set eyes.

Much of the property surrounding Bend, he has at some point owned and developed and sold, to the Inn of the Seventh Mountain, the Bend Athletic Club, Widgi Creek, River's Edge. He has been married three times—his latest wife one of those types who pencils in her eyebrows and dyes her hair blond to the point of invisibility—and his unstable taste for women seems to match his obsession and then abandonment of property.

Long ago there must have been many like him, particularly in these Western territories. Men, wild and hopeful, who chased after stakes and claims, their eyes always focused on the horizon and whatever goldness glowed there.

It is because of Bobby that Justin and his father find themselves in a side room of the county courthouse, attending an open meeting for the

Planning Commission. The windows are thin and tall, admitting only a little sunlight that deadens against the pine-paneled walls. They sit at a long wooden table that runs the length of the room and gives off a glow from the wrought-iron chandelier that hangs above it. A good number of men wearing leather vests and black string ties are crowded around the table, and at its head stands Bobby.

He has a too-tan face that is finely wrinkled around his eyes and mouth. He keeps his white hair a little long and parted in the middle so that it waves out from his forehead. His eyes are a chalky blue and his gaze direct and calculating. Today he wears a collared khaki shirt tucked smartly into his jeans, while around his neck hangs a bolo tie with silver-tipped strings.

Slowly he unrolls the map and when he tries to lay it flat, to smooth it with his hand, it snaps back, curling up again. His lawyer and a few other men, Justin's father among them, help him set Starbucks coffee cups upon its corners to hold down the paper and make it tense and visible to everyone.

It is a map of the Ochocos, its topographic lines like the swirling patterns of some great and elaborate fingerprint pressed down on it. Sketched onto the map in red pen is the perimeter of an area around twenty miles long and ten wide—and at its heart, the cavity of a canyon with a river curling through it.

Next to the map he unrolls another, this one a magnified version of the red-inked area. From where Justin sits, near the middle of the table, he can barely make out the words that run across its top in black swirling script: Echo Canyon. Here, in this black-and-white rendering, the trees have been logged, the brush cleared, replaced by a lavish development. The choicest lots border the top of the canyon and overlook the golf course and paved biking trails that fill the canyon below them.

After a time Bobby says, "There it is." He raps the table with his knuckles and brings his hand under his chin and jogs his eyes across the room, briefly settling his stare on each of the men. He has that special talent of connecting with people, of making everyone in a crowd of listeners feel singled out. "One unbelievable—and I mean truly magnificent—iron-and-timbered lodge, three hundred lots, and the fastest, truest putting greens in all of Oregon."

Everyone leans forward and glances between the maps as if trying to imagine the asphalt roads, the river-rock driveways, the sand bunkers, and water hazards set on top of all that wildness.

Justin can see in Bobby's erect posture the gladness to finalize these proceedings, to settle the thousands of decisions and compromises—the rezoning, the development permits, the traffic and environment and water issues—and all the rest of it, all the seemingly endless hassles he has pursued the past few years.

Then the door jerks open. There is a sudden shifting of attention, as everyone turns his head at once to observe Tom Bear Claws, followed by a bald-headed *Bend Bulletin* reporter clutching a notepad. They find a place at the table and Tom knocks his knuckles against its wood as if asking to be let in. "Sorry we're late," he says.

"You're not late," Bobby says through a thin smile. "You were never invited."

"Hey. That hurts my feelings."

Justin knows Tom. Most do. For the past few years, ever since Justin took over Honors English, he has invited Tom into his classroom as a lecturer for the unit on Native American literature. Justin enjoys his playful cynicism, how he rarely takes anything too seriously. He will drag a stool to the front of the class and settle his bulk onto it and smile at everyone with his broad and craggy face—his skin the color of tobacco—and talk about Coyote and Mouse and Thought Woman and the Great Spirit, the Maker of all things.

Once he kicked off his boot and peeled off his sock and showed the rattlesnake tattooed across the sole of his foot. It gave him the power to sneak up on his enemies without a sound, he said. "So you better keep an eye out."

Another time he read aloud a poem. He had written it on a yellow legal tablet. He pulled a pair of bifocals from his breast pocket and settled them on the end of his nose and made a barking noise into his fist before reading in a voice that rose and fell and lulled them all into a mystical reverie. Justin doesn't remember precisely how it went. Something like this: "The light of the forest is red. The night's wolves run through it and the day's men recoil from it. Under the dark cover of the trees, things get lost and trapped and eaten. The light of the mind is red, too."

When Justin later asked if Tom had written the poem himself, he said, "Mostly."

Justin has never asked but guesses him fifty. His hair is the color of a spent charcoal briquette and he keeps it tied in a braid. Around his neck hangs a leather necklace jeweled with elk teeth, but so does he wear sport coats and drive a BMW and regularly golf at Widgi Creek. Regularly he's quoted in the paper, the mouthpiece of the Warm Springs Reservation.

He made his money in fishing. Peer into any lake, any river, and along its bottom—like coins in a dirty fountain—you will find bottle caps, the brightest things in the water. The idea came naturally: beer and fishing go hand in hand. Punch two holes on opposite sides of the cap, pinch it into a clam shape, and attach a hook to one end, leader to the other. The shiny spinning color draws the fish to strike.

For a long time after college he worked for the Forest Service, but on the side, he started recycling beer caps from local taverns—the Elusive Trout, Big Dick's Halfway Inn—selling his lures on the Internet. Then Miller called. Now his six-pack retails for thirty dollars in just about every outdoor store and bait shop in the country. With the money he helped fund Kah-Nee-Ta—the Warm Springs resort and casino—where coins clattered from slots and waterslides spiraled into pools. For several years he has pushed for another resort—an off-reservation site at Cascade Locks, along the Columbia. In '05, the governor signed off on a tribal–state compact, the first step in establishing a trust for gaming, but since then, nothing has happened, the project tangled up in a web of red tape. There is talk of Tom managing Cascade Locks, but some say talk is all it is.

Talk is what Tom is best at, and Justin observes him with the same bemused pleasure a patron of the local theater might feel when an actor takes on a new role.

His voice has a somber petitioning tone, and beneath the fluorescent lights his face appears shadowed and cut sharply from clay. "My grandfather hunted Echo Canyon. My grandfather's grandfather, too. For so many families, not just mine, it's a sacred place. To build there ain't right."

Bobby clears his throat and everyone looks at him. On either side of his mouth, from his nose to his chin, runs a deep set of wrinkles, like parentheses that imply he always has something hidden behind what he is saying. "Everything you just mentioned, we need to consider and honor, of course." He seems to direct this more at the reporter than Tom. "We all appreciate—"

Tom holds up the flat of his hand. "You make it sound like the commission hasn't made up its mind yet. Give the bullshit a rest. We been talking about this for a year. What's left to talk about? What's next? Will there be a swimsuit competition?"

Bobby smiles. It is a smile you aren't meant to like. He is normally a pleasant man, but Justin once saw him blow up at a backyard barbeque party when he got into a screaming match with a very liberal, very outspoken pediatrician about drilling for oil in Alaska. The fight culminated with Bobby throwing a beer bottle against a fence, leaving behind a starburst of suds and shattered glass. Since then Justin has looked at him differently, always wondering about the anger that simmers just below the smile of his surface.

Right now a muscle in Bobby's jaw jumps. Then he lays both his hands on the table, on either side of the map, and brings his face close to it. The silver tips of his bolo tie swing back and forth like two tiny wrecking balls, knocking down paper forests, gouging open paper canyons.

"One thing I've never liked about this town," he says in a whisper he wants heard. "All the goddamned Indians."

Everyone goes still, too afraid or embarrassed to even look at Tom, who makes a noise like he is holding back a sneeze. Then he stands up so quickly he knocks his chair over. His boots crash against the floor. His lips peel back from his teeth. He cocks his arm to strike Bobby. Justin knows what will happen before it happens. There isn't a day that goes by his father isn't looking for a fight. He almost says, "Don't," but it's too late: his father is rising now to obstruct Tom, reaching out to seize his fist midair. There is a sound like a baseball falling smartly into the basket of a mitt. Their arms shake with the tension between them. Then Tom gives up. He lets his hand drop and rolls his shoulder like an injured pitcher and stares Justin's father in the eye. "Shut up, Paul," he says, though Justin's father has said nothing.

Bobby regards Tom and puts his hand over his mouth as if to keep from saying something. Then his hand falls away and he smiles tightly and says, "This certainly isn't helping your cause."

"Whether we're nice or not, I already know how they'll vote. So I might as well not be nice." Tom lets his shoulders rise and fall in a shrug. "I might as well fuck with you, you know?"

"Look." Bobby glances at the reporter and says in a voice that tries to communicate his reasonableness, his tolerance, "You realize this is all going to be very natural, very much a tribute to the landscape. An improvement even. And do you have any idea what it will do to property values in Prineville and John Day?" This last part he says to the Planning Commission—and the old men nod their heads and raise their eyebrows and purse their lips.

Tom looks as if he might rush Bobby again to offer another blow to the face. Then his mood seems suddenly to brighten and he sidles toward where Paul still stands with his hands clenched, a few paces from the head of the table. Two of the commissioners lean away as Tom leans between them and peers at the blueprint for a moment. "There's a trick the timber industry plays. It's a good trick. They clear-cut thousands of acres of pines and firs, but along the roads they leave the trees real thick to camouflage the baldness. Makes everybody believe those Weyerhaeuser ads when they say, 'Oregon will never grow out of trees.' But you climb up a mountain and you take a look down and you know what it looks like? It looks like shit." He thrusts his chin at the map of the development. "Like shit."

He turns to the reporter, whose pen hurries across his notepad. "Don't write that down," he says. "Write this down. You ready?"

The reporter nods even as he keeps his eyes on the notepad, the words bleeding blackly across it.

"Now I'm going to say some proud Indian nation stuff they can put in the paper. Okay? Here we go." His voice takes on the timbre of a dream as he tells everyone, "It took fifty years for white people to nearly wipe out the Tasmanians. About the same for the bison. And when you look around at Warm Springs, when you look at the Cree and Sioux and Chippewa and all the rest of us, what you see is the carcass of a once proud Indian nation. And the white establishment continues picking at our bones, chewing up what's left of us until there's nothing left of us. That canyon's what's left of us. But not for much longer." He looks at the reporter and his voice returns to its normal tone when he says, "You got that or you need me to say it again?"

The reporter brings his finger and thumb together in the *perfect* sign.

Bobby checks his watch and then looks to the Planning Commission. They have the dazed look of children who have just suffered through a parental lecture. They have heard all of this before. With respect to Native complaints, Bobby had hired on a group of UO archaeologists for a two-month survey that failed to turn up anything more than a few broken projectile points and a single petroglyph chipped into the basalt wall of the canyon.

In the end, the commission votes in his favor and when Bobby removes the coffee cups from the map, it slowly curls up on itself like a fist.

His father never took Justin to Hawaii or Disneyland or Mount Rushmore. Instead, he would load up the bed of his pickup with camping gear and they would drive to Christmas Valley or the Umpqua River or the Malheur Preserve, some still-wild place where they would hike dry-mouthed across a desert flat or fish a snake-shaped river or scour the forest floor for mushrooms to cook. It was in Echo Canyon—high in the Ochoco Mountains, among the big pines and bear grass meadows—that they hunted every November. Though Justin hasn't been there in years, he feels a strong connection to its woods, as does his father.

Which was why, a year ago, when Bobby tried to contract Justin's father's company—the Paul Caves Hand Hewn Log Cabin Company—his father said, "Yes," but with a red line of frustration underlining his voice.

Justin first learned about this in his father's backyard, where with a longbow his father shot arrow after arrow into a polyurethane buck he had arranged where the lawn met the woods, twenty yards away. He wore a leather quiver on his back. It was crowded with arrows carved from a Norway pine he imported from a Baltic Sea forest, where the cold stern weather made for slower growth and splendid spiny wood, or so he said. He fletched them with red cock feathers.

In a fluid series of motions he reached behind him to pluck an arrow, fitting its hardwood notch onto the bowstring, drawing tight and firing without hesitation, again and again, the arrows all hissing across the mowed space of lawn to find their target with a satisfying series of *whizzes* and *thunks*. For a big man, whose hands were so leathery and broad they looked like tools, he could move quickly and with a kind of grace.

Justin cannot remember where his mother was during this. possibly in the kitchen, doing dishes. Or maybe at the table, carefully cutting her asparagus into bite-size pieces. When he thinks of her he often thinks of her through the window of his father. She remains indistinct in many of his memories, backgrounded by his father's loudness, his hairy massiveness.

Justin said, "You don't have to do it, you know."

His father loosed another arrow, this one missing its target, rattling off a pine tree as it entered the woods. He sighed his frustration and lowered his bow and plucked at the string as if seeking out the first note of a sad song. "And then what? Then another company gets it and the job gets done anyway. The other guy gets money in the bank, gets his name out there, gets the call the next time a job comes up. And where does that leave me? You don't know politics." He withdrew another arrow from his quiver and examined its broadhead. The metal caught the sun and a thin gleam played across his face. "You think I want to see that nice country ripped up?"

"There's a lot of nice country out there. We can find another canyon."

"Is that how you feel?"

"Maybe. I don't know."

"I don't know," he said, parroting Justin in a singsong voice, then again, *"I don't know."* He pointed the arrow at Justin, bringing its razor point within an inch of his chest. "You should get that tattooed across your heart. *I don't know.* No, you don't know. You don't know much at all."

Paul is not the sort of father who goes to church and plays golf and whistles Christmas songs year-round. He is the kind of father who enjoys saying things like, "Pain is weakness leaving the body," and "Knowing you could die tomorrow, don't buy any green bananas." He smells like motor oil. His huge hands seem capable of tearing phone books in half and uprooting trees with a tug. His fingernails always carry dirt and bruises beneath them. He often keeps a sandwich in his pocket and withdraws it intermittently for a bite. His idea of a good time is to go price pistols at Bi-Mart.

Paul doesn't need to work so hard. Business is good. Justin knows this because he has taken care of the company paperwork since college. His father could easily hire more men, could spend his days sipping coffee and negotiating contracts and letting his hands go soft, but if his name appears on the letterhead, he ought to be the one dangling from a thirty-foot ladder, driving home the first and final nail—or so he insists. It's a general-on-the-front-lines sort of mentality.

And so right alongside his crew he pilots the cement truck and lays a concrete foundation. He uses broadaxes and table saws to hew down logs on all four sides until they are square. He chisels notches. He cuts lap joints. He uses an auger to bore holes.

For him, every day is a mechanical storm of chain saws snarling and sandpaper sizzling and hammers cracking. Sawdust hangs in heavy clouds. When Justin was a boy, his father would sometimes take him along. Justin would spend the day uselessly hammering nails into planks of wood, darting in and out of doorways, and climbing onto the roof and imagining the cabin as his own. He remembers everything smelling like the memory of a sawmill. He remembers watching his father as he worked, shirtless, sometimes with steam rising off his body in the cold mountain air.

His father lays floors. He stacks walls, cutting dovetail notches for the corners. He cuts the rafters, he cuts the joists. He bolts down a steel roof to shrug off the snow. He cuts out the windows and the doors, and his blacksmith digs a hole and fills it with pinewood and burns it down to an orange bed of coals and sets up his forge to bang out some wrought-iron hinges, doorknobs, banisters. Then comes the paneling, the chinking, the sanding, the varnishing, the caulking, the masonry, the plumbing and electricity.

And Paul does all this while maintaining a mostly meat diet and drinking his way through a six-pack almost every evening. To Justin, the heart attack comes as no surprise.

His father later tells him what it felt like. He says a belt seemed to tighten around his chest and the world darkened abruptly. He ran slantingly and stumbled with a half-fascinated terror at what was happening to him, at the way his body seemed at once to constrict and expand. When his legs gave out beneath him and he pitched forward, he tried to stop his fall with his arm but it had gone numb and he crashed to the ground unguarded and opened up a gash in his forehead.

This happens in late spring—a few months after the meeting with the Planning Commission—when Justin moves through the electronic double doors and into the emergency room at St. Charles Memorial. The air smells of disinfectant and tapioca and old fruit. When the doors *whir* closed behind him, the noise of traffic falls away, replaced by hushed voices and gurney wheels and heart monitors and Muzak pouring softly from the sound system. In the waiting area, people lie sprawled out in chairs with dazed looks on their faces as if they have been dropped from a great height.

At the reception desk, the nurse takes a long time in acknowledging Justin, finally raising her eyes from her clipboard when he clears his throat. "You hurt?" she says. "Or you here to see somebody who's hurt?"

"Do I look hurt?"

She gives him a bitchy half smile and says, "Name?"

"You want mine or his?"

"*His* name."

Outside, somewhere far off, a siren wails. He tells her his name and she taps a few keys at a computer terminal and directs him down a long buttermilk-colored hall lined with stainless steel tables on wheels. He hurries there and the noise of the siren follows him, growing louder, rippling through the town, through the concrete and the metal and the glass like a quick breeze over water, to settle on him with shocking volume. He passes a doctor with a brown mustache. The doctor moves at a quick trot toward the emergency room and whistles along with the ambulance, as if summoning it.

When he visited the hospital for his wife, he felt fear. When he visits for his father, he feels hate. He hates this place that keeps trying to take people from him. He wants to splash black paint all over the too-white walls. He wants to rip out the throat of an orderly who pushes a gurney one way, then the next, as he tries to get past him.

And then, just like that, the siren stops, as Justin arrives at room 343.

He pokes his head in the door, and just as he is about to withdraw it and continue on, the man on the bed raises his hand in greeting. "Dad?" Justin says, hesitating in the doorway. "I didn't recognize you."

His father does not look like his father. He looks like a pear that has begun to darken and collapse. Upon Justin's entrance he picks up the remote control and turns off the TV and then immediately turns it on again. It hangs from the ceiling corner and shows on its screen a weatherman standing on a Florida beach with twenty-foot waves crashing behind him.

At a wedding, Justin once heard Bobby Fremont tease his father, saying he looked like a beast trapped in a double-breasted suit. And this seems especially true now—hairy and brown-skinned and so large every corner of him hangs off the bed—the vision of him offset by all that antiseptic whiteness. Once, when Justin and his father stood side by side, his mother pointed out that they were the same height. It was true, but Justin never believed her. It has something to do with his father's build—so much broader than his own—but even more to do with his personality, which even now seems barbed to a gleaming point.

Above his bed hangs a black-and-white photograph of a dead juniper tree. Its trunk appears twisted, each bare branch straining up toward the sky.

"Where's Mom?" Justin asks.

"I told them to call you. I didn't want to worry her."

It is hard for Justin to look at him. His eyes are ringed by heavy shadows. His nose has a pinched look to it. His lip trembles a little when he speaks, as if he needs to cry but won't allow it. He turns his head from Justin and looks out the window where the sun is setting. Justin watches his face change from red to pale in the fading light, as if, having colored with embarrassment, he has composed himself.

A few minutes later a doctor enters the room. He has a domed forehead and silver hair and wears a white lab coat with an assortment of pens in the breast pocket. He withdraws one of them now and holds it like a weapon. "How do you feel?"

"I feel great." Paul claps his hands together. "Ready to go home."

"That won't be happening anytime soon, I'm afraid."

"Says who?"

"Me. You'll need to spend the next few days with us."

"But I need to get back to work."

"You'll have to take some time off."

"Quiet." He says it like a curse. "I'll do no such thing."

"You will."

A conflict plays across his features and he heaves a great sigh.

An hour later Justin's mother arrives, crying out from the doorway and knocking over his IV as she rushes to his bedside. "I'm fine," he says. "The doctor said I'm fine. He said I'll be up and out of here in no time."

Justin says, "Let's hope anyway."

His father holds up his hand, its index and middle fingers twined, and then the hand continues upward to his forehead, touching the bandage. For the next three weeks the bruises will linger there, eventually shriveling into a red pucker that he will often finger and remark that he can feel his heart beating along it.

BRIAN

Brian haunts this stretch of the river to learn the passages the beavers travel between their lodge and seed caches. He places the trap in a black, glassy section where the water runs deep and where the bank is slick from their bellies and tails slithering along it and where the beavers heap little piles of mud with castor secretion beneath them. The trap—a double long spring jumper—looks like some metallic species of moth. He baits it with willow twigs basted with musk sacs that smell of a vinegary unwashed groin. He places the trap a foot beneath the water and attaches it to a drowning line.

Normally he is patient. He knows he should wait until late winter, early spring. He knows their pelts are glossiest and thickest then. But he has a project—a sewing project—he is working on that cannot wait.

This morning a cool wind blows steadily and shakes the pines and looses from the birch trees golden leaves that scatter across the surface of the river and glitter like coins on their way downstream. The sky is ghost-gray, thick with clouds that carry rain in them. From where he stands along the bank, his boots sinking slowly into the mud, he can see the trapped beaver, a black shadow the size and shape of an oversized football. A twenty-five-pounder, he guesses, its hind leg seized by the trap, its body floating in line with the current. The water bulges over it, making a small rapid.

His father taught him how to trap, how to skin and gut the animal, how to cook its meat and boil its tail, how to prepare its pelt and sell it at auction. Every winter they woke together before dawn and pulled on their insulated coveralls and trudged through the snow and chipped through the ice to check or set their traps. He remembers the chimneys of steam rising from the holes in the river, the hot coffee splashed from a thermos, the blood looking so bright in the snow.

In his pocket his cell phone chirps to life, its ringtone the song of a chickadee. He digs it out and studies its screen and sees there a number he does not recognize. He has not spoken to anyone yet this morning and the coffee he drank earlier has not fully crawled through his system, so he takes a moment to clear his throat, orienting himself in the human world, which feels so far from this choke of woods and rush of water.

"This is Brian at Pop-a-Lock Locksmith."

He stands only five feet three inches but his combat boots cheat him some height. He wears black jeans and a matching denim jacket. His face is squarish, his eyes large and ghostly turquoise, his mouth regularly downturned in a construction of seeming gloom or discomfort. He keeps his hair in a high-and-tight buzz—a habit maintained from his time in the service—that draws attention to the dent in his forehead, a pinkish saucer-shaped place that looks like a third eye socket sealed with skin. He has a nervous habit of tracing its outline with his finger, as he does now, when the voice on the other end of the line belongs to a woman.

Her name is Karen—she feels so stupid, she *knows* she ought to keep a key hidden outside—her name is Karen and she just came back from a run to find the door locked. It was her husband, the idiot. She can't believe he has done this to her. He drives her crazy sometimes. Now she is at a neighbor's house. She has to get to work soon. She asks Brian to hurry, if he can.

"I can," he tells her, "but I'm in the middle of another job." He wonders if she can hear the clean rush of the river, the wind sighing through the pines. "As soon as I finish up, I'll be right there. Maybe twenty minutes?"

She gives him the address. "I'll be across the street, so I'll see you pull into the driveway." She comes from someplace else, he knows. Her voice is flat-toned, without the clipped consonants, the long vowels, the almost brutal rhythm that inflects the speech of a local. He imagines, from the soft pop her lips make at the end of a sentence, that she is wearing lipstick. A woman who wears lipstick to run. Maybe this is why he leaves the beaver dangling in its trap, knowing the glacier-fed water will preserve its carcass until he returns.

He is parked along the edge of a Forest Service road west of town. In square black lettering the name of the company runs along the sides of his Ford F-10, along with its motto: "Who has your keys?" The brochures show his father—clean-shaven and muscular, someone Brian hardly recognizes—handing a blond woman and her blond-headed boy their freshly cut keys. Everyone is smiling because they know the house is now safe, a fortress. No one will trespass. This is what Pop-a-Lock emphasizes more than anything: fear and trust.

Their customers are generally new homeowners who worry a prior resident will return some night and slide his old key into the lock and find that it fits snugly, so that he might step into the house without a sound and remove all the jewelry and silver and then perhaps step into his former bedroom with a knife in hand and a smile cutting his face. Or someone will lose his keys and suspect them stolen. Or someone will lock herself out of her car or her house and not have a spare key hidden under the geranium pot. Brian makes locks, he defeats locks.

He keys the ignition and drives the truck along a network of dirt roads that spill into wider cinder roads that finally connect to asphalt thoroughfares. The rain begins hesitantly, with a few thick drops splatting his windshield and thudding the roof of his truck, so many seconds passing between each impact, sounding like a conversation that can't quite find its rhythm. And then, in a rush, the world seems made of water.

Brian slows his speed to forty. He clicks on his headlights. He turns on the air to chase away the fog creeping along the windows. His wipers flash back and forth to carve away glimpses of a gray world. Lightning flashes. Thunder growls.

Most people are wise enough to stay inside, hunkered down in their recliners with a mug of coffee, a newspaper folded across their lap, every now and then standing up to approach the window and say, "Still blowing." Brian can see them silhouetted in their windows, pulling aside their curtains, as he drives along Highway 97, and then Empire, and then O.B. Riley, on his way to her house.

Through the steady curtain of rain he spots a dump truck, bright orange and flashing its hazard lights and coming toward him, no doubt coming from one of so many developments throughout the city, carrying the rubble of a hill flattened by dynamite or eaten by excavators. When he passes it, its engine growls and its tires tear through a puddle and send up a four-foot wave that hammers his door.

She lives in a wooded neighborhood where each home is set back on a piney lot. The houses are modest. Ranches mostly, with rugged arms of lava rock hugging their bottom half so that they appear to grow from the ground.

The road rises up a hill and loops through a series of basalt outcroppings decorated with streaks of guano and tangles of roots. Aside from a few cars, the road belongs to him alone, so he can afford to take a corner a little too fast. He experiences a moment of weightlessness as the truck hydroplanes, drifting into the next lane—and then the tires find their purchase and the truck stutters forward. To either side of the road, trees sway in the wind. Beyond them he can see the fast-moving gray-bottomed clouds, though barely, with so many fresh drops speckling the window and his wipers only able to swipe so fast.

The house is a two-story neocolonial with a brick facade. He knows this because in a former life he took a history of architecture class at Central Oregon Community College. He still has the books on his bookshelf, from that class and a few others, to paw through occasionally. That was before he enlisted, back when he planned on becoming—he doesn't know what—*some*thing.

She wears pink running shorts, a white tank top, a visor through which her raven black hair rises into a high ponytail. She marches toward him. Her arms pump, her hands made into little fists. The muscles in her thighs, dramatically etched, explode with every step as if trying to shove their way out. "Thanks for coming," she says, closing the distance between them.

"No problem."

She is a few years older than he, early thirties, and about the same height. For this he is thankful. He finds it difficult to speak with people, especially women, when they stand much taller than he. He will often position himself on a stair or a curb or the upward lift of a hill so that he can be the one to look down.

He almost extends his hand for a shake, but doesn't, remembering what his father told him: a woman must offer her hand first or she views it as an invasion. Still, the desire to touch her is strong. He turns away to yank open the hopper and pull down the tailgate and retrieve his toolbox, a big red Craftsman with a mucky rectangle on it, the remains of a Marine Corps bumper sticker he shaved off with a knife and spit.

She moves under the open canopy to shade herself from the rain. She has her arms crossed. She barely manages a smile, her face pinched with embarrassment and anger. "It's so annoying, paying somebody to let me into my own house."

"Sorry."

"No, no, no." She extends a hand to briefly touch his forearm. A candle flame of warmth lingers there. "It's not you who's annoying. I didn't mean to insinuate that. Obviously it's not you. It's my husband."

He doesn't know how to respond to this, and they stand there for a moment, looking at each other. Above them a rain-drenched basketball net hangs like a chandelier. The wind gathers speed and hurls a wall of rain at them, darkening their clothes.

A shiver works its way through her body and she glances over her shoulder and he follows her eyes across the street to a white ranch with green shutters. In the picture window stands an elderly couple, watching them. "My neighbors," she says. "They don't have much to do."

He raises his arm to give them a wave and they retreat from their window as if he just slung a rock at them.

"I guess I'm scary," he says.

She gives him an appraising look, the corner of her mouth hooked up in a smile. "I guess." The rain sticks to her eyelashes. Beads run down her bare shoulders.

"Listen," he says. "You better head back to the nosy neighbors. This might take a minute or it might take thirty."

"Please hurry," she says in an exaggerated whisper. "It smells horribly of mothballs over there."

"Oh, and I thought that was your perfume." He is not normally clever. The line surprises him.

"You." She scrunches up her face in mock anger and lifts her fist as if to hit him, then realizes they don't know each other at all. "Okay. I'm going now."

He watches her move away from him, her running shoes kicking up tails of water. A varicose vein trails up the back of her leg like a worm nested there.

On the front porch he sets down his toolbox and hunches over it. Nearby sits a wooden bench stenciled with ivy designs, and to either side of it, two clay pots crowded with red geraniums. A withered pumpkin is seated on the bench, left over from Halloween. Its sunken eyes and its sagging grin have black mold in them. Brian can smell the sweet smell of its rotting. A slatted wooden railing surrounds the porch. Beyond it, a half-moon garden of chrysanthemums, autumn crocus, and goldenrod. He imagines her squatting out there, deadheading flowers, pulling weeds. In the rain, mud rises up from the mulch and splatters the side of the house.

He observes all of this while slowly unloading his tools, finally selecting a hook pick. He tries the door. The knob turns freely. He pushes and the door catches against the deadbolt. He slides the hook pick into it. Carefully, like a dentist skimming the plaque off a sensitive tooth, he counts the number of pins within the lock. Then he selects a blank key and polishes the top of it—the part the pins will come into contact with—before shoving it into the deadbolt and turning it, binding it with the lock. He jiggles it several times before withdrawing it. The polished brass carries perpendicular scrapes from the pins. He uses a rat-tail file to etch the key, following the scrapes, carving away only a few millimeters of brass before polishing the blank again and returning it to the deadbolt and repeating the process several times over. Wet weather makes for stubborn locks. After twenty minutes, the lock gives and the door yawns open and he peers into the shadowy foyer before turning to wave his hand, to give the all-clear, only to see her already jogging toward him.

She bounds up the stairs and runs a hand across her face, wiping away the rain. "You're my savior." She is smiling. He can't help but feel there is something joyless about the smile. Her lips are red. Her teeth are long and white; they remind him of bones seen through a wound.

He nods. "I'm your savior." He can't seem to stop himself from nodding. She has her head cocked, watching him curiously, waiting for him to say something else—probably good-bye—but he likes standing on her porch while the rain hisses and the pine trees sway. He likes feeling the heat of her next to him. He likes smelling her sweat mixed up with the dank sage riding the breeze. So he tries to prolong the moment by saying something to keep himself here longer—the first thing that pops into his head: "You like to run?" He barely holds back the flinch he feels ready to seize his face.

"I run every morning."

"And you like that?"

With almost a frown, a brusque shake of her head. "It makes me feel better."

His hand begins to rise toward his forehead, to circle the dent there, but at the last minute he stops it, not wanting to call attention to the injury. In the air his hand hangs, as if he were reaching out to her.

Her grip closes around his like a trap, surprisingly strong. She thinks he is offering her a parting handshake. He is so thankful for her mistake he blurts out, "On the house!"

She releases his hand and looks to the roof with a startled expression. "What is?"

"Me." He crouches on the ground and begins collecting his tools. In the distance thunder rumbles. "This service, I mean. The unlocked door."

"Oh. You scared me for a second there." She gives a nervous laugh and puts a hand to her breast. "I thought you meant—are you sure? I'm happy to pay. It's my fault after all." Her smile falters. "My husband's."

He drops the lid and snaps the clasp in place and stands up. The weight of the toolbox makes him lean to one side. "I wouldn't feel right about it."

"Why in the world not? This is your business."

"It's my pleasure." He gives her a nod before clomping down the porch, into the rain, where he runs his thumb along the teeth of the newly sharpened key before sliding it into his pocket.

The rain surges, blending the world into a single gray element. Thick tongues of mud lick their way across the road. Windblown branches paw at his windows. It is always this way in the fall. The parched yellow summer gives way to a sudden gray as the storms crawl over the Cascades carrying bags of water drawn from the Pacific.

Which means the blasting white of winter will come soon enough. How he hates winter. Everything hurts more in the cold. A fingernail caught on the head of a raised screw. A knee banged against an ice-cobbled sidewalk. A knuckle scraped over asphalt when changing a tire, losing your grip on the tire iron. His head. Especially his sunken head.

He imagines the inside of his body as a cave with a red river flowing through it, and when the temperature drops, the river hardens into a red ice floe and red icicles hang from every corner of his insides, so that when he knocks into something or something knocks into him, the ice cracks, the icicles bite. And in a place like Bend, where winter glooms the sky and frosts the roads for the better part of five months, there's a lot of hurt.

Today feels like the beginning of the hurt, a throbbing reminder of what waits around the corner. A severe thunderstorm and flash flood warning is in effect until early evening. The temperature hovers around sixty but the wind makes it feel like fifty. Three inches of rain have already fallen—with two more inches to come before the storm lurches into eastern Oregon, where it will steadily lose power, falling apart in the desert.

This is what he hears when he flips the radio stations—the excited voices of weathermen talking about changing pressure systems, wind flow patterns, surface temperatures, and dew points—interrupted by syrupy pop songs. Nothing about Iraq. There never is.

He fingers the dent in his forehead. It has begun to throb, as if his pulse has focused there all the blood in his body. In the corner of his right eye he sees a flashing he at first mistakes for lightning. But no thunder follows. And the flashing—a white flashing that blinks in and out of sight—continues, worsens. He navigates the road with one hand while using the other to press into the dent, trying to relieve the pressure there, trying to think about something pleasant—the woman, Karen—but the rain and the winding road and his head, his aching head, prevent him. This is how his migraines always begin.

Soon his mouth will taste like metal. Soon the nausea, a sour turning in his belly, will boil over. Soon his right eye will go completely white as if veiled by a holy cataract. The pain, beginning behind his eyes and slowly clawing its way through his body until it hums at the ends of his fingertips, will grip him completely.

Ahead he spots a BP gas station, the familiar green shield floating out of the rain-swept murkiness. He snaps off the radio. He slows the truck to a crawl and grips the wheel with both hands and concentrates so intensely on an empty parking space that he doesn't see the black BMW pulling away from the pump. He cuts it off and the driver brakes with a squeal and lays on the horn and yells something fierce out his window that Brian cannot register.

He yanks the gearshift into park and pops the glove box and withdraws a bottle of Excedrin. He thumbs it open and shakes three pills into his palm and jams them in his mouth and chews them down into a bitter paste, wincing at the taste but knowing the medicine will work its way into him that much faster.

A shadow appears in the driver's side window—a man, Brian realizes as a face comes into focus—the man from the BMW. He wears a yellow polo shirt dotted with rain. "What's wrong with you, you fucking prick?" he says and slams his fist against the window and leaves behind a smear of rainwater. "What's wrong with you?"

Brian makes no response and the man retreats from view and the rain drums and the truck rocks and the windshield appears scalloped as the wind dashes over it. He closes his eyes and waits for the pain to pass or arrive in full.

When his eyes are closed, when the world is dark and he has nowhere else to retreat except the caverns of his mind, he thinks of Iraq: outside Ramadi, in Al Anbar Province: 2nd Battalion, 34th Marines. He was a staff sergeant. He has difficulty remembering days in particular. They swirl together and become flits and flashes of one big maddening day in which nothing changed and everything was bleached of its color. Same watery potatoes slopped on a tray for chow. Same games of euchre, five-card stud, seven-up. Same rusted bench press in the fitness tent. Same desert cammies with salt stains around the collar and crotch. Same Humvees growling and helicopters stuttering and mortar rounds snarling and small-arm fire popping. Same conversations about pussy and basketball and action movies and pimped-out cars. Same three-hour outpost guard shift—chewing his fingernails and smoking Camel cigarettes and flipping through porno magazines and kicking a hole in the ground and jerking off into it and watching the cum soak into the sand—leaving him half stunned with boredom. Same nosebleeds and cracked skin. Same Porta-Johns with flies and shit-soaked heat fuming out of them. Same sandals, robes, turbans, beards. Same eucalyptus trees and elephant grass and prayer mats and crows on telephone wires. Same black eyes floating from behind black hijabs, a sea of black ghosts swirling in and out of sight. Same everything. And everything with sand in it, from his Diet Pepsi to his M-16 to his pubic hair.

Of course there were moments that punctuated the even passing of the days, that punched holes in his cyclical memory of Iraq. The boy in a tattered brown robe hurling a rock at him and darting down an alley. The old woman who touched his face with her hands and spoke what sounded like an angry song. The camel shot with a flare as a joke, its hindquarters on fire, braying and galloping in circles, trying to outrun the burning. The deaf man flex-cuffed and hurled to the ground because he wouldn't respond to their commands. The charred carcass of a Chinook chopper trucked into the outpost with the body of its pilot still melted into his seat.

The bomb that opened up in his skull.

There were bombs everywhere. Tucked under cars, overpasses, trash piles. Buried beneath a dirt road. Sewn into a vest. Stuffed into the carcasses of dead dogs. They were soaked in napalm or packed with black powder or gummed with plastic explosive. They were decorated with nails and stainless steel balls that tore through a body like buckshot through a stop sign.

That day is like a series of broken images, a torn film strip flapping through a projector. Forty clicks west of Baghdad. Fallujah. Two Humvees. Eight men, Brian among them. They were carrying supplies to the base under construction there, growling through a blond-colored collection of buildings that might have been carved by the shamal winds from dunes. The day had been quiet, the streets relatively empty. Whenever they did pass a car, he remembers holding his breath for a minute to survive the dust it threw up, making a game of it. He did not hear the explosion nor did he see it. One moment they were driving. And the next moment they were not. One moment the sky was a pale blue—and the next moment, red with fire, black with smoke.

He remembers slumping away from the Humvee and sitting down in the middle of the street and watching his shadow grow darker with the blood leaking from him. He remembers looking at the twisted snarl of flaming metal and seeing the bodies hanging out of it and crawling from it and thinking somebody ought to do something. He remembers the sound of distant gunfire that could be for a wedding or could be for a funeral or could be from another patrol. He remembers the rotorwash of the Blackhawk that sent the dust swirling from the street and the flies buzzing from his head as it touched down to carry him to the CSH in Baghdad. The IVs, the damp towels, the white sheets, the fog of painkillers.

He was lucky, they told him. He wasn't dead. And he wasn't like Williams, who suffered a spinal fracture and will spend the rest of his life limp in a motorized chair. He wasn't like Jones, who was unable to pull himself out of the gun turret and whose skin melted away in a rush of flaming gasoline. He wasn't like Carlson, who lost his legs and who gets around on prosthetics known as C-Legs with microprocessors that sense movement and adjust hydraulics.

The shrapnel peppered his arm and shoulder with small pieces of metal later dug out with tweezers. Today, he has to hunt among his hairs to even find the scars. The real damage came to his skull—a section three inches in circumference, gone, carved away by a piece of metal driven through the air.

Here his second stop-loss tour ended with an honorable discharge and a Purple Heart and a photograph of him in the *Bend Bulletin* shaking hands with the mayor, his face half obscured by bandages, his mouth unsmiling, his eyes staring into the camera with a kind of deadened resolve as if it were a 60 x 80mm scope trained in his direction. Those first few months back in Oregon he would wake up feeling as though he had taken the wrong plane and arrived at a place where no one knew him and where he should not be and where his anxiety could at any moment take command of him. He knew he was being paranoid, knew his black-veined fear to be unreasonable—but he could not help himself despite this knowledge.

The high desert landscape didn't help, central Oregon reminding him so much of Iraq. The sandy soil that rose up in clouds and clung to skin, to cars. The stark sections of land where no life could be found except a vulture circling the sky and range steers feeding off bunch grass. The daytime heat giving way to nights so cold you could see your breath. And so he straddled two regions at once, occupying a gray territory. He startled at loud noises: a train whistle, a backfiring car, a dynamite explosion from a hilltop community under construction. He peered carefully at the underbellies of bridges and overpasses when he drove beneath them, hunting for the IEDs he knew were not there. If someone walked by him quickly in the mall or on the sidewalk, he imagined striking them in the windpipe with his fist, dropping them, demanding to know the rush of their business.

No one ever asked him about the war. Not one neighbor, not one friend or former teacher, not even if they carried a Support Our Troops ribbon on their lapel or bumper. They only said, "It's good you're home." It was at moments like this, especially when their eyes lingered on his forehead—at first the bandages, later the scar tissue, bubblegum pink—that he felt on the verge of collapse. Alone. Inapt. Not a part of Iraq, not a part of Oregon. Not a marine and not a citizen—just a vessel of blood and bone and gristle floating and turning in the air. For a long time he did not feel he was capable of continuing to live a normal life, of achieving any sort of sense of comfort. He felt that he had lost more than a section of his skull. He had lost himself as well.

He blames his frontal lobe. He remembers the doctors telling him about the spider-shaped lesion there. This was why he had such initial difficulty putting words together, solving math problems, maintaining an erection. This was why his expression rarely changed, stoned-faced, dead-faced. There was a numbing effect, as if someone had excised a certain nerve from his body. He remembers in the weeks after his discharge, sitting in a Shari's restaurant, sipping coffee and forking into a piece of strawberry pie, when a mother and her child—a round-faced toddler with a black shock of hair—sat down at a nearby booth. When the toddler broke a green crayon and began crying inconsolably, a high-pitched wailing that made him think of an air-raid siren, he imagined smashing the kid's skull against the edge of the table until it cleaved in two and spilled forth a red mess not so different from that of his pie. He wasn't sure what he felt in that moment, a half-chewed bite of strawberry softening on his tongue. Anger? No. Anger was a word with too much octane in it. He felt an impulse to strike out. That was a better way of thinking about his mind and its rewiring, as something that responded to impulses. He knew he was not normal. He knew people would hate him if they were privy to his thoughts. He knew he ought to feel guilty, regretful, about the child, about the thousands of tiny nightmares that went through his head every day. But he does not.

He remembers when things didn't feel so dark, when life seemed bright with beauty, with possibility. He remembers sitting in his desert cammies on a Curtiss Commando transport plane—on his way out of Romania after a refuel, on his way to Mosul—when he peered from the window and beyond the green rolling hills and sparkling lakes and saw the Carpathians mantled with snow and felt completely alive and connected to the two hundred men around him who would face horror and frustration and who would die for one another.

That feeling is unavailable to him now. He does not see himself as part of anything, only apart. His company is best suited for the woods.

Sometimes he drives out into the desert and parks in the shadow of a juniper or a monolith of rock whose shape suggests a fossilized animal. When he sits in his truck with the country sprawling all around him, when he hears the wind moaning through the canyons and whispering through the sagebrush, when he observes the sun ride up in the sky and burn the color out of stones and the moisture out of soil, when a cluster of ants carries a grasshopper carcass into their swarming nest, when a hawk drops out of the empty blue and strikes a rattlesnake and carries it off to a fencepost to peel apart, Brian understands he is a part of the scenery—simply an animal, a complicated animal—and as an animal he can be either prey or predator, a target or the arrow that hastens toward it.

Now, at the gas station, when he opens his eyes again, he finds the bleak weather departed, the clouds blown off into the desert. The rain has clarified the air, revealing the mountains, dusted with fresh snow that gleams in the sunlight. He can appreciate their beauty only distantly, distracted as he is by the faint throbbing in his temple. At moments like these, he cannot help but feel someone has bored into his skull to burrow around, picking at his mind like a careless locksmith.

JUSTIN

Justin has not spoken to his father for three months. Not since he returned home from the hospital and began weight lifting in the living room, shirtless, his chest cloven by a zipper-shaped scar. "Got to get back into it," he said. When Justin scolded him for this, his father told him to fuck off, mind his business.

Paul has always been like bad weather—relentless, expansive, irritating—but since the heart attack he has grown even wilder and more unreasonable, as if, having cheated death, the laws of life no longer apply to him.

The long silence is not unusual. Over the years, their conversations often begin on a normal note—how's work, how's the fishing. Then their voices rise in argument, though usually they can't remember what about after a few weeks pass. Such is the natural rhythm between them—every season for them like the emotional course of a year for most fathers and sons, where the small pangs of affection felt during the holidays are inevitably followed by arguments followed by long silences followed by making peace.

Which is why, when November nears and his father calls and invites Justin to join him camping and hunting in Echo Canyon, he only hesitates a moment before saying yes.

"You're sure?" his father says.

"Sure I'm sure." And suddenly he is. He looks forward to leaving behind the traffic that hums through the town, the exhaust-spewing trucks and SUVs. He looks forward to getting some clean air in him and some motion under him. And he looks forward to spending one last weekend in Echo Canyon, so that he might say good-bye, as Bobby Fremont plans to break ground next week.

"Good. I think . . ." His father's voice falls off a cliff here, uncharacteristically uncertain.

Justin tries to fill in the sentence for him. "Some guy time would definitely be healthy."

"Exactly," his father says, relieved, his voice rising to a manly pitch reserved for taverns and locker rooms. "We'll drink some beers and raise some hell!" He clears his throat. "And, you know, shoot the bull."

Several silent seconds pass as Justin wonders what kind of conversation qualifies as *bull:* hunting stories, dirty jokes, drywalling advice?

"And bring that kid of yours," his father says before hanging up. "I'll make a man out of him yet."

That night Justin dreams a dream he has not had in a long time.

He is in a meadow lit by silvery moonlight. From the surrounding forest a song plays, a children's song, "Teddy Bears' Picnic." It sounds muted and scratchy, as if played on an old gramophone. "If you go down in the woods today, you better not go alone. It's lovely down in the woods today, but safer to stay at home." The lyrics, sung in a lazy baritone, have always bothered him. His mother claims he howled and clapped his hands over his ears and ran from the room every time she tried to play it for him as a child.

From the trees, a half circle of black hunchbacked figures emerges, advancing into the meadow. Their shapes seem to waver, shifting like smoke. After a few loping paces they stop and sway to the music and lower themselves, as if crouching. From them comes a noise Justin recognizes—a scream—a scream of pain brought on by an animal caught in barbed wire while his father roughly whispered, *Shoot, shoot, shoot.* He is flinching, as if subject to some blunt force, flinching before the shadows of the forest of his mind.

The figures move forward again. As they come closer, he recognizes them as bears, all of them walking upright, wobbly-legged. Strands of barbed wire hang from them like the wires of a lurid marionette. Their fur is damp with blood. Their eyes are black. Together their chests swell in a collective breath, the prelude to another scream that goes on and on as they continue forward, spreading out into an irregular crescent that will, in a black knot, enclose him.

He jerks awake with the song still looping through his head and his father's face taking shape in every shadow of the room. Outside the moon creeps higher in the sky and his fear gives way to an uneasy state of anticipation as he thinks about the trip—his ability to steady his rifle and his father.

KAREN

Tonight she grills steaks. She thinks her husband ought to do this—she thinks he ought to do a number of things, like lift weights and scream at football games and take a wrench to leaky faucets. These are, after all, things that men do. But he isn't very handy and doesn't have time for the gym and the only sport he watches with any interest is soccer. She doesn't know what the right word is for him. Tame? Maybe this is why he doesn't have many friends?

Whenever she asks him to grill, he plays dumb, fumbling with the knobs and dropping the tongs and sighing loudly, saying he doesn't remember the temperature for pork, questioning whether he needs all the burners on and how high. The meat is always dry and rubbery by the time he is done with it. Long ago she stopped asking for his help, and now she stands on the back patio, tending the three-burner, stainless steel Ducane grill with the steaks sputtering and hissing inside and the smoke rising off it to mingle with the smoke rising from their chimney. The evening is cool and Justin threw into the fireplace some split pine from the tall pile of firewood his father cut and dropped off earlier in the week.

She uses a dry rub of garlic salt, black pepper, cayenne pepper, and cinnamon, a little sweet to balance out the spice. She tosses the steaks—big porterhouse cuts from a grass-fed Angus they had slaughtered to fill the freezer in their garage—on the grill for ten seconds, then flips them, sealing in the juice. She snaps off the flame for the central burner and closes the lid and the grill becomes a kind of convection oven. Waves of heat come off it, but she doesn't step away, even as her skin goes tight and she feels as if she is going to split, as if her inside is bigger than her outside.

When the steaks are done—she can tell just by pushing the tongs against them, the give of the meat—she drops them onto a plate and carries them inside, where at the kitchen table her husband is grading papers and her son is reading the latest issue of *National Geographic.*

"Heads up, mouths open," she says and sets down the steaming plate next to the wooden salad bowl full of spinach and romaine lettuce, the homemade multigrain bread wrapped in a cloth. Everything is organic. Beef hormones cause cancer and cause girls to have their periods at nine. Pesticides on lettuce cause cancer and autism. The preservatives in bread cause cancer. The preservatives in croutons cause cancer. The preservatives in mayonnaise-based dressing cause cancer and the trans-fat in it causes coronary heart disease. She subscribes to e-newsletters like the *Daily Green* and subscribes to RSS feeds from Safemama.com. She shops mainly at the Bend co-op. She belongs to a community-supported farm. She believes she is taking care of her family—she is keeping them from harm. For this, she receives no thanks. Her husband whines about the money she spends on food and her son whines about wanting a McDonald's burger, a Mountain Dew.

Now the two of them glance up at her. Without saying a word, they fill their plates and begin to eat. Justin neatly arranges his meal into three even sections. "I don't like my food to trespass on other food," he once said—her husband, who now holds a pen in one hand and a fork in the other, at once munching his salad and scribbling some marginal comment in green ink on a student's essay. The table is quiet except for the sound of their chewing, their silverware clinking and sawing. In the fireplace a pitch pocket pops, and for a moment they all look there, where orange flames lick their tongues across the half-blackened wood, before returning their attention to their plates.

When Karen cuts her steak, the center is as purple as a plum, just the way she likes it. A well-done steak is a steak charred through with carcinogens. Blood pools on her plate and she soaks it up with her bread. Before bringing it to her mouth, she says, "Doesn't anybody want to talk? About something?"

Justin slows his chewing, swallows, licks his lips. "What do you want to talk about?" Spinach clings to his teeth.

"Surprise me."

Justin's eyes go to the window, where shadows gather in the failing light. "I can't think of a single thing to talk about." He returns his attention to his salad. "Sorry."

Graham sets down his fork and wipes his face with his napkin. "Dave Jasper got busted at school." Karen and Justin look at him and under their gaze he stutters out, "You know Dave. From soccer. From fifth grade—"

"For what?" Justin says.

"For killing coons." His eyes dart between them. "His brother goes out in his truck, down dirt roads, and into alfalfa fields, his brother and his brother's friends, and they take Dave with them. They spotlight the coons and the coons freeze and they jump out of the truck and kill the coons with baseball bats."

Karen's hand falls to the table and makes the plates clatter.

Graham's voice gets faster; he is excited by her disgust, she can tell, like a boy handling lizards, worms, things that make her shriek. "In shop class, Dave was making this bat with nails in it. It was totally medieval-looking and Mr. Steele asked him about it and Dave told him and that's how he got busted."

"That's disgusting. That's like, serial killer in the making. You've heard about how they torture animals when they're young?" Her tone is at first almost amusedly horrified, but as it grows more severe, the smile on Graham's face fades. "I don't think you should be anywhere near that kid, that Dave—"

"Karen." Justin gives a half wave of his hand. "Don't overreact."

"I don't think I'm overreacting. I don't think I'm overreacting."

"It's disturbing, I know. But boys do crazy stuff. *I've* done crazy stuff."

That's rich. Her husband, who scolds her for leaving out her shoes, who folds his socks into tidy little balls, thinks he's a wild man. She crosses her arms and gives him a bitter twist of a smile. "Like *what*?"

"Thrown frogs under the wheels of cars. Shot squirrels and rabbits with BB guns. When I was in high school, a few of us used to kill marmots for money. Ranchers would pay us two bucks a marmot. We'd fill the back of a pickup. I'm not saying I look back on that fondly. I'm saying it's the nature of boys." He has his knife out before him. Its point is aimed at her.

Graham takes a drink of milk and says, "I had this—I—"

"I'm saying that Dave Jasper did something stupid, but one day Graham will probably do something stupid, because boys do stupid things, and you don't want people labeling *him* a psycho."

"Graham is *not* that kind of boy."

"I had this dream last night," Graham says, almost yelling. Karen goes quiet and turns her attention to him, trying to smile and not quite pulling it off. But she'll listen. He's trying, after all, to salvage their dinner, to turn the conversation. "It was a crazy dream."

"Let's hear it." Karen neatens her silverware.

"I dreamed about us going hunting." He nods at his father. "About when we go to Echo Canyon. I dreamed I got shot. Some man was hunting me through the forest and I kept trying to outrun him but he was always there, around every corner. At one point I looked down and noticed I was naked." He blushes here as if imagining them imagining him stripped of clothes. "And my body was totally covered in fur. Not hair. *Fur.*"

"That sounds more like your grandpa." Karen's joke has an edge to it. She does not like, not one bit, the idea of her son away for the weekend with his grandfather. She believes him to be more than a bad influence, someone who finds the faults in everything, who makes fun of organic food and fair trade and liberal pantywaists, who speaks of blood and weaponry with smiling relish. He is those things, and those things are bad enough, but he is also half bent with the same kind of madness that would send someone into the night with a baseball bat jeweled with nails. She doesn't trust him. And around him she doesn't trust her husband, so easily cowed.

No one laughs at her joke. If anything, Graham's voice grows more earnest when he says, "Finally he got me." He indicates where, right beneath his left breast. "When I woke up it hurt." He rubs the spot. "It still hurts."

At that moment something drops down the chimney and onto the fire. There is a terrible screeching, the noise a nail makes when drawn harshly across metal. Something moves there, a black thing surrounded briefly by flames—an owl, Karen realizes—a great horned owl the size of a toddler.

She can barely register the seeming impossibility of such a thing—when the owl opens its wings and hurriedly flaps them and launches itself into the air. Its claws are open and its beak is open and it flaps and screeches its way through the living room, battering the walls and windows, seeking escape, its feathers smoldering, leaving smoke in the air like contrails from a jet. There is an old wedding photo sitting on the mantel and the owl knocks it from its perch and it shatters on the floor. Then the owl makes a beeline for the dinette. Justin releases a scream to match the owl's and Graham falls over backward in his chair and Karen ducks down and runs for the front door and throws it open and not ten seconds later the owl departs through it, disappearing into the evening.

Karen has her hands over her heart to settle it, its beating like a hammer wrapped in cloth. "Holy shit." She closes the door and leans against it.

Graham pulls himself—and then his chair—up from the floor. He opens and closes his mouth but doesn't seem to know what to say. The house smells as if it is cooking. A few feathers—clear and incandescent, the color burned out of them—float through the air like the lost wings of wasps.

"What the hell happened?" Karen says. Her breathing is tough, like she just got back from a run.

Justin shakes his head as if he doesn't know even as he says, "When I was a kid, starlings would fall down the chimney. They liked the updraft. The warmth of it. Sometimes they'd get high on the fumes and pass out." He stands and walks to the fireplace and picks up the fallen photo—he and Karen are smiling in the back of a limousine—the glass from its frame now sprayed across the hardwood, reflecting the fire and seeming to emit an orange glow. "I guess we ought to get a chimney cap."

"Why don't we have one? Shouldn't you have installed one? You know we didn't have one, so you must have thought about this?" She cannot stop herself. Her shock has turned over like a black dog and become anger that grows worse when he only half tunes in to the upset buzz of her voice as it rises between them like the smoke of the burning owl. "Seriously, Justin," she says, moving toward him, snatching the photo and setting it roughly on the mantel once more. "The windowsill has dryrot. The outlet in the bathroom doesn't work. There are bees' nests in the soffits. One of the porch steps feels off-kilter." Her voice is close to cracking with emotion. She hates when she comes undone, but lately it happens more and more, her temper flashing, taking over.

Sometimes she feels like two women. One of the women is a mother and wife. And after Graham takes his nightly bath—after he brushes his teeth and pulls on his jammies and climbs into bed—he calls out for this mother and she walks down the hall and pauses in the doorway of his bedroom. He lies there, the covers pulled up to his chin. At the sight of her, his eyes scrunch shut and his mouth trembles with the start of a smile, as he pretends to sleep. She walks slowly to his bed—slowly because every footstep scares a shiver or a giggle from him—and then she—again, slowly—drags the sheet from his body until he is completely exposed. They both are laughing at this point. At the base of his bed, with two hands, she then snaps the sheet and it hangs in the air a moment before sinking into the shape of him. And then it is time for the kiss—one on each eye, the nose, the mouth.

This last Christmas she bought him a digital camera. Since then, he was rarely without it, its carrier clipped to his belt. He studied its manual as if he would be tested—dog-earing pages, highlighting passages. He would snap photos of things she thought strange. A damp mass of hair pulled from the drain. A dead chipmunk by the side of the road. His big toe after he accidentally rammed it into the coffee table and brought a half-moon bruise to the nail. He talked seriously about aperture, megapixels, the light being all wrong. She thought he was so funny, not really a boy but a funny little man. When she asked him what he liked so much about photography, he brought his hand to his chin and rubbed it, completely earnest, unaware of how theatrical he appeared. Many of his movements and speech patterns were like this, like he was putting on a show, playing adult. Finally he said that he liked the way the camera stopped time. "It's like a superpower. I can freeze something forever, exactly how it was. Do you know what I mean?"

She knew. She kept a shoebox in the back of her closet. In it were trinkets from the past—her retainer, pressed flowers, a pencil sketch of a horse, love letters from old boyfriends, a blue ribbon from a district track meet, and some photos, among them a shot of her soon after she graduated from high school. That summer, with a group of girlfriends, she had climbed South Sister. The photo caught her at its summit, among the clouds, balanced on a knob of basalt. She wasn't facing the camera, but staring off at the ragged jawline of the Cascades. She wasn't smiling, but looked happy, satisfied, and stared hard into the distance as if she was about to journey there and only needed to steel herself to the idea.

So there was the woman who tucked her son into bed each night, who baked cookies and dirtied her knees in the garden—and then there was the other woman, the one on top of the mountain, the one Karen lately couldn't get out of her head. For years she had been neglecting that person, shoving her down into a hole, containing her behind walls mortared by makeup and casseroles and laundry detergent.

That used to be me, she thought when she sat on the edge of the bed and studied the photo—or sometimes, in disbelief, *that's me?*

That's who the anger belongs to, the woman who climbs mountains, who wants her life to count for something, to mean something, and these past few years she has steadily come to believe that isn't the case.

Now her husband walks past her, through the living room, across the short hallway, to the dinette, where Graham is again seated, watching them. Justin pulls up his chair and retrieves his napkin off the floor. With his fork he stabs at the remains of his salad. "I'm so busy I can't get my own work done. It bothers you so much, call someone."

She follows him as far as the hallway and stops there, between rooms. "Don't you think that's your job?"

"I told you I'm too busy."

"To call someone? You're too busy to call someone?"

"No. I thought you meant—" He closes his eyes and takes a deep breath. "If you want me to call someone, I can call someone."

"I want you to call someone."

"Okay. I will." His eyes are still closed. "Let's change the subject, okay?"

"Okay," she says and means it. She doesn't want to be angry. Especially in front of Graham. She steps into the dinette and goes to her son, puts her hands on his shoulders, squeezes. "It's okay." He bends his neck to look up at her and she puts her hand to his face, which seems to change every time she looks at him. When he was younger, he used to walk around the house in his woolly socks and shoot lightning bolts from his fingertips—zapping her on the elbow, the knee—and one day he startled her in the bathroom and she jerked a hot curling iron to his forehead. He still carries the scar, a little reminder of the moment, just above his left eyebrow. It was an accident—she kept telling him that—it was an accident. But she had hurt him, and when you hurt your child, it doesn't matter whether you meant to or not. The hurt is there, imprinted on them, because of you. The wrong word or a raised hand no different from the toxins in so many foods, working their way into them, changing them for the worse. She touches the scar now and then kisses it. "Everything's okay."

She spots a bit of gray in his hair. "You've got something," she says and seeks the something with her fingers. When she recognizes it as a feather, she flicks it away. "Jesus," she says and sticks out her tongue. "I hate birds. I've always hated them ever since I saw that bird movie—what's it called?"

"*The Birds?*" Justin says.

"That's the one." Again she shivers at the memory of the owl. "*God.* Nature."

BRIAN

Sometimes the biggest challenge of the day seems to be figuring out what shows to watch. He sinks into the couch and flips through the five hundred channels available to him and shoves Doritos into his mouth until the bag is empty and his camo shirt is dusted over orange. A few months ago, on the Discovery Channel, he happened upon a program about skinwalkers. These were Navajo witches who scrabbled about on all fours while wearing wolf hides. Their eyes burned against their pale faces like red mites pressed into fungus. They chanted backward chants to raise evil spirits and they unearthed graves and they stole hair and skin and fingernails from the dead and ground them into a corpse powder that they blew in your face to give you a ghost sickness.

He had always been fascinated by the supernatural. As a child he used his allowance to buy *Tales from the Crypt* comic books and he snuck from his father's bookshelves novels by Stephen King and he asked to spend the night at a neighbor's house only because he could rent R-rated horror movies. Nights he often spent with his blanket wrapped around him like a cocoon, the breathing hole at his mouth the only part of him exposed.

In eighth grade he dressed up as an ape for Halloween. He had a full-body suit with shaggy black hair and a mouthful of teeth. No one at school knew who he was. He would walk up to girls and stare at them and say nothing and they would press their backs to their lockers and hide behind their friends to give him a wide berth. Some people laughed but with a nervousness that made their laughter come across as forced and wheezy. It was the first time he felt powerful.

He kept the ape suit in his closet and sometimes he would put it on and stare at himself in the mirror and thump his chest—once, twice—while breathing heavily into his mask. He did not know why but it gave him an erection. Normally his father would not return from work until dinnertime, so he felt safe to walk around the house in the ape suit and watch television and do his homework at the kitchen table, but one day his father came home early and because Brian had the television volume up he did not hear the growl of the engine or the crunch of gravel or even the rattle of keys. When his father pushed open the door to the garage with a pizza balanced in one hand, Brian sprang up from the couch. This startled a yell from his father and he dropped the pizza box on the floor—its cardboard mouth burped cheese and pepperoni.

Moths—Pandora moths the size of hands—fluttered in from outside while his father leaned against the open door and observed Brian with hooded eyes that revealed his curiosity and disappointment. "What's wrong with you?" he finally said. The ape suit went in the garbage that night, but Brian hasn't stopped thinking about it—the way an amputee will never stop thinking about a lost limb—remembering the sense of power that came with it.

Over the past few months he has trapped weasel and pine martens and coyote and beaver and even a wolverine. For all except the beaver, which required an open-cut dissection, he sliced around the hind legs below the hock and sliced up the back of the hind legs to the anus and from there stripped the pelt off the hind legs. He removed the tail bone by slicing from the anus along the bottom side of the tail to its tip and then worked it free from the bone. He pulled the skin delicately off their pink bodies as if pulling a damp nightgown from a woman, pausing at the head, where he had to cut through their ear cartilage and around the eyes and through their lips to slip off the pelt completely.

Then came the fat, the flesh, the gristle—scraping it off—and then washing the pelt with soap and water and patting it off with a towel. He keeps several wooden stretchers in the garage and he centered the pelts on them and pulled them taut and waited a day for them to dry and then turned them and waited another day and then wetted their underside with vegetable oil to keep them pliant and brushed their fur with a dog comb so that they appeared fluffy, shiny.

From the Goodwill he bought a mannequin to use as a frame. He had learned how to sew in the service, but never with leather. The Internet told him everything he did not already know, such as how to keep the holes clean by lightly dampening the stitch groove and polishing the diamond awl blade with a block of beeswax before every punch. With a waxed five-cord linen thread that runs from a thousand-yard spool he used a saddle stitch method, pulling snug so as not to break the thread or rip a stitch.

He made the leggings first—from four gray-furred coyotes—and then puzzled the rest of the pelts together to match his upper body, binding the variant furs and their colors to make a patchwork coat that hung from him loosely and would not tear if he ran and contorted himself oddly when climbing a tree or leaping across a canal.

And now he is nearly done, tying off the final stitch for the helmet or mask—he isn't sure what to call it—made from the beaver he trapped the other day. He is in the living room—seated on the same lumpy couch and watching the same wood-framed Mitsubishi television as he was when his father surprised him so many years ago. *Wheel of Fortune* is playing. Pat Sajak is making small talk with a contestant, a man from Kentucky who has a wonderful wife and dreams of one day taking a cruise to Alaska. His hands are deformed. They look like fleshy lobster claws. Another contestant spins the wheel for him.

The sun has set. The curtains are closed. The mannequin stands nearby, draped in the hair suit. Its blue eyes stare into a void and its pink mouth puckers into a dead smile. On television the wheel is spinning, and in the living room Brian is scissoring off a loose thread and knotting its end. The category is Action and the puzzle is three words. Brian sharpens a pair of scissors on a whetstone, then holds his fist inside the furred mask to brace it as he scissors two eye holes and carves open a slit for breathing.

The wheel is rattling its kaleidoscope of pie-wedge colors, glittery numbers. It nearly comes to a stop on bankruptcy but clicks forward another notch to the silvery promise of a thousand dollars. "Touching you naked," Brian says to the television. And then, more loudly, "It's *touching you naked,* you idiots."

The man closes his eyes and lifts his deformed hands as if in benediction. A moment passes before Brian realizes the man is crossing his fingers. "Thumbing your nose," the man guesses. Lights flash. Bells ring. The audience claps and Pat Sajak smiles and the man does a little dance and throws back his head and opens his mouth to reveal a black cave of laughter that seems to swallow up the screen when Brian punches the remote and everything goes dark.

Brian stands from the couch and approaches the mannequin. He stares into its blank blue eyes a moment before fitting the mask over its head. He surveys his work as a tailor, tidying a sleeve, brushing his hands across the fur, petting it. A musky smell rises off the suit, somewhere between a groin and a wet dog—a smell that surrounds him, minutes later, when he strips naked and steps into the pants and tightens their belt and then pulls on the jacket and finally the mask. The noise and the heat of his breathing surround him and he experiences that old familiar feeling of power and excitement. An erection throbs to life. It is his first in months.

He walks from the living room down a narrow hallway and into his bedroom. There is a full-length mirror mounted on the closet door and he studies his reflection in it. The only source of light is a 40-watt bulb glowing above him. It has about the same effect as a flashlight, throwing long shadows that squirm all over his body when he moves. He likes the way the mask fits snugly to his face, like armor.

When Brian was young, his father took him to a Noh drama playing at the community college. The music was unlike any he had ever heard: the calm murmur of the bamboo flute backgrounded by the sometimes slow, sometimes manic tapping of the taiko drum. And he remembers, more than anything, the masks the actors wore.

In every Noh drama there are five types of masks—gods, demons, men, women, and the elderly—meant to depict the essential spirit of the character. And these five masks were sold afterward in the lobby. He remembers picking up the demonic mask, with its red skin and bulging white eyes. A thin mustache framed its mouth, trailing to its chin. Horns rose from its forehead. In the way of little boys, he loved it precisely for its ugliness. He begged his father to buy him one as a souvenir, but they were too expensive, so he settled instead for a cassette that featured music from the production.

He still has the tape. Its cover is faded and its sound is bothered by the occasional hiss of static, but it plays. His boom box from high school still sits on his dresser and he inserts the tape into it now and turns up the volume.

The reedy whistle of a flute fills the room, followed by a gunshot chorus of drumbeats. He begins to dance. The hair suit weighs probably thirty pounds and at first he slings his arms and bends his legs with some clumsiness, getting used to this second skin—and then he becomes more comfortable, his motions more fluid. Sweat begins to trail down his back and stomach. Beneath the mask his breath is like a great wind.

As the music plays, as he leaps about his room, there is a kind of darkroom going on inside his skull. Pictures get dipped in briny solutions. At first they are white. Then they darken in places to reveal a naked woman with a paper bag over her head, a pistol growing out of a man's crotch, a Muslim laying down a prayer rug made of human flesh, a camel burning, a six-fingered hand giving him the finger.

And then he goes to the boom box and hits the stop button and feels trembling all through his body a quiet sense of power. He pulls on a pair of white tube socks and then his combat boots, shined to a black gleam.

"I'm going out," he yells to the house and pauses a moment in the doorway as if awaiting a reply.

Years ago, they decided to have a reunion, his friends from the war. They came from scattered corners of the state but they arrived in Portland at the precise hour—at 8:00 p.m., at twenty hundred hours—at the Irish bar called the Book of Kells whose vast, dark-wooded interior reminded Brian of the belly of a ship. All three were members of the same unit, and though they had not seen each other for many months, they felt instantly comfortable for the history they shared. Two-handed handshakes gave way to hugs gave way to meaty backslaps. Jim was a round-faced man who worked for the Tigard postal service and kept his head shaved and offered an apologetic laugh at the end of every sentence, while Troy was tall and slight with his receding hairline pulled back into a weak ponytail, with punch-colored pouches under his eyes from the long hours he worked as a manager at Kinko's. They said, "So how the hell are you?" and "You're looking good," when they worked their way through the bodies and the tables and found a snug at the back of the bar. A dim light hung over the table and made their skin and their teeth appear yellow.

A waitress in a black skirt and a white collared shirt asked them if they needed a menu and they told her please and then ordered burgers and a pitcher of Bud Light and when she asked if Carlsberg was all right instead, they said, "Sure, sure," and then gave Jim—who had suggested they meet here—a hard time for choosing a joint too good to serve Bud for crissakes.

At first Brian joked and laughed along with them, when they mashed through their burgers and popped fries in their mouths and licked ketchup off their fingers, but then the beer began to take hold of his mind and his thoughts dimmed along with the lights and he said less and less, simply nodding along with the conversation, rubbing the depression in his forehead.

Troy spoke constantly and had difficulty sitting still. He had always been a nervous man, but Brian noticed now his fingernails chewed down to blood. "You remember that time," he said. "You remember? With Big Back?" He told the story of the hotel compound where they were stationed briefly. There was no running water, so to reduce the stink, the Porta-Johns were set outside. This lance corporal—a former high school football star who went by the name of Big Back—was in the john with a *Hustler* when the compound came under mortar and rocket attack. With the smoke whirling and the air shaking and men running in every direction, he blasted out of the john with his pants around his ankles and his dick still in his hand. "Quite possibly the funniest thing in world history."

Brian had been looking forward to seeing them—he really had—but watching Troy tell rapid-fire stories with a mouth full of food and listening to Jim chuckle—*huh-huh-huh,* a kind of heavy breathing—made him feel empty, as if the hole in his forehead had opened and his fluids had drained from it and his body could blow away at any instant, a mere papery husk. He had expected the very opposite; he had expected this meeting to bring him some kind of sustenance, like the rare burger that bled on his plate. These were, after all, the men he showered and shit with, the men he bunked beside, listening to them snore and mumble in their dreams. Together they had stood rigidly in formation and played poker with nudie cards and watched burnt-orange tracer rounds hurry through the night sky like falling stars. "How sick are you, motherfuckers?" a lieutenant had asked them during their second tour. "Sick. We're sick motherfuckers, sir," they had said. "We bleed green. Corps to the core." All had tattooed in black ink the eagle, globe, and anchor across their left shoulder.

When the waitress came by to ask if they wanted a third pitcher, Brian was the last one to say yes.

All his life he has lived in this house—this three-bedroom ranch with the lava-rock chimney and the red cinder driveway—located in Deschutes River Woods, a thickly forested development on the outskirts of town. There are no streetlamps here. Only the stars spiraling above him, the moon staring through the trees like a scarred eye from another world. For a moment Brian stands in his driveway, letting his eyes adjust, before loping off into the trees.

In so many ways he seems to lack some retinal nerve capable of seeing the world as others see it. He knows that most people, in the middle of the woods, in the middle of the night, would feel some level of fear. He does not. If anything, he feels comforted by the black solitude it offers him. When you have seen what he has, and when you know a world away other people are going to the mall and throwing frisbees in the park and drinking coffee in an outdoor café, you come to accept that everything you have ever known to make sense makes probably no sense.

An owl hoots. The wind hushes it. The moon appears balanced on a high remove of rimrock. The world, awash in its blue light, appears drowned in water. He scuttles through the trees, pawing aside branches, dodging roots, leaping over logs and landing on all fours and continuing a few paces as a hunched figure before righting himself. He feels a dark wind moving through him like a cold bellows.

His boots shoosh through the sandy soil and thud against the pitted basalt, keeping time with his heart as he moves north, orienting himself by the stars and the blue-hued mountains glimpsed between the trees. And the moon, always the moon, following his passage.

At the Book of Kells, in the far corner of his booth, his glass sweated in his hand and he shaved the moisture from it with his thumb. When he lifted the glass and brought it to his lips, it left behind a ring on the table, a damp eye peering up at him through the wood grain. He wondered what it saw, what they saw, as they watched him, tried to include him in their conversation. They asked him if he dreamed about the war and he said, "Some nights." They asked him if he remembered that time Eugene shoved a paper towel up his ass and lit it on fire and did the Dance of the Burning Asshole. "Yeah," he said after a big mouthful of beer. "I remember." They were trying to cheer him up, to make him feel good. But he wasn't giving them anything back, so after a time they stopped asking, glancing at him now and then with expressions made of equal parts concern and annoyance. He was ruining their night. This was supposed to be the time when they found a common medicine in their stories and their bottomless glasses.

He wondered if the war bothered them at all, if they felt damaged by it. Troy had taken some shrapnel to the leg. Jim had lost the hearing in his right ear. But otherwise, they seemed fine. They seemed like men who taught their dogs to roll over, who read the labels on jars of spaghetti sauce at the grocery store and dug dandelions from their lawns with special tools sold for that purpose. He wondered if they felt comfortable and safe, happy. He wondered if they kept their bathroom cabinets stocked with Zoloft and Trazodone. He wondered if they kept guns hidden throughout their houses—behind the silverware, next to the toothpaste, shoved between the mattress and box spring. He wondered if they ever blunted the memories with a six-pack of Bud, a chaser of Jim Beam. He wondered if they ever woke up in the middle of the night and called their wives Iraqi pigs and tried to strangle them. He wondered if they ever dropped to the ground and covered their heads after mistaking gravel popping beneath tires for machine-gun fire.

"So I pull into the parking lot across from the Foreign Ministry and park next to this tan-colored Iraqi Army truck." Troy is speaking loudly, gesturing with his hands, his fingertips ragged and clawing the air. "I walk across the street and I hear this blam—*ka-blam*—so loud I can feel it inside me, in my bones. I turn and see the truck still in the air, flipping forward, with a cloud of smoke and fire surrounding it. And my Humvee is toast—all fiery and snarled up. I was *that close*—a minute away from seventy virgins and a thousand cheeseburgers, whatever's waiting for me on the other side. IED rigged by magnets to the underside of the truck right next to me. Doesn't get any closer than that. Except it does. Check this—I feel this heat, this stinging—and I look down to find a hole in my cammies, a quarter-size hole right through the groin burned by a piece of shrapnel." He bugs open his eyes. "*Holy* shit."

It was a story they had all heard before. Brian wondered if at Kinko's, maybe in the break room, with his jaw thrust forward and his purple shirt tucked in to his khaki pants and a Sierra Mist clutched in his hand, Troy told the story to his employees. "You're home now," Brian wanted to tell him. "Stop pretending to be such a badass." His mouth opened with a spackle of saliva, but the words would not come.

His face felt warm and his mind felt loose and his bladder felt ready to burst, so he excused himself and went to the bathroom and found a stall and sat down on a toilet because he didn't have the energy to stand. He sat there long after the piss surged and dribbled from him. He rested his head in his hands and listened to the sinks sizzling and the blow driers roaring and the men talking too loudly to each other at the urinals. The bathroom door pushed open and swung closed with the passage of so many bodies sounding like the slow whapping of chopper blades. "I'm tired," he said to no one, everyone. There was a throbbing behind his eyes. He closed them for what could have been a minute or could have been an hour.

"I'm tired." The voice was not his. The voice came from the CSH, from the bed next to him, where a man was cocooned in gauze. He had worked as a combat tracker in Saqlawiyah. A sticky IED had melted away the left half of his face. The bomb had been planted in a roadside drain. There was soap powder in it, so the fire stuck to him, leaving behind what looked like chewed gum splashed with red paint. The doctors called him Two Face. He only lived three days and during that time he never spoke except to whisper, "I'm tired, I'm tired."

His father had said the same thing. His father, who had been drinking, who had lost his wife to another man, the whistle-blowing, flat-topped gym teacher, Lonnie M. Wise, at the elementary school where she taught. It wasn't anything Brian's father had done. She simply fell out of love with him. It was as easy as that. She and Lonnie had moved to Eugene to begin a new life together, leaving Brian and his father to their frozen dinners and humps of rank laundry. Brian was a teenager at the time. One night he woke to the noise of glass breaking and his father yelling. He crawled from his bed and poked his head from his room to see a sliver of yellow light in the hallway. He followed it to the kitchen, where he found his father sitting on the floor, his back against the fridge. He was pinching his nose between his thumb and forefinger, trying to loosen some pain there. The room was cold and when Brian looked to the window above the sink he saw half the glass missing, a sharp-toothed hole made by the beer bottle hurled through it. Outside snow fell and the flakes carried through the window into the kitchen, where they swirled about and made the scene before Brian appear like some sad and shaken snow globe.

"Dad?"

His father's hand dropped and his eyes—hooded, red-rimmed—regarded Brian.

"Dad? Can I do something for you?"

"No." His father's voice, gravelly. "There's nothing you or anybody can—" Here he attempted to sit up, rolling forward with a groan, and then fell back into his seat at the base of the fridge. And no wonder:

the kitchen counter was cluttered with bottles of Coors Light, many with their labels peeled off. When his father shook his head back and forth, he knocked aside some magnets that fell clattering to the floor. He laughed without humor. "Look at your old man," he said. "Just look at him. And listen." He wagged a finger at the air before him where Brian did not stand, where snowflakes fell like damp pieces of shredded paper. "Listen to him when he says if you're not careful you can end up in a place you hadn't expected. You got choices in life. And you can make the wrong choices that seem like the right choices—you can easily do that—and before you can remedy your error you find yourself . . ." He looked around as if to find the word he sought. He picked up a magnet—a clown with a fistful of balloons—and weighed it in his palm. "You find yourself not living the life you expected to live."

He fell silent for a long time. He bit his lip, as if to chew back the thing he had said, which he maybe realized was not the thing to say to your son, who was only a boy and still blind to the pain of the world. Perhaps he realized that Brian would forever remember this moment, thinking of it off and on throughout his life, the memory crystallized like a snowflake that wouldn't melt. Memory was his gift and his disability. He remembered everything. He even remembered his dreams so that they blended together lucidly with his waking life. And this moment in particular he remembered because his father had always seemed such an optimist, always smiling, whistling, saying, *Look on the bright side.* That he carried such sad thoughts inside him haunted Brian and helped him understand the difference between the surface and the core of things, the truth of things. So that when years later, when his father shyly inquired whether Brian might want to come work for him, when Brian said he was thinking about college instead, and his father responded, "I'll be happy either way. I'll be happy so long as you're happy," Brian recognized this as a lie. If he chose to buckle himself into the white pickup truck and peer into locks and sharpen his tools on doorsteps across Deschutes County—if he chose that life—his father could mend that broken kitchen window, could erase those words uttered from the base of the fridge. His life would be something worth pursuing and those choices he worried over so long ago, those wrong choices would have seemed like the right ones again. Brian understood this and offered up his own lie in response to his father's, saying he would, he would, in fact he had always planned on working for Pop-a-Lock, but first he wanted adventure, he wanted to learn, so he planned to sign up with ROTC. They would pay for his college tuition and he would give the Marines four years and then he would return to Bend, to his father. He never intended to keep the promise. At the time, whenever he went to McDonald's for a burger or whenever he saw a garbage truck rumble by on the street, he experienced a horrible kind of empathy, where he imagined his life as theirs—hunched over a grill and flipping patties and smelling like their grease or hanging from the back of a truck that chewed up waste and leaked chicken blood and sour milk, nothing to come home to except a wide-bottomed wife and three squalling children. In Bend, this was the trap that awaited him, no matter what his career. So he pushed it aside and signed the paperwork, never guessing that the towers would fall and in that fiery instant what had seemed like the right choice turned horribly wrong as it left him at this juncture of life, in this bar in Portland, among these men who reminded him of everything he wanted to forget, with a punctured skull and a scabbed brain that could not process friendship or love or any human desire except for want and not-want.

And there was his father again, sprawled out on the kitchen floor with snow drifting in the window, dusting the floor, swirling around the overhead light so that it looked like one of Van Gogh's stars. "Just go to bed, Brian," he was saying. "We should both go to bed. I'm very tired." He again struggled to rise and Brian held out his hands and his father took them and squeezed them, massaged their knuckles, and said, "Don't pay any attention to your old man. I'm drunk. You can see me, but I'm not here."

When Brian looked at their faces, he knew this was what they thought: We can see you but you're not here. You're not Brian. And in a way they were right.

Troy said, "Feeling okay?"

"Fine. Tired is all."

They sat in silence for a time, bringing their glasses to their mouths, chewing on the few cold French fries that remained on their plates. Then Troy launched into a story about how after he came home from "the theater"—that's what he kept calling the war, *the theater*—he had taken to wearing his uniform. "You guys ever do that? Just put it on to remember the feel of it, the smell of it? Fill up your ruck with stones and march around your backyard and snap off salutes to a tree?" He smiled, embarrassed at what he had said. His eyes concentrated on the yellow depths of his beer, where the bubbles came from, rising up to escape the glass, as thoughts rose up his throat to escape his mouth. "Anyway. I wore it to the grocery store one time. There's a charge you get, you know? A certain power." His words were dank and soft, blurring together. "When you're walking around and everybody's smiling at you and looking at you with, like, you know, a kind of awe? It's like you're somebody, not just anybody. So I'm at the Safeway and this little old man comes up to me and shakes my hand and says, 'I'm proud of you.' That was a good feeling." He gnawed at his thumbnail, clipping it with little bites of his teeth. A line of blood ran from it and he licked it away and then wrapped the thumb in a paper napkin.

Troy was proud of himself, of what he had done over there, whereas Brian felt nothing—not pride and not resentment—only a certain blankness, like the space on a chalkboard run over by an eraser, the words ghostly visible beneath a scrim of white. He took the pitcher and poured another pint. He had to concentrate to keep his aim steady, to keep the beer from overflowing.

Jim and Troy started in on a story about this marine they knew who guarded the U.S. embassy and who went dogshit crazy and drove his car off the edge of the Grand Canyon. "The theater," Troy kept saying. "The theater." Brian wondered if Troy heard the word on a news program or read about it in a book and thought it sounded important so made an effort to include it in his vocabulary, the theater. The word bothered Brian horribly—yes, the pretentiousness of it—but more so the way it made him think of Iraq as a kind of stage where they all donned costumes and spoke their lines emptily and drove cardboard tanks you could punch a fist through while blank-faced people sat in the audience and yawned and checked their watches, impatient for the performance to end.

If anything, *this* was the theater—this world he had inhabited since returning. Like an actor he must think about how others perceived him at any given moment, forcing a smile when a customer cracked a joke, pretending interest when asked about the Trail Blazers, feigning remorse when he accidentally backed his truck over a toy poodle. And on an even deeper level—getting up each morning, putting on clothes, swallowing food, fighting the urge to walk into the forest and find a cave to occupy—all of it a contrived facade. People faked a lot of human interactions but he specialized in a more elaborate kind of fakery. He was faking it now, sitting here, grinding his teeth, making every effort to control himself, knowing that he *should* feel happy, he *should* wear a smile, he should not slam his hand palm down on the table so heavily that their pint glasses jump and slosh, as he did now when Troy once again uttered the word *theater*.

Troy put out his hands as if to catch the pint glasses and the napkin fell from his thumb to reveal the raw wound there. "What the fuck, Brian?"

"Stop saying that." He only recognized the words as belonging to him after they were uttered.

"Saying what?"

"That word. Theater."

"You're really not acting like yourself. You're acting—"

"Stop saying that word."

"It's just a word. What's wrong with it?"

"It makes me want to kill you."

The noise of the bar fell away and a stare hardened between Jim and Troy, heavy with meaning, before their eyes swung toward him again. "Where you staying tonight?" Jim said. "We'll call you a cab."

"I don't need you to call a cab. I need you to stop pretending you're war heroes." And with this being said, the bar vanished and in its place stretched a great desert where the windblown pumice ate at your skin and the heat made your skin peel away and revealed a redness, your interior. The feel of Iraq settled over Brian, the vastness of the desert and the blue sky hanging over it, the hot wind like the breath of a clay oven, the scorpions napping under every stone. It was a place that did not care about him or about any man because in its age it had seen so many die and so many born only to later die.

Right then the waitress appeared next to him with a smile full of teeth. "You guys doing all right here?"

His hand answered her, leaping off the table to grab her by the forearm. "Have you ever heard of Fallujah?"

Immediately her smile fell from her face. Her eyes crinkled up with pain and panic. She tugged against him. "Please let me go."

"Al Anbar?"

"Please."

Her arm was so thin and tender. He knew if he squeezed only a little harder—twisted—a damp snap would come. "See?" he said to the table. "She's got no clue. Nobody knows there's a war going on. Nobody cares."

"Let her go." This was Troy, his voice deep and punishing. He made a manacle of his hand, locking it around Brian's wrist, the pain sharp where he dug his fingertips into the veins and tendons.

Brian released the waitress and threw all of his weight across the table—concentrated into a fist that connected with Troy—his mouth, his lips bursting against his teeth. Instantly, blood. His mouth appeared terribly lipsticked. He did not scream but the waitress did, a scream that went on and on like a siren and made every face in the bar swivel toward them.

There was a moment—before his knuckles started to throb, before Jim pinned him to the wall, before Troy ripped a handful of napkins from the dispenser and pressed them to his face, before the bartender pulled the phone from beneath the bar and punched 9-1-1—there was a moment when the world seemed to freeze, everything pausing for the barest instant, as if Brian could still turn around and go back to a more peaceful time.

He hadn't meant to punch Troy. This was not to say he regretted it, only that he hadn't chosen to strike him. So many of his decisions now seemed instinctual, processed only on the most basic level, as when the bomb had detonated, when he had thrown up his arms to defend his face—and suddenly he found himself on that road again, when the explosion first took hold of the Humvee, lifting it, ripping it open, making him feel surprised, not fearful or angry or anything else, only surprised, with the first sparks of adrenaline racing through him, as if this were a sudden drop in a carnival ride, metal screaming, the sky and the ground confused, something he would laugh about later.

And then the world was back in motion, careening forward, with Troy yelling at him through a mouthful of blood, "You're wrong in the head."

He reaches a meadow, a circle of moonlight, and hurries to the far end of the silvery space where the forest resumes. The shadows are waiting for him there—so dark they seem palpable, like cloaks, something he could wrap himself up in. The shadows are where he feels safest. They slide across his body as if licking him, happy for their reunion. It is difficult to see under the trees and now and then he can hear things crashing about in the undergrowth, but he does not feel afraid, only occasionally startled, such as when an owl swoops through a column of moonlight, its wings silent, its face as broad and white as a dinner plate.

He sometimes stomps through Manzanita thickets and sometimes follows game trails—about a foot wide, packed and furrowed dirt—that curve left and right, rarely straight, an always bending corridor that finds the holes in the walls of the forest. Branches claw at him but his suit protects him, a pliant armor. He smashes through a huckleberry thicket and the smell of the plump, late-season berries stays with him, his fur blackened with their blood. The ground occasionally goes soft with sudden patches of mud, the remains of the storm. The mud sticks to his boots and he stops now and then to scrape it off against a log. He can hear the hiss of the river long before he sees it and when he rounds a curve and descends a slope the trees fall away and the moonlight is all around him. The river is the color of mercury. He jogs along its shore until he reaches a fallen tree broad enough to scuttle crabwise over, into the woods again, now closing in on O.B. Riley, her road, her neighborhood, her.

Something is shifting inside him. Since meeting the woman, Karen, he has had what can only be described as feelings. For the first time in a long time he feels like more than a machine of reflex, more than someone who only wants or does not want. In this case there is want, unquestionably, but underlying the want is a certain human tenderness, maybe. It is a maze of emotion whose end he does not know and whose course he follows through the woods.

He is outside, leaning against a squad car, his hands cuffed behind him. A pool of pink vomit steams at his feet. His mouth tastes like acid. His mind is blistering. A block-shaped officer stands nearby—another twenty yards away, scribbling on a pad, speaking to Troy and Jim, who stand with their arms crossed. Night has settled over the city. Despite the streetlamps, the headlights, the alternating flashes of blue and red thrown from the squad car, the shadows are thick enough that everyone looks like a threat, all the people walking along the sidewalks staring at him, their faces sharp and toothy, their shirts and jeans dark, so that they appear to blend into the night, to fade and reappear from one instant to the next. A car full of teenagers roars by and, red-faced, they howl out the window at him like skinned jackals.

His forehead throbs in time with his heartbeat. His vision rises and falls on yellow waves of drunkenness. He doesn't feel angry anymore. He feels numb, deflated. So when he hears Troy speaking—when he hears Troy trying to convince the officer not to arrest him, saying, "You can't go from no law to law. You can't"—he isn't thankful so much as hopeful that soon this will all be over, soon, and then he can sleep.

Her house looks different in the dark—squatter, more forbidding—its windows square sockets of yellow light. He crouches in the bushes, thinking he is in the right place, but it isn't until he glimpses her inside—ponytailed, frowning—that he scurries on all fours into the yard and huddles next to a hedge that runs below the picture window.

He rises inch by inch, so as to appear part of the landscape, and once over the sill peers in the window, beyond the living room, and spies her standing framed in a lamplit doorway. It is as though she is packaged by it, waiting for him.

The moment is fleeting. The kitchen sits to the left of the living room and from it comes a man—a tall, thinly built man with his shirt tucked into his pants despite the late hour. He has his right hand in his pocket and from the way it bulges beneath the khaki fabric Brian imagines him a coin jangler, the type who rolls quarters and dimes around with his fingers, making a song. He addresses Karen without looking at her directly, his eyes flitting back and forth between her face and the floor. Brian cannot perceive his words—they come across only as a low-voiced murmur—but he can read in Karen's expression an obvious distaste.

This is the husband responsible for locking her out—the idiot, she called him. He certainly looks like an idiot. He looks like an insurance salesman who reads the *Wall Street Journal* and plays golf on the weekends and keeps careful score with those tiny pencils. Brian feels assaulted by his presence. He looks wrong in the house—he looks wrong next to Karen—like a mismatched piece of furniture.

The man turns to the window as if he senses Brian's searching stare. But Brian does not duck or scamper off into the woods. Yes, he knows the man cannot see him, can see only a window full of night that reflects a ghostly image of his living room—but even if he could, even if the sun were high and an alarm sounded, Brian would remain footed to this property, unafraid.

The key gives him that sense of access, ownership. He can picture himself inside the house—sitting on the sofa, eating off the wedding china, spitting toothpaste in the sink, shoving his thumbs deep into the eyes of the man until blood wells from them. The vision brings with it a shifting sensation, as though the drudgery of his life is about to change, to take on a new dimension, all because of her.

JUSTIN

In the morning Justin and his son load their gear into the Subaru wagon and drive to his father's house. His father's house. It is his, even though he shares it with Justin's mother, even though Justin grew up there alongside them. Decidedly his.

Along the way Graham plays his Nintendo DS—something called "The Legend of Zelda"—where a young elf fires arrows and casts spells to battle his way through an elaborate wilderness maze. Justin asks Graham if he is excited, and he says he is, though he never lifts his gaze from the screen, nor do his thumbs cease their frantic dance across the control pad.

"You'll be leaving that thing in the car. You know that, right?"

His eyes remain intent on his work. "I just wanted to get in one last game."

"And then you're going to shut it off and for three days forget it exists."

"Yeah, yeah, yeah," he says, and then, "Dad?"

"What?"

"Define *guy time.*"

"Say again?"

"You keep saying guy time. We're going to have some guy time. That's what you keep saying."

"You know what I mean. Hunting, fishing, camping, *hanging.*"

"Hanging?"

"You know. Bathing in a river. Sitting around a campfire. Scratching your armpits. Eating beans and farting and not caring if Mom hears. It's fun. Stepping outside your comfort zone and challenging yourself. Becoming a man." Justin flits his hand in a half circle as if trying to conjure something in the air, maybe a vision of Graham twenty years from now. "And all that stuff."

"Mmm." Not looking up from his video game.

They pass through what was once a forested area, razed down to stumps that used to be tall healthy ponderosas—thousands of them—standing like sentinels along the road Justin has driven all his life. Now they are gone and everything looks absent. For a moment he forgets where he is, not recognizing this place, the sky revealed in a way he has never before seen.

And then, just as abruptly as they disappeared, the trees begin again, thickly clustered, the sunlight filtering through them in strobelike flashes that brighten the way. He hangs a right down a long driveway that opens up into a clearing. In the middle of it crouches the cabin, two stories tall with a red steel roof. Smoke curls thickly from the river-rock chimney and spreads into a thin gray haze.

A pea-gravel path leads to a set of rough stone steps that rise up to the porch. Next to the railing sits an old Maxwell House coffee can, the damp grounds within it looking a lot like chewing tobacco, soon to be shaken throughout the garden for fertilizer. A sheep skull hangs above the front door like a gargoyle. They scrape their shoes on the welcome mat and enter without knocking. There are bone-work pegs by the door from which hang camouflage hats, rain slickers, a Carhartt jacket. Beneath them sit boots caked with mud and whiskered with grass. The honey-colored hardwood groans beneath their weight as they move across it, down a short hallway that opens up into the living room. A wooden hutch stands against the wall. Inside of it sits an arrangement of bone china and finely decorated teapots, one of the little touches his mother made to call attention away from the bear hides and trophy fish and skull-and-rack mounts crowding the walls. There are two bay windows in the living room that let in the light. This is where Justin finds his father.

He is sitting in a lotus position in a square of sunlight. He wears faded blue jeans and a long-sleeved thermal. He has disassembled his rifle and spread it across a Budweiser beach towel. The room stinks of gun oil. When he looks up, his eyes catch the light like glass from an old bottle. He smiles genuinely and rises to greet them. On Justin's shoulder he lays his hand, warm and enormous. "Ready to face the day, troops?"

"Sure thing," Justin says.

"And what about you?" He squats in front of Graham and his height is such that even when balanced on his haunches they are eye-to-eye.

Graham nods his yes. He has a blush oval of a face, almost eggish, topped by straight blond hair that he keeps parted severely to one side. His arms and legs are thin, the knobby joints like knots in a pale rope. Delicate is a good word for him. Around his neck hangs a lariat attached to a digital camera, his most prized possession. He wears safari pants and a fishing vest with many zippered compartments. A narrow-mouth Nalgene water bottle dangles from one side of his belt, and from the other, a Leatherman tool. Aside from the camera, he is fully outfitted with things Justin bought for him last week at Gander Mountain. Graham has seemed anxious about the trip—his first hunting trip, his first time away from his mother for more than a night—but once outfitted he must have felt armored because the furrow between his eyebrows vanished and he stopped chewing incessantly at his fingernails.

"You're always so quiet," Justin's father says to him. "Why are you always so quiet?"

Graham shrugs and gives him a shy smile and Justin's father locks his hands behind Graham's neck and draws him close until their foreheads touch roughly. "Come on. I want to teach you something." His knees pop when he straightens himself out and again when he returns to the beach towel. He pats the floor next to him and Graham joins him there.

"Don't suppose your old man ever showed you how to clean a gun? No? I didn't think so. Time to listen up, okay?" He explains how all firearms—"I'm talking about rifles, handguns, shotguns, even bazookas"—are exposed to mechanical wear as well as the abrasive effects of weather and unexpected handling problems, such as being dropped in a river. "Which your old man once did, you know. He ever tell you that story?" Again, the flash of his eyes.

You would think, after so many years, Justin would feel a certain numbness to his father's jabs, like a nerve deadened by repeated hits. But no. Even if he keeps his arms crossed and his expression composed, a part of him flinches. His father is always going for the seams, hoping to tear Justin open and let his stuffing fall out. Sometimes Justin fights back, but mostly he tightens his lips into a thin line, holding it all in, hoping to avoid the several exhausting weeks it takes to repair a breach between them.

His father shows Graham how to make certain the weapon is unloaded, how to check for possible obstructions, holding the muzzle toward a light source and looking from chamber to muzzle. He takes a brass bristle brush and runs it down the bore to remove any grit or burs. Then he soaks a patch in solvent and attaches it to the end of the cleaning rod and runs this down the bore as well, followed by a dry follow-up patch meant to detect traces of rust, followed by a patch with a light coat of gun oil on it. Then they clean all the exposed parts of the action, the inside of the receiver, the face of the breechblock, with a stiff toothbrush. "Mirror-clean," he calls it.

It is a lecture Justin heard many times growing up. Seeing it directed at his son, who watched his grandfather with wide damp eyes, makes Justin feel nostalgic and worried at once. He remembers the words Karen spoke to him that morning. "Don't let him bully Graham the way he bullies you."

"I'll do my best," he said and she said, "Try. Please."

At the time she was standing in front of the sink, drying her hands on a flour-sack dish towel. The light was coming in through the window, surrounding her in a kind of spotlight, and he remembers looking at her, really looking at her. She had a young body whose age you recognized only if you looked closely at her face. The crinkling of skin around her eyes and mouth. The veins trailing faintly across her temple. The constellation of age marks on her cheek. It was as if she were several people cobbled together and he was uncertain how much of her still resembled the woman he had fallen in love with.

"What?" she said. "What are you looking at?"

"Nothing."

Graham came into the kitchen then and set his cereal bowl on the counter and she kissed him on the forehead and asked how he was doing—"Good"—and if he was excited—"Yes." She smiled faintly and said in a voice meant for them both, "Please be careful."

"I'm always careful," Graham said.

"I know you are. I know. Just remember that your grandpa doesn't know his limits anymore. In many ways he's more of a child than you are."

Justin watches his father now as he begins to gather up their gear and march back and forth from the cabin to the Bronco, so weighed down with rifles and ammunition and knives and fishing gear that his movements produce a metallic ringing, like the movements of keys on a ring.

They follow the red-colored road into the desert, with Bend behind them and the Ochocos ahead. The big orange circle of the sun seems to have the sky to itself. It floats above them, casting a hazy light.

A few minutes into the drive, Justin looks back to see Graham sitting quietly in the backseat, and beyond him, a multitude of houses, already growing dim and gray in the distance. Past them the land gathers into foothills and the foothills rear up into snowcapped peaks that block out vast sections of the sky. The Cascades forever keep Justin oriented. All his life, if lost, hiking through the woods or driving along some strip of county two-lane, he needs only to spot the familiar crowned point of North Sister or the flat-topped Mount Bachelor. They breathe over him. They help him find his way. Now he adjusts the side mirror and in it observes the mountains growing smaller behind him. He places his hand on their reflection.

Karen made a pan of sweet rolls and they eat some now and drink from a thermos of coffee, when they drive this arrow-straight road. The desert is dotted with sagebrush and stunted juniper trees and little else. Under the sun everything looks faintly yellow, like something jaundiced. Every now and then they pass an unincorporated town or a trailer park called Frog Bottom or Pine Hollow. Each doublewide has a satellite dish mounted on its roof. And in the front yards Justin inevitably spots a collection of weeds and red cinder, soggy-diapered children, dogs choking on their chains, snarling at every car.

Then they pass through a region where no one lives. Lava, born out of some ancient eruption, stretches all around them like some vast black lake with wind chop making it rise into sharp edges. Here and there a bone white tree pushes up through its crust.

His father walks the Bronco up to seventy, eighty, as if to hurry past this place, where the desert lies ahead and behind and to either side of the road. The engine shudders. The tires hum along the reddish blacktop. Clumps of sagebrush whip by. A red-tailed hawk roosts on a telephone pole. A bunch of Mexicans moving irrigation pipe. A tar-paper shack with its door gaping like a crooked tooth. Two coyotes sitting in the shade of a dead tree. All of this fuses together in the white-hot air. Their tires eat up the road and for a while their talk dies out and gives way to an uneasy kind of anticipation.

Graham has recently developed an interest in computers and a few weeks ago announced at the dinner table he would grow up to become either a programmer or (his old standby) a photographer for *National Geographic.* Justin's father is now trying to figure out what this means—to become a programmer—asking in a loud voice that carries over the noise of the radio and the engine—what exactly the Facebook *is,* what exactly an iPod *does?*

Graham does his best to answer his questions, speaking with quiet assurance, using his hands to mimic typing. What Justin's father doesn't understand, he normally labels worthless and sweeps aside with his fist and a few select words. Which is why, when Justin notices his eyebrows coming closer and closer together in confusion, his knuckles growing whiter at the steering wheel, he decides to change the subject to one his father will enjoy.

"How's Boo working out for you?" Boo is the hunting dog he always wanted, a lab-retriever mix his father bought a year ago from an alfalfa farmer.

"Oh, he's a good boy." His father smiles and adjusts the rearview mirror so he can spy on Boo where he sleeps in a horseshoe shape next to Graham in the backseat. "Boo?" he says. "Hey, Boo Bear?" At the sound of his name, the dog perks his ears and lifts his head from his paws and thumps his tail a few times. "You ready to hunt, Boo?" he says and Boo barks sharply.

He then begins to explain at length how raising a dog is no different from raising a child. He claims a man who fails to sufficiently and constantly train his dog, to test it, to *discipline* it—from its weaning to its death—is in for a rude awakening. "Boo wasn't even a month old when I first introduced him to water, to various types of cover, and of course to game birds," he says and runs a hand across his beard, neatening it. "When it comes to dogs, you got to develop their obedience and hunting desire from the get-go or they won't grow up right."

Here he gives Justin a look full of judgment and love and Justin pretends not to notice, knowing they have a long weekend ahead of them.

His father tells them how he first coaxed Boo into water. "I took my fly rod, see?" His hand mimes casting. "And with a pheasant wing dangling from it, I shot it off into the shallow part of the pond and let Boo chase it and sight-point it."

Then he baited Boo with a dead bird, and then a live lame bird. "At first, my boy got afraid when he felt the bottom disappear under his legs, but I got in the pond with him and showed him how safe it was. Now he can by God hardly go by a puddle without wanting to jump in it." Justin remembers his father shoving him off a dock and demanding he tread water for sixty seconds and laughing much as he laughs now when looking lovingly at his dog.

"No," his father says, as if responding to some conversation Justin wasn't a part of. "Boo won't be much help to us deer hunting, but he's good company."

The green huddled shapes of the Ochocos grow larger before them as they pass through Prineville and then Mitchell and John Day and Justin continues to listen and his father continues to speak until the final distance—where the sagebrush gives way to juniper and then pine trees—becomes the near distance and the ground begins to steadily rise and the evergreens filter the sun into puddles that splash across the highway. At last the heat is gone, replaced by cool mountain air that makes breathing feel like drinking.

Among the big pines crouches a minimart with two rusty gas pumps. Out front, a hand-carved sign with white lettering reads GAS & BAIT. For exactly what they advertise, Justin has been stopping here since he was a child. They turn off into its gravel lot and park next to a pump manned by a thin man in greasy coveralls and a clean white pair of Payless knockoffs. Justin quickly hums the banjo line from *Deliverance* before his father leans out the window and says to fill it with regular.

The minimart is a sunken and derelict structure, constructed from a gray, salt-colored wood and asphalt shingles either ragged or missing. A neon Budweiser sign flickers blue and red in the window. On the porch stands a cigar shop Indian with a hatchet nose and a feather headdress. He stares woodenly at the men as they stomp up the stairs and under the drooping brow of a roof and push through the door. A bell jingles to announce their presence and they pause to orient themselves, blinking in the dimly lit space.

There is a smell to stores like this—worms mixed with tobacco mixed with hydraulic oil—that is not Justin's favorite smell, but close to it. Like the smell of cherry Coke or a plastic toy freshly torn from its package, it's the smell of his childhood.

The man behind the counter is built like a plow horse. He is something like thirty years old, but with that creased look that comes from too much time working under a hot sun, roofing or framing or holding a sign that reads, STOP. He wears a tank top that was once a shirt, the sleeves scissored off. His arms and shoulders roll with muscle when he lifts a dumbbell with one hand, and then the other, doing bicep curls. He exhales sharply. A hula girl tattoo seems to move when the muscle beneath her moves, sending her hips shaking across his deltoid.

He does not stop his workout, nor does he turn to look at them, except glancingly, his eyes intent on a small-screen television tuned in to an old episode of *Bonanza*. It sits on a shelf behind him with cartons of Camels and Winstons stacked all around it.

The paneled walls are busy with lacquered trout and skull-and-rack mounts of deer, elk, antelope. The gaps between the floorboards are wide enough to lose a quarter through and they groan as the men make their way up and down the aisles, grabbing a six-pack of Pepsi, a bag of Fritos, Oreos, beef jerky. A packet of Panther Martin spinners. Justin's father says something about his filter being on the fritz when he grabs a gallon jug full of water.

There is a waist-high wooden bucket in the back corner. A piece of paper taped to its top advertises ten minnows for a dollar. Justin lifts the lid and he and Graham peer into its water to see hundreds of minnows darkly swarming. Justin dips his hand in and Graham does the same and the fish make a writhing sleeve around their arms and their eyes widen with pleasure. Graham asks, "Can we get some?" and Justin tells him no, they are river fishing, not lake fishing.

By this time his father has made his way to the counter and Justin joins him there, assembling the groceries on the counter. The man behind the register finishes his set before lowering his weights to the floor with a clatter of metal and wood. Justin can hear one of the dumbbells rolling along the uneven floor, finally coming to a rest—with a *ding*—against something metal. A shotgun or an aluminum baseball bat? Justin wonders. Something this man would curl his hand around before doing damage.

The man regards them now with his square-shaped head, taking them in with what seems like a glimmer of anger—because they have interrupted his workout or because they are obviously not from here, Justin doesn't know.

"Gas, too," Justin says and the man says, "Yeah," in a voice that implies he already knows.

The total comes to $53.35, a lovely palindrome of a number, and Justin pulls out his wallet at the same time as his father. They then begin the familiar game of tug-of-war they play whenever they go out, each of them insisting on paying, trying to nudge the other aside, until Justin finally says, "I want to pay. I *want* to."

His father holds up his hands in mock surrender and then grabs the bag of jerky and tears it open with his teeth. He pops a wedge in his mouth and passes another to Graham and they exit the store together, talking about the weekend ahead with their mouths full of rough meat.

The cashier repeats the price and then lets his eyes wander to the television, where Hoss and Little Joe Cartwright spur their horses into a gallop and with pistols drawn take chase after a whooping throng of Indians they have surprised in a dry canyon. When the cashier looks back—Seth, his name tag reads—Justin lays a hundred-dollar bill on the counter. "I don't have change for that." His face tightens like a fist. "What makes you think I have change for that?"

"Oh," Justin says. "Sorry." He pulls his VISA from his wallet. "You do take credit?"

"Long as you got a driver's license."

Justin produces the cards and with a huge blue-veined hand Seth snatches them and examines them side by side. "You're from Bend." He snorts. "That explains it."

Justin doesn't need to ask what he means by that. He is talking about the network of streets growing ever wider and longer, forking off westward into the foothills and eastward into the desert, followed by telephone wires, their shadows lining the land like lines on music paper. He is talking about the ridges of condos, motels, big-box stores. He is talking about how steadily, incessantly, juniper trees come down and houses spring up, houses with whirlpool tubs and granite counters and rugged pine columns flanking their doors, and among these houses, as if some massive pen has flung green ink, will appear a golf course, each green splash mowed in long perfect strips of light and dark turf, constantly irrigated so that the grass will not fade to the blighted yellow found naturally here.

It is common knowledge, the resentment felt toward Portland and Eugene and Bend, especially among the dairy farmers and cattle ranchers, the mountain towns. The money comes out of the cities. The votes come out of cities. They make a red state blue.

Seth wears a ring on his index finger. It is a class ring—gold with a red gem surrounded by lettering that probably read John Day High, Class of 1992, or something like that. It catches the light and winks when he runs the VISA through the reader and stares carefully at the register as if he hopes it will announce the account stolen or closed. Only after the receipt spits out and Justin signs it does he return the cards.

When Seth reaches beneath the counter, part of Justin expects him to withdraw the shotgun he knows waits there. Instead Seth grips a paper bag. With a snap of his wrist, he opens it and begins to fill it with groceries. "What are you doing out here anyway?"

"Headed to Echo Canyon."

"Hunting? Fishing?" He pronounces these in a clipped-off manner, without the g.

"Little of both."

"Expect you know they're tearing it down, tearing down the canyon, come Monday."

"Yeah." Justin makes a motion with his thumb, indicating the space his father filled a moment ago. "Actually, my old man is part of the crew. His company, this log cabin company, they—"

"You say he's part of the crew?" All of Seth's muscles seem to tense at once and he leans over the counter, close enough so that Justin can feel his breath, can almost taste it, flavored with the ghosts of a hundred cigarettes. "That's great. That's just lovely. Tell him thanks for pissing on my porch, will you?" His smile is not a smile.

After a stunned silence, Justin says, "I don't understand."

"Course you don't," he says. "You're from *Bend*." He lays heavy emphasis on the word, as if to break it.

Justin understands and doesn't. He rolls his eyes at the way big-box stores sprout up like fungus, at the way Californians outnumber Oregonians, at the way MapQuest can't keep up with all the development, but at the same time, he likes Gap and Starbucks, likes not having to drive to Portland for the things he wants. He knows he shouldn't say anything more—he should grab his groceries and go—but his mouth is already stammering out a question. "I mean, in a way, aren't you glad?"

The word seems to disgust Seth. "Glad?"

"You'll get more business, won't you? You'll have people lined up at the pumps. It will bring you no end of good." As Justin speaks, Seth's eyes narrow, reducing Justin, so that his final sentence trails off into a kind of whimper. His face has contorted into an expression of pure hatred. Justin hasn't been on the receiving end of *that* for a long time, and it sends him reeling back several steps as if the emotion has a palpable force.

There comes from the television the noise of gunfire. Smoke swirls and parts to reveal dead Indians lying scattered in the sand. Justin's eyes wander to observe the action, but Seth's do not. They remain fixed on Justin. "No end of good," he repeats, as if to make sense of the phrase.

If Justin tells his father about Seth, he will react in two ways at once. He will be dismissive—"So he didn't like you? So what? You were going to invite him to prom or something?"—even as he goes rigid, reminded once again of the reluctance he felt in his backyard, more than a year ago now, when he loosed arrow after arrow into a polyurethane deer, wondering if he has betrayed himself, this place. So Justin says nothing, though the conversation weighs on him heavily as they pull away from the station and continue along the winding mountain pass.

Around a corner comes a Chevy Malibu, a tiny car with a big deer lashed to its roof. The wipers are going, cleaning away the blood that runs down the glass. The vehicles pass each other so slowly it is as if they are passing each other on a river. Justin's father offers them the old fingers-off-the-steering-wheel salute and they return the gesture.

The highway forks and they take the northeastern branch. There is a barricade here that during the depths of winter blocks entrance to the snowbound roads. It is swung open now, yawning like a mouth. When they pass through it, his father makes a noise and turns around in his seat to observe something.

"What?" Justin says and puts his hand on the wheel, maintaining a straight course, while his father's eyes focus on the world behind them. "What did you see?"

"I saw—I swear I saw—though it couldn't have been—a wolf." He takes the wheel with one hand and combs his beard with the other. "Must have been a coyote." He says *coyote* as many of Justin's students say it, as if it consists of two hard syllables, the first rhyming with pie, and the second, goat.

Justin looks but sees only forest, a wooded maze of shadow and light. Along the side of the road there are strawberries and green corn lilies and patches of snow and boulders encrusted with rough gray-green lichen, appearing as if they have been rolled across a cellar floor. They pass an old lumber camp, the sheds sunken, the equipment rusted over and forgotten. The trees give way every now and then to reveal a vale with a river running through it or a thin waterfall trickling in silence down a wall of basalt. "Are you seeing this?" Justin says over his shoulder, and when his son does not respond, he turns in his seat to observe him reading a book—*Wildlife of the Pacific Northwest*—a hearty softcover with plastic binding and slick pages the rain will run off. Justin picked it up at Gander Mountain, a last-minute impulse buy near the register. Its pages are filled with photographs and illustrations and descriptions of everything from sword ferns to mountain goats. Justin feels a small pang of irritation—as his son ignores the beauty all around him—but keeps from scolding him, knowing that he will hear in his voice his father's.

"Graham," he says, loudly, his voice demanding his son's attention.

His face rises from the page, pale and startled. "Yes?"

Justin nods at the window. "What do you think?"

For a moment Graham stares off into the woods before saying, "It's pretty." As if to confirm this, he lifts his camera and it clicks and whizzes and captures the green blur of their passage.

The pavement gives way to cinder, deeply rutted and soft where over so many years the snow melted and didn't drain.

At the top of the canyon, they pass a payloader and a backhoe and a collection of tractors, and his father slows and turns his head to study them as though observing the scene of an accident. He opens his mouth as if to say something, but then the road pitches at about forty degrees and he returns his attention to steadying the wheel. He downshifts. The engine flutters briefly before falling into gear. He feathers the brakes and adjusts the rearview mirror and glances into it.

"You know, it's good luck to see a wolf," he says. "Or is it bad?"

BRIAN

From two wooden hangers he hung the hair suit, a clotted mess of mud and cheatgrass and pine needles. This morning the smell of it fills the room, a pungent mix of paint thinner and wet dog that has seeped into the sponge of his skin so that even after his shower, when he fingers shampoo through his hair and soaps his armpits, the smell lingers, reminding him of her, helping him keep his focus when three people call this morning. "I'm sorry," he says. "Things are just crazy around here. So many locks to pick." He gives them the name of a competitor and wishes them well.

He spoons through a bowl of oatmeal and drinks a half pot of black coffee before walking to his father's room. The bed, with its duck-and-cattail-patterned comforter, is crisply made. The green-carpeted floor is vacuumed. The clothes—jeans, flannel shirts, Gold Toe socks—are folded neatly in the drawers of the oak dresser his father built in the garage. The mirror above it reveals Brian as he walks to the night table and picks up the clock radio. The power went out briefly the other day, during the storm, and the clock flashes red, a nonsense code of numbers. He checks his watch and sets the clock to 7:36 and blows the dust off it—a wisp of yellow, like some sorcerer's magic dust, cast into the air to conjure the dead. "I met someone," he says to the clock. Somewhere within it a wire-tangled brain hums with electricity.

By eight o'clock he is driving along O.B. Riley. The road cuts through a great hump of earth and basaltic bedrock, exposing strata, the thickest of them the gray cake of Mazama ash, nearly eight thousand years old, expelled from the belly of what is now Crater Lake. He imagines the air swarming with fireflies of ash, the ground bubbling over with a red porridge of magma—a world so much different from this one—the evidence of it imprinted below the calm surface, seen only when the earth is stripped back to reveal its red-muscled, white-boned interior.

There is a cindered track of Forest Service road fifty yards up the hill from her home. He parks there, hidden among the pines, and waits. He keeps a rifle scope in his glove box and he withdraws it now to study the windows, where lights glow but no bodies move. The pumpkin is gone from the porch. There is a two-door garage and one of the doors is open. In it sits a white Subaru wagon. The hatch is open and full of what looks like camping gear—bright-colored backpacks, the blue pupae of rolled sleeping bags. A minute passes before a door opens and the husband—the idiot—appears in the dim light of the garage, struggling with the weight of a plastic cooler. He heaves it into the back of the Subaru and then pushes the bags around to accommodate its size. He is wearing jeans and a red thermal long-sleeve under a gray T-shirt. He slams shut the hatch—the muted thump of it audible even to Brian—and then yells something into the house before reentering it, absent a few seconds before returning with a boy. He looks about ten, pale and slightly built. Brian catches a glimpse of him before he climbs into the car, joined by his father. The engine coughs to life and before long they are a sun flash in the distance, traveling away.

His phone rings and he turns down another customer and thanks her for her time and just when he hits the red button, END, the door to the house opens and Karen appears. She pauses there, half in, half out, testing the door, making certain it is unlocked, before closing it. She wears a white visor and tank top, the pink running shorts from the other day. Brian lifts the scope to his eye once more and observes her as she grabs one foot—pulling it back, stretching her thigh—and then the other. She does a few lunges. She rotates her head and windmills her arms. She uses the porch stair to do some calf raises. And then, with a small jump, she is off, her fists striking the air while her feet beat the ground, as she approaches the end of the driveway. There Brian entertains a wish no different from that of a girl pulling petals from a daisy, murmuring, *Loves me, loves me not.* Karen will make a choice—left or right—either moving toward her husband or moving toward Brian. He *wills* her to turn right, clenching up his face in concentration, trying to manipulate her muscles, her very bones, and when they appear to listen to him, sending her up the hill, toward him, he feels his expression go through a remarkable transformation. His eyes go wide. His face loosens, slack with bewilderment. And then his lips pull back and a smile creeps up his cheeks. He is smiling. He touches it as if to marvel at its rareness.

Karen grows larger in the scope until he can see a crooked lower tooth, the pores on her nose, flashing in and out of sight as the trees interrupt his view. She is moving closer. Soon she will pass the road where he is parked. But he doesn't worry about her spotting him. He almost welcomes it, imagining her pace slowing, her arm rising in a wave, the bright flash of a smile on her face to match his.

JUSTIN

His father is a creature of habit. Anything outside the familiar he labels "different." Sushi. Soccer. Rap music. Even in the wilderness, the place he goes to escape, he seeks out what he knows. *There,* he will point out to Justin, a thatch of willows from which they once chopped branches for roasting marshmallows. Or *there,* at the top of that tree, the tangled nest that looks like steel wool, where the osprey returns year after year.

For as long as they have been visiting the Ochocos, they have made their camp in Echo Canyon, along the South Fork of the John Day River. Aside from the occasional Forest Service truck grumbling down a nearby logging road, they rarely see anyone and his father considers the spot his own.

To remember the exact location, he has blaze-marked a pine with his hatchet. "Keep an eye out," he says now—and then yells, "There!" indicating the tree with the wound scabbed over by hard orange sap. They pull off the road and park under its branches.

Justin climbs from the Bronco—followed by Graham and the dog—and pauses. It is the air. It feels, it tastes, so good to breathe. Whenever he comes here, he can't get used to it: how the air somehow seems older than other air, like the breath of a stone drawn from a glacial stream. It seems to carry sounds farther, more sharply. A pinecone falling. The whisk of an owl's wings when it leaves a branch. The wind sighing through a spiderweb. A coyote gnawing on a bone.

A deer. Justin can hear it coming from a long way off, pushing its way through the trees. And then it appears at the edge of the road and steps cautiously onto the gravel. None of them moves and the buck doesn't see them. It has a heavy, lengthy throwback rack that forms a crown. Its eyes and its snout are black and damp. Even from a distance of thirty yards, they can see its muscles tightening and loosening beneath its hide.

They stand like this for some time, and then his father tires of the reverie and bangs shut the driver-side door. The buck startles at the sound, stepping clumsily backward, before trotting away, back into the forest, vanishing between the trees midleap, as if its antlers fit just so. Justin watches his father watch it go. His expression carries a mixture of envy and hunger. Even as he dreams a bullet into its hide, he admires the beauty of its architecture, its speed.

He comes around the front of the Bronco and joins them. In the way of fathers on 1950s television shows, he brings his hand to Graham's head and messes his hair. "Maybe we'll run into him tomorrow, hey?" he says.

Graham plays the dutiful grandson, smiling even as he tries with his fingers to comb his hair back into its proper place.

Before they set off into the woods, Justin glances back at the Bronco. Anyone who drives by will see it and will be able to find them, if they wanted to, something he might have once found reassuring. But not today, not with Seth's hateful face lingering in his mind.

They tramp along, loaded down with rifles and poles and tents and backpacks, his father casually listing off every piece of vegetation, the wild white onions and yarrow and Queen Anne's lace. He knows the name of everything. When Justin was a boy, his father would quiz him regularly. Doing so brought order to a wilderness that would have otherwise appeared swarming and impenetrable. Now Graham has his book out and is frantically leafing through its pages, following up on everything his grandfather tells him.

The trees open up. Justin expects to find the vast bear grass meadow that runs up into the thatch of willows growing along the South Fork, and next to it, their old fire pit, probably with a few weeds growing through its ashes. They find something else entirely.

A hundred yards away, at the far edge of the meadow, near the old logging road, stands a backhoe holding in its scoop a block of dark earth it extracted from the neat hole beneath it. Nearby squat two diggers, a payloader, and a bulldozer, their broad metal shovels gleaming dangerously in the sun, like sabers lifted before the charge of a squadron. Next to them stands a bright blue Porta-Potty. The grass of the meadow has been spray painted in great hieroglyphic designs that predict what will become of the canyon.

Normally they would veer right, toward the nearby river, but without a word Justin's father continues forward, flattening a path in the grass. Justin and Graham follow while the dog wanders around, sometimes ahead and sometimes behind, always panting. His whole body seems to wag along with his tail as he sniffs at a clump of lupin and pees on a molehill and pops his jaw at a grasshopper and barks at a yellow-bellied marmot that chatters its warning from a nearby burrow.

They tour the work site silently. All around them the grass is trampled down and decorated with trash. A crumpled-up bag from McDonald's. An empty Skoal tin. Cigarette butts. Justin's father picks up a crushed Coke can, examining it as if it were some curious artifact, before tossing it over his shoulder.

Justin's wife often teases him for the way he blinks rapid-fire whenever taken aback. And he is aware of the habit now, when his eyelids shutter open and closed repeatedly, as if to remove some grit from his vision. Blinking is all he can think to do. He has always thought of this place as the very definition of wild. To see all this human evidence overlying it seems wrong, mismatched, like green grass poking through a snowdrift.

A tall stand of pines edges the meadow and each tree has a pink X spray painted across its trunk. A dozen have already been sawed down—their stumps pulled from the ground, leaving behind gaping cavities a man could lie down inside—to accommodate the passage of the equipment from the road to the meadow. Justin can smell sap and damp soil. Sawdust, nearly white, decorates the ground like freshly fallen snow. Survey markers are planted here and there. It is difficult to imagine what will happen within the next few weeks, months, years.

This coming Monday a legion of men in Carhartt jackets and steel-toe boots will swarm the canyon, logging and brush-clearing. Bobby wants the entire canyon cleaned out before Christmas, beginning the project before the year turns over for tax purposes. And then, come spring, after the snow melts, roads will be laid down on a primitive basis, followed by utilities. As soon as electricity hisses beneath the forest floor, Justin's father and his crew will tap into it and begin work on the lodge, which Bobby wants to house a pro shop, a restaurant, a bar, a banquet hall, and fifty rooms. By next fall the spec homes will go up and retired Californians wearing polo shirts will begin buying up the lots.

Graham approaches a spray-painted pine. He reaches his camera to his eye and snaps a photo.

"What did you do that for?" Justin's father says.

"What for?" With the camera still poised to shoot, Graham rotates on his heel and takes another photo, this one of his grandfather hooking his thumb in his belt.

"What kind of picture is that?"

Graham lets the camera hang loose around his neck and shrugs.

"You want to be working for the *National Geographic,* you should be taking a picture of an elk on top of a mountain or something. Now *that* would be a picture."

Graham stands there another moment, waiting to see if his grandfather has anything more to say, and then asks what the X means.

"It means it's marked," his grandfather says. "Like a buck in the crosshairs." He kicks vaguely at the shovel of a tractor. The impact creates a dull *bong* that sends Boo into a barking fit. "Shut up, Boo." By some trick of the light he looks ten years older. There is a distant expression on his face that betrays feelings of regret or sadness or something else. Resignation, perhaps.

The pine doesn't know what will happen to it. It will remain unsuspecting, pumping its sap and stretching its roots farther and farther into the soil, until the saw hits its bark. And when that happens, when the saw screams and the wood chips fan from the cut, its future will disappear. The wind will no longer run through its needles like fingers through hair. Birds will no longer roost in its branches. Hunters will no longer pause in its shade to pull from a water bottle or a cigarette. Instead the tree will be felled, its branches sliced off. The log will be collected, stacked on a flatbed, and choked with chains, driven to a mill and sectioned into boards that will end up part of somebody's dining room or fence or pool cue or gun cabinet or maybe the dresser drawer where they keep their socks rolled into balls. And isn't that the real mystery of life: who you'll end up being consumed by? Or what you'll end up consuming?

Justin's father looks around him as if the canyon has been made suspect, as if he will never see it correctly again. It bothers them both to think of the canyon as a hazy memory that they'll struggle to organize a year from now: *Where was that place we used to camp? That bend of the river that offered the best trout?*

"Fuck," he says.

"Dad."

"What?"

Justin jogs his eyes at Graham. "Language."

His father dismisses him with a wave. "Nothing wrong with dropping a cuss here and there, so long as you keep your mouth clean around the girls."

"You never let me swear growing up."

"Look what happened." Again he messes Graham's hair, and this time, when Graham goes to neaten it, his grandfather snatches his hand and shakes his head, no. "This little guy could use some roughness about him."

Maybe it is the builder in him, the way he determines the weakness of things, looking at people the way he might look at houses, noting water intrusion or uneven flooring. It certainly informed his parenting. Justin remembers when his father took him to a slaughterhouse. At the time he was a little older than Graham. He had left out a package of hamburger that spoiled and his father saw their field trip as a remedy for such carelessness.

He remembers the smell of the slaughterhouse—of animal sweat and shit mixed up with the minerally sourness of blood. He remembers the clattering of hooves and machinery, the high-pitched screams of the dying—all of it echoing throughout the vast chamber like a horrible music played from red-lunged accordions and drum sets constructed from bone.

BRIAN

His first few weeks back in central Oregon he spent much of his time changing bandages, applying salve to the wound that continually dried out and cracked and sent a trickle of blood into his eye so that his vision went red, and then with a blink, clear.

Every day he would crawl into the Jeep he had bought thirdhand in high school and drive around, needing the speed, the distance between him and the rest of the world. He kept the windows down and let the air bully its way into the cab, down his throat, hot and dry and flavored with the familiar taste of sage and juniper. The world tasted the same but looked different, the plateaus and buttes stacked up like slabs of meat, the ponderosas scabbed over with bark the color of dried blood. The bandage that patched his skull would flutter against the wind and one time tore off entirely, sucked out the window, into the day, where a clump of rabbitbrush caught it and june bugs and fire ants and bluebottle flies drank of the red wetness collected in it.

During this time it was difficult to shop for groceries and order a burger and get mail from the mailbox and even speak to people—about weather, politics, the price of gas—those things that seemed so irrelevant. Being ordinary was difficult, almost startling. He felt as he used to, as a teenager, after a long day of skiing Mount Bachelor, when sprawled out on the couch or lying in bed, his thighs would seize up, his knees would bend, imagining the rise and fall of snow-groomed trails. His body couldn't realize that it had slowed down, that the white huddled shapes of trees weren't rushing past.

This was why he drove and stomped his foot against the accelerator: to maintain his speed. And then his father died and slowed everything down again.

He found his father in the driveway, in the truck, the engine still running. He had backed up into a juniper tree and remained there long enough for the tailpipe to scorch the bark. His body slumped against the door. Slowly Brian approached the truck. Through the window he could see first his hair, the color of cigarette ash, and then below it, the emptiness of his face, and knew him to be dead. His mouth was open and his tongue hung from it. His left eye was a tiny red planet. A rope of blood ran from his nose. An aneurysm, the doctor said.

His father had put the truck in reverse and turned around in his seat to eye the long curve of the driveway and a vessel at the base of his brain burst. Just like that. Something he had done a thousand times before—the safest thing in the world—had killed him. It was like getting lung cancer from pouring cereal or choking to death when checking e-mail: it didn't make sense or seem fair. Especially considering what Brian had walked away from, dented and spoiled, but alive. At the funeral many people said his father was with God, which meant God was death. Afterward he did not cry. He only felt profoundly lonely and staggered around the house, peering into rooms, trying their doorknobs to see if they were locked.

JUSTIN

When they approach the river, Boo freezes. "You see that?" Justin's father says, nodding in the dog's direction. "He's sighted something. Maybe a ptarmigan or a grouse."

It is another thirty yards to where Boo points, his body black and rigid, his snout indicating something hidden along the edge of the meadow, where the bear grass gives way to willow thickets. "At ease." The dog relaxes his pose and wags his tail but keeps his eyes focused ahead of him.

Here is a stand of willows, and beyond it, their fire pit. A tent crouches next to it, a brown vinyl dome tent, the kind that might have been purchased from a hardware shop in the late seventies. Its front flap is unzippered, gaping and fleshy and trembling, like an old man's mouth.

The tent appears to be empty, but they can hear a scritching sound from inside it. "Hello?" Justin says and then says it again, this time raising his voice to make sure he is heard over the river, its waters hissing. The scritching stops.

They set down their gear and slowly approach the tent and draw aside the flap to peer into its shadowy interior. A dark shape comes at them and takes to the air shrieking—a crow, he realizes when his senses overtake his alarm.

The dog barks wildly. His son runs off a few paces before turning around with his hands raised protectively before his face. His father simply stares after the bird—still visible but departing from them like a curl of ash blown by the breeze—before regarding the tent once again.

"Should we camp somewhere else?" Justin asks when his heart settles. "Is there somebody else staying here?"

His father continues to stare at the tent for a minute and then lays a hand on it, as if checking for a pulse. "No," he says. "There's nobody here."

"How can you be sure?"

He raises his hand. Its palm is coated with pollen.

"Why would they just leave their tent?"

"Your guess is as good as mine."

Right now Justin hears silence. It's like a mistake in music—the way it makes him cock his head and listen—like a finger losing its place on a guitar, the wrong note so much more striking than the right note. The steady sigh of the wind, the intermittent birdsong, the chipmunks rustling for pine nuts, has stopped. There is only the river, murmuring in the background.

Then, from the nearby forest, a mass of swallows starts up into the sky, frightened by something. They wheel overhead and their shadows speckle the meadow and their frantic chirping fills the air. With that the spell is broken.

His father wipes his hand on his thigh and inspects the palm.

By this time Graham has returned to the campsite. "Did you know pollen never deteriorates?" He is always saying things like this, listing off trivia he has committed to memory when surfing the Internet or reading the encyclopedia. "It's one of the few naturally secreted substances that lasts indefinitely."

"Indefinitely," his grandfather says and snorts, amused by the word.

"Do you know what that word means?" Graham says, not condescending, but eager to explain.

"Do you know what it means to be a know-it-all?"

"Did you know that certain types of plants can eat meat?"

"Where do you get this stuff?"

"I read it."

"Where?" The beginnings of a sneer grow beneath his grandfather's beard. "On the *Internet*?" He enunciates it like a foreign dish that once gave him indigestion.

"No," Graham says. "The back of a cereal box."

"Oh." The sneer turns into a smile and his grandfather lifts his arms and lets them fall, defeated.

They make their camp fifty yards upstream from the other tent. Even though they understand it to be empty, there is something about it that makes them uneasy, so that camping beside it is a little like picnicking downwind from the rotting husk of a beached whale.

While Boo splashes along the banks of the South Fork, chasing the silvery flashes of fish, Justin sets to work digging a new fire pit. His father and Graham make another trip to the Bronco, carrying the cooler and a duffel bag and lawn chairs and his old army-issue canvas tent. It leaks and smells like mothballs and mildew. Every night Justin has ever spent in it, he wakes up swollen and sneezing.

Last Christmas he bought his father a new tent from REI—one of those fancy waterproof, windproof four-man deals with a lifetime guarantee and a screened-in moonroof. "What happened to the new tent I bought you?"

"This has been a good tent for us." His father pats it fondly. "I like *this* tent." He does not look at Justin but sets to work unfolding the canvas and planting the stakes.

His voice goes high and he tries to control it. "That tent cost me nearly three hundred dollars. You're just going to let it rot in the attic?"

Paul finishes hammering a stake into the ground and stands up and straightens his posture to accentuate his six-foot frame. Beneath his stare Justin feels as if he has shrunk a good five inches, as if his chest hair and muscles have receded—and he becomes twelve all over again.

His father eyes Justin with a hand resting on his belly. "I didn't ask for the thing. And I didn't want it." He begins to rub his belly as if to summon his anger from it like a genie. "And when are you going to learn that quality doesn't always come with a price tag? Just listen to you. You're as bad as a Californian."

"Graham has allergies, you know. I hope they don't get set off by the mold."

"Graham has allergies." He sniffs his amusement. "More like you've got allergies."

"We've both got allergies."

Paul sniffs again. He has never suffered from the watery eyes or shortness of breath that come with fall and spring, so he always views allergy symptoms with suspicion, as though they were invented for sympathy. He passes the hammer to Graham forcefully enough to make him stagger back a step. "Here's a job for you. Pound in the rest of the stakes."

Along the banks of the South Fork, willows crowd together. The world tries to reflect itself in the water but can't. The clouds and trees and sun fall into the surface and vanish, swept away by the white water, along with their faces when they stand at twenty-yard intervals along the rocky bank and plop their spinners in the water. They have to be careful not to tangle their lines in the branches, snapping their wrists with short sidearm casts.

Justin watches his son. He can see in his face a certain excitement he recognizes. There was a time when, upon entering the woods and following a game trail to the river, with the sun falling through the trees in angled shafts, with the air cool and pine-smelling, with his fishing pole in one hand and tackle box in the other, he would dream about trout with freckled backs and bright white bellies and feel his heart turn over with excitement.

He feels something similar now. The dark forest. The green meadow. The pitted, unscalable walls of the canyon surrounding them. Seeing it, he realizes he has actually longed for this place. It is like hearing an old song on the radio. One you loved but forgot existed. Rediscovering it made you happy.

He wonders what his wife is doing. Maybe crunches on the living room floor while watching a DVR recording of *Survivor.* He has not thought of her since they left that morning, when she hugged Graham tightly to her chest and then gave Justin a quick squeeze that felt more like a handshake and said, "Take care of our boy."

There had been an argument earlier. He can't remember exactly where the anger came from—something trivial—maybe his carelessness with his bowl, chipping it in the sink when he went to splash the milk from it. But before long each of them was slamming cupboards, heaving sighs, looking for a way to cut the other with a sharp word or glare. "Fucking excuse me," he can remember saying as he pushed past her with the cooler.

He hadn't wanted to leave like that—with their anger unresolved. He remembered their wedding day, when the line of family and friends had exited the sanctuary to tearily offer them hugs and handshakes in the breezeway, his grandmother had whispered to him, "Never go to bed angry. Best advice I can give." That's what driving away this morning felt like, like going to bed with their backs to each other, anger spoiling their dreams. He had thought about calling from the road, had even fingered the phone. But then he thought of his father listening in on the conversation and slipped the phone back in his pocket. He was ashamed to call because there was something to be ashamed about. There was history here: no matter what the situation, even if he felt completely innocent, he would always apologize, always, just to end it, to put a stop to the tension that made him so distracted and headachy. Not this time.

There was a time when they would make up with sex—no, fucking was the word for it. In the middle of a screaming match, one of them would get a hungry look and shove the other against a wall or to the floor, ripping off clothes, enough to bare a breast, to bite a thigh, their kissing more like eating. Any bared skin would go red from carpet burn and the crosshatching of fingernails. And then their grunts would rise into mewls and their mewls into the best kind of screams and they would collapse, emptied, satisfied, breathing heavily. He missed those days.

His attention drifts to the river, from which he pulls three rainbow trout, each the size of his forearm. When he stares into their pearly eyes and rips the hook from their mouths, he cannot help but feel a strange pleasure even as he recognizes a thing yanked from its home into a cold white space it did not know existed until that very second. They gut the fish and throw their heads in the river.

When they return to camp, Graham goes to the tent to get a jacket. From inside comes a fierce buzzing, like a dozen maracas violently shaken. He jumps away with a scream and Justin hurries toward him.

"There's something in there," Graham says. There comes a sound like the thump of a stick against the canvas.

"It's a snake," his grandfather says. "It's a goddamned rattler is what it is."

His father retrieves a long stick from the forest and with his knife hurriedly whittles its end into a yellow point. With this he beats at the outside of the tent. "Hey! Hey, snake! Get out of there, you snake!"

Eventually a western rattler slides from the tent, pausing to taste the air with its tongue, and then begins its fast slither through the ankle-high grass. Justin's father chases after it, hooting with excitement, and Justin chases after him, certain someone will be bitten. At the sound of their footsteps, the snake coils up like a pile of rope to face them. Its tail buzzes out another warning that Justin's father silences by whipping the spear forward as though it were an extension of his arm. It pierces the rattler cleanly through the head and tacks it to the ground.

He gives Justin a big grin before uprooting the spear and holding it out before him. From its tip hangs the rattler. It twists into an S and slumps into a diamond-backed line more than five feet long. Its beaded tail drops down to zigzag a trail in the dirt.

Justin must look spooked—he is spooked—because his father laughs a little when he toes the snake off the end of his spear, its head now a peculiar saddle shape with a hole through its middle. A lot of blood and clear fluid comes out of it.

Graham says, "If that isn't the biggest rattler in the entire universe, I'd be surprised," and his grandfather smiles at him like a big dumb cat with a mouse in its jaws.

The snake refuses to die. It does a dance instead, twisting and knotting itself into calligraphic designs, its tail rattling, its mouth sometimes closed, sometimes open and as bright as bubblegum. Justin believes it is staring at him. As if it can open its mouth *that wide.*

Minutes pass and the snake continues to knot itself into an ever-moving tangle. Every now and then Justin's father pokes it with the spear. "Can I try?" Graham says and for a while he and his grandfather trade the spear back and forth, stabbing, prodding.

Watching a snake die is like watching a campfire, a controlled menace.

A long half hour passes and then it is done moving, no matter how hard Justin's father pokes it. The sunlight has begun to retreat from the canyon when he carries the snake to the campfire and lays it out on a log and goes to work with a boning knife, chopping off its head and setting it aside. Then he pries open the body to eviscerate it and strip off its skin and dice its meat into cubes and put them in a pan to cook with a slice of bacon.

They stand around the campfire and watch the meat hiss in the bacon fat. It smells fungal.

"Did you know," Graham says, the initial nervousness of his voice giving way to an academic tenor. "Did you know that when you see a dead snake you're supposed to bury it, because the yellow jackets and wasps will eat the poison and when they do it becomes their poison so that when they sting you they sting you to death?"

"You read that on the back of a box of cereal?"

"No." He purses his lips, terribly serious. "I saw it on the Discovery Channel."

His grandfather picks up the head, a soft jewel, with his thumb and forefinger and squeezes. Its mouth opens. Little clear beads hang off its fangs' tips. "Did *you* know the Chinese believe venom is an aphrodisiac? And that the Indians believe it has healing powers?"

"Indians?" Graham says. "Or *Indian* Indians?"

"Both."

With his knife Paul widens the snake's smile and removes the poison sacs. A see-through whitish yellowish color, they appear made from spider filaments. He drops them into a bottle of Jack Daniels. "A snack for later."

Once cooked, the meat turns bright pink, like plastic. He seasons it with salt and pepper before forking it onto a dish. "Dig in." They fill their mouths with the snake and the snake is so good—like a rougher sort of pork—it creates in them an appetite. They feel it uncoiling in their bellies and rattling and asking for more. So they feed it.

They throw the trout filets in the pan where they sizzle as if angry. Justin's father turns them with a telescoping spatula, cooking them through in less than five minutes, serving them up on tin plates already dampened by the snake. They eat the crumbly meat with their fingers and spit out the splinters of bones while the canyon darkens all around them.

For a long time the only sound is the rushing of the river and the occasional *crack* of a Coors can being opened. "I thought Dad told me your doctor said you weren't supposed to drink anymore," Graham says and his grandfather says, "That doesn't mean I'm going to drink any less." He settles into his own separate silence and appears like a still-life painting, his hand on Boo's head, motionless and watching the fire with a detached expression.

Justin collects the dishes and carries them to the river and goes to work scrubbing with sand and a dash of biodegradable soap that goes frothing downstream. Back at camp, he packs the cooking materials into a large canvas bag they will later hang from a tree.

By this time the air has grown heavy with the shadows that come with early evening, earlier each day now that fall is deepening into winter. A great bunch of honking draws Justin's eyes skyward where he observes a flock of geese, arranged in a capital V, headed south. One of them appears drunk, swooping and circling away from the rest who continue along their determined course. He realizes it is an owl, snatching moths from the air.

And then he spots another. And another still. He takes his beer and wanders away from camp and in the deepening gloom watches the owls as they fly in and out of the high branches where they make their roosts.

His father appears beside him. "What are you doing?"

"Just looking. At the owls and the trees and everything else."

"You always liked trees," he says. Justin can smell beer in his breath and can hear it in his voice, the friendlier, looser tone of it. "I remember when you were a baby. One night you wouldn't stop crying. So I took you outside and we stood underneath a tree and you fell right asleep."

Justin looks at him as if for the first time. "I've never heard that story before."

"You always liked trees."

"I did?"

"Sure."

The darkness comes right up to the fire. Justin's father sits on a lawn chair while Graham and Justin take to the logs they dragged earlier from the forest. The pyramidal arrangement of firewood glows yellow at its top and orange in its middle while the charcoal at its bottom gleams with the black, glassy quality of obsidian. The flames throw shadows upon the willows surrounding them and toss sparks into the air and the night becomes a flickering vision of orange gleams and shifting black shapes. From way off in the distance comes a mournful scream that interrupts all other sounds in the canyon.

Graham stands up. "What's that?"

"That's an owl," Justin says.

"It sounded like a dinosaur. I mean, like the dinosaurs in the movies."

Boo moves to the periphery of the camp and huffs once. Having proved himself, he hurries back.

Graham lowers himself to the log. A few minutes pass before the screeching begins again. From the forest sounds another owl, then another, some of them with voices like a metallic rasp, others a twittering hoot. Graham looks over his shoulder, perhaps wondering if later tonight he will wake to find some phantom looming over him. "They sound sad," he finally says.

His grandfather nods and pulls from his beer. "That they do."

For a time they sit there, listening to the owls sing, their remote wailing.

"If I could sing a song like that," his grandfather says and pokes at the fire with a stick and the sparks float up and grow smaller and smaller until the darkness encloses them. "A song about the way I feel. Well, it would be quite a song."

From his belt he pulls a Gerber buck knife and flicks open its seven-inch blade, the blade stained and chipped from so many years of skinning animals and gutting fish and carving wood. With it he begins to whittle his stick down to a point. "You got any stories, Graham? Scary ones?"

Graham thinks about it for a while and then launches into a story he heard at school. It's about an old hunchback who lives underneath the city and pulls boys down when they reach into sewer grates to fetch their runaway baseballs. "You know how Pepto-Bismol turns your poop black? Well, this guy is so evil, he poops black even when his poop doesn't have Pepto-Bismol in it." He goes on another minute, and then his grandfather interrupts him, saying, "I've got a story."

A moth flickers by and vanishes.

"Go on then," Justin says.

"A long time ago," he says, as slow as breathing, "something terrible happened here." He studies Graham and Justin, making sure he has their attention. "It was the summer of Red Morning's fifteenth year, and like every Indian boy, he went on a vision quest." At this point he has had six beers and from the sound of his voice they are beginning to affect him. "In this very canyon." He aims his knife at the ground for emphasis before lazily returning to his whittling.

"Now when you go on a vision quest, you're not supposed to eat or drink or sleep. You're supposed to just sit there—on your buffalo hide or whatever—and get in tune with nature and eventually, supposedly, your spirit animal will shuffle out of the forest and tell you something you won't ever forget, at least not for a little while. And then you'll go back to your village a man. So this Red Morning, he finds a nice meadow and he waits for the spirits to call, maybe two weeks, before—"

"You can only last four days without water," Graham says. "Then you die."

"Indians are made of different stuff. They're tougher." He aims the knife at Graham. "And if you interrupt me again I'm going to throw you in the river."

Graham smiles and then covers up the smile with his hands.

"So he waits there three weeks. Lips cracking. Skin blistering. Spiders and ants and mosquitoes biting him. And finally his spirit animal comes. When it first comes out of the woods, he thinks it's a man, draped in furs.

But it isn't. It's tall and naked and covered fully in coarse, black hair. It smells like spoiled meat. And it has long yellow claws. But Red Morning doesn't feel afraid. He knows it's going to tell him something important. It says only one word before returning to the woods: 'Kill.'"

He falls into a reverie, speaking softly, telling them how Red Morning stands up then and stretches his aching muscles and is about to gather up his buffalo hide, when he sees in the near distance, just around the bend in the canyon, where his village is, tentacles of smoke rising into the sky.

He runs home as only a fifteen-year-old Indian boy can run, so fast that his feet leave the ground and he is actually flying. He no longer feels hungry or thirsty. There is still a pain at the bottom of his stomach, but it's a different kind of pain, as if all the blood in his body is pooling hotly there.

Near the village, he climbs up an embankment so that he can see what the trouble is before he faces it full-on. He stares in disbelief at the scene below him. The smokehouse is burning. The sweat lodge has been kicked in. Several wickiups have been kicked open, slashed apart. Bodies lie strewn about everywhere, his mother and father among them, with holes the size of fists in their chests and stomachs. Then he spots the soldiers. They wear gray pants and blue coats that fork in the back like a devil's tail. There are five of them and they stand in a half circle, smoking rolled cigarettes and laughing quietly.

These are the white men he has heard rumors about but never really believed in. The ones who kill elk and deer only for their antlers, sawing them off and leaving their bodies to rot. Here, they have killed everyone and filled their leather satchels and saddlebags with dried venison and bone necklaces and carefully carved pipes and blades and arrowheads. Anything that shines prettily or promises to fill their bellies, they take. They are led by a hawk-faced man wearing a white hat.

At that moment Red Morning remembers the word the creature whispered to him. *Kill.* His pulse takes to the rhythm of it like a drumbeat. *Kill.*

Justin's father pauses here to wet his throat with another sip of beer.

His face is red and hollow-eyed from the fire. He has whittled his stick down to a splinter. Shreds of wood decorate his thighs.

He continues, telling them how Red Morning cups his hands around his mouth and howls a war cry, opening up his throat and bouncing his tongue, so that his voice fills up the canyon, echoing off its walls and trees, making it sound as though the whole world is full of Indians hungry for the scalps of white men.

The soldiers throw down their cigarettes and look in every direction. They seem ready to fight at first, but what are they fighting for? They have taken everything there is to take. So they leap onto their horses. When the hawk-faced man urges his horse into a gallop, the strap of his satchel breaks and it comes loose from his shoulder and disgorges itself upon the ground. The food and the jewelry and weaponry fall as a mass that breaks into many pieces that roll and bounce among the hurrying hooves of his horse. It stumbles and kicks and throws him from his saddle. His men continue a good thirty yards and stop haltingly because all around them the canyon still vibrates with Red Morning's war cry.

The shadows on Justin's father's face move when he talks. But that's it. That's the only thing that moves. His body stays absolutely dead still. Even his voice is a level drone, so slow you can pick each word from the air and examine it.

"Stop!" the hawk-faced man cries to the men, scrabbling across the ground to where his rifle has fallen. "Come help!" He is about to yell for them again when an arrow strikes his neck and takes away his voice and sends him reeling. His hat falls off and soaks up a jet of arterial blood that escapes from him. He struggles to right himself. Another arrow shaves him narrowly. And then another, this one finding its mark and dropping him.

"The other men leave him there, but each in his own turn meets death, some with their throats slit, others brained by rocks. He finds all of them." Justin's father's voice rises and falls and levels once more. "And then he skins them and guts them and eats their meat and breaks their bones and sucks the marrow from them. And with every bite he takes, his skin grows hairier and his nails grow longer, as long and sharp as talons."

Graham laughs and his grandfather gives him a severe look before his attention drifts off toward the dark forest and the less dark sky. "If you're walking through the woods and if you see a tree with scratches on its bark?"

They follow his gaze, expecting to find such a tree. "The Indian once known as Red Morning has been there, sharpening his claws and teeth. He wanders the forest, still hungry for revenge, searching for men with rifles, someone to blame for what happened to him and his family."

Graham makes big eyes even as he grins to prove he isn't afraid.

For the next few minutes they sit quietly. Then an owl swoops near the fire, its wings arched against the warm updraft, exciting the flames with the air it displaces. Justin shifts his legs. His feet have needles in them, having fallen asleep. And the log beneath him feels suddenly cold and hard and unwelcome.

Justin awakes with a full bladder and ventures out of the tent and into the evening stillness. The moon is gone, the canyon lit only by the glow of the stars. He pauses after a few paces, his last breath and footstep the only lingering sound. The hair on his arms prickles as it does when you feel you are being watched. He thinks of his father's story, able to believe in it for a moment, his mind drugged with sleep. Then he shakes his head and in doing so shakes off his fear like a cobweb. He moves hesitantly forward, away from the campsite, to the place they designated their toilet.

When he lets loose a steaming arc of piss, his eyes wander the sky. An owl banks and wheels, its silhouette blacking out the stars in the shape of a mouth. He follows it until it vanishes against the backdrop of a fast-moving collection of clouds. They come from the west. He stands there awhile—half-asleep, entranced by the gray mystery of the night—and for five minutes, maybe more, watches the clouds become a thunderstorm crisscrossed with wires of lightning. Soon the canyon will darken with rain. He shakes off and hurries back to camp and observes nearby the abandoned tent. Its black hump makes it appear like the huddled remains of a beast that has run and run only to collapse exactly there, perishing where it lies, like the shadow-filled skeletons of cattle in John Wayne movies.

He lies awake until the night fills with the dull, even noise of rainfall. The entire world seems to hiss. The wind flares up for a moment and the canvas rattles and flaps, joined by a sound like the crack of whips as branches break off trees. He clicks on his flashlight, revealing their four bodies crowded into a tent that droops and breathes around them with many damp spots dripping and pattering his sleeping bag.

When you put your head on your pillow and listen—*really* listen—you can hear footsteps. This is your pulse, the veins in your ear swelling and constricting, slightly shifting against the cotton. He hears this now—an *under*sound, beneath the rain—only his head is nowhere near his pillow. He has propped himself up on his elbow.

There it is. Or is he only imagining it? The rasping thud a foot makes in wet grass—one moment behind the tent, the next moment in front of it, circling.

The front flaps billow open with the breeze, the breeze bearing the keen wet odor of rabbitbrush, a smell he will always associate with barbed-wire fences, with dying, with fear. Outside, thousands of raindrops catch his flashlight's beam and brighten with it. He imagines something out there, rushing in—how easy it would be—its shape taking form as it moves from darkness into light.

His father releases a violent snore. Justin spotlights him with the flashlight, wanting to tell him *shh*. His father's fingers twitch like the legs of the dreaming dog he drapes his arm over. His mouth forms silent words, his eyeballs shuddering beneath his eyelids, and—not for the first time—Justin wonders what is going on in there, inside him.

Morning, a sneezing fit wakes Justin. He wipes his nose and then the gunk from his eyes to see that his father has already risen, his sleeping bag left crumpled and empty on his cot like a shed skin. Justin can smell wood smoke and hear the crackle of the campfire made from the wood they kept dry by storing it in the tent.

His son still sleeps, an arm thrown over his face, so Justin rises as quietly as he can, pulling on his jeans and the Patagonia longsleeved crew he paid way too much money for the other day, when he and Graham went shopping at REI and got carried away, spending over four hundred dollars after an overeager saleswoman wearing a green vest bullied them into a family membership while dragging them rack to rack, talking at a fast clip about how important gear was—that was the word she kept using, *gear*—emphasizing, among other things, dry-core weave as an essential component in any shirt, the way it wicked moisture away, etc. He wishes he had spent the money instead on an air mattress. He hasn't been camping in years and he's not used to the time away from his bed. His spine feels like the hinges have gone stiff, like the oil has leaked out of them.

He steps outside and pops his back and takes in the morning—the trees that remain in shadow down low, while sunlight ignites their upper branches. He then notices the dewy grass trampled down in a path that leads around the tent. He follows it, slowly, as if expecting something to leap out at him around every staked corner, until he has made a full circle. Then he steps out of the ring of trampled grass and stares at it for a long time, the memory of last night surfacing in his foggy brain. He does not feel the fear he felt before, but a mild discomfort brought on by this observation: whatever has visited them—whether deer or bear or coyote, he wonders—hasn't simply prowled near for a sniff. The wide path of tramped-down grass indicates a continuous circling that reminds him of vultures wheeling in the sky.

A pitch pocket pops and draws his attention to the campfire, left unattended.

He looks around for his father, looking to the east, where the last of the clouds move slowly away from him, seeming to drag the blue weight of the sky behind them. The rain has left behind a dampness that creeps from the ground as a milky mist. A quarter his height, it covers the meadow and makes everything farther than ten yards away gray and indistinct. As he peers into it a red-winged blackbird darts out, flashing past him, toward the river, where he hears a dog bark.

He walks a few paces from camp, toward the hum of the South Fork, until it becomes visible. Along it the mist drifts thickly riverward. He spots his father, naked along the shore. He appears as if upon a cloud. A sudden whirl of mist hides him for a moment. And then, while running his hands through his wet hair, he emerges from its dense vapors as if throwing off a shroud.

The cold water has tightened and pinkened his skin and his dampened hair looks completely black, flattened like seaweed against his head. Justin sees him for a moment as he was, so many years ago. The picture of health. He remembers how his father used to lift weights in the basement and how the house would shake when he swung 250 pounds over his head and then back to the floor in a power lift. He remembers how his father once broke a wrench when wrestling with a rusted-over bolt. How, one winter, after his woodpile receded faster than he knew it ought to, he drilled a hole deep into a piece of firewood and filled it with gunpowder and sealed it with putty—and when the living room of his neighbor, Mr. Ott, exploded several days later, Justin's father called FTD with a smile on his face and ordered flowers to be delivered to the hospital.

In this way he is like a force of nature, moving through life with reckless abandon, wiping away any kind of opposition as a storm would wipe away a village, the low growl of his voice like a distant shout of thunder that makes you pause in whatever you are doing and look up.

Now he dries off his body with a towel and then spins it into a whip to snap Boo, who barks eagerly and runs a few paces away from him and back. He drapes the towel over a boulder where his clothes lie in a pile. He pulls on a well-worn pair of Wrangler blue jeans and a thermal shirt whose long sleeves he pushes up to his elbows. And then wool socks, Browning boots whose laces he double-knots. Once dressed, he tosses the towel over his shoulder and moves toward Justin. As he does, he seems to grow older, the wrinkles fanning out from his eyes and the yellow creeping into his teeth when he smiles his hello. Age spots dot his skin. Plum-colored pouches bulge beneath his eyes. He says nothing but lays a damp hand on Justin's shoulder. The chill remains after he takes it away.

Boo follows the circle around the tent, his nose to the ground, sniffing excitedly. He pauses now and then to press his snout fully into the grass, his tail wagging. And then he stiffens and whines and regards the woods a moment before returning to whatever invisible tendrils of scent he discerns.

"He was doing that earlier." Justin's father rubs his head and beard with the towel before tossing it over a log near the fire. "Something prowled close for a sniff last night. That right, Boo?" He squats down next to the dog and pulls him into a headlock and kisses him on the snout. "What do you smell, Boo Boo? You smell a raccoon? You smell a possum? You smell the big bad wolf?"

He hikes to the edge of the forest, twenty yards away. Here he hung a red canvas bag shaped like a huge sausage. It contains their dirty clothes and cooking supplies, anything that might carry the smell of food. There is a handle on the hind end of the bag and he has run the forty-foot rope through it and made a slipknot that he choked tight. He then threw the free end of the rope over the lowest branch, twenty feet above the ground and yanked at it until the bag hung suspended just below the limb, like a massive cocoon. The free end of the rope he secured to the trunk in an anchor hitch he undoes now, lowering the big bag until it impacts the ground with a metallic clatter as the pots and pans and plates readjust themselves.

Justin's father asks him to fetch some water for coffee. He unzips the bag and rifles around in it until he finds the kettle and throws it at Justin, who catches it fumblingly. There is a cold spring in the nearby forest. From it bleeds a marshy stream, one of so many that trickle to the bottom of the canyon and feed the South Fork. Justin pushes his way through the woods. By this time the mist has mostly burned off, only a few skirts of it surrounding the trees and billowing in his passage. A swarm of tiny brown toads hops away from him when he approaches the spring.

Here it is—the size of a hot tub—surrounded by willows and sun-sparkled stones. And there, next to it, a pair of tattered boots, one of them lying flat against the ground, the other pointed skyward, like a gravestone. He has paused without realizing it. Now he takes several hesitant steps forward to see beyond the boots, where a strewn puzzle of bones and cartilage come together and form a body.

The kettle falls from his hand to the forest floor with a *thunk.*

The man has been dead a long time. So long Justin can only identify him as male by his clothes and even then he cannot be certain. His jeans and flannel shirt have been torn open and scattered in pieces as though he has exploded and left the shrapnel of his person lying here and there among the weeds. The vultures and the coyotes and the flies and the worms have had their way and licked the skin clean off his bones. His bones are the color of old paper, a yellowish black, their surface scored from the gnashing of teeth. Justin imagines the coyotes howling when they ate his remains, fighting over the juiciest cuts of meat.

His ribs look like the legs of a dead spider, curled upon itself. Crab grass grows through his knuckles and around his skull like hair. He seems to have grown out of the soil and is now receding into it. A moth lands on the skull, flexing its wings and tasting from the black pool of an eye socket, before taking flight.

At that moment the world seems to stop. The moth ceases flying, frozen in midflight. A tree limb, bowed by the breeze, stills. A pinecone falling from a branch hangs motionless in the air and an immobile chipmunk watches it not fall.

Justin feels a fist-sized pressure in his chest that comes from holding his breath. With a gasp, the pressure vanishes and the world unlocks and resumes its flow, as the moth flutters away and the pinecone crashes to the ground.

And then he runs. He runs and probably makes it fifty feet before he stops and finds his cool and steadies his breathing and returns to the spring, slowly. There is a taste like salty pennies in his mouth and he realizes he has bitten a hole in his cheek. He swallows the blood and calls for his father. And then again, before a voice faintly calls back to Justin from the campsite, "What?"

"I need you to come here. Come here right now."

Something in his voice must alarm his father because a moment later Justin can hear a crashing in the woods and then breathing beside him. Boo trots forward and Justin's father grabs the dog by the collar before he can disturb the corpse.

"This is bad," he says. He is wearing a John Deere cap with a chewed-on brim. He removes it now and stares into its hollow. "This is a hell of a thing." He looks like a man who has woken from a nap and cannot find his bearings.

Justin takes his cell phone from his pocket and hits the power button. It chirps to life and the screen glows with greenish light. No surprise: there is no service here, far from any tower. "If we drive to the top of the canyon," he says, "if we get a little higher, I might be able to get a signal. It's worth a try anyway."

"No." His father puts his hat back on and straightens it.

"Excuse me?"

"No."

"He's dead."

"People do that. They die." He lifts his hand and lets it fall and slap his thigh. "I tell you something: *he's* in no rush."

Justin understands this completely and not at all. "Dad?" he says. *"No."*

There is concern on his face, but Justin genuinely believes this has more to do with having to abandon their hunting trip than with the dead man sprawled before them. His father puts a hand on his shoulder and squeezes just hard enough so that Justin knows he means business.

"Look. It turned out to be a beautiful day, didn't it?" And he's right—it is—the kind of bright blue day that bleaches everything of its color. "How about let's enjoy it?" He regards the dead man and Justin notices his cheek bulge, his tongue probing the side of his mouth. "Probably died of a heart attack. Nothing to be done about something like that.

Tomorrow evening, when we leave, we'll drive to John Day and tell the police. But not today."

His father releases Boo then and the dog creeps toward the dead man, his muscles tense, his body low, as if certain the blackened pile of bones and sinew will leap up at any moment and attack. When it doesn't, his movements loosen and he begins to pant happily and wades into the spring to drink.

"Okay, Justin?"

Justin looks at his feet—something he does when gathering his thoughts—and there discovers a weather-beaten pack of Marlboros, the cigarettes that could not kill the dead man quickly enough. Next to it sits something shiny. It has the look of a mud-encrusted marble. In mindless curiosity, Justin picks it up and wipes the dust off and turns it over. A faded green pupil stares at him. An eye—he realizes—a glass eye. There is a chip in it where a coyote clacked it between its teeth or a crow pecked at it in the hopes that it would burst. When he shouts his disgust and drops it, it bounces a few times and rolls to a stop with its pupil upright. With no fleshy pocket to retreat into, it does not blink, ever watchful.

"Justin?" his father says again, his voice calm, as if he finds none of this unusual.

Justin wipes his hands on his pants and wishes for a handful of soap. "Okay," he says in a voice he recognizes as the voice of his childhood. "Fine." This is what his wife was talking about, he now knows, his father's ability to bend him into whatever shape he wants. Justin has grown so used to following his direction, he does not think to question, except briefly, whimperingly, such a gruesome decision.

They go silent and side by side stand watching for a time. The way they are standing there, with their spines so stiff, they must look like part of the forest, a stunted group of trees. Finally Justin kicks a mass of dirt over the eye. It does not lessen the feeling of being watched, as he hoped it would. He remembers the feeling from last night and imagines the eye rolling toward him in the moonlit meadow.

From faraway comes the sound of a diesel horn, a logging truck rocketing along a distant highway, reminding him that no matter how much this feels like the middle of nowhere, it isn't.

When they return to camp, Justin checks on Graham and finds him staring blankly at the ceiling of the tent, his chest rising and falling with a faint wheeze. Already the sun has soaked into the canvas, making the air inside the tent warm and humid; he feels as if he has stepped into a mouth.

"Graham?"

His son lifts his head to look at Justin with eyes that are red-rimmed and watery.

"Feeling all right?"

"I think I need my inhaler." His voice has that dreamy quality that comes from not getting enough oxygen.

Justin digs around in his backpack and finds the Albuterol alongside his toothbrush and soap. Justin hands it to his son, who sits up and shakes the inhaler and breathes deeply of it when it spurts into his mouth. He keeps his chest puffed out and holds the medicine inside for thirty seconds before letting it escape with a winded pant.

Justin rubs his back. "Better?"

He nods before taking another puff.

Justin holds back the desire to tell him about the body, to tell him to pack his things. Another minute and the boy dresses, pulling on a white waffle-print thermal, stepping into a pair of khaki-colored nylon pants with many pockets and a zipper around each knee so that you can pull off the legs in hot weather. They step outside to find Justin's father adding a log to the fire. Last night he set up a grill and now the flames rise through it to warm the kettle. From its mouth comes a line of steam.

"I hope you're happy," Justin says.

His father keeps his eyes on the fire, poking the coals with his boot. "Something the matter?"

"Graham woke up feeling sick."

He more grunts than says, "Flu season."

"Not that kind of sick. Allergic sick."

His father heaves a sigh, but upon studying Graham—the redness of his eyes and the black smudges beneath them—his face softens. "You know what's good for allergies?"

"Pills?" Graham says.

"No. Coffee."

Graham has a Pendleton blanket wrapped around his shoulders and he draws it a little tighter when he squats next to the fire. "Coffee tastes like dirt puke."

"Well, this is different. This is cowboy coffee." He waits for Graham to ask for an explanation, and when he doesn't, he gets one anyway. "A pot of water. Three cups of coffee grounds. Boil for an hour. Drop a bullet in. If it floats, it's ready."

"Really?"

"No. Not really." He takes an old sweatsock and holds it tightly over the mouth of a tin mug, and then, with his free hand, removes the kettle from the grill and pours. The black and grainy coffee filters through the sock and fills the mug. "But it's strong."

For breakfast they fry up a pan of bacon and boil a pot of beans and sop up the grease with a bag of wheat bread. When finished, they sit around for a few minutes, rubbing their hands fondly over their bellies like women in their final trimester. Justin's father pours himself another mug of coffee and uses his knife to stir it, though he has put nothing in it, preferring it black. He removes the knife smoking from the mug and sets it on the log next to him and raises the coffee to sip.

He then breaks their daze when he turns to Graham and asks, "You know anything about guns?"

"Not really." Graham digs a hole in the dirt with his shoe and covers it back up. The tense look on his face seems expectant of another lecture.

Justin's father finishes his coffee and sets down the mug and slaps his hands on his thighs and rises from his seat. "I've got a gun I want you to take a look at."

He vanishes into the tent and when he reappears he carries a box of shells and a brand-new .30-30 lever-action rifle. It is crafted out of walnut and blued steel. He sits down next to Graham with the rifle laid across his thighs, smoothing his hands up and down the length of it.

He explains that this particular gun, the Model 94, once known as the Model 84, has been around for 110 years. "And still going strong." His voice takes on an exasperated tone when he says there are those out there who feel it isn't a powerful enough gun, those who had taken it hunting and either missed or wounded an animal and then immediately gone to trade it in for a .243 or some other high-stepping number. "I suppose it's easier to blame the gun than to admit you're a lousy shot." He pats the stock. "But this gun works and it works well. It was my first gun. It was your dad's first gun."

There is something about a lever-action carbine, he says. Your meat tastes better—your trophy looks handsomer on the wall—when you hunt with it. He stands up and demonstrates how the rifle comes easily to the shoulder without you having to think about it. "See? It points naturally. It's light. It's handy. It's easy to shoot. It's got a real light recoil but plenty of punch."

Whenever he speaks of guns his voice takes on an almost professorial tone, carefully explaining intricacies his audience can appreciate only distantly. The terms he uses must make little sense to Graham, but the boy listens eagerly and stares with an enchanted expression on his face, as if the rifle were a long shapely leg capped by a red high heel.

Justin's father explains that it was chambered for several other cartridges more powerful than the .30-30, such as the .38-55, the .32 special, but he prefers the Barnes 150-grain flat-point X bullet. It has a deep hollow-point designed to expand at .30-30 velocities. "Let me tell you something," he says when he opens up the box of shells and handloads the magazine. "This will penetrate like there's no tomorrow." The shells slide in and the breech closes with an oiled snap, the sound teeth make when biting air.

He holds it out to Graham and Graham stands up and licks his lips and wipes his palms on his knees before taking it. The weapon is strange to him—but gives him immediate confidence. Justin can see this in the widening of his eyes, the straightening of his posture. Justin remembers the first time he held a gun. The feeling—the power, the lurking pleasure of the cold metal fitting into his warm hand—is unforgettable.

"Do you like it?" Justin's father says.

"I do."

"Good." The skin around his eyes crinkles like tissue paper. "Because I bought it for you."

Graham says, "No way," and a second later so does Justin, only with a different emphasis.

Graham turns to him with the rifle gripped tightly in his hands. "Come on, Dad. Don't be such a—" He meets Justin's eyes easily, his stare ugly and powerful. Justin is surprised by his reaction. He is one of those children who eats his vegetables when told to, who shuts off the television after his program ends, who never asks for more than his allowance. To hear such a challenge makes Justin feel momentarily off-balance.

"Don't be such a what?" Justin says.

"Come on, Dad."

"Come on, Dad, *nothing.*"

The stare he gets back—a dark forbidding stare—reminds him very much of his father. Justin wonders what has happened to the pale-faced trembling asthmatic of a few minutes ago. His son opens his mouth, as if ready to say something, and then, having thought about it, pinches his lips together in a line.

Justin approaches his father until he stands only a foot from him. "Got something to talk to you about." His voice has a crack running through it.

"Now?"

"Right now." Justin tries to drag him—grabbing his shoulder, as solid as wood—but he will move only when he wishes to move, so Justin releases his grip and walks away from camp and into the meadow and waits. Justin hears his father say to Graham, "Better give that back for a sec." And then, with the rifle in hand, he slowly makes his way through the grass. On the way he stops to pick a flower and smell it before tossing it away.

"You know what you're doing?" Justin says.

"I'm giving him a gun. You had a gun when you were his age." He waves his arm as if the memory of Justin—a boy, hunting—lies out there in the woods.

"Yes, but I'm not you and he isn't me. He hasn't taken a hunter's safety course. He doesn't have his hunting license. And—"

"For Christ's sake. When's the last time you saw a ranger out here?"

"And." Justin holds up his hand, indicating that he needs to listen. "His mother specified he wasn't to shoot anything but a picture."

"His mother," Paul says through his nose. "You realize you cut your teeth on this sort of thing? Will you listen to—"

His father doesn't know anything about the trouble with Karen. He doesn't know that Justin often sleeps on the couch, that Karen often speaks to him through Graham, that Justin often limits himself to touching her shoulder and only when he feels the need to offer a reassuring squeeze or indicate that she ought to move aside so he can grab a glass from the cupboard.

"Look," Justin says. "Forget her. *I'm* the one who's going to make the decision about when he's ready." Despite his effort to control his voice, it comes out in an almost whining tone that makes the attention in his father's eyes give place to a dismissive parental stare. "You're undermining my authority, Dad."

"You worry too much. You're a nervous guy." He smiles and shuts one eye and aims the rifle at the hawk circling above them. Sunlight reflects off the gunmetal and for an instant lights up the side of his face. "Bam." He hands the gun to Justin and says, "How about you give it to him? Say it's from both of us."

"A little late for that."

"Still. You give it to him."

He starts back to camp, pausing after a few steps to dig in his pocket. "Here," he says. "Have a Werther's Original. It will make you feel better."

"Thanks." He absently takes it and unwraps it and puts it in his mouth and then remembers he doesn't like Werther's Original.

Graham's eyes are a pale shade of gray, almost colorless, regarding Justin when he stands before him. "What do you think?" Justin says, running his thumb along the Winchester's stock, tracing the wood grain, its color like cream ale. "Do you think it's a good one?"

"Yes," Graham says, eagerness creeping into his voice. "I think so."

Justin regards the rifle. Its barrel is twenty-five inches long, a beautiful black that is almost blue, cold to the touch. He checks the safety and wipes a smear of dirt off the muzzle before holding it out.

Graham lets it hang there a moment, his eyes considering Justin. "So it's okay?"

"Yes. I guess. But let's not tell your mother about this. Not yet. Okay?"

He takes it gingerly, with two hands. He keeps his grip a moment longer before letting go. Like all weapons, the Winchester has surprising heft—as if something large, a living creature, is contained within it. His arms lower with its weight. "Nice!" he says, letting the word trail out with a hiss. Immediately he holds the rifle to his shoulder and aims down the line of it.

Justin's father stands a few paces behind him. When Justin turns to look at him, his face crumples up in a smile. He gives the thumbs-up and Justin shakes his head disapprovingly in response, even as he feels a certain excitement for his son.

"How about let's shoot something?" Justin's father says and Graham says, "Okay," and approaches him, ready to hand off the weapon.

"What are you giving it to me for? Your gun, after all."

"It's my gun," Graham says in a soft voice, as if to himself. He holds the Winchester at his hip and pivots quickly, carving a silver arc in the air when he draws a bead on this tree, then that tree, the hidden threat among them. Justin imagines the dead man collecting his bones and rising up to greet them.

"Come on," his father says. "We're going to see what kind of gunslinger you are." He motions for them to follow him, and they do, out into the meadow, where he instructs Graham to click off the safety and then points at a nearby pine tree with an X spray painted across its trunk. "How about you shoot—"

"Hold on," Justin says, but neither of them chooses to hear him. The rifle looks so menacing in Graham's arms, like a snake that might turn on him at any moment, opening up holes from which blood will trickle.

"Shoot that tree," Justin's father says. "X marks the spot. Can you do that?"

"I can do that." Graham takes a long time staring through the sight before he pulls the trigger. Every other sound falls away, replaced by an ear-splitting crack that is lost a moment later in the calm of the canyon. Below and to the right of the tree, the earth splashes up, like mud under the blow of a sledgehammer.

"Holy crap is that loud," Graham says, putting a hand to his ear and cracking a belly laugh.

Boo runs to the divot and stares intently as if expecting blood to bubble from it. Justin's father whistles for him to return to his side and then comes up behind Graham and coaches his posture. "Try again. This time brace the rifle to your shoulder. Like this. Now bring your hand forward but not too far forward. And don't *hold* your breath. Shoot at the *end* of a breath."

To hear them talking about guns, laughing sadistically—acting like men are *supposed* to act—positions Graham suddenly in a new light, making him seem more mature than he ever has before, a little man. But shouldn't Justin be the one goading him along, making that happen? Wasn't he the teacher? With the knack for being alternately stern and jokey in the classroom, inspiring his students?

Again the rifle jumps and the report thunders, expanding and contracting in the space of a second, before rolling away down the canyon—

while on the tree trunk a white, pulpy carnation opens up in the middle of the X.

"You're a natural," Justin's father says, clapping his hands twice, before indicating where Graham ought to aim next.

He sends a stone skipping. He knocks a pinecone from a high branch. A stalk of mullein bursts into a pollinated cloud. Each explosion dissolves something or sends something briefly aloft. The coarse scent of gunpowder hangs all around them.

Justin's father stares then at the tractors parked along the edge of the meadow. At that moment Justin can see through his skull and into the gears of his mind as he considers ordering Graham to blast out the tires and windows. Instead he points to a dirt clod and says, "How about that—"

Gone before he can finish the thought. He curls his finger into his fist and brings it to his chest, protectively, as if Graham had tried to shoot it. "Jeez."

He clips a magpie and its wings open and close like a black hand. He shoots a marmot and it scurries a few paces with its sides gushing blood. Between shots he pumps the lever and the smoking brass shells land between his boots.

Low-throated laughter rises from Justin's father. He loops an arm around Graham's neck and squeezes him tight in what appears to be half headlock, half hug. "You're one good kid."

Justin watches from a short distance and notices the pink flush of his son's skin, so different from his normal complexion—the pale yellow of an onion—resulting from his spending so much time inside, tapping at the keyboard or Photoshopping his pictures or leafing through a book.

It is almost supernatural, how comfortable Graham seems with the rifle. Justin remembers when he was that age, the long hours he spent in the backyard, stapling paper targets to trees and firing at them until his shoulder darkened to a purple shade of bruise. Back then, he had always tried to obey his father, performing his best imitation of him, without ever pulling it off completely, like a clumsy marionette whose movements are obviously dictated by wires and wood. Graham is different.

He is not a mimic. He is a student. He learns what he needs to know by asking questions and listening, like he is doing right now—aim over the target when shooting uphill, hold low when shooting downhill—and Justin worries what this might mean for him—this education—and how he might emerge from it changed.

Justin's father says, gloating, "You see? And you didn't even want to give it to him!" He then picks up one of the shells and walks to the tree, the one Graham has shot. A yellow trail of pitch oozes from the bullet hole, sweetening the air. With a stick Justin's father digs a hole in the ground, maybe five inches deep. He drops the shell in it like a seed. "There," he says. "To mark the occasion. Now if we come back in ten years, the shell will still be there. It'll be the same, but we'll be different."

"Good job, Graham," Justin says.

Graham smiles and then gazes proudly at the rifle. "It's a really good gun."

"Sure is."

"Do you want to hold it?" he says, as if Justin were the child.

"Why not?" When Justin takes it, the metal is hot and he jerks his hand down to its stock and tries not to cry out.

BRIAN

When Brian was fourteen, he came home from school with a black eye. This wasn't the first time. The other kids would call him shorty, small fry, half stack, oompa-loompa, and he would try to shrug it off, try not to let their words bother him, but they would always keep at it and after a time he wouldn't be able to hold back.

This was soon after his mother lit out for Eugene, and lately his father had been trying too hard to be a father. Clapping his son on the back. Calling him buddy. Talking loudly about trucks and fishing and basketball. When he saw the black eye, he grabbed his son by the chin and eyed him closely and asked what happened. Brian shrugged and said, "Some shit." They went out then and bought some boxing gloves, black ones, so that his father might teach Brian the old one-two combo followed by a roundhouse.

In their backyard he told Brian, "Stand like you stand when shooting a gun." He placed one foot in front of the other. "It's the same principle." He lifted his right glove before his mouth and positioned his left next to his cheek. "Now put up your dukes. Now bend your knees and bounce on your toes. Good. Now hit me." Brian took a step forward and hesitated. *"Hit me,"* his father said. "Hit me, you puss."

This was the first time his father had ever called him a name. Brian felt a stab upon hearing it and jabbed his father in the belly. "Harder. Like you mean it." Brian swung with everything he had. His father stepped aside with his leg angled out to trip. The force of Brian's swing carried him over it and he lay sprawled out in the dirt. "Get up." Brian did as he was told, a bit hot and watery around the eyes. "You punch like a girl. Punch like you got balls." His tone was almost furious.

Brian forgot about his stance, his gloves, and lunged, swinging like a street fighter. His father's body, so huge compared to his, eluded Brian with a few quick steps. His father faked a shot to his chest and Brian flinched and cowered, pitched forward by the pain he anticipated.

"Come on," his father said. "I haven't even hit you and you're acting like I hit you. You're practically bawling." Brian tried to calm himself, to breathe. He assumed the classic boxer pose and sprang forward and his father short-punched him in the mouth. Brian didn't know if it was the pain or the shock or the humiliation, but he went down—with a clash of his teeth—and stayed down, crying.

He remembers a deep purplish blood rushing all over his gloves when he put them to his mouth, as if his father's fist had tapped the deepest blood in his body. "Oh, no," his father said. "No, no, no." Pulling off his gloves, pulling Brian into a hug. "I'm so sorry. I'm so, so sorry." Both of them crying.

Later, his front tooth turned gray, eventually fell out, and Brian woke up with twenty dollars under his pillow. His smile had a hole in it for over a year before the orthodontist implanted a false tooth whiter and squarer than the rest. During this time he learned not to smile. He learned how to talk by barely moving his lips.

Sometimes he thinks about the hole—how vulnerable it made him feel, how his tongue constantly probed it—when he hunches before locks to prick them with his tools. Every house is a mouth. Her house is a mouth.

JUSTIN

Justin's father fills his backpack and Graham's with Nalgene water bottles, bags of trail mix, peanut butter sandwiches, a first-aid kit, waterproof matches, a poncho, a compass, bungee cords, Bushnell binoculars. Justin will carry the Gerber Reserve Insulator, a bulky, many-pocketed backpack full of freezer bags and freezer packs, to collect and keep cool the meat they hope to harvest. Years ago, they never would have needed it, since by October a thin blanket of snow inevitably covered these mountains. He remembers icicles dangling like blue fangs from tree branches and rock overhangs. Frost ornamenting pinecones. The river clotted up with ice. This afternoon the temperature will rise into the seventies. Meat will spoil quickly.

His father pulls from his rucksack three blaze orange caps and tosses them to Justin and Graham and they try them on and then take them off to adjust their plastic bands and fit them snugly onto their heads. They pull on vests of a matching color. "The pumpkin brigade," Justin's father calls them.

Justin finds the bottle of Hawaiian Tropic his wife packed and splats a dollop into his hand. He dips his thumb into this and dots Graham on the forehead, nose, cheeks, and ears, and tells him to rub it into his skin, while Justin makes the same pattern on his own face. The smell of coconut fills the air and Boo trots over to sniff them. Justin offers the sunscreen to his father but he refuses it. "For kids."

Just as they are about to sling their packs onto their shoulders and set off into the woods, they startle at a noise—the burst and *scree* and tinkle of broken glass. It comes from the far side of the meadow, where a man moves among the tractors carrying a crowbar. Justin's father brings his hand to his forehead and makes a visor of it, watching the man climb onto the yellow hood of a bulldozer and cock his crowbar and swing and shatter the windshield so that the glass rains all around him and catches the light. He knocks the crowbar around inside the frame of the bulldozer, removing all the stray teeth of glass that have not come loose with his initial hit. Then he swings his crowbar in a half circle, as though it were a samurai sword, and pretends to sheathe it. He goes to the bright blue outhouse and gives it a shove. It rocks one way and then the other, teetering, finally toppling over with a *thunk* and *shoosh* when he heaves his weight against it a second time. Beyond him, through the trees, sits a cherry red pickup with jacked-up tires and a smiling silver grill.

Without a word, Justin's father snatches up his rifle and starts across the meadow at a fast clip. Of course he does not slow when Justin calls out to him. What choice does Justin have—now and so many times before—but to follow? His rifle rests on a log, as though sunning itself. His hand hesitates before grasping it. "Stay here," he tells Graham and then throws the strap over his shoulder, rather than carrying the rifle diagonally, as a soldier would, as his father did.

He recognizes the man—the cashier from the gas station. Seth, his name tag had read. Like the noise the snake in their tent made. *Sethhhh.* He remembers his arms, their surging muscle seemingly capable of cracking the bones that held them in place. He had obviously felt a lot of anger toward them, just as he had obviously gotten a great deal of pleasure out of frightening Justin, when he leaned across the counter with a forbidding look on his face. Perhaps now, watching them approach him, he is pleased again.

When they hurry their feet through the grass, it makes a whispering sound, as if the forest is, blade by blade, stone by stone, tree by tree, turning its attention to them. His father is breathing loudly, perhaps out of anger or perhaps out of exhaustion, winded by his fast pace and the thin mountain air. And then they are upon Seth, who waits with a guarded expression.

"Howdy," Seth says, wide-faced and staring hard at Justin's father and his rifle. He wears a red tank top and tight blue jeans, his muscles unnaturally large and defined, like a grotesque anatomy lesson. He has hopped down from the bulldozer and leans against his crowbar as if it were a cane.

A dripping sound comes from the fallen outhouse and fills the silence. All around them glass sparkles in the grass like glitter. On the bulldozer, where the windshield should reflect the orange glow of midmorning, a shadow lies instead, like an empty eye socket.

"You enjoying yourself?" Justin's father says in a joking, angry way.

Seth smiles and gives a slow-motion swing of his crowbar. "As a matter of fact."

All the joking has fallen out of Justin's father's voice when he says, "Get out of here."

"Funny, I was going to tell you the same thing."

Justin is standing a little behind his father, but he steps forward now. "I got a kid here."

"You think I care, Bend," Seth says. And Justin sees how it is: he is not a person, he is a stand-in for a community, a way of life that seems foreign and intrusive to so many who grew up around here. "I don't."

Justin's father lifts his rifle and draws a bead on Seth's chest. "I said get out of here and I meant it."

In this moment Justin has the sudden sense of the world shifting, of morals and laws and civilized human behavior knocked out of place, vanishing in the stead of something wilder. He's reminded now of Katrina. When the levees broke, so did social order. Rape. Pillage. Burn. Fire a .22 from your roof. Check the pocket of a dead man for his wallet. Doesn't take much to take us there, Justin thinks. Is his father capable of killing someone? Undoubtedly yes.

"You see my grandson over there." Justin's father humps his chin in Graham's direction without taking his eyes off of Seth. "You don't want him to see what the inside of your skull looks like, do you?"

"You'd never do that," Seth says. "I could walk right up to that rifle and stick my finger in it and you'd never do a thing."

"Come on and try."

"You're so full of it."

Then his father swings the barrel left and fires. The crack of the gunshot is followed by the chime of glass shattering, falling from the red pickup, its left headlight destroyed.

For a moment Seth stares at his truck. "You'll fucking pay for that," he says. Then, without even a glance, he walks away. He climbs into the cab and the engine roars to life. He crushes the accelerator and kicks up a plume of cinder and the sunlight twinkles off his side mirror when he retreats from them, lost finally among the trees.

Justin's father lowers his rifle. "I think I won that conversation." He is smiling. He is proud of what he has done. Sometimes Justin wonders if he sees his fellow humans as anything more than complicated animals, not so different from a deer or a wolf, knitted together with the same sinew but in another design.

They set off with their rifles strapped to their backs. They hike along the South Fork—past where it tears along in white rapids, groping at the boulders and logs, trying to carry them downstream—until it widens and calms and goes glassy with eddies in which pine needles pool.

Boo climbs out onto a scarred jawbone of a rock and drinks messily from the river before sniffing at its muddy banks where the tracks of a toad shorten and then vanish, surrounded by the fern-like impression of wings, where an owl swooped down to make its breakfast. They pause here to drink from their Nalgene bottles and while Graham studies the tracks in the mud Justin says to his father, "I don't know how I feel about leaving our camp unattended."

"Even if he did come back, which he won't, what's he going to do? Break one of our pots? Piss on our sleeping bags? Big deal."

"You pointed a gun at him."

"Ah," he says. "That kind of shit happens all the time out here. It's no worse offense than giving somebody the finger."

They step over roots and rocks and through the bright shards of sunlight lying like jigsaw pieces all over the ground. Every now and then a cloud passes over the sun at the very moment Justin steps into one of these jigsaw pieces so that its light goes out suddenly. One moment he is stepping into a square of brightness; the next he is pausing in a sudden dark. Camp-robber birds hop and flutter through the woods around them, unseen, like something pacing them.

Justin's father stops before a tree with a jagged black vein running down its middle. "You know the Indians used to douse their arrowheads with rattlesnake blood and charcoal taken from a tree struck by lightning." He licks his thumb and runs it across the trunk. It comes away black. He traces it along the lip of his rifle, as if it were a crystal he wants to bring a sound from. Then he faces Graham and stabs his thumb against his forehead, pushing him back a step and leaving behind an inky smudge. "Now we're ready."

They continue forward, stepping over fallen pinecones and branches, the litter of last night's storm. Chipmunks dart forward to investigate their presence, then scatter into the underbrush. Every now and then his father pauses to study some tracks on the trail, rain-blurred but recent. They see the places where the deer have peeled away strips of bark from the river willows, where they have left their stool, where they have bedded down.

Justin catches Graham looking off into the woods, as if sensing something, maybe worrying over the man with the crowbar or the story his grandfather shared with them last night.

The basalt walls are pitted with holes from wind erosion or from the bubbling of gases long ago. These holes catch the shadows and look like the eye sockets of the earth. They follow a zigzagging series of switchbacks toward the top of the canyon, and as they do, sagebrush replaces bear grass and the soil steadily loses its moisture and around their boots the dust hangs in heavy clouds. His father casts a great shadow that Justin steps on when following him up and up and up.

Finally they gain the rim of the canyon. Here the ground is cobbled with black lava rock that falls off into the long, wide, thickly wooded gulf. They stand gazing out over it. The sun has not reached a high enough angle to illuminate its bottom. It is a little like looking into the future, looking into the canyon. While they stand fully exposed in the daylight, below them it is already night. Or always night.

The wind rushes fast-moving clouds through the sky and makes a hissing sound in the branches. It whips their clothes tight against their bodies and traces patterns in the dust, making the ground seem alive with its subtle movement. Justin misses the calmness at the bottom of the canyon and wishes the wind would stop. It feels intrusive, almost threatening, like some heavy-pawed beast blundering through the woods, rustling bushes and straining the branches of trees in its hurried passage.

They continue along the edge for a good hundred yards until Justin's father stops next to a stone cairn. Justin imagines he is studying it and conjuring in his mind the pioneer or Indian who has piled the stones one on top of the other, while perhaps fancying that he sees some part of himself in them, trekking into an uncultivated territory to leave his mark with a bullet, and later, a building.

Justin doesn't say, "Dad?" for another few seconds until he notices his face has gone deeply red, approaching a sort of blackness, infected by shadow. Justin hurries to his side.

At Justin's touch he hunches forward, his knee knocking the stones loose from the cairn to scatter all over the ground, and when Justin says, "Dad?" again his father does not respond, lost in his private pain. One hand clutches his thigh and the other beats at invisible things in the air. He seems suddenly to lose weight, so that his coat hangs around his shoulders rather than hugging his broad back tightly. His skin goes from red to brown to gray-yellow in the space of a few seconds, those seconds like the turning of seasons, wintering his appearance.

And then he's better. He shakes his head as if to free some water from it, to clear his vision, and then he smiles weakly. "Just a little engine trouble. All better now." He takes a deep breath and then another and this seems to inflate him. "All better." He stands up straight, then hunches forward slightly, weighed down by pain or weakness.

"Look at me," Justin says. "Dad?"

His eyes are empty, his pupils dilated like bullet holes entering into the blackness of his skull. Graham grabs Justin by the shirtsleeve and says, in a choked voice, "What's wrong with Grandpa?"

"Everything's fine. Just shut up for a second." He shakes off his son, who reaches for him again, before withdrawing.

Justin calls out to his father several times before his body stiffens and he pushes Justin away, saying, "I'm here, I'm here."

"Should I call someone? I think I should call someone."

He raises his hand; it says as clearly as words, *Don't.*

"You're sure?"

"The day I come and ask you what needs to be done, you'll know you're grown up enough to tell me."

"Dad. Quit it. I need to know you're okay."

"I'm fine." Whatever has been bothering him—a clot that temporarily left him lightheaded or a lazy stretch of pumping from his ventricle—his shoulders have squared against it. It is gone. Boo whines and approaches him with his tail hesitantly wagging and Justin's father gives him a pat and says, "Good boy. Daddy's okay."

He then restacks the stones into their original design and forces a smile at Graham, who stands there wavering in his stance and moving his lips as if to say something. Then Justin and his father look at each other and look away and settle their eyes on the only thing moving, a distant hawk doing broad slow turns in the sky, hunting, suspended above them like a drifting flake of ash.

They rest awhile, drinking water and eating fistfuls of trail mix. Justin watches his father intently during this time and after a few minutes withdraws his cell phone. He doesn't know if it will work here or not. It is more of a gesture to partner his question: "Are you sure?"

He answers by giving Justin a flat look of finality and rising to his feet and clapping the peanut dust off his hands and readjusting his rifle and continuing down the trail, not looking behind him to see if they will follow, knowing they will.

A small fire not long ago burned through this plateau, making the trees sharp and black at their tops like diseased fangs. When Justin brushes against a pine, its shadow sticks to him. Boo races here and there, stirring up black dust and sniffing at invisible tendrils of scent.

And then, as if they have stepped from one room to the next, they are past the scorched section of forest, walking again in the shade of red-barked ponderosas and lodgepoles.

A basalt cornice juts from the canyon wall and his father climbs out on it. Far below him, in the spots the sunlight has not yet warmed, vapors float up and finger the air. The trees down there appear so thickly huddled, the river scribing between them a silver path scarcely visible. His father coughs something from his lungs and spits it over the edge and follows its fall and laughs softly.

"Please come away from there, Dad."

As if on cue, his father's boot scuds against a knob of rock. He stumbles toward the edge, then jerks his body backward and finds his balance. He does not cry out. He does not retreat from the crag. He simply clears his throat and brings the rifle to his shoulder to glass the canyon below. He is so natural and fearless, standing casually at the edge of a two-hundred-foot drop, peering through his scope and cursing the big stags for hiding from him, the goddamned chickens.

"Would you come away from there?" Justin says.

"Why?"

"Because you're making me nervous. And because there's a better place over there." Justin points to a nearby shady spot, a collection of boulders arranged in a kind of half-moon shape with several feet between them, where they could rest their rifles. "How about we go over there? Please."

Sometimes dying in bed seems like the only thing that scares his father. He acknowledges what Justin said with a sigh and retreats from the ledge and tramps toward the boulders, where he says, "Now this is a good spot," as if it were his discovery.

For the next hour they crouch behind the boulders, bracing their rifles upon them, glassing the canyon floor. Every now and then Justin glances at his son, sometimes reminding him to be careful, to keep his finger off the trigger unless he plans to shoot. "Do I look stupid?" he says to Justin and Justin says, "No. You look twelve."

He remembers lying in bed with Karen, so many years ago, both of them naked and bathed in moonlight. At the time she was seven months pregnant and they were sweating, breathing heavily, having just made love. He was curled around her back, still inside her. One of his hands gripped her swollen breast and she grabbed it and pulled it down to her belly. "The baby," she said. He felt a flutter beneath his palm and imagined the baby floating inside her, encased in a watery sac, its little hands and feet fighting against it. He was not a religious man, but in the dark, with the baby moving and the warm buzz of sex playing through his veins, he could believe in anything, so he offered up a prayer for his son. He prayed that nothing would ever harm him, that the boy would grow into a happy, healthy man. He hopes the prayer somehow imprinted itself into his bones and blood, like something Karen consumed, its nutrients broken down and filtered through a cord into Graham, helping him along, even now.

The sun continues its slow path across the sky and casts its light into the canyon at such an angle that the west side is bathed in crisp yellow light, the east as dark as night. Through Justin's scope, among the columns of light between the shadows of the trees, he spots a buck, his color blending so perfectly with the stone and dirt Justin can only see him when he moves. There is great beauty in the way his muscles work under his hide. He is feeding at the edge of a meadow, and when he angles into it, Justin gets that feeling you get before you kill. Twitchy. His skin tingles. He experiences a warm rush of blood behind the eyes that feels a little like an erection. Everything in the world goes blurry except for his target, so distinct he can see every hair and sharp-edged horn. He could squeeze the trigger now, but something makes him pull his face away from the scope, wanting to share the moment with his son.

Here he is, expecting to advise Graham, maybe put an arm around his shoulder and guide the line of his rifle. But the boy has already spotted the deer. Justin can tell from the stillness of his body. He is like a hawk on a telephone pole, staring through his scope with utter attentiveness.

Justin watches him in silence. There is something in his son's face. A tightening of his jaw and a flaring of his nostrils that foretells what will come. He isn't going to ask permission. He is going to shoot. It makes him seem faraway and unfamiliar. He is so enchanted by the desire to kill—the same acute and forceful feeling that drove primitive man to bring a blade of obsidian to a stick and sharpen it—that his current life, his school and his bicycle and his bedroom with the desk scored from the snarl of his pencil and the giant beer mug filled with brown pennies and the movie-monster posters hanging on the wall, has become nothing but a tiny black fly he brushes aside with his hand before bringing it to the stock and tightening his finger around the trigger.

Earlier, his grandfather explained to him the importance of accuracy. "One shot," he said. "One kill." If you don't kill the animal straight off, it would twist and cry out and bound off into the woods and you would have to follow the puddles of blood until at the base of some tree you would find it, its eyes looking at you, asking *why?*

Justin expects him to miss. It is, after all, more than a two-hundred-yard shot, downhill. Justin again sights the buck with his scope and brings that faraway world closer and waits for the crack of the rifle. Before he hears the bullet, he witnesses its destination, as the buck jackknifes in the air, and, after it lands, takes off running in a crooked way. The gunshot follows, loud like the kind of sound the sky would make if it broke open.

"You got him," Justin says and puts his hand in Graham's hair, proud and saddened.

"I killed it?"

"We'll see. You got him. I know that much."

Maybe it is a trick of the light, a shadow thrown by the pine boughs that reach over them, but his face seems to have subtly darkened. He says, "But it kept running." Justin can't tell if Graham is bothered more by the possibility of its escape or its imminent death.

"That's the way it works." Justin explains that if he got in a good shot, the deer will run only a little while and then collapse and flop a few times before quitting. It strikes Justin as backward, explaining death to someone after giving them permission to kill. Not for the first time, he hopes he hasn't made a mistake, bringing the boy.

Justin's father stands beside them and scans the canyon below. "Somebody tell me exactly what happened."

"Graham shot a buck. Five-pointer, I think."

His father scratches absently at his belly. His mouth widens and tightens and can't seem to settle on a single emotion, expressing at once his elation and perplexity. "I didn't see anything."

"It was there. He shot it."

"So you saw it, too?" This seems to almost anger him. "Why didn't I see it?" A gust of wind comes along and pops his hat off his head. It rolls a few feet from him before he retrieves it and fits it back in its place. "I wish I had seen it."

"It's gone now." Graham raises the rifle so fluidly to scan the canyon, it is like a natural extension of his body.

The first time Justin killed anything—a robin with a BB gun—he felt a black stone in his throat and wetness in his eyes. He studies his son now. What Justin witnessed before in his face—hunger—has vanished, but Graham doesn't look as though he is going to cry. If his eyes are wet it is only from the wind. He looks pale and deflated and a little disappointed in himself, like a man who has run over a dog, who has listened to its body crumple moistly beneath the tires of his truck and now realizes he must park on the roadside and drag its body into the ditch.

KAREN

She isn't used to restaurants like this one, a former blacksmith shop renovated into a California-chic lounge and restaurant. The walls are brick and basalt, roughly mortared. The chairs are black leather. The tables, darkly polished pine. The dim lighting is made a little brighter by the many mirrors staggered throughout the dining area. In her water glass floats a slice of lemon that sheds pulp and leaks yellow blood. When the waiter lays her napkin across her lap, she isn't sure whether to say *thank you* or *back off.*

Across from her sits Bobby Fremont. Since last week, when he asked her out to lunch, she hasn't thought much about what she is doing—about what it means to secretly agree to a meal with a man other than her husband—but on the drive over she made herself imagine a scenario where they laughed about local politics, talked about their favorite television shows, and ate salads. But now here they are and his eyes never seem to leave her, his gaze hungry and probing, slipping her blouse over her head, unhooking her bra, hiking up her skirt. She feels at once flattered and debased. Maybe that's why she's here—to feel that way.

Bend is a small enough town that she looks around often, looks for a familiar, wondering face. What she would say to a friend or neighbor or colleague, she isn't sure. She lifts her water to her mouth. Ice clatters against her teeth. She has drained her glass already.

Her husband is several hundred miles away, and the distance feels good. It feels right. As though they ought to be separated. Justin prefers not to talk about how things have soured between them, but once in a while, when he is in a foul mood or has sucked down a few beers, she can get him to fight. "You're not the person I married," he said a few weeks ago. She didn't argue.

He thought it was about the baby. It wasn't. The baby was just a black doorway that took her into a far room of the house where the windows offered a different view. She is unhappy. She does not enjoy her life as it is, and she thinks her marriage has something to do with this. Sometimes she feels guilty about wanting to escape. She has, after all, what most would call an enviable life. A beautiful child, a good job, a nice house. She has her looks and her health. She lives in the shadow of the mountains. Sometimes she reviews this list, counting off on her fingers all the things she *ought* to be grateful for. She tries to smile. But when she smiles the smile feels more like a fissure that leads down her throat to some darkness inside her.

She likes to go online and plug in to Google terms like "bubonic plague" and "genocide" and "elephantiasis" and even "irritable bowel syndrome." She scrolls through the Web sites and gasps at the photographs and momentarily feels better.

The waiter—a red-haired twenty-something with sideburns—appears at their tableside and sets their plates before them: the ribeye for Bobby, pan-seared halibut for her. The waiter asks if there is anything he can do for them—more water? "Yes," she says. The same word spoken to Bobby when he called and asked if she was busy, if she would like to meet him for lunch. Yes. Automatically. Not thinking, just responding. She isn't sure what else she will say yes to—she isn't sure even what else she should say, as they sit across from each other, his gaze steadily trained on her, seeking out her eyes—her eyes darting around the room, focusing on nothing and everything.

She has known Bobby for years. Every time she and her husband went to a party or an opening or a fund-raiser, there he was, moving through the room, clapping shoulders, shaking hands. Some people complained about the way Bend has changed, the way Bobby has changed it, the big parking lots and boxy buildings of their new outdoor mall, the hurriedly constructed housing developments with the same five neo-Tudor designs replicated over and over.

The two of them had never exchanged a *How are you?* a *Lovely to see you,* until two weeks ago, when she met a girlfriend at Deschutes Brewery.

One pint turned into three. She never got out anymore and the beer was so cold and she was so thirsty and when she got off her stool she had to concentrate to keep from stumbling. She felt warm and loose. The music called down from the overhead speakers and made her want to dance. Minutes later, she walked out of the bathroom and directly into Bobby. "Oopsie," he said and caught her, his hands on her waist, his face an inch from hers. She could feel the heat coming off him. He is much older than she, but handsome and fit and powerfully confident. She kissed him then. Full on the mouth. And he had kissed her back, but first he laughed, and when he did, she could feel the laughter inside of her. And that was it. She pulled away and returned to her stool and grabbed her purse and said good-bye to her friend and didn't look back. The next morning she did not feel regretful so much as she worried that someone had seen them, that Bobby would say something or want more than what she gave him.

Now here they are. His smile, crowded with too-white teeth, is a dare. This lunch is a dare.

Her legs bounce beneath the table. She ran ten miles this morning and still she wants to move, to race along the sidewalks that snake through town. She has so much energy. She aches with it. She remembers feeling this way as a teenager. Growing pains, her mother called it.

"So?" Bobby says, wiping his mouth with his napkin.

"So."

He raises his eyebrows and she puzzles over something to say. She hasn't been on a date—is that what this is?—in more than a dozen years. "Tell me something you learned recently." This is what she usually asks Graham at dinner. She wants to hit herself, to bring the palm of her hand to her forehead with a smack.

"Ooh," he says. "Good question."

"Really?"

He saws off a hunk of steak and pops it in his mouth. He does not set down his fork or knife but holds them upright while chewing noisily. "Here you go. Here's something." He still hasn't swallowed but that doesn't stop him. "I was out at a real estate site the other day, a place

I'm thinking about buying. The owner took the agent and me down a narrow dirt road in the middle of nowhere—truly—middle of fucking nowhere—into a gulch. So we're poking around and find these wires and cans with holes drilled in them. Apparently the buckaroos used to use this as a place to catch wild horses. We're talking early twentieth century. They'd drive the horses into the canyon where other men would be waiting. As the panicked horses dashed in, the buckaroos pulled the wires taut from where they were lying on the ground. The wires had strips of fabric on them and cans filled with pebbles. The horses would believe they were suddenly fenced in. And if they brushed up against the wire, the pebbles would rattle loudly in the cans and scare them. Isn't that neat?"

"That is. Neat."

He swirls the wine in the goblet, sniffs deeply, sips, and pops his lips. When he speaks again, his tone has shifted from awe to contempt. "What a bunch of stupid horses. And what a simple concept to capture them." His eyes, already on her, seem to narrow their focus. "No need for trees or wood or axes or hours of labor or waiting for the smell of men to fade away."

She gulps some of her water.

"No riding broken horses to exhaustion chasing a bolting herd."

She gulps some more, and then her glass is empty again except for ice, the lemon buried beneath it like a drowned canary. She glances around the restaurant for their waiter and can't find him and when she looks again at Bobby she finds his eyes still on her.

"What about you?" he says.

She has to pee, she realizes. "What about me?" Her hair is down. She never wears her hair down anymore. It feels alien, brushing against her face, obscuring her peripheral vision. She feels masked by it, hidden. A good thing. With the restaurant full and people walking by on the street, there are so many chances someone might spot her.

"What have you learned?"

"Oh. Let's see." Her eyes drop to his plate, the forest of broccoli along its edge. "Did you know broccoli is one of the gassiest things you can eat?" Her mouth seems to belong to someone else. She cannot understand why she said this. Maybe because she doesn't care? But if she didn't care she wouldn't want to climb under the table right now in embarrassment.

His smile breaks for a second before reasserting itself on his face. "Note to self." He turns his plate so that the broccoli is at the far side of it.

"Sorry."

"For what?"

"I'm just not used to this."

"It's fine."

"Is it?"

Bobby knifes into the steak again. "We're just having lunch."

"Is that all we're having?"

She likes the way Bobby looks at her, so intently and so differently from her husband, whose eyes don't seek her out, always focused elsewhere, on a book, a pile of papers, the window. She sometimes wishes she could snatch them out of his head and train them on her. "Just *look* at me when I'm talking to you." But she also knows that when he does look at her—hungrily, as she steps out of the shower and pulls the towel off the bar—she wishes he would go away. Maybe because that's the only company of hers he seems to crave; otherwise, they could remain in their separate rooms for all he cared. That's what it felt like anyway. She's mixed up; they're mixed up. She knows it.

"You want to know what else I've learned? I've learned that everyone has two faces. There is the outside face, the mask they wear for the world, and the inside face, the one that comes out when the blinds are down and the doors are closed."

"Is that so?"

"It is. It is so. Let me give you an example. Do you know Tom Bear Claws?"

"The Indian. The one who hates you."

"The very same. Did you know that he doesn't hate me and I don't hate him? That we're in fact friends and business partners? Did you know that?"

"I don't understand."

"That's because you only know the outside face." He lifts his wine goblet and holds it up so that one of his eyes, oversize and bowled, looks through the glass at her. "Outside face, inside face."

"I guess."

She looks outside, where a cloud scuds over the sun, darkening the world. Her reflection takes form in the window. Her hair is covering most of her face, but she can see her lips and they're red and upturned in a strange smile. She hasn't seen this woman in a long time and barely recognizes her.

"You look beautiful, you know."

She barks out a laugh.

"What?"

"Say that again."

"You look beautiful?"

"I haven't heard it in a long time. It's nice to hear it."

In dreams, sometimes you have to run—something is chasing you—but no matter how hard you try, your body responds as if tied down by leaden weights. She felt that way a lot. She felt she was slogging through a waking dream. But nothing was chasing her. Instead she was chasing something, maybe just a feeling: buoyancy.

She wasn't sure what you called this. A midlife crisis. A seven-year itch that rashed out five years late. She feels bored, resentful, claustrophobic, weighed down.

Bobby says, "What's the most beautiful thing you've ever seen?"

She smiles and tips her head—she can't decide if he is being silly or charming. It is the sort of question a boy might have asked her, long ago, when parked on top of Pilot Butte, the stars above and the lights of the city below equally bright.

"I don't know." She wants to say her son pulled from between her legs and laid between her breasts, the blood still pumping between them through a cord, but she doesn't. Instead she picks up her glass and swirls the ice in it. "You?"

"You."

"Oh, boy. You know how to lay it on thick, don't you?"

"Hey, I mean it."

"Uh-huh."

"You're stunning. You really are."

She realizes she is toying with her hair, tossing it, coiling a strand of it around a finger and letting it swing loose. "I'm married, Bobby."

"I don't really believe in marriage. I've tried it three times, you know, so I'm kind of an expert on the matter. And in my mind, it doesn't make sense. It's not how we work. You want to wear the same pair of pants—or eat the same meal—your entire life? I love this ribeye, but I'd hate it if I ordered it every day."

"So I'm meat to you?" She isn't sure of her tone, whether flirting or mocking.

"We're all meat, Karen. But I only meant it as an analogy."

When the check comes, she reaches for it even though she knows he will insist. Reaching for it momentarily reasserts some sense of control. And then his hand is there, on top of hers, heavy and tanned and wormed over with veins. "That's mine," he says.

She concedes the check by withdrawing her hand.

"Let's go back to my place," Bobby says, not asking, telling. "Get a drink?"

She glances at her watch without even noting the time. "I don't think so."

"You have something better to do?"

"I need to go running."

JUSTIN

It takes half an hour to leave the sun-lit rim of the canyon and descend the switchbacks into the cooler hollow below. The wind abates and the temperature drops. Springwater makes the ground marshy.

Justin glances over his shoulder often, scanning the ridges, unable to shake the feeling of being watched, especially when they move through a clearing and abandon the protection afforded by the trees. He thinks about Seth returning to the camp, potentially following them, with his scope trained on their backs. It makes him feel the same way the glass eye did—itchy—as if crawled over by a prickly-legged fly.

They approach a stretch of the South Fork where the white water roars over boulders. They hike upriver until they find a glassy tract interrupted by a humpbacked arrangement of boulders. They clamber across them, using their hands and feet, while Boo plows through the water and shakes off on the far shore and barks his encouragement.

Justin's father stands on a sandy mound for a time, turning in a circle, before pointing in a northeasterly direction. "I think it's this way," he says and Justin can only trust in him, as he has lost his bearings.

Without any trail to follow they hike through the woods, dodging under branches, stepping over logs, banging their shins against stumps, scaring screeches out of the chipmunks that forage in the shadows. The trees and ledges mostly shelter them from the sunlight. The ground, flat at first, begins to slope upward. Horseflies buzz around their bodies and bite the blood from their skin. Justin's father slaps a hand to his neck and curses, as if the forest were conspiring against him.

At one point Justin turns around to see how his son is doing, to ask him if he wants a pull of water, and finds nothing except the trees and a spattering of Indian paintbrush. His mouth opens and closes as if seeking out a question, finally finding one in "Dad?"

Twenty yards ahead his father pauses and regards Justin with raised eyebrows.

"We lost Graham," Justin says and in a hurry starts back the way they came, knocking into trees and calling out for his son, feeling that familiar needle jab of panic. His arms push aside branches that swing back to claw his cheeks.

He has run only a short distance when he finds the boy sitting on a log with his elbows on his knees and his pack on the ground before him.

Justin feels the simultaneous urge to hug him and smack him. "What the hell are you doing? Are you hurt?"

"Kind of."

"What do you mean, *kind of*?"

"I'm tired."

Justin glances back to see his father come crashing toward them with Boo bounding beside him. His belly swings when he runs and his breath comes out in a blustery pant. "What's the problem?"

"There's no problem." Justin shrugs off his pack and pulls a water bottle from a mesh side pocket and tosses it to Graham. He catches it and it sloshes in his hands when he uncaps it and takes a long drink. "Graham was just tying his shoe."

"Why didn't he say something?"

Over the rim of the water bottle, Graham is looking at Justin, who gives him a wink and hopes his son understands what he is doing, protecting him from the bite of his grandfather's criticism. "He did," Justin says. "We just didn't hear him."

"Speak up next time." His father swats at his forearm and leaves behind a black smear. "You get lost, you'll be pissing your pants and crying for mama."

Boo goes to Graham and licks his knuckles. Graham offers the dog a scratch behind the ears and then caps the water and throws it back to Justin with a look of damp gratitude in his eyes.

"Let's go." Justin slides the bottle back in its pocket and hauls up the bag again and snaps its chest and waist buckle into place and tightens the straps. "There's a buck out there with your name on it."

Justin checks on Graham often, as they stagger up the hillside, sometimes slipping on the pine needles, pressing their hands to their knees with every step to give them that extra boost upward. The trees fall away as they come to a rocky embankment that reaches darkly upward and stretches to either side. It is colored with green and yellow lichen that crumbles into a chalky dust against Justin's hand. Fissures run through the rock and brown grass grows in them. His father says, "If we follow this east, just a little ways farther, I'm almost certain we'll find the meadow."

Coming from a man who seems certain about everything, *almost* carries a lot of dead weight. Justin doesn't like to hear him say it, especially with Graham so tired and the sun so high and hot. He pulls off his hat and runs his forearm across his brow to wipe away the sweat.

They move along a narrow corridor, with the forest to their left and the wall of vertical rock to their right. Loose rock crunches beneath their boots and makes every step sink and slide, as it does with snow. More than once Graham almost falls and each time Justin throws out an arm and affords him what security and balance he can. Water escapes a cloven section of the rock wall and trickles down an algae-ridden runnel that disappears into the forest; in their passing they pull handfuls of its icy water into their hair and onto their faces and feel revived.

They work their way around the corner and the trees open up into a bear grass meadow with autumn-blooming bitterbrush and snarls of blackberry vines along its edges.

"Thank Christ," Justin says.

His father crouches next to Boo and whispers something close to his ear before yelling, "Scent!" a command that sends the dog bounding into the meadow, the sun sliding over his slick black fur, making it appear almost metallic. Even from a distance Justin can hear the sniffs and snorts as Boo bends his snout to the grass. The dog runs erratically at first, zigzagging his way through the grass, and then his tail stiffens as he picks up on something that interests him. From there he paces out a wide circle that eventually loops in on itself. He then pauses and lifts his head and gives a throaty moan.

They discover there a splash of blood already beginning to go brown around its edges. They follow its trail—a splatter on the ground, a smear along a trunk—through the woods and over a moraine and around the curve of the canyon, where it vanishes. In the permanent twilight of the forest, they spend the next few minutes circling, like one big huddle of dogs eager to find a scent. Sometimes deer will circle around and return to the place they came from, feeling safer in familiar territory. And sometimes they will circle into the wind so they can smell danger ahead of them during their flight. But more often they will run fifty yards, stop, look, and listen for what injured them, and then bed down if they observe no threat.

Boo seems confused, sniffing eagerly in one direction and then another, growling and whining in a way that makes him sound almost human. He pauses at the base of a dead ponderosa and licks his chops and barks as if asking a high-pitched question.

Justin's gaze reaches upward, following the trunk twenty feet until it breaks off in a splintery mess that looks like a jagged set of incisors. Its top half lies downhill from them, thrown there years ago by a windstorm. The forest has since claimed it. Vines strangle its fifty-foot length. Yellow-orange conch fungi rise here and there from the rotted wood, their size and shape similar to the plates that would grow along a stegosaurus's back, giving the log the look of a slain dinosaur. As do the gouged-out sections of wood that run its length. They appear damp and gray with piles of fresh splinters beneath them.

Graham walks over to Boo. With his hand on the head of the dog, he studies the stunted height of the tree. What Justin dismissed at first glance as worm- and weather-riddled wood, he now recognizes as decorated by the graffiti of claws. Graham glances at Justin then. He has the look of an altar boy told to beware the devil. Justin can see the story from last night—the story of the Indian—racing through the caves of his mind.

"Don't worry," Justin's father says, as if reading the question before it is uttered. "It's just a bear. That story was just a story some old geezer made up." He has been studying the ground for tracks, but apparently the hard-packed dirt reveals nothing to him. Now he too approaches the torn-up tree and runs his fingers along the slashes that crisscross it. He swings an arm slowly, pretending his fingers into claws, and then reaches his hand to its limit and Justin sees that he would need another arm yet to reach the highest slashes. "Huh," his father says as he breathes inward, as though speaking to himself.

"Huh what?" Justin says. "What are you thinking?"

"No bear that big around here." He takes off his hat. It has smashed a sweaty ring into his hair. "Must have climbed up and left those scratch marks."

Leaning forward, heads down, they form a loose rank and circle the area until Justin's father spots a smear of blood marking the way into a small space between leaning rock columns.

This turns out to be the entrance to a slim chute of basalt that gradually widens as it crookedly draws them deeper into a side canyon. A thin stream trickles along its floor. It makes a gentle tinkling sound. A cold breath, the breath of a place deep underground, reaches up from the water as it pushes its way through the headstone-sized rocks that lie scattered everywhere, split at sharp angles and decorated with lichen, so that they hardly know where to put their feet. The blood—once visible in infrequent splatters—now becomes a red watercourse.

They know they are close. After fifty yards, the chute opens up and dead-ends at a circular clearing the size of a chapel. The ground here is messy with the skeletons of so many animals, their bones knee-deep, crushed and scattered and bleached by the sun and picked at by crows until there is nothing to be got from them. Jawbones. Rib cages. Spines welded together by ragged strips of cartilage. Skulls with moss growing like hair along their bone plates. Teeth—big teeth—clattering loosely in jaws or lying scattered across the ground and reminding Justin of the pale, forked-bottom tubers his rototiller unearths every spring when he preps his garden for planting.

Some of the bones are frail and brittle and paper white and snap beneath their approaching footsteps. Others are fresher, their color like the grayed flesh of the elderly.

The buck is sprawled out among them, against the far wall. The blood trail leading to it is like a loose thread vital to its stitching. It doesn't stir as they clatter their way through the carpet of bones; the pure stillness of death has seized it. Justin looks up and forty feet above him sees a round circle of sky, and at the top of the high basalt walls birds sit in black ranks, waiting.

Art decorates the walls. From the floor—to as far as Justin's hand can reach above him—every inch of stone has been chipped or painted. Here is a series of bear track petroglyphs climbing sideways along the wall. A pictograph of a fat-bodied snake rising up a stone column, its rattles like a bunch of grapes. Another shows a gang of Indians astride painted ponies, their faces chalked white and their long hair plaited and their hands gripping lances Justin imagines he can hear rattling across the wall, joined by the drumbeat of horses' hooves and the low chant of a war song.

Like the bones, the images seem staggered in their age, some of them faded, others so bright they might have been painted the week before. Here the paint is a richly hued red, made perhaps from chewed berries with fat as a binding agent. It depicts a scene similar to their own, a reflection in a stone mirror. Three men stand over a deer. They carry spears in their hands. They appear to be dancing, bent-legged, bow-backed. In a splotch of color Justin recognizes his father's face, with his own in blurry red just beyond it.

"I thought Fremont sent archaeologists through here," Justin says.

"The man pays well," his father says.

Justin continues to circle the room—the bones snapping beneath his steps, releasing a chalky dust that bothers his nose—as his mind circles back to that moment at City Hall when Tom Bear Claws barged in and spoke his mind with the reporter in tow. He must have known about this place, and if he did, he could have put a stop to the development, but he didn't. Which meant he was in on it; the tribe was in on it. His presence at the meeting was a matter of theater, no different from a cowboys-and-Indians shootout on the screen. He wonders what Warm Springs has to gain and guesses it has something to do with the long-delayed Cascade Locks Resort and Casino.

He scans the walls and spots scenes similar to the one previously studied, where men chase and stab and eat animals, deer and bear and coyote. There is the occasional portrait of the sun. And the recurring illustration of waves meant to interpret the river. Then he detects a lone figure, off to his right, a hunch-backed, dark-colored figure whose large black silhouette could be a bear or could be a man and among all the redness makes everything else seem an artistic splattering of blood.

They stand over the deer. Somewhere beneath it, and beneath the tangle of bones, the source of the stream gurgles unseen. The deer's eyes are open and reflect the sky in their black gaze. Its mouth is open, too, and its tongue hangs out, almost comically, if not for the blood trickling from it. Boo comes over and sniffs at it and laps up some of the blood in a kind of kiss before Justin's father gives him a nudge with his boot and the dog scurries off and busies himself with some bones.

With his finger Justin's father traces the path of the bullet as it entered the shoulder in a red starburst and traveled the length of the deer through bone and muscle to exit the rear ham on the opposite side. "Not a bad shot."

Justin looks at Graham, expecting to see his chest swollen with pride. Instead his head is bowed and his hands are folded before him. The deer is no longer something seen distantly through a scope, like some computer-generated image in a video game. The deer is *right here* and they can smell the brassy blood mixed up with the damp green hay smell of its fur. Weak-eyed and sunk-shouldered, Graham says, "Dad?"

"Yes."

"Can I ask you a weird question?"

"Yes."

The words come slowly. "Does that deer know he's a deer? Or is he just like a tree. Or something. Like, does he even think about anything? When he got shot—"

"You shot him," Justin says, the English teacher in him interrupting, wanting his son to take ownership of his language and recognize what he has done. Not to shame him, but to edify him.

Graham nods and chews a dried strip of skin from his lip. "When I shot him, did he think *I'm dying?*"

What does it feel like to be hunted—he wants to know—to be a deer staring down the wrong end of a rifle, to feel a bullet puncture your skin and mushroom inside you, ripping open your guts, breaking through bone? It is an important question.

His grandfather answers. "Graham. Listen to me. This is what it thinks: I'm hungry. And I'm tired. And I'm going to shit now. That's what it thinks. But it doesn't think like you and me think. It's just meat and bone." And then he sighs and runs a hand thoughtfully through his beard and surprises Justin by making a leaf-in-the-wind motion with his hand. "Come over here."

Graham goes to him and his grandfather takes him under his outstretched arm. "I want you to do something for me. I want you to get down on your knees. And then I want you to put your hands together. Now say a prayer. Be thankful."

Thankful for the deer's sacrifice or thankful for his true aim or thankful for the thrill of the hunt—Justin isn't sure—but they bow their heads and close their eyes, praying an old family prayer—"The Lord has been good to me, and so I thank the Lord"—while the blood soaks into the soil and Boo chews his way through a femur and the birds sequestered above them mutter among themselves.

Afterward, Graham seems a little better. Rather than choking the barrel of his rifle with both hands, as if trying to wring the oil from it, he slings it over his shoulder and examines the deer more closely, running his palm along its fur and prodding the bullet hole with his thumb.

They take pictures. Justin's father borrows the camera from Graham and instructs him to stand behind the deer and rest his foot on top of its shoulder.

"There. This is a great angle. You in shadow, the deer in the sun. It's a great picture. Seriously." He takes the camera away from his eye a moment and studies Graham with a directorial gaze. "Do me a favor? Take the rifle and brace it against your hip, so that it's aimed upward at, like, a forty-five-degree angle."

Graham does as he is told and his grandfather says, "Now look like a badass."

Graham stares at him blankly. And then his face slowly changes shape—his eyes narrowing, his upper lip curling—as he tries to make it an Eastwood moment.

"Perfect." His grandfather raises his free hand, his thumb and forefinger coming together as a circle. The flash blinks three times before filling the air with light and Graham's eyes glimmer red for an instant, like an animal surprised by headlights on a nighttime country road.

His grandfather studies the camera, turning it over in his hands, before approaching Graham. "Now push the button that lets me see it."

Graham takes the camera and fiddles with its controls until he brings the photograph up on the screen.

"Now *that's* a picture." His grandfather massages his shoulders. "Taking photos like that, you'll make it into *Field and Stream* no problem."

"National Geographic," Graham says.

"*National Geographic,* eat your heart out."

They regard each other so that for a moment Justin feels excluded. And then, from above, comes a great flapping and cawing as the birds fly suddenly from their perch. Justin looks up in time to see their departing blackness and what might be a dark, massive head leaning over the edge and then pulling back out of sight. Justin remembers the claw marks and remembers the seemingly fresh pictographs and feels his skin tighten all over. Dust and pebbles fall all around them with a hissing and ticking and then everything goes quiet.

Justin's father stares skyward for a long time, waiting for something. When it doesn't come, he pulls his knife from his belt—its blade scored with cuts and its handle stained by so many years of blood—and says, "Time to open this deer up and see what it's made of."

Justin's father guides Graham through the cleaning. First he jabs the knife into the deer. The moist insult of metal connecting with flesh has always made Justin cringe, but Graham leans closer to watch as its belly unzips and his grandfather reaches inside the incision to withdraw the gut sack, holding it out before him like some freakish birth, gray and oblong and bulging, then laying it aside. Graham prods it with a bone and it breaks open and makes the air rank with a smell like wet feathers and spoiled gravy.

Justin occupies himself by clearing away a section of the boneyard, enough to reveal the narrow stream that comes to life beneath it so that they might wash the blood from the meat and the viscera from their hands. He wears an insulated backpack and shrugs it off now and pulls from it a box of ziplock freezer bags. Into these he drops the liver and the heart, still warm even after Graham dunks them in springwater.

Later, Justin's father will hoist the deer onto his shoulders and with blood oozing down his back carry it through the chute and into the main canyon, where they will find a skinning tree. He will tie a noose around its antlers and hoist it into the air and show Graham the whitish membrane that binds the hide to the muscle and bring a blade to it and make a sawing motion until enough of it comes loose for him to grab and pull and force apart with a sound like a big Band-Aid pulled slowly off a damp wound. And the deer will hang naked, its muscles' color somewhere between red and purple, its rump padded with white fat.

But that will come later.

Right now, with his hands gloved in blood, he rises from his crouch and stands before the wall of the grotto. He appears to be studying the rock art. Then he lifts his hand to the basalt and begins to add his own cipher, dipping his hand occasionally into the deer to refresh his paint supply. After a time Graham copies him. And then so does Justin—all of them going to work on the rock. They start in with soft hesitant strokes that turn rougher and before long their hands move as fast as their muscles will allow, painting bloody swirls and bloody blobs and big bloody eyes that come together in a kind of mural.

Justin feels gripped by a reckless idea. The darkness of the woods and the thrill of the hunt and the wildness of his father have torn away some protective seal inside him; he cannot control himself. For a moment, just a moment, he forgets about his mortgage payment, his shaggy lawn, his Subaru and the groaning noise it makes when he turns left, his desk and the pile of ungraded papers waiting on it. All of that has gone someplace else, replaced by an urge, a wildness.

"Hey, Dad? Know what I think would be a good color on you?" His father gives him a fleeting look just as Justin scoops up a handful of blood and palms it into his face as you would a pie. "Red!"

His father recoils until the wall stops him. Justin was smiling, but now his smile fails as he wonders what kind of spirit has overtaken him, as he tries to read his father's expression, a red mask. He runs his fingers along his cheeks and they track flesh-toned lines through the blood. "I always knew you were crazy," Paul says. Blood oozes into his mouth and he spits it out. Then he reaches into the pile of viscera and laughingly hurls a lung at Justin and it knocks the hat off his head.

And for a while, they are close as his father has always wanted them to be close, in that old-time way, like the men in Western movies, affectionately slugging each other, belly-laughing around the campfire.

The dried blood makes a gruesome brown lacework of their skin so that they hardly recognize each other when they return to camp carrying their insulated packs laden with quartered meat. They empty the venison into their five-day cooler and arrange the freezer packs throughout the stacks of chops and steaks and roasts to preserve them.

Then they rummage through the tent, joking about snakes, as they collect clean jeans and T-shirts and underwear and go down to the river and peel off their blood-encrusted clothes and step naked into water so cold it takes away their breath and makes them whoop and shiver. They splash at each other and then take up handfuls of sand from the river bottom and use it to scrub away the blood and sweat until their skin glows clean and pink. As the red husk falls away from Justin, dissolved and carried downstream, he feels his earlier wildness subside, his senses return.

Around them, as the afternoon wanes, the land mellows into green and gold colors. In the fire pit they arrange a knee-high teepee of sticks. His father strikes a wooden match and drops it into a cluster of brown pine needles and they catch flame with a crackling noise. The flames work their way up the sticks and when they burn a white-hot color Justin sets a log into the fire and the flames take to it, too. His father retrieves some Coors from a rock cairn he built in the river. He hands one to Justin and another to Graham.

"Um," Justin says. "How about no?"

"Come on," his father says, his voice taking on a confidential buddy-buddy tone. He cracks the tab of his can. Beer foams out the top and when he slurps at it some of the foam sticks to his beard. "What's wrong with you? Come on. Let him have a beer. Don't be a puss. Don't be a girl. We've got to make him into a man. That's why I brought him out here. That's why you brought him out here, isn't it?"

Justin isn't sure he can answer that question; it's what he's been struggling to answer since they climbed out of the Bronco.

"Why else, if not to—"

"Fine," Justin says. "But just one." He holds out his index finger to indicate the number and then drops it into a point aimed at Graham's chest. "Again, your mother, she shouldn't hear about this."

"I won't tell." He turns the beer over several times as if he has never seen one before. He opens it gently, the tab hissing, then popping. When he takes his first sip, his face registers some displeasure at the taste, but he doesn't complain.

They drink the beers—so cold—and then Graham and his grandfather go into the surrounding woods to gather fistfuls of wild onions. They chop them into fingernail-sized bits and fry them with butter until they caramelize, and they taste good, like candy, alongside the venison steaks browned over the fire. Even as they take pleasure in their dinner and enjoy the pleasant burn in their muscles, Justin scans the long dry ridges that hang over them, unable to shake the feeling that they are being watched by eyes they cannot see.

"You're eating what you killed," Justin's father says to Graham before popping a forkful of meat into his mouth. "That's responsibility. That's something to be proud of."

Graham cannot help but smile at the compliment, at the beer in his hand. Justin imagines his son has experienced today a glimpse of adulthood in all its loveliness and ugliness, the ugliness mostly forgotten as he rams his knife into his half-eaten steak and saws off another slice.

The sun sinks through a reef of clouds and into the mountains and the sky flushes. The trees are green when they start dinner and as the sky grows darker they turn purple, then black. He pulls off his boots and his socks and enjoys the feel of the grass and the dirt, the prickly mound of it beneath his arches. His skin burns and so do his muscles, but in a pleasant way. An *earned* way. It has been so long since he has spent a full day under the sun, sweating, relying on his muscles as much as his mind. He thinks about this often: how the day-in, day-out routine of the classroom—the lectures, the papers, the conferences—feels insubstantial. Evenings, he looks back on his day feeling vacant, headachy, uncertain, and uncaring of what he has accomplished. Whereas now he feels very full indeed.

He remembers how, when he was a child, he would often eat his dinner alone with his mother. He would ask where his father was, when he would get home, even though he knew the answer. He was at a construction site—operating a payloader, smoothing concrete with a trowel, telling somebody to do something. He would come home after dark and collapse on the couch with an exhausted smile on his face and a beer balanced on his chest. Justin always wondered about that smile; it wasn't until he was an adult that he understood it. If his father experienced this sensation at the end of every day, well, there is something to be envied in that.

BRIAN

He wears the hair mask and nothing else when he goes to the hallway closet to drag out his dumbbells. He knows sleep is a long way off for him. And he knows that when he feels the poisons building up inside him, the best solution is to throw some weights around. He learned this in the military, the mindless rhythm of weight lifting, the therapy of it. He picks the weights up, he puts them back down, pleasuring in the heavy breathing, the *clank* when he slides another plate on the bar, the bright red explosion when a capillary bursts in his eye.

The dumbbells weigh forty pounds each and he slings them up and down, working his biceps. The veins rise jaggedly from his neck and forearms. Beneath the mask his breath goes hoo-*hee*, hoo-*hee*.

The television is tuned in to one of those shows where a poor family gets its home ripped apart and built again to suit its needs. Right now the host, a hyperactive man with bleached blond hair, is running through the demolished house with a bullhorn, yelling at the construction crew in a happy, psychotic voice. "We've got to hurry, people. We've only got two days to change this family's lives."

He does push-ups. He does military press. He does squats and lunges and calf raises. He does triceps extensions followed by shoulder presses followed by upright rows followed by lateral raises, the weights growing heavier in his hands, making his palms go as red as the tip of his erection throbbing before him.

He gets a beer. And then another. He drinks between sets and the living room takes on a hazy dreamlike quality. When he finally sets down the dumbbells, the show is nearly over. The family—six kids and a single mother with cancer—cries when touring its new home. It has a big-screen plasma and an aquarium built into the wall and a fire pole that reaches from the second story. Everyone has his or her own bedroom. The host has his arm around the mother, who smiles with tears racing down her cheeks. "This is a new beginning," she says. "This is the life I always hoped for."

Brian shuts off the television and examines his reflection in its darkened screen, his muscles now pumped up with blood, trapped beneath his skin. Then he goes to pull on the rest of the suit.

The drive takes ten minutes. In town, the streetlights give off tired circles of light at regular intervals, soon replaced by the darkness of the outlying roads. He has to focus to keep his wheels trained precisely. More than a few times he swerves onto the shoulder and the cinders tacking and clinking against the wheel startle him into correcting his course. He parks a hundred yards away, on that same service road as before. When he gets out of the truck and moves into the woods, toward the house, he doesn't hurry or throw anxious glances over his shoulder. The night feels like such a familiar place for him. And the suit makes him feel invisible.

The living room window swims with watery blue light cast by the television, like a nighttime pool. He creeps up to it and peers inside. He cannot find her at first. He looks for her in the usual places, on the couch, the recliner. Then some movement catches his eye and he rises up a little to find her on the rug, doing crunches. She wears a black sports bra and yoga pants. She is watching a food show, some sort of competition involving people with knives and white chef smocks. Her face is scrunched up in a look of pain, but she doesn't pause, doesn't rest, just keeps pulling her knees to her chest, holding her arms out for balance. Brian watches her do at least fifty before she finally falls back to the floor with a thump.

Brian ducks behind a bush when a car grumbles by. Then he climbs the porch, trying to step as softly as he can. He expects the doorknob to be locked, and it is, and so he slides the key from his pocket and works it into the knob, which turns with a soft click. And just like that he is in the house, standing in a short hallway with a coat rack and mirror in it, the same collection of shoes he saw before. Outside another car goes by, its headlights sweeping across the house and making the mirror flash. Right then Brian's reflection moves from shadow into light—the mask on his face suddenly evil and snarling—and he almost screams.

Instead he takes a deep shuddering breath. As he does he can smell the smell of Karen: something lemony underlined by sweat. It's the kind of smell he imagines a taste for.

The lights are all off except in the kitchen. Just ahead of him, to his left, an archway opens into the living room. He peeks around it and takes in the layout of the room. Bookcases line the walls. A couch with laundry piled on it and a recliner with an end table carrying an unlit lamp. The television in the corner. And Karen on the floor, hurrying through another set of crunches.

Her body is angled away from Brian so he can step into the room without being observed. She makes a little contended grunt with each crunch, her noise and the noise of the cooking show hiding his footsteps as he moves forward, crouching behind the loveseat. In the dim light of the television her skin looks soft, pale, like the inside of a wrist. Brian imagines clearing his throat to announce himself. He imagines what would happen next. She would scream and grab something—a lamp maybe—to brain him with, but then he would peel off his mask and she would say, "Oh," and he would say, "Yes, it's me," and she would set down the lamp and look at him curiously—anxious, yes, but curious more than anything. After she scolded him, saying, "You could have knocked," and after he apologized, saying, "I'm sorry. I just wanted to watch you. I like to watch you," she would make a drink for both of them and before long he would lean in for a long sweet kiss that grew into something hungrier. The thought excites him. His erection is jammed painfully against his pants.

And then the phone rings.

At first Brian thinks the noise comes from the television—the two-note chime sounding similar to the local Z-21 weather warning—but when Karen reaches for the remote and the television blinks off, Brian ducks behind the chair just as Karen jumps from the floor. She hits the chair in her passing and it rocks back and Brian catches it with his hand.

He tries to hold his breath, to seem as if he is part of the room, when Karen appears next to him, looming over him in the near dark.

Brian feels stinging spots on his skin, certain she can see him. But she can't. Her eyes are foggy from staring into the light of the television. And she is moving across the living room now, through the archway, down the hallway, into the kitchen, where her phone calls to her.

Brian tries to move quietly when he hurries to the other side of the chair and crouches down. He can hear the scrape of the phone as she lifts it off the counter, the click as she flips it open, her voice saying, "Hey, Rachel," and then, "Did he?" and then laughter.

Brian feels suddenly cut off, separate from her. His erection withers. The beer is wearing off, replaced by tiredness. He feels the urge to run, to return home and take a cold shower and crawl into bed, alone. Alone is where he is meant to be. The laughter in the other room continues. It oppresses him, makes him feel limp, somehow defeated, her connection to someone else. He knows he could never make her laugh like that.

He rises from his hiding place and then spots on the couch the folded clothes, her underwear stacked into a neat pile, some of it lace, purple. He grabs one, and then a few other things, a shirt, a skirt, whatever rests on top, before he retreats from the room, sneaking his way out the door, clomping down the porch, hurrying to the place where he parked his truck.

He is careless in his rush. He runs up the road instead of through the woods. His fast breathing fills up his mask and drowns out the noise of the world, including the engine of the truck, the crunch and hum of its tires as it moves toward him. About a second before it turns the corner, he notices a glow, growing brighter. And then the truck appears thirty yards ahead, its high beams arresting him. Maybe it is the beer, which has settled over him like a heavy cloak, but he doesn't react quickly enough. He simply stands in the middle of the road, holding up one arm to shade his eyes, until the brakes squeal and the truck lurches to a rocking halt. Only then does instinct kick in and he reels into the forest.

The truck stays there for a long time and from a far-off vantage in the trees, Brian crouches, growling, *Stupid, stupid,* to himself, *so stupid.*

JUSTIN

After Graham finishes his dinner and sets his plate aside, he pulls out his book—*Wildlife of the Pacific Northwest*—and begins to flutter through its pages before settling on one. Justin asks him what he is reading about and he says, "I'm reading about mule deer."

"When you get a second, tell me what it says about bears."

Graham flips to the glossary and studies it a moment before finding the correct page number. Then he thumbs open the book to that section and presses down on the spine so that the pages lie flat. His eyes lift to meet Justin's. "You want me to read it to you? Out loud?"

"Sure."

When he reads, he traces each line with his finger, telling them in an almost singsong voice that bears have shaggy fur and rudimentary tails and plantigrade feet. They have acute hearing and a keen sense of smell that can decipher dead meat at a distance of at least seven miles. He tells them how a bear's ears don't grow with its body—remaining the same size, from cub to silverback—so you can measure the age of a bear like so: the smaller the ears appear in relation to its head, the older the animal.

They are among the most behaviorally complex of animals. "Practically as smart as humans," Graham says and his grandfather emits a low growl as if in agreement.

Justin says, "Out of curiosity, what does it say in there about grizzlies?"

His father says, "Why?"

"You remember how a few months ago those girls got attacked by a bear? At Cline Falls? People were saying it was a grizzly and—"

"No grizzlies in Oregon."

"I know, but—"

"Not since the Depression. That's the last time anybody bagged one anyway."

"I'm just curious, okay? What's the harm in looking it up?"

In response his father takes a swig of beer and then rolls his head around on his shoulders, cracking his neck.

"Just look it up," Justin says.

Graham waits for his grandfather to object and then turns a few more pages and begins to read again. "'*Ursus arctos horribilis*.'" He butchers the pronunciation, but when he looks at Justin for approval, he nods so that the boy will continue. Graham tells them how grizzlies feed on berries, bulbs, roots, rodents, pine nuts, moose, elk, mountain goats, sheep, and the occasional human. "Basically everything." They have concave faces. Their paws are black with wrinkled skin on the pads and their claws are long and curved and used for digging up roots and excavating den sites. They have a distinguishing shoulder hump. This hump is actually a mass of muscle that enables them to swing their paws with such remarkable striking force. They live in Alaska, Canada, Idaho, Montana, Washington, and Wyoming. "So we're safe, huh, Dad?" He pauses here to take a sip of beer as if it were the most natural thing in the world.

A minute ago his grandfather scraped up a handful of dirt and now he is flinging pinches of it at Justin, dirtying his chest, his lap. Justin brushes it away and ignores him until he reaches for another handful.

"Why are you doing that?"

"Dunno."

"Well, quit it."

He smiles and readjusts his weight and looks around as if for something else to throw.

"Hold on," Graham says. "There's a footnote." His eyes drop to the bottom of the page. "'The North Cascades Recovery Area is located in Washington. Its ten thousand square acres are bound by the Mount Baker-Snoqualmie National Forest, the I-90 corridor, and the east border of the Wenatchee-Okanogan National Forest and the Loomis State

Forest. The grizzly population here has more than tripled in the past ten years and the Forest Service predicts the number to grow exponentially and for the bear to eventually reclaim its place in North America.'"

Boo stands up then and studies the forest as if heeding a way-off call silent to all ears but his own. His tail wags hesitantly and then he huffs, an almost bark. Justin's father pats the dog on the head. "Good boy." He doesn't seem the slightest bit curious about what the dog has smelled or seen. He is too busy concentrating on his beer as it rises from his thigh to his mouth. The dog regards him before whining again and running his tongue across his snout as if he can taste as well as smell something in the air.

"Listen to this," Graham says with the trace of a smile on his lips. "'You are a hundred times more likely to die of a bee sting than a bear attack, and a hundred thousand times more likely to die in a traffic accident.'"

In this halo of fire surrounded by so much darkness, Justin does not feel reassured. If their bear is a grizzly, he wonders what has drawn it down from Washington—the warmer weather? The endless supply of garbage cans and Dumpsters? The trout-filled rivers? Hunger has to be the reason. It is always the reason.

His father stands from his chair and moves about the fire and it throws his shadow on the woods like the shape of a prowling animal. "I need a drink."

"You've already got a drink."

"A real drink." He rifles around in their makeshift kitchen until he locates the bottle of Jack. He holds it up and examines it, like a translucent agate, then gives it a swish. The poison sacs swirl whitely in the whiskey. "Anybody thirsty?" he says with a sickle of a smile cutting his cheeks.

"I think that's a really, really bad idea."

"Always the life of the party," he says, as if to himself. "My son."

"Let me remind you what happened earlier today." Justin is using his paternal voice, he realizes, the voice he uses on Graham when he forgets to take out the trash or neglects to mow the lawn. "You, bent in half, unable to breathe, with something—I don't know what—going haywire inside of you."

He finds his seat again. The lawn chair groans beneath his weight and Boo lifts his head from his paws to regard him, then yawns and clacks his teeth. "I'll just take one tiny little sip," he says. With his fingers he indicates how small a sip it will be before unscrewing the cap. "For medicinal purposes. It'll burn all the badness out of me." He raises the bottle in a toast and takes in a mouthful of liquor and smacks his lips and shrugs his shoulders. "Don't taste any different."

He grows quiet after that. Warily, Justin watches him. A minute later, his eyes blink and reblink as if to find their focus. The occasional shiver runs through him. He shakes his legs and stares into the fire, as if ready to race away from the flames should they flare up and singe him. The cocktail has affected him in an unsettling way, but Justin doesn't see what any further pestering can accomplish save elevating his heart rate, so he keeps his eyes sharply trained on him, waiting for him to slump over.

He never does. It no doubt helps that he weighs two-sixty and carries around a belly full of food. After twenty minutes, the worst of it has worked through him, and he grows still and meditative. His stare burns through the haze of the heat waves rising from the flames. "I can't feel my lips," is all he says during this time, so softly Justin isn't sure he says anything.

When some wood cracks and pops, sparks swirl up to join the stars. Justin looks up in time to see one of them fall and go sizzling across the sky, briefly brightening the night like autumn lightning. Then comes another. A meteor shower. Justin tells everyone to look. Each flash of light is perpetually renewed by another star and then another star coming loose and streaking into brightness and then nothingness.

"There's one," Justin says and Graham says, "That was a good one."

Then the moon rises and blots out the stars. It has a white ring around it, making it look like a great celestial eye, staring down on them. An owl swoops in and out its light.

Graham rises to his feet, a little unsteadily. Justin remembers his first beer. He drank it on a hunting trip such as this. His joints had felt oiled. His head, warm and cloudy. When he coughed he saw fireflies floating around the edges of his vision. Funny, how people go numb over time. How, when they're young, such a small tease can affect their systems so powerfully. A can of beer reducing you to giggles. A glimpse of an underwear ad in the newspaper furnishing you with a hard-on so rigid it feels as though it's going to snap.

"There he is," Justin's father says, talking about Graham but looking at Justin. "There he is—all grown up. That's my boy."

Graham has a hollow-boned build, like his mother. From the dopey grin sliding across his face, Justin can tell he is feeling what Justin would feel after working his way through a six-pack. "How about a picture?" he says, with a kind of sway and swing to his voice. "I haven't taken many pictures. And I'd like to take one."

Graham walks to the other side of the fire and Justin readies to catch him, but the boy makes it there without stumbling and lifts his camera to his face and says, "Cheese." He smiles as if he were the subject of the photo and Justin leans toward his father and lifts his beer as the light of the flash washes over them and temporarily keeps the night at bay.

Just then Boo comes trotting out of the dark, grinning around a bone with a strip of denim sticking to it. Justin's father says, "Release," and takes the bone and stands there, holding it, staring at it, not knowing what to do. Boo pants and wags his whole body along with his tail and Justin's father looks at him. What he is feeling now, Justin doesn't know. His emotion is masked, hidden behind his beard.

Justin wakes in the small hours of the night to a vivid sense of danger. He reaches out and touches his son, not to rouse him but to feel him, to know he is there. Every nerve in his body has gone alert. The frogs seem unnaturally loud in their drumming and the darkness beyond the flap of his tent seems too still.

It is that old hair-on-the-back-of-your-neck sensation. You just know. Justin knows something stands outside, maybe only a few feet away, studying the tent. He concentrates on his ear, opening it up to accept every sound, trying to blot out the rumble of the river and determine whether it is a hand or a paw or the wind brushing up against the tent.

He might wait ten minutes or he might wait an hour—it's hard to tell, as he floats in a gray zone between waking and dreaming—and then he notices, only inches away from his cot, the tent wall is moving, denting inward. This is not the wind. This is a compacted pressure—rounded and growing in size, coming slowly toward him. A snout or a paw. A snout, he decides, when he hears a sharp exhalation—*huff*—against the canvas. He is sitting up in his cot and leaning away from the indention, only an inch from his face. It has stretched the canvas to its limit. A stake is preventing it from going any farther. He imagines it coming loose in the soil, allowing the snout to press forward, into him. He imagines what is waiting on the other side—a muscled head—wider than his torso—bearing a button black nose that he can presently hear sniffing and blowing as it explores the scent of the tent and guesses at what lies hidden inside it. And he imagines, finally, his face snatched off like a mask, swallowed in a lathery slurp.

He feels a scream in his throat and dampens it to a whimper by clamping his jaw so tightly that something clicks behind his ear. It is all he can do to keep from rolling out of his sleeping bag, shouting a warning, waking his father from his slumber, so that they might snatch up their rifles and fire in tandem.

Instead he does something he doesn't completely understand. His hand rises. He watches it climb, shaking, like a bird blown by an updraft, toward the snout, which has by this time darkened the canvas with its saliva, making a design like a melted bat. His hand pauses and he holds his breath before touching it as gently as he has ever touched anything.

Immediately it pulls away and the canvas returns in a slow snap to its original shape. He waits for what must be the longest silence of his life, certain the tent is about to collapse all around them or tear open with a sudden slash.

Then he hears what must be its tongue licking its chops—the saliva popping and hissing in an almost electric way. The clacking of big teeth coming together. A snort. And a shushing as it slinks away, its paws dragging through the grass.

After another minute he rises from his cot and draws aside the flap and peers outside. There is no moon. The stars offer meager light. The darkness seems anchored among the woods and so the woods seem to possess the night.

He thinks of the Cline Falls attack—and how one of the girls granted Z-21 an exclusive interview after she was discharged from the hospital. Her parents sat on either side of her on their living room couch. They held her hands and nodded along with her account with concerned looks on their faces. She wore a ball cap when she talked about waking up to a growling noise. She remembered the tent collapsing all around her, the weight of the bear pressing down on her. She remembered its huge black shape against the starlit sky, knocking her down when she tried to run. Its hot breath when it took her head into its mouth, gnawing, trying to find a way into her. She could not feel anything at this point, she reassured the reporter. She was too jacked-up with fear to feel. She could only *hear.* Its heavy panting all around her. And the noise of its teeth against her skull, like a rake dragged over concrete. Eventually it spit her out and shambled off, leaving her alone and weeping. She took off her hat then and showed the reporter how her scalp had healed into a vast scar that looked like chewed bubblegum of flavors strawberry and grape.

The black obscurity of the night invites thoughts such as this. And Justin cannot help but imagine a fate far worse than the girl's. Someone, months from now, will find his jacket at the mouth of a cave, torn and spotted with blood. In a pile, maybe near a primitive hearth, there will be bones, piled one on top of the other, all of them scarred with spindly little lines—from teeth—cracked open with all the marrow sucked from them.

KAREN

When she rolls over in bed and her arm flops across the empty stretch of mattress, her hand in the hollow of his indented pillow—when she pulls aside the blankets and walks naked through the house, the blinds pulled, only the sunlight peeking around the edges of them—when she grinds only enough beans for half a pot of coffee—when she paws through the newspaper and scatters its sections messily—she finds she does not miss her family, not at all.

For breakfast she eats an apple sliced over cottage cheese. She washes this down with a short mug of coffee. The apple is organic and the cottage cheese is organic and the coffee is organic and fair trade. With every swallow, she imagines she can feel the goodness of the food breaking down inside her, dissolving into nutrients that build her body up instead of break it down. Then she pulls on her sports bra and shorts, slides her feet into her sneakers, and double-knots the laces. She is out the door, on the porch, where she spends the next few minutes stretching, the bands of her muscles as tight as her skin in the cool mountain air.

She hopes Graham is doing all right, especially with that son-of-a-bitch grandfather, who bullies him as if he were his own, just another version of Justin, one he can mold to his liking, make into more of a man. She really wishes his heart would just give out. The world, she thinks, would be better off. She knows this is an awful thing to think, but she can't help but think it about him.

She will run ten miles today—pounding up and down Awbrey Butte, looping past Drake Park on her way through downtown—and then walk another mile to cool down. She checks her watch and expects to be back in a little over an hour.

She starts by jogging a slow pace. After the first hundred yards, her joints—at first stiff, as if clotted with rust—stop clicking and protesting. Her muscles go warm and loose with blood. Her pace quickens, her legs and arms arranged in sharp angles, scissoring the air. The sound her sneakers make on pavement matches the pounding of her heart. She takes in deep lungfuls of cool air that breathe out hot.

She is in the best shape of her life. Sometimes she stands naked before the mirror and studies her body. She is deeply tan except for the starkly defined paleness from her shorts and sports bra, her skin as white and damp after a hard run as something drawn from a shell. She stretches or walks in place just to see her body move and ripple, as if there was something trapped beneath the thin sheath of her skin.

She likes the way she looks. And she knows other people do, too, knows her effect on men. She cannot go to Blockbuster without being trailed by a clerk asking if she prefers comedies or romance, cannot visit the grocery store without a stocker asking if she needs help finding anything. She likes the way she can turn a head, earn a smile. But there is a very thin line that divides feeling powerful and powerless, like now, when the man in the red Dodge truck slows to pace her. She tries to ignore him. He makes that impossible by rolling down his window, yelling, does she know how to drive stick?

She doesn't look at him but yells back, "I know how to read a license plate number."

With that he curses something, lost to the wind and the roar of the engine when he stomps on the accelerator. She wonders why so many men go through life thinking of themselves as predator and women as prey? She wonders where this comes from, this hunger, whether it is taught or inborn, a tooth-and-claw impulse that comes from that far-off time when we loped through the woods and slumbered in caves. Maybe this is why she enjoyed the locksmith so much. She could tell he desired her—but he was so small, which made his desire feel like a child's, almost cute, certainly harmless.

Of course she sees the same cruel hunger even in children, sees it in the schools she visits as a nutritionist. The other day, she was at Obsidian Junior High, seated at a table in the cafeteria with a junk food display. She had all sorts of gross-out trivia available, including a pile of fat, candlewax yellow, in a glass container—and a sign that equated it to a Whopper, large fries, and chocolate shake at Burger King. Every once in a while a student would stop by and say, "Gross," or "How's it going, Mrs. C?" but mostly they ignored her, walking by, their trays piled high with Tater Tots and fried chicken tenders. In the swirl of bodies, one girl caught her attention, a pimply girl with frizzy brown hair and a hen-shaped body. She looked already middle-aged, though couldn't have been more than fourteen. She sat with her friends, all of them a little off, their eyeglasses thick and their teeth crooked, their haircuts and their clothes homemade. They were playing some sort of game—Pokemon or Magic, one of those—and the hen-shaped girl was standing up, bending over to study a cluster of cards. At a neighboring table, a group of boys wearing Nike apparel began to hoot and snicker and point their fingers, and at first Karen thought they were just being boys, just making some mean idiotic boy joke about a big ass. Then she noticed the red stain that crept down the thigh of the girl; she was wearing pale blue jeans against which the blood looked impossibly bright. She was having her period. She was having her period and didn't realize it, hadn't worn a pad, maybe never needed one before now.

At first Karen did nothing. She wasn't a teacher and wasn't permanently based at any school, so she felt sometimes separate from what went on in the hallways and classrooms. So she watched the boys laughing and sneering, watched one of them dip a Tater Tot in ketchup and hurl it at the girl, watched it strike her head, clinging wetly to her hair. And then he threw another, and another, and soon the rest of the boys joined in, pelting the girl, her hair and back and ass. Karen watched all of this as if it were happening on television, as if the girl were a lame wildebeest and the boys long-jawed crocodiles. It was only after the girl began to stagger away with a slack expression on her face—wiping her hands across her shirt and pants, trying to clean away but instead smearing the ketchup—that Karen jumped up and raced toward the boys and slammed her hand down on their table and said to stop it—stop it, damn it—they ought to be ashamed of themselves.

She fears for the girl. She will grow paler and fatter as time progresses. She will go to the community college. She will move into a one-bedroom apartment, and in its living room, an old wood-paneled television will stand along one wall, and along the other, guinea pigs, cages and cages of them stacked up like apartments. The carpet will be littered with wood shavings and shit pellets. She will work at the library or the DMV and her co-workers will talk behind her back about how she smells like celery and cedar and urine. She will die alone. This depresses the hell out of Karen. Because she knows the girl could do better. There are so many routes to run, so many paths to choose.

Karen thinks about that often, the many different lives that could have been available to her. She could have married the boy she dated in high school, Doug, the lineman with the blue eyes, small teeth, and long, thin penis, in which case she might have stayed in Portland and died with him when a few years ago he head-onned a logging truck coming over the Santiam Pass. Or she might have used her college fund to travel to Europe, where she imagined herself walking slowly through museums and wearing tight black jeans and eating chocolate croissants at outdoor cafés. Or a few years ago she might have forgotten to change the batteries in the smoke detector and not known soon enough about the grease fire she started when she left the bacon on the stove too long and maybe the smoke inhalation would have left her brain damaged or maybe the flames would have scorched her face and made it appear melted. And within each of those possibilities nested a million other possibilities, every one of them dependent on whether a phone was answered, a step was icy, a door was locked, every one of them resulting in a different Karen, all the different versions of herself branching outward through time like the jumble of roadways and dirt paths available to her now, so that sometimes she feels she truthfully shouldn't even bother and might as well lie on the couch all day and shovel Cherry Garcia ice cream into her mouth.

Trees wall the roads she runs. Sunlight flashes through their branches and through the sunlight fall browned needles from the ponderosas and yellowed leaves from the birches and aspens. The rings on a tree, she knows, tell a story. A wet year brings a fat ring. A fire or disease or drought brings a thin ring. The tree grows around barbed wire, around stones, around snapped saw blades, swallowing them. She once heard a story of a logger who found a tooth deep inside a tree. She didn't used to be so poisonous in her thinking. When she thinks of the toxins built up inside of her from so many years of eating carelessly, of the resentment that has grown steadily over fifteen years of marriage, of the stretch marks and the varicose veins that came from two pregnancies, only one of them fulfilled, she thinks the inside of her body must tell a story like a tree. Were she to break open a bone, perhaps it would look like the inside of a coffee mug—riddled with lines, stained with brown blotches.

She runs on gravel shoulders and she runs on mountain bike paths and she runs on county two-lane. The tunnel of trees opens up—cut away in squares of browned grass that extend to porches busy with pumpkins and straw bales—and next to the narrow asphalt lane a sidewalk appears and she runs along it as the houses grow closer and closer together. Five crows balance on a fencepost, watching her approach. When she passes by, one of the crows opens its wings and makes a high, keening sound.

Her feet thud against cement. She once read that every time she took a running step, her knee absorbed eight times her body weight. That was over nine hundred pounds. She is amazed by this, the thousands of pounds she forces upon her body every run, the resilience of her body. It makes her feel powerful. Not like her job, her marriage, where she sometimes feels like a mannequin made out of clear plastic, insubstantial to the point of translucence.

There was a time, of course, when she felt differently, felt most alive when with Justin. She liked to pretend she was in the inky clutch of one of those poems he used to read to her in college, that time when the world was defined by laughter and pleasant moans, bars and coffeehouses, reading and talking deep into the night, showering together, taking turns shampooing each other's hair. But that was before.

Now they fell asleep early and watched television when eating meals. And there were little things that over time made her want to scream. The way he hummed along with the radio. The way he neglected to turn on the fan, so that she had stand there and breathe in the smell of his shit when putting on her makeup. The way he insisted on reading the paper in order. The way his snore began as a putter before deepening into a full-throated roar, like an outboard motor unmooring from a dock and heading into open water. The books in her office had shifted from a mishmash of Sylvia Plath and Kate Chopin and Danielle Steele to the purely clinical, *Nutrition for Life, The F-Factor Diet, What to Expect When You're Expecting,* nothing fun or meaningful.

Romance, once the most important thing, had come to seem the least. Romance belonged to the selfish part of her; the part that responded to its own hunger, that fed itself and not others. Marriage, children: they made her look increasingly outward instead of inward. It was as though, long before she lost the baby, she had lost herself. The old Karen—whom she occasionally spotted in a photograph, blowing cigarette smoke between her lips or reclining on a beach towel in a red bikini—had steadily shrunk over the years, replaced by someone who served others. Even at work, counseling the girls who shoved fingers down their throats, the boys who gnashed down whole bags of potato chips in one sitting, she was selfless, allowing herself to get snarled up in their pain and neglecting her own.

But lately—through her running, as she sheds the sweat and fat that feel like years of accumulated poison so that her body feels lighter, almost buoyant—she is reclaiming herself, kicking her way greedily into the world again as she did so many years ago at the jumping bridge.

The jumping bridge was a suspended railroad track that ran over the river near her high school. The smell of oil and formaldehyde rose off the ties when she and her girlfriends stood on them, suspended forty feet above the water. They would strip down to their underwear and their naked skin would go tight with goose pimples when they curled their toes over the edge of the timbers and said, "You go," and "No, you go."

Karen remembers stepping off the edge, the wind roaring in her ears, the river rising up toward her, the feeling of weightlessness before her body broke the surface of the water. She would bring her feet together tightly, trying to needle her way downward and touch the muddy bottom, not knowing what was down there, not caring. She remembers one time making it all the way, feeling the cold mud suddenly sucking at her feet. She opened her eyes in the gray-green murkiness and saw next to her a broken cement block with tentacles of rebar coming out of it. She had laughed at the sight of it, thrilled at how alive she was, and the laughter took the form of a wobbling bubble that rose from her mouth to the sunlit surface of the river.

She thinks of this when that old smell rises up to greet her, when she approaches the north-south train tracks that split Bend like a zipper. Fifty feet from them, the lights begin to flash and the gates begin to drop. She keeps running and glances down the tracks and sees the freight train, a big steel snake, approaching. For a moment she considers trying to outrun it, dashing across—for the same reason she used to leap off the bridge into the river, the thrill and danger of it. She stutter-steps forward and then reconsiders, slowing her pace, pausing a few feet from the tracks, jogging in place. The whistle sounds. The ground begins to tremble beneath her. She feels her pulse ticking in her neck.

A car pulls up on the other side of the tracks, a black BMW with a license plate that reads, THE MAN. Its horn beeps and she looks a little closer, looks through the tinted windshield to see a face she recognizes—white teeth, white hair—Bobby. Someone else is in the car with him, a dark silhouette larger than the passenger seat. The driver's side window goes down and Bobby gives her a wave. She returns the gesture, then glances around: the road behind her is empty except for a white truck parked two blocks behind her, its engine idling, a crooked line of exhaust rising from its tailpipe.

The train grows closer. The whistle shrieks again and the crossing bells clang and the wheels clatter. Bobby leans his head out the window and shouts something she can't hear. And then the engine is upon them, blasting past them, hauling so many flatcars stacked high with timber. The logs are stripped, a patchy mix of brown and white, what looks like a whole forest whittled down to toothpicks. A hard wind comes off the train and knocks her back a step; it smells of oil and resin. A swirl of dirt and cinder rises up and bites her skin. She stops jogging and stands flat-footed and feels the ground shaking, feels the train's power rising up her legs, pounding her heart. Through the boxcars she glimpses flashes of Bobby, still leaning out the window, watching her, smiling.

And then the train is past them, the noise of it rattling away, like a toolbox tumbling down basement steps. And the lights stop flashing and the gates rise and the world seems suddenly so quiet, with the engine of Bobby's car purring softly, the only noise between them. She starts forward and when she crosses the tracks feels a sudden lurch in her heart, as if she is about to be struck, as if another train might roar along and plaster her to the tracks. But nothing happens.

She passes the car and glances in the open window and spots the Indian there—the Warm Springs Indian—Tom Bear Claws—the guy who visits Justin's class every year as a guest speaker, the guy who regularly appears in the newspapers railing against Bobby developing Echo Canyon, the guy they talked about the other day at lunch. She had forgotten about that until now, seeing them together, their eyes on her. "Need a ride?" Bobby says.

She hesitates a step. "Nope."

"Good seeing you."

"Yeah," she calls over her shoulder, already past him.

She tries to hurry but his voice follows her, catches her. "You look good."

She closes her eyes and runs faster, and when her feet beat the ground, pushing her forward, she imagines she can feel the train's force still surging through her, like another heart beating out of rhythm with her own.

JUSTIN

A dream about a big black bird flutters away with his waking. This morning is worse than the last. His eyelashes are caked with gunk, and his pillow, damp with snot. There is a swelling beneath his jaw, each of his glands feeling like a watery marble. He massages his sinuses and feels something draining down the back of his throat. With a groan, he pulls off his sleeping bag and steps into his jeans. The cold has crept into their fabric and makes his skin pimple with gooseflesh.

His body feels as though it has calcified during the night. Just outside the tent, he snaps his neck and pushes his knuckles into his lower back until a juicy series of pops loosens him some.

The night has left the world dewy with its afterbreath. A light mist clings to the ground, coiling around tree trunks and floating along the river, soon to be burned away by the rising sun.

He notices then the grass around the tent, freshly trampled down, and the boot lying before him. Its leather is badly torn and discolored, as if it has passed through the digestive tract of a large animal. He recognizes it as belonging to the dead man. He stands there for a long time, staring at it, trying to make his brain work, still foggy with sleep. The sight of it is as disconcerting as a spider crawling across a projector's lens, magnified on the screen. A frightening interruption to the half dream of dawn.

He remembers what Graham said before—about bears being practically as smart as humans—and wonders what kind of animal would leave a warning. No kind of animal.

It must have been the dog. The dog found it and set it there. That is the only reasonable explanation.

As he approaches the fire pit, he steps around the boot, keeping an eye on it as if it might spring up and kick him. He kindles some wood with balled-up pieces of newspaper and before long has a fire crackling.

He thinks about last night. It has taken on a black-and-white quality, like a scene vaguely remembered from an old movie. The danger he felt then no longer seems substantial as he breathes in the cold morning air and observes the air growing brighter all around him. But this sense of passing safety vanishes when he walks to the edge of the forest to retrieve the canvas bag and finds it missing.

The branch hangs crookedly, torn from the tree, leaving a tear-shaped gash of bright white wood along the trunk. Near the ground, where the rope was anchored, he observes a pattern of worn-away bark, chewed and clawed until the last thread snapped. The grass lies trampled all around the tree and into the woods. In the air something lingers. If he flares his nostrils and breathes deeply, he can smell it. It smells a little like Boo when he comes out of the river and shakes off. Spermy. *Hairy.* With a touch of fryer-grease musk.

He listens, but hears only birdsong and the river, so he lifts his foot and takes one hesitant step, moving across a border, from the steadily brightening meadow to the shadow-clad forest. He feels a tingling in his feet as he does, as though the heat of the bear's passage lingers below him. He moves forward, picking his way through a cluster of bushes, stepping over a log, and taking care not to snap a branch or trip on a root. After only a few yards he encounters the rope, lying among the browned pine needles like a snake. He follows it through a tight corridor of trees and find at its end the bag, still attached, but torn open, its contents strewn all over the forest floor.

A package of Oreos lies in tatters beneath a bush, chewed open and emptied. Several empty cans of Pepsi rest here and there among the trees, their thin metal ragged from the bear chewing it open to lick the sugary residue. The handle has snapped off the frying pan.

Clothes, their dirty clothes, have been stomped into the dirt and draped oddly over bushes. Shirts and socks and jeans. At his feet he finds a pair of underwear. Kid-size tighty whities. He picks them up. They are still damp with saliva and ripped along the butt. He imagines his son inside them, the teeth gnawing on him, opening him up.

That is what bothers him most, the sight of the underwear. Immediately the image of his wife's face rises up before him; it is closed, locked, like a door he doesn't own the key for. He wonders how much more wooden she will become when he tells her about this, their time in the canyon.

He inspects the bag. It will remain functional, so long as he hugs it to his chest when he walks, to mend the long, tattered wound torn into it. He goes about collecting their clothes and garbage and cooking utensils. When he lays his hand on the frying pan, its coldness creeps up his arm, along with the feeling he is being watched. He scans the forest for any movement. A chipmunk worries at a pinecone. A camp-robber bird flits among the trees.

As he returns to camp the feeling doesn't go away.

His feet feel cold and bloodless while over the fire he boils water for coffee. The smell of grounds wakes his father. He emerges from the tent in his white T-shirt and his holey BVDs. He stretches and yawns dramatically and the noise brings Boo from the tent. Boo promptly picks up the boot with his teeth and presents it to Justin's father as a cat would a dead mouse. "Goddammit, Boo." His father picks up the boot and shakes it at him. "Bad dog. *Bad* dog."

Boo yips once and cocks his head in confusion and his father examines the boot. "Thing looks like a hay baler got it," he says before hurling it thirty yards into the river. It bobs in the water a moment, traveling away from them like a slow-moving target in a shooting gallery, and then sinks from sight.

Justin tries to keep his voice at a reasonable pitch. "I think we should go."

"Don't tell me you're scared."

Justin tells him about last night—the visitation—and then this morning—the torn tree limb. As he speaks, his father approaches the bag where it lies near the tent like a gutted animal. He kicks at it and it lets out a rattle as the pans and plates within it shift.

"I want to go. Okay? Can we go?"

"We will."

"When?"

"We will."

"But when? We will when?"

"Tonight. Like we planned." His father is almost smiling, Justin can tell. It's the possibility of danger that excites him, the courting of it.

"Think about Graham."

"Don't you remember? You're a million times more likely to die of a bee sting. Remember that?"

"A *hundred* times."

"A hundred. A million." He shrugs as if there weren't any difference. "Over fifty years, I've been coming here. Never had any troubles."

"This is trouble." Justin points to the bag as evidence. "You've got your trouble right here."

Justin must be gazing at him with naked fury on his face. To defend against it, his father crosses his arms. "This place won't be here tomorrow," he says. "I got a few hours left to enjoy it. I'm going to eat a nice breakfast. And I'm going to breathe some nice fresh air. I'm going to listen to the birds and watch the clouds and hike around some. Then I'm going to bag a deer, a big one." With his tongue he reaches for a tuft of beard, pulls the hair into his mouth, and chews. "And there's nothing you or any redneck or bear in the world can say to convince me otherwise." He slaps Justin on the thigh—once—as though punctuating a sentence, indicating a definitive end to the conversation.

Graham wakes up with a wet rattle in his chest. He sits next to the campfire and coughs into his fist and moves to another lawn chair when the smoke bends with the breeze and billows into his face and worsens his coughing. When he can, he sucks on his inhaler, taking two hits of Albuterol. This helps him to eventually expel several globs of mucus from his lungs. He spits them into the fire, where they sizzle.

When his coughing finally ceases, the morning's sounds are waiting. The river. A crow's wings fluttering in the brush only a few yards away. The chittering of a marmot. The noise of something losing its purchase from a tree and clattering through its branches to hit the forest floor with a deadened *thump*.

The sun drives through the trunks of trees and throws a lurid red light upon everything. It is almost painful to the eye, the canyon everywhere crimson and cut with shadows.

"Red sky morning, sailor take warning," Justin's father says, his eyes regarding the woods.

When his father goes down to the river to splash some water on his face and scrub his armpits, Justin draws near to where Graham sits, his elbows on his knees and his camera in his hands. "What are you doing?"

"Looking at my pictures."

On the screen Justin sees the shot Graham took last night, when they sat around the campfire—only Justin isn't present. The focus is on his father, his lips moist with liquor and arranged in a crooked smile.

"Where am I?"

"I guess I didn't include you."

The words sting in the way they fittingly capture the weekend. Justin begins to feel what every parent feels—when his or her child enters that special phase of life defined by locked bedroom doors and profane music and theatrical eye rolling—betrayed by the growing distance between them. "Oh," is all he can manage in response.

Then Graham points to the place above his father's shoulder. "Do you see that?" He leans in and uses the zoom feature, bringing the background closer, until the screen reveals a pixelated silhouette with two firefly eyes, watching. "What is that?"

"I don't know," Justin says. About last night, he has mentioned nothing—nothing about the pressure of the snout against the tent, nothing about the canvas bag torn from the tree—knowing he will only frighten the boy. "Probably a possum." Justin's gaze rises to the forest, to the place where the eyes were. There, among the pines, shadows play.

"You don't think it's a bear?"

"No. I don't think that."

Justin's mounting sense of alarm collapses and folds up inside him when Graham punches the button that shuts off the camera and makes the screen go dark. That he, a mere child, can dismiss the possibility of danger makes Justin inwardly scold himself for being so easy to scare—even as the eyes burn faintly in his mind.

"Dad?" Graham says, looking at Justin now, really looking at him. Steadfast, concerned, sensitive—this is his son—and Justin puts an arm around his shoulder as if to welcome him back. "I miss Mom."

"We'll see her soon."

They look at each other for a time. His eyes are that beautiful shade of gray you would pick for a gem in a meaningful piece of jewelry. Justin sees in them a resolve unavailable to him at that age, when his weaker parts would crumble easily and he would always do as he was told without any self-possession. Justin gives him a pretend punch in the chin and draws him close and claps him on the back with a half-violent affection.

"But first there's today to get through. And I'm looking forward to today," Justin says, even as his eyes drop to the camera. "I've got a feeling it's going to be a good day."

BRIAN

He was afraid of this. When he turns on the television, the screen lightens to reveal a reporter standing in the woods. His handheld microphone reads Z-21 across its handle. On these local stations you'll always find a different guy wearing the same bad tie and ill-fitting JC Penney suit, all of them either fresh out of college and hungry to prove themselves or else old and tired with yellow teeth and black dye jobs, their hunched posture indicating their grim acceptance of never making it out of minor-league news. This reporter is no exception, no older than Brian and stuttering his way through a report of a Bigfoot sighting. When he gestures to the pine forest behind him and says, "It was near here, in these very woods, that the alleged creature was allegedly spotted," his tone is alternately fearful and joking, as if he doesn't know quite how to pitch the story.

The live shot cuts to an earlier interview. The reporter stabs the microphone at a man with a silvery beard stained orange around the mouth from tobacco. He wears a camo hat and flannel shirt with a gray hood sewn into it. "Can you tell us what you saw?" the reporter asks off-camera.

"Well." The man—*Jim Ott, Witness,* the white tape at the bottom of the screen reads in black lettering—takes off his hat and scratches his head before saying, "I don't want to say it was or it wasn't. *Him,* you know. Sasquatch. I don't know. This is all very strange. But this thing, let me tell you about it, was bipedal." Here he squares his shoulders, proud of the word. "And for those out there who are saying, oh, it's a bear—nothing but a bear—let me ask, you ever seen a bear do this?" He departs the screen now and the cameraman takes a moment to find him again, out there in the road, mimicking the movements of

Brian, lurching along with one arm before his face, like some hillbilly Nosferatu.

Then he comes back to the reporter, laughing and shaking his head. "Swear to God. Cross my heart. Honest to goodness. All that. I mean it. That's what I saw. I tell you what, though. They always say Bigfoot is tall, but this one was short." He puzzles over this a moment. "Maybe it was a infant."

The report continues but Brian doesn't hear any more of it, doesn't even seem to breathe until the newsbreak ends and a National Guard commercial takes over. A man with a grease-painted face leaps from a plane and into the night sky, lost to the darkness as Brian punches off the television.

By the time he dresses and chews his way through two bowls of cereal and drives to O.B. Riley, the road is lined with trucks and the woods are busy with men toting rifles, oiled and ready to fire. There are dogs—pointers and labs—everywhere, some of them leashed to bumpers, others darting freely through the trees and the slow-moving traffic. He rolls down his window and the cool breeze carries the noise of dogs baying, rifles firing, and men speaking in low voices. He overhears one man saying a Bigfoot head would look real nice on his office wall, among the lacquered trout and trophy bucks. Another asks if it would be a kind of cannibalism, eating Bigfoot.

They are and they are not talking about him. He cannot help but imagine them as his enemies. Running a knife along his neck to make a blood necklace. Pulling the guts from his belly and hosing down his insides. Peeling the meat from his bones and rubbing garlic salt and cayenne pepper into his rump before grilling it over hot coals. When a man in a Carhartt jacket looks at him, Brian glances away in a hurry, very nearly expecting him to yell out, "There! He's the one we want!" And then they would swarm toward him and beat at his windows with their fists, the butts of their rifles, shaking the truck and finally turning it over and dragging him from the cab to cook on a bonfire spit while they danced around and stomped their feet.

His guts roil and his breath quickens with a panicky feeling that convinces him he will die if he doesn't quit this place. It is then, when rounding a bend in the road, when fluttering his boot above the accelerator, that he spots her house. He hates to see it this way, through the invading traffic, with so many men tromping about as if in competition with him. But such thoughts are short-lived as he notices the garage door descending and the white Ford Focus pulling out of the driveway.

Two cars are between them, so he feels anonymous in trailing her, through this hilly section of forest and into town, where she pulls into the Safeway parking lot. He maintains his distance, heading to the other side of the lot, waiting to kill the ignition until she pops out of her car and disappears into the store.

JUSTIN

So they set off for the day, their last in the canyon. Once they are under the trees, bright flakes of sunlight move across their faces and the noise of the river falls away, replaced by the hush of the forest. Today they will stake out a different location, a clear-cut situated at the southern tip of the canyon. In previous years, Justin's father has killed five big bucks there, among the shorn acres of stumps, and he considers the place lucky and his own.

They follow a hard-packed game trail, a narrow ribbon of dirt, its dirt polished from years of hooves trampling along it. Boo leads the way as they hike its wandering length for one mile, two. They find the river and walk along it. The water rushes toward them, seeming to slow them, to push them back the way they came.

Every now and then the dog approaches Justin's father with a stick and he will hurl it into the woods and the dog will dart after it, crashing through the underbrush, loudly sniffing for his treasure. Graham looks like he wants to join in their game without quite knowing how. Eventually he finds a stick of his own and peels the bark off it and rattles it against the tree trunks as he passes them until his grandfather gives him a glare that indicates he needs to quit it.

Midmorning, Justin's father starts up one of his monologues. He has so many theories—about 9/11, weaponry, homosexuals, antiperspirants as a cause of Alzheimer's—and this particular theory concerns the end of the world. Justin doesn't know what triggers the subject—maybe some question Graham asked him or maybe his own determined want to share those bricks that when stacked and sealed together make up the architecture of life as he sees it.

"I'm thinking, thirty, forty years from now, we'll be gone. It's the cycle of things. Nature finds a way to cure itself of pollutants, assailants, junk that disrupts the harmony of it all. That's what we are. Junk." His voice slows and deepens to accompany the prophecy. "Could be a virus. An asteroid. A bomb. And *poof*—problem solved. The human problem."

Justin tunes out his father's voice as he picks his way through a cluster of thorn apple bushes and in place of his chatter hears Boo mewl. The dog has gone still, his hackles raised. A series of shivers work through his fur and make it ripple like some black tributary of the river they stand alongside.

And then, from somewhere across the South Fork, comes a sound—a deep groan that goes on for several seconds—and all of them are stilled. Boo's head points like a compass needle to the source of the sound, the woods.

"Quiet!" his father says when Justin opens his mouth to speak. He has one hand cupped around his ear, while the other holds his rifle. When after a moment they have heard nothing else, Justin says, "You think it's the bear?"

He does not have an answer, because right now Boo breaks away from them and leaps into the river. The dog, wild with energy, swims surprisingly straight and clean through the torrent of the rapids. But the water is fast-moving and foaming and pulls the dog a good thirty feet downstream before he makes it across. Once there he shakes off quickly and rushes the sandy bank and enters the woods, and then a moment later appears again on the bank, barking at something in the trees.

"Boo," Justin's father yells. "Boo, goddammit, get over here!"

The dog does not acknowledge him but continues barking when he runs in a wide circle and then vanishes into another section of underbrush. His bark is sharp and loud so that they can hear him, over the noise of the river, long after he is lost from sight into the woods. Branches snap. Bushes rustle. And then a silence sets in that in this deep shadowed canyon seems too silent.

Dust clings to the air and drifts across the river. Some of it sticks to their skin. His father cannot stop shaking his head. He bites his lip and

Justin half expects blood to leak from it. His eyes are burned spots in a face flickering with sunlight thrown this way and that by the breeze-blown branches.

His father immediately wants to ford the river and search for Boo.

"What about Graham?" Justin says.

His father tugs at his beard and then tightens his hand into a fist that shakes a little. "We've got guns."

"It's just a *dog,* Dad."

His father shoots back at him before the last word leaves his mouth: "Shut up. Will you just shut up for one second?"

"Try to think about your real family right now."

He looks at Justin with a mystified expression, as if thinking, *You mean you?* And Justin wonders, were he the one missing, would his father so keenly seek him out?

Then his father fixes his gaze on some point across the river. Justin would slap him except for the brutal expression on his face. "No," his father finally says. His voice is soft, but snake soft, as if it could uncoil powerfully when provoked. He blinks at Justin quickly, sending a message: no, no, no. They will not leave the canyon without Boo.

So Justin suggests to his father, since they are so close already, that they might make their lunch at camp. He is not hungry—not in the slightest—but he tells his father sincerely that with food in their bellies, they can *think* this through, they can determine what to do next, his secret hope being that his father will come to his senses in this time.

And who knows, he tells his father, the smell of cooked venison might bring the dog from the forest.

"Or something else," his father says.

His father puts two fingers to his mouth and whistles that special ear-zinging whistle Justin has always wished to master. When Boo does not respond he mutters, "Damn," and kicks stupidly at a tree and then tightens his lips in pitiful defiance and begins marching toward camp with his rifle held at his side like a spear.

BRIAN

Above him a red eye blinks. The glass doors split open. He grabs a cart and circles it through the fruits and vegetables, and then the bakery, spotting her there. She wears black fleece and blue jeans, her hair tied up in a ponytail that bobs when she walks. In one hand she carries a basket weighed down by oranges and bananas. She stops to inspect the baguettes before tucking one under her arm like a child pretending to be slain by a sword.

She starts off again and he pushes his cart forward in such a hurry that he nearly strikes a boy who comes wandering around a table stacked high with boxes of doughnuts. He has a bowl-shaped haircut and sad brown eyes. Maybe he is eight, maybe eleven—Brian doesn't feel particularly apt at judging the ages of children. "Sorry," both of them say. And then the boy is on his way, but not before putting his hand up in a gesture of apology and departure.

His arm is covered in a raw-looking birthmark. It is hard not to stare. The skin appears smeared all over in raspberry jam. Brian forces his gaze elsewhere. He picks up a box of maple bars and pretends to read the label affixed to its packaging. Then his eyes jog back to study the mottled flesh. He wonders whether the children at school tease the boy, call him a freak, single him out at recess to throw sticks at and chase. He feels a sudden compulsion to rush over and tell him what to do, how to fight back, where to hit them and make them bleed so they will never bother him again.

But Karen is nearly out of sight, so he silently wishes the boy good luck and tosses the maple bars in his cart. The aisles are crowded with people. He has difficulty negotiating between them as his cart has a wobbly wheel that makes it veer constantly right. He abandons it near the meat counter, where he pauses, ten yards away from her. She is squatting, studying the stacks of chicken breasts.

The butcher—short, round-shouldered, his eyebrows as thick and arched as crowbars—comes toward Brian. He wipes his hands on his apron, leaving red smudges on the white fabric. Brian looks to her, looks to the butcher. "I'll take—I'll take some meat."

The butcher pulls on a pair of white plastic gloves with a snap. "Afraid you got to be more specific than that."

"Sorry. Steaks."

"Sirloin? Rib eye? Filet? What?"

"Yes."

"Yes what?"

"I'm sorry. One second." He makes an effort to study the glistening rows of meat. "I think I'll have some New York strips. Two of them."

The butcher doesn't bother asking him to pick out a pair, snatching two on his own, wrapping them in butcher paper, shoving them across the counter, yelling, "Next!"

By this time she has noticed him. He takes the steaks and pretends to examine them while watching her out of the corner of his eye—when she rises from her squat and shakes her baguette at him. "I know you." She is smiling. It feels good to be smiled at.

"Yeah?"

"You're the key guy."

"That's me. Brian."

"Brian the key guy."

"Who unlocks the hearts of women all over central Oregon." He isn't sure where that comes from, but he says it in a silly voice and hopes it won't be taken seriously. He imagines a glint of mischief in his eye and hopes it will find a reflection in her.

Thankfully she laughs. "Good line."

"Thanks."

This, he is thinking, this is what I always want life to be like. And then he notices her gaze, the way it bounces between his forehead and the rest of his face, uncertain what to focus on, what represents him, as when you speak to someone with a lazy eye and cannot determine which eye is the one that sees you. Under the fluorescent lights the scarred crater of his injury must be inescapable, like a cup carrying a shadow. "You're wondering what happened?"

"What? Oh, no. No. I'm sorry."

"I saw you looking at it."

"I'm sorry."

"Don't be. It's hard not to look at. You'd have to try not to look at it."

"No. That's not—"

"Yes." He brings his feet together as if the memory of the war alone makes him stand at attention. "You've seen the reports about roadside bombs, read the articles, though they're harder to find these days, buried on page seven." He forces a smile. "Anyway. That's me. That's my story."

And now what must he seem like? A half-wild man with his skull carved out as if by an ice cream scoop, with no expression and who knows what thoughts? He should have worn a hat.

Then she does something unexpected. She rushes her hand to his, squeezing it, not a handshake this time but the smallest kind of hug, its warmth rising up his arm and seizing his heart like a drug. "I'm sorry."

He remembers Portland—the Irish bar, the waitress pulling away from his touch, her teeth bared in fear. But Karen isn't afraid of him. There is something about her, like the boy with the birthmark, something wounded, that makes her different.

"I think you're—," she says and he closes his eyes and holds his breath, waiting for any of the number of wonderful ways such a sentence might end. "I think there's something wrong." Her hand releases his and he snaps open his eyes to see her step away. She is looking at the floor and he follows her gaze there, to the linoleum glow, darkened by a pool of blood. His hand is wet with it. The steaks, poorly wrapped, are leaking from the butcher paper.

He holds them out as an explanation. "Don't worry," he says. "I'm not hurt." He looks around as though to find a paper towel or a wash basin. Blood continues to patter the puddle, making it larger, the red tongue of it reaching out to lick his boot. He can smell its vinegary odor. She continues to step back and he calls out to her, "I'm totally fine!"

JUSTIN

Clouds begin to pile up above them. They move and meet each other, closing the blue gulfs between them, like hands slowly weaving a spell of grayness over the day. The sun filters through the thinner clouds and shapeless sections of light roam across the canyon floor and walls.

Graham coughs raggedly into his fist. "What are we going to do?"

It isn't a question Justin can answer, so he concentrates instead on the woods around him, where everything seems suspect. Every branch an outstretched claw. Every moving shadow like a sudden, sneaky dodge into concealment. He wishes his way out of the canyon and in doing so looks to the sky, his eyes lingering a second too long on the sun, so that when he looks away he sees a white dot, like the last of a television image when you hit the power button, bothered by a program you would rather not watch.

They return to find their camp not as they left it. The cooler is open, its contents scattered across the camp. The lawn chairs are tipped over. The tent has collapsed and Justin's sleeping bag sticks halfway from its opening like a stuck-out tongue.

"*What* the hell," he says as adrenaline-soaked panic hums in the background of his brain. "I mean, what the hell, Dad?" Justin knows this sounds like a line from a bad book, and he wants a line from a good book, but there is nothing else to say. "Dad?"

His father picks up the sleeping bag and smells it, clearly lost in thought. "Mmm."

"Mmm what?"

"Mmm the bear didn't do this."

Justin waits for him to say something more and soon he does, when walking about the campsite, kicking through its remains. "Bears don't unscrew a jar of peanut butter. They don't unpeel a stick of jerky. Bears don't drink Pabst Blue Ribbon and neither do I." He peers around the cooler and knocks closed its lid. "And bears don't steal whiskey."

The thought of Seth—who else could it be but him?—in their camp, sucking on a beer, rummaging roughly through their things, seemed trivial considering what had already happened. He felt only distractedly angry. If Seth were to walk out of the woods now, Justin could kill him without a second thought, throw his body in the river, and turn before the white water sucked it away. He knows this is completely outside his way of thinking, but that's where the day has brought him. He wants to punch holes in trees, throw boulders around.

"Let's go now," Justin says. "Can we just go? Now?"

His father goes to the fire pit and squats next to it and begins to arrange fresh kindling. "Not without Boo, we won't."

"We'll go to John Day and—"

"Not without Boo, we won't!" This is said at a scream. A freakish look comes into his eyes that Justin doesn't want to argue with, so he lifts his hands and lets them fall, as he seeks an explanation and gives up on one all in the same motion. "We'll eat something," his father says, his voice calm now, "and then we're going to find him, like you said. Like you said we were going to. We're going to track him. And if we run into anything else along the way, we'll kill it."

Soon flames crackle and venison steaks sizzle in butter and Justin's brain feels as if the clouds have dropped down and seized it.

After they eat, Justin looks at his father, but his father is looking at the woods. His hope that his father will come to his senses fades when his father stands and moves away from the camp and arranges his rifle so that it runs behind his neck and parallel to his shoulders. His posture is that of a scarecrow stapled up in a dead cornfield. The rifle carries the weight of his arms or he carries the weight of it.

Justin fishes a Pepsi out of the river cairn and hands it to Graham. He accepts it without a word and drinks it hesitantly, and then in a gulping way, as if he didn't realize how thirsty he was. Justin pours the dregs of the coffee into a tin mug and drinks from it. It is horribly bitter but he swallows it down like medicine meant to purge something from his body.

Birds chirp. The river makes a hissing sound. Patches of bush shudder in the breeze. The shadows of clouds move across the canyon floor. A june bug clacks its wings and he follows it with his eyes as it flies off a short distance and lands on a spray-painted patch of grass and tastes of it. The spray paint sharply turns like the elbow of the arm of a big body outlined by chalk.

He tries to recall everything he knows about bears and a television show comes hazily to mind, something he watched on the Discovery Channel. Over footage of grizzlies pawing salmon from rivers—and black bears wrestling in meadows—a throaty British voice explained that all bears are originally descended from a creature the size of a small dog. That bear shoulder blades were used as sickles for reaping grass. That polar bears weigh some two hundred pounds less than they did fifteen years ago, due to diminishing feeding grounds. These are facts. Facts are manageable. Facts are things you can wrap your mind around and file away on your mental bookshelf and share with classrooms full of students. Facts calm him.

His father must hear Justin approach, but he does not turn to greet him. "Come on," Justin tells his back. "We'll go get the police, the Forest Service, whomever. And then we'll come back here. We'll find Boo then."

His father says nothing. He has fallen into a stubborn silence no word of Justin's can break. So Justin lays a hand on his shoulder, gives him a shake. His father swings around and stiff-arms Justin's chest with one hand and slashes at him with the other, his knuckles glancing off Justin's cheek. Justin stumbles back a few steps and his father tries to dodge his way past him. Without realizing it, Justin has made his hand into a fist, and now he swings it, stopping his father with a blow to the face that sends them both staggering back a few steps. Hot nails of pain feel driven between his knuckles and along his wrist. He experiences something similar inside his chest where the sensation of victory and shame mingle in a stabbing way. The slack look on his father's face indicates he feels equally stunned; he brings his hand to his mouth, where blood already runs.

Then his father rears back and lunges forward, his hands shooting out to seize Justin by the head. His father hurls him to the ground and the breath escapes his lungs in a gasp. Immediately his father falls on top of him and strikes him with a straight right followed by a series of short punches to the cheek. Justin feels a white hot pain in his ear. Sparks dance along the edges of his eyes. Justin grabs wildly at his father's leg and drags him down and they lie crumpled together, giving each other a rough sequence of blows to the neck, the stomach, the face. Justin's muscles knot against the force of his father's fists. When his father elbows him in the nose, a sudden pain boils in and around his eyes that brings tears. Justin knees him in the groin and his father groans and strikes Justin's forehead with his open palm, knocking him back into the ground with such force Justin literally feels his brain batter his skull and his vision goes black for a moment and then returns to the Technicolor sharpness brought on by the adrenaline humming through him.

Graham abandons his place by the fire and runs to them. Their only noise is their wheezing breath, the occasional muffled grunt, the slap of fists against flesh. In this way they fight as brothers would, quietly, so their mother couldn't hear.

When Justin was a child, his father would wrestle with him, sometimes laying a knee on the side of Justin's head or fishhooking his mouth with a finger until he begged, "Uncle." But there isn't any sort of satisfying close to this fight. Graham says, "Stop it," softly at first—and then louder, "Stop hitting him! You're hurting him." Justin isn't sure who Graham is referring to, but his voice is strong enough to break them apart. In this way nobody wins or loses. They just stop—satisfied somehow—climbing away from each other, panting, bleeding.

Amidst the pain, there is a feeling of vacancy. As if a great room inside Justin, once cluttered with hard-angled furniture, has suddenly been emptied—with relief. They now look at each other with a resentful kind of understanding—and then at Graham, who stands with his arms cradled against himself, his elbows in his hands. "Just stop it," he says.

Justin presses his thumb to one nostril and blows and a thick strand of blood comes from it and clings to his thigh. He tries to wipe it away but it only smears into the denim like a gash of its own. "So?" Justin says. "Have we come to some sort of decision here?"

"You tell me." His father leans over to spit and then uses his forearm to wipe his mouth.

A thin stream of blood trickles from Justin's nose to his mouth and he swallows the metallic taste of it.

"You already know the answer."

They move in the direction Boo has gone, toward an unknown danger. Justin tries to conjure in his head a vision of Karen, her hands on her hips, her lips pursed in vicious disapproval—but the image of her trembles at the edges before dissolving, as if part of his brain has come unplugged, the same part that once cared about the sale at Target and vacuuming under the furniture.

They wade the South Fork with their rifles held above their heads and Graham clinging to Justin's back. In the deepest part of the river, where it is coldest, the water comes up to Justin's belly and threatens to pull his son away. Justin tells him to hold on tight. His arms are around Justin's neck, constricting him like a tight-fitting backpack. Every step is a sliding uncertainty. Beneath the water, his boots stumble along slowly and blindly. The rocks are slick and uneven and occasionally seem to clamp down on his boots like teeth that will only let go when Justin heaves his boot from their grip and then tries to find another foothold even as the current yanks his foot riverward. The water rushes against his body, forming a white frothing collar around his waist, its force tremendous, so that he has to angle his body against it and make a diagonal path toward the shore. All it will take is one clumsy step on one algae-ridden rock and they will be lost to the river, carried downstream in an icy torrent.

His father's fists have left a headache pounding against his skull and he tries to ignore it now. He tries to concentrate every fiber of his mind on finding a proper foothold and slogging forward. His father arrives on the far bank several minutes before Justin and spends those minutes glancing back and forth between Justin and the woods, his face dense and compacted. He yells his encouragement when they near the shore, or so Justin guesses, since he sees his mouth move and his arm wave, though his words are lost to Justin, muted by the roar of the rapids and Graham panting nervously in his ear.

Once across—once he pulls his foot from the water and sets it on the muddy bank—he tries immediately to shrug Graham off, though at first he doesn't seem to want to let go, and they both very nearly keel over. "Get off," Justin tells him, not unkindly—and at last the boy releases him. Justin breathes heavily and moves a few staggering paces from the mud to a stony embankment and more falls than sits down.

Despite the chill of the water, he feels hot all over. His lungs burn. Two long fingers of fire rise up his back, reminding Justin of Graham's unwieldy weight. His neck feels so rigid he wonders if he will ever turn it again. His quads and calves in particular feel warm and wooden, like lumber left in the sun. He massages them with his hands, hoping he won't cramp up. A shadow falls over him and he looks up to see Graham observing him with a dismal expression, his eyes wide and moist. "Sorry," he says.

"It's okay," Justin says. The spray from the river has dampened his hair and he runs his fingers through it and regards his father. A tree long ago fell from the forest and now its rotting husk lies across the embankment. His father has one foot on it and one foot on the ground, as though he is already stepping into the woods, pausing midstride only to see if they will follow. "Well?" he says.

"Just give me a minute."

He checks his watch and says, "One minute."

Justin stares at the river, its gray water foaming over white, and remembers its interminable power as he struggled pitifully against where it wanted him to go. Over the noise of it, he can hear little, except for the distant *tock* of a woodpecker, like a clock that indicates a perilous appointment drawing near.

He settles his breathing and by the time he does, his father has started into the forest without a word. Justin rises to follow him, leaning at first on his son as he shakes his legs and makes a hula-hoop motion with his hips, ironing the cricks from his muscles. His boots squish and his pants cling to him uncomfortably and when he enters the woods the light falls away as if in a sudden dusk. There are prints everywhere—as if exactly *here,* all the animals of the forest have decided to scribble in the dirt the graffiti of their passing—mostly the forked depressions of hooves, mingled with the long, thin, and vaguely human imprints left by raccoons and possums, all of them blending into each other. They bend their heads low to the ground and push their way through the thick underbrush and try to find among this ghostly procession of creatures the pattern of a dog's paw. "Here," Graham yells and waves them over and he points out a print like a scaly pear with thorns rising from it. It is located in a sandy pocket surrounded by a barren stretch of lava rock, so it takes them several minutes more to find another track, and then another, a series of them eventually coming together to reveal the dog's flight. The prints wander through the woods, around stumps and over logs and through rabbitbrush, but with a definite northern direction. Eventually the brush opens up into a thin game trail and the tracks continue along it, less obvious now against the hard-packed dirt.

His father takes the front of the line and Justin takes the back, with Graham guarded between them. They hunch along wordlessly, studying the ground and forest. Birds sail around them, squawking and inspecting them, but otherwise they see no living thing as they plod along, a slow-moving progression of tired joints and fearful hearts, following Boo's prints as best they can.

Justin's eyes sweep back and forth across the trail, as you would do when driving a narrow passage of road, worried something might leap out and threaten your course. He feels confined, condemned. He tries to think of other words that begin with *con.*

Condone. Concede.

What did that prefix mean anyway? With. It meant with. Or together. Or something like that. He really ought to know these things, as a teacher. There was always some smart-ass kid calling him out, waiting for him to trip up, and he needed to be ready for them.

Contradictory.

Consequence.

He hears a sudden rumble and flinches before glancing up. There, in a patch of blue sky, he sees a jet with a long white contrail following it. He imagines himself inside the jet, among all the passengers, reading their magazines and eating from their single-serving pretzel bags, all of them heading someplace civilized, safe, contained by fences and lit with bright lights.

He closes his eyes for a second and it almost seems possible. He is almost there. Then he opens them and sees the woods all around him and feels his life spiraling down as if into a cave.

They climb a steep grade and enter a wooded ravine with a stream rushing through it. It is a tight corridor—filled with shadows and jutting knobs of basalt and stunted juniper trees that somehow grow through the stone, their roots groping for leverage—and when they leave this place and enter a wider gulch, it is with the relief of a deep breath and a loosened belt.

They find a pile of shit, like a muddy wig jeweled with berries, resting nearby. The ground as Justin steps around it feels unstable as though it might break open up to his knee. So he walks tenderly, as you would when bringing your foot down on the edge of a frozen lake, depressing your weight gently, watching the cracks appear around it like sudden black creeks. Beneath the ice, the paralyzing grip of fear awaits. When he thinks of the first body and its blackened bones—when he thinks of the circle tamped around their tent like a bull's-eye—when he thinks about the safety of his son—the cracks widen.

His father walks ahead of Justin and stops, his head lowered, his eyes searching the ground. "Do you see it?" He squats as he asks them this. Justin and Graham huddle beside him and follow his arm when he holds it out and indicates the path. "He's running along at a good clip and then . . ."

He does not need to say anything more. The soil tells the story, still marshy here from the storm the night before, as easy to read as print on the page. The bear. Justin sees where the pads touch each other and the toes fall close together and nearly in a straight line. Far in front of the toes, impressions from the claws gouge the ground so that they look like something separate from the main print, its size equivalent to a catcher's mitt.

His father lays his hand over it and for the first time in his life Justin thinks of him as small. A wince passes over his father's face and a flush follows it. He draws his hand away from the print and brings it to his eyes. He pinches the bridge of his nose as if to relieve himself from a hidden pain.

"No grizzlies in Oregon," he says under his breath.

"Keep saying that, maybe it will come true." Justin feels his heart expanding and the blood quickening through it. He imagines he hears the ghost of a yelp still lingering in the air. He looks up the trail and tries to envision the great shape of the bear, shambling through this thin corridor of trees, with Boo trapped between its jaws, the dog flapping like a salmon pulled from the river.

At a crashing in the trees very close to them, Justin and his father both raise their rifles. Justin's panicked thoughts flutter inside his skull like owls trapped in an attic. But nothing comes out of the dimness except a mule deer, a six-pointer, a big beautiful animal that rips through the pines and over the fallen timber and into the open trail, where it halts, watching them, swishing its tail, not ten feet away—so close Justin can smell its musk. Its rack is a big and tangled basket.

Justin has not yet processed his relief. The air is remarkably still as he stares down the length of his rifle. It feels cold in his hand. He considers firing—as much for the trophy as for the release, the explosion—but doesn't. He doesn't have it in his heart—and apparently neither does his father, who sighs—as if to say, *Why bother?*—and lets his rifle fall and the movement sends the deer bounding up the trail and around the corner.

His father moves forward twenty paces and then freezes. He crouches and sets down his rifle and lifts something from the ground. There follows a tinkling noise, such as would come from a tiny bell. He holds in his hand a nylon collar. Boo's. Torn in half, into a long red strip. The tinkling comes from its tags, knocked together by the wind. His father holds it out, not for Justin to take, but for him to look at. For a long time they stare at it. It is torn in places and its color, naturally red, is made redder by the blood that rubs off on his hand when he holds it.

After a long purposeful silence, he casts his eyes on Justin without looking at him, looking through him. His eyes are red and watering, from smoke or from sadness. Justin notices a small patch of white on his beard that looks like a tiny egg nested in it. "My dog." His voice is thick and watery. He twists and squeezes the collar, as if to wring the blood from it. His face fills with lines of pain and a vein worms across his forehead. A minute passes before he picks up his rifle, his finger curls around the trigger, his voice wild and fast when he says, "I'm going to . . ."

But he doesn't know what he is going to do.

He looks at Justin through a fog of shock and anger and fear and confusion, finally saying, "What now, Justin? What are we going to do now?" He speaks slowly, each syllable occupying its own time and space.

Up to this point, Justin felt small and vulnerable on this dark game trail, a piece of meat among the shadowy trees. Now the sensation worsens. His father, who always knows what to do, doesn't know what to do. He needs his son to think for him, and Justin admits to feeling something like paralysis then, as his mind determines the miles they have to travel before the sun sinks from the sky.

"You don't want to say it," his father says, "but you're thinking it."

A tense silence follows his words, broken by a branch cracking somewhere in the distance. Both of them flinch.

When he finally speaks again it sounds like a reply. "What you're thinking is we're going to die." He smiles without humor. "That's what you're thinking, isn't it?" He laughs harshly at this.

Justin first glances at Graham—who stands a few feet away, his eyes scrunched closed, seemingly deaf to their conversation—and then to the collar. In its blood-soaked fibers he thinks he can see the oily sheen of unreality, shimmering in the same way the mirror shimmers just before Alice steps through the looking glass. Nothing seems possible and everything seems possible. Life seems possible. Death, too.

Justin says, "Maybe you're the one who—"

"You're wrong for thinking that!" He laughs like someone who never shows emotion, explosively, wretchedly, so Justin knows it comes from somewhere deep inside. His laughter goes on and on until it finishes with a sob.

Justin has seen him at funerals—has seen him break a leg after falling from a tree stand—but this is the first time Justin has seen him cry. Before he knows what he is doing, he puts an arm around his father's shoulder and draws him close—and his father is utterly overcome.

Justin thumps him on the back. It is a strange sensation, comforting his father, just as it is strange to look back upon yesterday—it lies so distant, so irrevocable. "I'll be glad when we get out of this canyon," Justin says.

His father lets go of his grasp and wipes at his eyes with the insides of his wrists. "Tell me about it." He does not gift Justin with a smile, but his voice has some forced measure of humor in it.

Graham still has his eyes shut. He is chewing at his thumbnail, pulling at slivers of it hungrily. Justin gives him a squeeze on the shoulder. The boy's eyes snap open to reveal his curiosity and fear.

"We're not going to die?" Graham says. He touches his fingers to his belly, just below his breastbone, something he always seems to do before he cries.

"We're not," his grandfather says, though his expression carries darkness.

"All right," Justin says. "Let's go."

His father remains footed in his shadow. "We're not going to die because we're going to kill that bear. We're going to find it and we're going to kill it good and dead." He then takes a deep, quivering breath that helps steel him against whatever he will face. "Come on, Graham." He continues up the trail and Justin stops him by beginning a series of broken sentences—but each thought loses its grip in the empty air. He becomes very aware of his father staring at him.

"Are you done?" his father says, and when Justin doesn't say anything, he resumes tracking, now following the bear and not the dog. "Come on, Graham," he calls over his shoulder. "It won't be much longer. We'll kill it and we'll cut off its cock and cut out its heart and we'll be back in camp by nightfall." He stops and again says, "Come on, boy." Not even looking at Justin but holding out his hand to Graham. His hand, roughed over with calluses from gripping hammers and levels and saws, from shaping the world. "Come on."

Justin knows that this moment—when his son will or will not respond to that hand's charge—means something. His family hangs in the balance. The family he came from and the family he has constructed. Justin readies to make a grab for the boy, but there isn't any need: Graham is stepping back, retreating, ducking behind Justin.

Justin's father drops his hand and balls it into a fist. "Just look at the two of you." His voice has hate in it then, but also the hardest kind of love. "Go then."

Nothing else occurs to Justin to say. Not good-bye or good luck or be safe. He is entirely out of conversation. He can only watch as his father departs them, growing smaller as he moves away, until they can't see him anymore.

"What else did that book of yours say?"

In a whisper, Graham says, "Book?" He seems not to know who Justin is, let alone what he is talking about. His chin is quivering and he is looking over his shoulder as if the trail will at any minute pull out from under him and roll up into a secret closet and leave them stranded there in the middle of the forest.

Justin says, "Let's head back to camp, okay?"

Graham nods and they return the way they came. They hurry through the trees, a place where shadow is interrupted by columns of light, as it is at the bottom of the ocean. With every step, they seem to move a pace faster—the forest blurring by—even as Justin's muscles ache and his legs feel as though heavy weights hang from them. They duck their heads to avoid tree limbs, like thick arms swatting at them. They sweat and their sweat streams in muddy paths down their cheeks. Even the birds seem hushed as the two of them hurry along and speak only in whispers and peer now and again over their shoulders.

Justin's mental switchboard plugs in to its many fearful circuits. He fears for his son and his father. He fears for himself, for his lack of judgment in putting Graham in harm's way. The short-breathed alarm he feels grows with the steadily slanting light. He feels played with. He feels that soon, any moment now, when they are on the very verge of safety, some *thing* will rise from the forest and strike them down.

The river surprises him. One moment he is surrounded by woods, the next he teeters on the bank of the South Fork's fast-moving waters. He had not heard it, his mind noisy with so many fears and doubts, all of them black-clawed and draped in fur. He puts one boot in the water and then withdraws it, as if testing a bath whose water proves too hot. "I don't know if I can make it across again."

"You don't have to carry me," Graham says, his voice and his face cast in doubt. "I can do it on my own."

"No, you can't. The river's too strong. We'll have to go upstream until we find a calm stretch."

"Okay."

"It might be another mile."

"Okay."

Another mile when the other side of the river beckons only twenty yards away. Justin heaves a sigh and begins to walk upriver, his boots crunching over pebbles.

"I remember something," Graham says.

"What's that?"

"From the book."

"Okay."

"For their dens, they dig a tunnel beneath a tree or beneath a rock face. The tunnel leads to a chamber where they sleep." Up to this point, he sounds unthinking and emotionless, almost academic—but when he says, "I'm scared," he becomes twelve again and picks up a spear-sized stick and examines it, as if unsure whether he ought to consider it a toy—something to clack against tree trunks—or a weapon.

PAUL

Paul follows the bear. Steadily the trail rises up an incline, and ahead, in scattered glimpses seen through the treetops, he sees a sheer canyon wall. The trail is messy with tracks and piles of lumpy excrement—decorated with berry skins—evidence of the bear's frequent passage, and Paul tramps through them both. The thorns of prickly ash carry clumps of fur in them. Here and there a stump or a log appears to have gone through a shredding machine, torn apart by claws in search of grubs. He kneels next to one and stares into the woods as if they were a mirror and listens for a time, waiting for a grunt, a snap, some noise that will indicate he is not alone. Nothing. In the log, in a hole burrowed by a woodpecker, he spots a cache, some pine nuts, a highbush cranberry. He digs out the cranberry and pops it in his mouth, a little sweetness on his tongue, before spitting out the seed and moving on.

On a rise, the ground flattens out and the pines give way to a twenty-foot wash of broken basalt that has come loose from the cliff side in big and small pieces like some vast gray puzzle shaken from its board. Beyond it lies the cave—in a half-moon shape—as tall as Paul and twice again as wide. Blood leads into it, like the tacky trail left by some enormous red slug. He searches for movement but discerns only a short expanse of cave wall that slopes sharply downward before darkness overcomes it.

The smell—a heavy, oily smell—hangs in the air like a shambling presence. He brings a hand to his nose to guard against it. He stands there, his eyes fast on the cave, waiting for a decision to come to him. A chill wind blows through the gulch, momentarily dragging the smell away from him and making the pines send out a roaring whistle. Just as quickly, it stops, as if the forest has taken a deep breath.

He lifts his right arm over his head and stretches it out and lets it back down, and then does the same with his left. He snaps his neck sideways and it makes an audible pop. Readying for a fight.

It won't be his first. When he was a teenager—at the Deschutes County Fair—among the shooting galleries and dunk tanks and horse stalls and pigpens, there was a ring of sawdust with a sign next to it that read *Bear Wrestling.* In the middle of the ring prowled a big black bear with a leather muzzle. The bear was chained to a stake. For a dollar, you could wrestle it. If you pinned it for ten seconds, you won a stuffed animal, a sack of caramel corn. Paul watched several men—thick-necked ranch hands—try to grapple the bear down, all of them reduced to screams, some to tears, as the bear overcame them. He had a plan. He would walk out there and punch the bear as hard as he could in the snout, as if it were a dog or a bull, something that he could teach to submit. He remembers the crowd of people surrounding the ring, laughing, hollering him on, as he approached the bear at a sprint. It rose on its haunches to greet him. He swung and struck the bear in the nose. Which served only to piss it off. It loosed a pained roar and wrapped its shaggy arms around him and dropped him flat with six hundred pounds of hair and muscle and stink pinning him. The muzzle pressed against his face. It was laced leather and he could see the teeth snapping on the other side of it, less than an inch from his nose.

He laughs at the memory and feels a little braver. From his pocket he pulls a book of matches and studies it in the palm of his hand. The Pine Tavern, it reads in green lettering. He imagines the whine of his son's voice next to him. "What are you going to do?" he would say.

"I'm going to smoke it out," Paul would say to his son, to no one.

"You're crazy. And then what? What are we going to—"

"We're going to kill it. That's what we're going to do."

There is no response. Because he is alone. He retreats down the trail, swinging his head left, then right, until he spots what he is looking for, a rotten pine whose branches sag and whose bark hangs grayly off it like an ill-fitting coat. A woodpecker flies from a cavity in the tree when he approaches it. He grabs at a low-hanging branch and it sheds many browned needles when he yanks at it and finally tears it from the trunk. The *crack* makes him startle and he clicks off his safety and lifts his rifle and holds his breath, certain the bear will come lumbering from the cave and curl a clawed paw around him and drag him down into a darkness that carries the thunderous aroma of wet fur and animal shit and blood both old and new. It is the smell of something wild—and right now, in his mind, it fills the world and becomes the only smell.

But the darkness of the cave remains uninterrupted. Still, the idea lingers—and seems even to intensify—when he moves slowly forward, his steps uneven over the rocky surface. One hand grips his rifle, the other the branch. His head feels hot and his hands feel cold and stiff and doomed to a slow response when he needs their action.

Ten feet from the cave he kneels and lays down both the rifle and the branch. He removes a match and scratches it into a flame. The flame gutters, growing blue and then vanishing in a black puff as the wind drags it from the matchstick. He strikes another and cups a hand around it. The flame dances as he lowers it, but, shielded from the wind, it hugs the match and then the branch when he touches it to the tuft of needles where it flares and makes a noise like torn fabric. A blue-yellow color sputters and crawls along the branch.

He snatches up his rifle and then the flaming branch and rises from his crouch and charges the cave entrance. At the last minute he hurls the branch inside and turns to run unsteadily along the cliff wall before circling back to where he first stood, observing the cave.

His heart is like a hot hammer in his throat. The cave glows orange. Shadows play across its walls. It is the kind of place witches would gather, stirring their cauldron, speaking the darkest prophecies. He is glad Graham is not here to see the stuff of nightmares. All the rest of the world falls away, his attention singular, so that when a flock of geese passes closely overhead, he notices them only vaguely, their honks sounding like music from another realm, the way the distant ring of a buoy no doubt sounds to an exhausted swimmer pulled far from shore by the riptide.

At any moment he expects the bear to explode from the den, the smoke swirling around it like a wreath. He is ready to fire. But he is ready to run, too.

A minute passes. Then another. And still the bear does not come. The flames have died out. Smoke still billows from the cave but weakly, like steam pluming from a gray-lipped mouth on a winter's day. He sighs and starts forward, this time with the intention of entering the cave.

He no longer moves with the caution he exhibited earlier, his rifle in his hand but gripped carelessly, an umbrella on a sunny day. At the cave entrance, he pauses and looks back over his shoulder. Then he descends into the smoky dimness.

He gropes around in the smoke, the embers offering some light but not enough. His feet clatter against rocks and his hands claw at the ground until they discover something damp, a collection of bones and blood, the remains of Boo. He scoops up what he can. He has by this time held his breath to the limit. His lungs demand air and he breathes in a great gasp of smoke and begins to cough, at first hesitantly and then miserably as the burn overtakes his throat and lungs.

He staggers from the cave, hacking, clutching to his chest a skull with some spine still attached to it, a gruesome sculpture upholstered with patches of hair. He pets the remains and they smear away against his hand. He is crying again. There is nothing violent and shuddery about it, not like that embarrassing moment with his son. Tears are simply leaking down his cheeks.

Boo listened to him, never rolled his eyes or whined at commands, always greeted him with slobbery kisses and a wagging tail. His loyalty was unconditional. If only humans were more like dogs, Paul is certain he would have loved more of them in his life.

KAREN

She isn't worried, not really, about her husband and son. Not even when her call goes directly to Justin's voice mail. They're still in the canyon, still hunting, making the most of the weekend. He warned her that they might not return until midnight. The concern she initially felt for Graham has been relieved by the calming solitude of the past two days.

She kindles a fire and pulls on a sweatshirt and fixes a dinner of turkey breast and steamed carrots and whole-grain bread. The plate is now empty, a smeary mess beside her, when she sits at the computer—Googling gangrene, blastomycosis, human intestinal parasites. She barely hears the doorbell the first time it rings. She is too busy reading, her lips pursed, her head cocked. She feels strangely serene, she feels good and normal, after clicking through so many images and descriptions about toxic secretions, rotting flesh.

Earlier, when searching "animals attack," she came upon a story about this couple who owned a snake, a python. They kept it in a glass cage in the living room. They fed it rats and mice, and after it had eaten, they allowed it out of its cage and let it wander the house. It would slide through their legs, over their laps, always friendly with a full belly. They considered the snake a part of the family and began sleeping with it at night. It would curl up between them and pleasure in their warmth. In the morning, when they readied for work, they would open up the top of its glass cage and the snake would pour into it, piled up at its bottom like a thick rope. But after a while, the snake resisted their prodding—it didn't want to leave the bed—even when they tempted it with squealing mice.

And then the snake refused to eat altogether. This went on for several days until one morning they woke to the snake turning over and over again, twisting into knotted designs, opening and closing its mouth as though to clear a yawn from its throat. They called over the veterinarian, who walked into their bedroom and observed the snake from a distance and said, "Do you know what's wrong?" and they said, "No," and he said, "I'll tell you what's wrong. Your snake is getting ready to eat you. He's stretching out his body and his jaw so that he can curl around one of you and strangle you and swallow you in the night."

The doorbell rings again and she minimizes the window and rolls away from the desk and wonders only vaguely who could be at the door—the UPS man, another reporter asking about the Bigfoot sighting, the Jehovah's Witnesses she saw scouring the neighborhood when on a run the other day.

There was a time, after she lost the baby, when she dreaded answering the door. On the other side of it she would always find someone—a friend, a neighbor, a co-worker—with a pitying look on her face and a plastic container or glass dish in her hands. A casserole. Cinnamon rolls. Chocolate chip cookies. "Take this," she would say. "And please let us know if you need anything. Do you need anything?"

No. She needed nothing. Except for them to leave her alone.

One day she opened the door and found a Bundt cake resting on the porch. No note. No one in sight. She picked up the cake and carried it across the yard and hurled it into the woods. For two days afterward, when she left the house, she could hear the faraway buzzing of the flies that feasted off it.

And then one night Justin said, "Mary Elizabeth said she dropped off a Bundt cake."

"Oh, so that's who left it. There was no note."

"Where is it?"

"I threw it in the woods."

He was quiet for a long time. "You shouldn't have done that. She baked it just for us," he said. "And I happen to like Bundt cake."

The sun is setting when she pulls open the door to find Bobby on her porch. He is smiling. His teeth are very white against his tanned face. He has a dangerous look to his eyes, that kind of squint when there's no sun. He wears khakis and a cornflower blue oxford cloth shirt with a pocket on the breast. He holds a red rose in his hand.

She feels a hitch in her chest, the heart-stopping sensation that would come if she reached for a light switch in a dark room and encountered another hand instead. She steps back and the walls grow momentarily taller, the ceiling higher, the floors longer. It is one thing, meeting Bobby at a restaurant—and it is another, allowing him into her home.

"Knock, knock," he says and steps inside without invitation. Without hesitation. Her husband is defined by hesitation.

"What are you doing here?" She feels a scuttling in her guts, some mixture of guilt and excitement that feels like bugs eating their way through her.

He plants the rose in her hand. "I was in the neighborhood. I thought we'd celebrate."

"What?"

"Echo Canyon. We break ground tomorrow. Big day. Big deal. Hey, do you have any wine?" He explained how thirsty he was—so thirsty—from speaking to Tom all day.

"Um."

"Or a beer? I'm not picky. Something. I'm just thirsty as hell."

"All right. I guess." She walks into the kitchen, walking sideways, so that she can keep an eye on him. At the sink she fills a glass with water and drops the rose in it and it totters for a moment as if it will tip over. "He was with you in the car the other day?"

"Tom. Yes. At the train crossing. You looked amazing by the way. I wanted to kick him right out the door so that you could take his place and we could just drive and drive and drive."

She crosses her arms and asks about Tom. She still doesn't get it, what he was saying the other day about them being friends, partners. "That doesn't make any sense."

She fixes him a drink—finding a bottle of Chardonnay from Sokol Blosser in the back of the fridge, uncorking it with a pop—and he wanders around the house, rotating a vase of dried flowers, peering into a cupboard, picking up a book and setting it down, all the while chatting, telling her how this all started when the governor and Warm Springs tribal council signed the compact for Cascade Locks Resort and Casino. Tom asked, after a few years of trying to negotiate the legal circuit, for Bobby's help and he found himself always on the phone with lawyers. The tribe needed a fee-to-trust transfer to put in trust twenty-five acres of the sixty-acre site for gaming activities. And then there was Section 20 of the Indian Gaming Regulatory Act, which required the secretary of the interior to determine whether the resort would (a) be in the tribe's best interest and (b) not be damaging to the surrounding communities, which was particularly difficult to get past, since Hood River had nothing good to say about casinos and the type of people they would attract to their hamlet of apple orchards and fir-clustered hillsides.

And then there were complications, due to the proximity to the river, concerning site drainage and utilities. And then they had to figure out how to alter the transportation routes to access to the development, which would involve a new interchange off I-84. And on and on it went, so complicated that his head felt as if it might cave under the weight of it all.

After phone calls and dinners with lobbyists and lawyers and contractors and bureaucrats and politicians, after a fraternity brother of Bobby's from Sigma Chi became the new secretary of the interior, they made Cascade Locks happen.

"You did all this for an Indian casino? You got, what? A stake in it?"

"No, baby. I got Echo Canyon."

"What are you talking about?"

This was what he was talking about. Every now and then the Forest Service offers up isolated parcels of federal land in an effort to raise money—and now was such an occasion—in an effort to offset the shrinking revenue of timber sales. The Ochocos were filled with Indian gravesites, with petroglyphs and pictographs etched and smeared onto basalt. The Warm Springs Indians fished and hunted there. The tribe would have first bid at the land and they would take it.

"So I tell Tom not to bid. Or to fuck up the bid. File the paperwork late. Send it to the wrong address. Make it disappear altogether. What, after all, are they ever going to do with that land? Fire an arrow into a deer? Smoke a peace pipe next to the river? They aren't sentimental. It didn't take any arm wrestling. A canyon for a gorge. A golf course for a casino. Tit for tat."

She doesn't feel any sense of scandal, disapproval. There is too much guilt and nervousness roiling inside her to find fault in anyone else. If anything, she feels more vulnerable than ever. Every time she turns around there seems to be one less thing that makes Bend different from anywhere else in the country—and Bobby has a lot to do with that. Just being with him now, she feels a humming in the air, a prickling in her skin, as if she is about to change too, stripped down and built back up, a willful act of reconstruction. She doesn't know whether to want it or not.

He takes the wine glass that she didn't realize she was holding out to him. "Thank you," he says and raises the glass in a toast. "May your blessings outnumber the shamrocks that grow and may trouble avoid you wherever you go."

"Let's hope." She brings her glass to her lips and drinks heavily from it, several long swallows that leave her warm-bellied.

On the counter sits a wooden bowl full of red apples. The apples look like hearts, waxy hearts encased in paraffin. He selects one and tosses it up in the air and catches it. "Let's go to the living room, yeah? Sit down by the fire? Get comfy?" He departs the kitchen—not waiting for her to respond, knowing she will follow. And she does. And when he plops onto the sofa and pats the empty space beside him, she follows him there as well. The fire is snapping and crackling and over the faint smell of wood smoke, she can smell him. He smells like something from a bottle.

"What are you doing here, Bobby?"

He stares at her with some larger predatory perception, a slight flaring of the nostrils. "I told you. I was in the neighborhood."

"But what are you *doing* here? What are we doing?" Her voice sounds sad. She knows how easy it would be to say she doesn't care—she doesn't care about the past, she doesn't care about the future, she doesn't care about her family, she doesn't care about anything except herself, what feels good to her, what she wants *right now.* She deserves that, doesn't she? A little change. A little vacation. But every time she thinks this—I don't care—she feels as though she has swallowed a pebble and now her belly is weighted with stone.

The momentary pleasure isn't worth the aggravation. Right? She is almost certain. When her gaze travels around the room—anywhere but his eyes—and itemizes the framed photos of her family, her son's tennis shoes, a bookmarked novel of her husband's—the same thought teases her: you're not up to this.

Then he rests his glass of wine on the coffee table and puts a hand on her knee. She wants to say no, but the word feels hazy and won't take form on her lips. She crossed an invisible line the other day at lunch—and he crossed another line now when stepping into her house—and she isn't sure if there's any going back.

The television is like a watchful gray eye and she sees in it their half-light reflection.

He brings the apple to his mouth and noisily chews. It makes a crunching sound that sounds like a broken bone. A bit of pulp sticks to the corner of his mouth. His tongue arrows out, grabs it, disappears.

Then a strange noise fills the room. A violent fluttering, a rapid-fire succession of hoots that draws all their attention to the fireplace.

"The hell?" he says.

There is a crumbling rush of soot and the flames dampen briefly. And then a dark shape flutters there—in the middle of the fire—an owl.

Its hoots give way to a panicked screech so awful it makes Bobby drop his apple and bring his hands to his ears. And the owl escapes the fire with a sweep of its wings that sends smoke and cinders in every direction. It circles the room in pained terror, flying around them with its feathers smoldering.

In this panicked moment, when the owl swoops toward Bobby with its claws outstretched, he races from the couch, knocking into the coffee table, knocking over his wine and shattering it into a long dribbling tongue of glass. His voice is somewhere between a whimper and shriek when he says, "Leave me alone! Leave me the fuck alone!" He is hunched over and loping around in circles and swinging his arms feebly at the great bird—and then it noisily flaps down the hallway into some secret corner of the house. Bobby trips over his feet and drops heavily to the floor, and when he does, something falls from his mouth and clatters on the hardwood.

At first Karen thinks it is a chewed hunk of apple, damp and white and sickle shaped. And then she realizes—when Bobby raises his head and looks at her, his mouth arranged in a snarl—that the left side of his mouth appears oddly black. He is missing his teeth. Those square white teeth. He wears a dental plate. He claws it up now and rams it into his mouth and stands up in a hurry. He is panting. His hair is mussed and falling across his face in white tendrils and he runs a hand back through his hair in an effort to neaten it.

Toward the back of the house comes a screech and Bobby looks wildly to the hallway as though certain the owl will return for him. He only glances at Karen before rushing to the door, throwing it open, and running out into the evening.

Karen remains on the couch with her wine glass gripped in her hand. The weird jolt she felt when the owl appeared—a power surge of a jolt—is followed now by a draining sensation. She feels incredibly heavy, barely able to lift herself from the couch and walk with leaden feet to the open door.

Bobby is still there, out in the gloaming, one foot on the bottom step, the other on the short pea-gravel path that will take him to the driveway. He looks, from this vantage, small and old.

He lifts his hand to point at his car. "So I guess I'll—"

"Yeah," she says and closes the door and goes to find a broom to scare the owl from her house.

JUSTIN

Once in camp, Justin pauses only for a moment, and then moves on, having come to a decision: he will take his son to John Day and then return with a warden. He can be there and back within an hour. As he jogs across the meadow, a few hundred yards from the Bronco, he glances up to see that the sun has only just begun to sink from sight, and for a second he watches it, the decreasing brightness of it, and wishes it would stay there, wishes it would remain day, when everything seems a little safer, even if it's not.

And here is the Bronco. The tires are slashed. The windows are smashed in. The hood is thrown back and wires rise crookedly from the engine block like alien weeds. Perhaps, if he flays the wires and reattaches them, the Bronco might come alive with a loud *chuff,* but there is only one spare, and no matter how he bullies the steering wheel, the tires will only spin out and cut half-moon shapes into the cinder road.

They stand arrested by the sight of it—horror struck is the only word—barely crediting what they see. For a moment Justin's mind regresses and he becomes four again. A monster has done this, he feels certain. A bear that is more than a bear. It walks upright and speaks in a guttural voice and hungers for boymeat. It is possessed by the spirit of the forest. It watches them, near and invisible.

And then, when he spots the crushed PBR can gleaming in the grass, his imagination dissolves and he becomes forty again. Of course Seth did this. In his panic, Justin forgot he even existed, but now imagines him clearly, as if he stands next to him: the smile on his face when he swings the crowbar into the windows, when he plunges his knife into the tires, pleasuring in the sound, the crash and hiss orchestrated by an anger that seems to come from nowhere but comes in fact from the outlook of someone who perceives himself to be drowning while others float by comfortably on their pleasure boats. It is an outlook Justin can no longer sympathize with. He wants Seth unemployed, foreclosed upon, shoved out of his hometown by sky-high property taxes. He wants a fluorescent-lit travel plaza cemented over that shitty gas station/bait shop where they first met. He wants this canyon gutted, burned, made into a mall where grandmothers walk every morning in purple jumpsuits.

Justin's heart is beating hard. His hot face feels as if it has been electrified and his mind feels full of damp-winged wasps. He realizes how much the last few days have touched him—so incrementally he has not noticed their cumulative effect until now—with absolute fear.

For one horrible instant, he slips into an imprecise state of mind during which time he fears he might crumple into a heap—suddenly weighed down by fatigue, shock, horror, all of that bad stuff—and rock back and forth and shake his head and scrunch shut his eyes and not speak for a very long time—months, maybe years—and then only with the aid of medication. It seems such an attractive option, compared to the alternative, acknowledging the spasms racking his son's face as he tries to control his emotions.

Tears cover the boy's cheeks. He has his hunting cap off, as if mourning something. And Justin knows that to save his son's life he first has to save his own; he has to keep a lock on his sanity. A black cloud has descended on them and to dispel it he needs to say something, to blow it away with a comforting word or two. "Everything is going to be fine," is the best he can manage.

"Oh." His son's voice sounds uncertain but his features relax and he looks to the top of the canyon as though leaving is now a reasonable possibility. He uses both hands to wipe away his tears. "But the truck is dead."

Justin nods a reluctant yes.

"So what are we going to do?"

That is a question with many branches forking from it. *Will we live?* is one of them. *Will it hurt when I die?* Those are the questions that matter and the answers Justin has to avoid to keep the fear outside and a single-minded courage in.

"Don't worry."

"But what are we going to *do*?" Graham is stuck on these words, their barren possibility. "It's that ghost story Grandpa was telling us, isn't it? That's why this is happening? Because we shouldn't be here? Because they're tearing down the canyon?"

It is a child's response, and Justin loves him for it. Despite all that has happened, he remains a child and carries a child's superstition for how the world throws its good and bad luck at people. "No," Justin says and hugs him tightly, smothering him. When they pull away, Justin does his best to give Graham a hopeful smile and pluck at his shirt collar and tug at his sleeves as much to keep his hands busy as to neaten him. "You going to be all right?"

Graham nods, not favoring Justin with his eyes, but setting his shoulders and his feet so that he appears erect. An impression of being all right.

"Good," Justin says. "That's good. That's how I need you to be. Now let's go back to camp. Let's wait for your grandpa."

Graham fits his cap on his head and starts back to camp and Justin follows him there and adds wood to the smoldering fire until it catches flame. Then he adds another log to chase away with bright orange light the approaching dark.

A thistle grows next to Justin. Without really thinking about it, he pulls it from the earth and shakes the dirt from its roots and thumbs open its clenched flower and mashes the purple crown of spores into a cream. His hands need to do something and his eyes need something else to look at, so he continues to destroy it, peeling the leaves off the stem and letting them fall one by one and pausing only when he notices an egg sac, encased in silk and deposited in that narrow space where the leaf meets the stem so that the bees and the birds cannot disturb it. He makes a clumsy attempt to return the thistle to the crater he has pulled it from, but after a moment it falls over and he leaves it lying there.

A noise makes Justin look up. It comes from nearby, from the woods.

A thud. As much a vibration as a sound, like the blunt end of an ax striking a tree or a bird in full flight hitting a window. A sound that reminds Justin of barriers and the pain of their forceful collision. A warning?

He tries to imagine a happy ending to the day. It isn't easy. His father will either return or he won't. If he doesn't, if he doesn't by midnight, then they will leave and head back up the gravel road until it gives way to asphalt and leads to town. And if his father does return—and wasn't that still a possibility? Wasn't it? Perhaps even with Boo panting beside him—then they would all laugh and slap each other on the back and head off into John Day, where they would stop for burgers and fries drowned in ketchup. Graham would show them the pictures he had taken and they would all agree it had been an adventure, something to bring up ten years from now at Thanksgiving dinner. This is the happy ending he stores in his mind when he goes to the river and fishes around in the rock cairn and withdraws a Pepsi and carries it to his son. "Looks like you need one of these."

Graham takes it and sets it down between his feet.

More noise comes from the nearby forest. At the rustle of motion Graham looks at Justin quickly. He is dirty and red in the face. The panic in his eyes infects Justin, who grabs his rifle and stares dimly into the trees and spots a form of black shadows moving. These become two possums, one chasing the other, both hissing, as they leap from branch to branch and then hurry down a tree trunk to the forest floor and then pause to regard Justin with their black eyes as if to remind him they are not to be feared.

"It's nothing," Justin says and settles back into his seat with his rifle resting on his thighs.

PAUL

He looks out over the river with red-rimmed half-lidded eyes. His fingernails are broken and clotted with dirt from burying the dog. He feels empty, carved out. His heart seems to beat too sluggishly one moment, too hurriedly the next. Several times he had to sit down in the trail, dizzy, with what looked like black flies twirling around the edges of his vision. And now the river seems too, too wide and full of rapids, an impossible distance. He has never believed, not really, not even when waylaid in the hospital, in his own mortality—and the possibility of it these past few hours has finally disturbed his peace of mind. He is like a man who wakes from a nightmare and stares at the room around him in silence, wondering if the threat has passed, if the closet will bang open and reveal a glowing set of yellow eyes.

Walking upriver does not occur to him. Nor does firing his rifle to draw his son to aid him. There is only the riverbank before him. He sees it as if through a tunnel. His mind chugs through a slow series of calculations before he finally shrugs off his backpack and unzips it and pulls out two twenty-foot nylon ropes and fastens them into a sheet bend. His hands are clumsy and his mind foggy, so this takes time. His fingers can't maintain their grip on the rope. He examines his left hand as you would a failed tool you're considering tossing aside. It is red and peppered with bits of dirt and shaking slightly. His fingers look alarmingly swollen. He tries to flex them. They are at a loss. He closes his eyes. There is bile at the back of his throat and he swallows it down.

Around his waist he slowly, slowly tethers one end of the rope in an anchor hitch. Then he walks to a nearby tree and again ties the knot, this time around its trunk. He leans against the tree for a pained, breathless minute, then takes a deep breath, steadying himself, and goes to the river.

He glances over his shoulder, expecting to find the bear shouldering its way out of the woods. And then he enters the water, his boots and then his legs disappearing into it, until the river creeps up to his belly. Normally he finds the cold invigorating, better than a cup of coffee for waking him, but right now he begins to shiver. His pace slows considerably here, in the middle of the river, where the water rolls over white. He winds the rope around his wrists and allows only a little slack, ready for the worst to happen. All around him boulders peer out of the water, their surface as black and slick as sealskin. When his body hitches to the left and stumbles a pace downstream, he tightens his grip on the rope, ready for the river to swallow him up. But he finds his balance by bracing himself against a boulder, hugging it, gasping.

During this short period of time, he feels very alone, the river seeming more like an ocean; the boulder is an island and the surrounding reef is busy with the shadows of sharks and the riverbanks are thick with jungle that camouflage long-tusked boars and colorful, poisonous snakes.

He cannot imagine letting go of the boulder. It is more than his legs, so sluggish and rubbery. It is the ache in his chest, his heart feeling punctured, as if it were deflating. And it is his mind, thick with exhaustion and on the verge of collapse. Everywhere he looks he sees an echo, another hazier version standing next to it. The clouds have an echo. That tree has an echo. The canyon has an echo.

The shivers working through his body finally convince him to release the rock, to push forward, knowing he is growing hypothermic. He staggers forward and when more than halfway across the river his foot slides out from under him. He goes sprawling and slams his knee against a rock and cries out in pain but loses the cry in a garble as water fills his mouth.

The river sweeps him up and drags him several feet before the rope goes taut and he spins and struggles limply against the anchor of it. He thinks he can pull himself from the water, but the current's force is too great. He thinks the rope will swing him toward the shore, but it has caught against a collection of boulders. He tries to find his footing, each time with no success. His feet hang downstream. He can feel the water pulling on his boots and thinks that they might come loose from him and float away like little boats. He knows now what the hooked fish feels. The weight of the water threatens to bend him backward, to snap him in half, against the rope, which has worked its way above his beltline and below his shirt, so that it digs directly into his skin with a burning pressure that matches the feeling in his chest, a combustion working toward a red explosion.

He imagines he can see Justin and Graham on the shore, can see them in flashes interrupted by the gray oblivion of the river. Graham is waving his arms and Justin is rushing into the water to save him. And then Paul heaves himself upward—he makes one last stubborn lunge—reaching for them, his mouth hanging open, his head sidelong like a fish resisting a hook. He reaches for his son.

And then he collapses into the water and the river boils over him for another minute until the sharp-edged boulder bites through the rope and sends his body wheeling downstream like a piece of driftwood or any other part of the forest. Aside from the rope anchored to the tree, you never would have known he was there, as the river continues to gurgle and hiss, hiding beneath its surface snags and rocks and creatures drowned and alive.

JUSTIN

There is a perimeter of light and warmth around the fire and they stick to it. The darkness is like smoke slowly settling over them, a black vapor ever-thickening. The trees begin to look less like trees and more like cloaked wraiths. While Justin sits in the twilight and watches for his father, he feels as though time is slowing, thickening. Seconds feel like minutes, and minutes like hours, and the thing he most wants to happen—for his father to step out of the forest with a wave—won't happen. He wills it to happen and the effect is like willing yourself to sleep—any second now, yes, all right, soon, here it comes—in only making him more twitchy, overcome by a fatigued anger.

His father is out there. Justin shouldn't have let him go. His father had been crying—like a lumbering child—had succumbed to a bracing hug. He had not acted like himself. Justin should have been stronger, louder, should have demanded his father return to camp. He has food and water in his pack, a first-aid kit, but a flashlight? Of course you don't need any of those things if you're dead, Justin thinks and immediately tries to banish the thought by shaking his head and grinding the heels of his hands into his eyes. He can't be. Not dead, not him.

There is too much to think about. There is so much in his head. And all of it bad. At school, when he faced a pile of student papers, a faculty meeting, parent-teacher conferences, a basketball game, he would make a list, write everything down, and then check the items off as he completed them. That always made him feel better, made the chaos more manageable. He wishes he had a piece of paper now. Then he could go over everything.

There is food—they really ought to eat something. Food will help him think, keep his energy levels up. And there is his father, who ought to be back by now but who could not be dead, not like the skeleton out in the woods, not like the dog whose collar was left behind like a warning. There is Seth with his smile and his crowbar. And there is the bear. The bear and Graham. He didn't want to think of them together, not in the same sentence, not in the same canyon, with night closing around them, but there you go, here they are.

As if that weren't enough. What about his wife? Of course his wife, who might or might not be fretting about them right now, glancing at the microwave clock. He has done exactly what she bade him not to do. How long will it take before she calls his mother? And then 9-1-1? No, not Karen. She is too practical for 9-1-1. She won't see this as an emergency, not yet. She will start with the Forest Service—but probably not until ten o'clock and only an answering machine will pick up—and then the John Day police—but only a patrolman will be on duty and after inquiring about their whereabouts he will direct her to the Forest Service. And when she says—in annoyance, more than panic, sharpening her voice—that she already tried them, damn it, the patrolman will chuckle and say not to worry, ma'am, boys will be boys, and sure as shit he can't count the number of times a hunting trip has gone on a day or two longer than planned, when the beer is flowing, when the bucks are hiding in the big pines.

Karen will spend the next few hours pacing through the house, flipping the television on and off, staring into the fridge. And then what? He told her they might not be back until late. She might simply fall asleep. Or she might call 9-1-1, but even then it will take a lot of effort on her part to motivate any sort of action, to convince them anything is out of the ordinary. And even if, by some miracle of persistence, Karen badgers a ranger out of bed and sends him grumbling through the Ochocos in his green truck, it will be dawn before he reaches the canyon and by then the construction crew will have arrived anyway. How long are they from help? A long way. They have a whole night ahead of them. And he doesn't think he can stand another night, not without his father.

Somewhere in the distance an owl hoots—followed by another. Their voices become a strange, sweet music. He imagines his frightened face seen dimly through the evening gloom and tries to harden his expression for the benefit of his son, grim and silent.

"Graham," Justin says. "I've got one for you. Did you know that the Indians believe owls and whip-poor-wills and a few other birds—I can't remember what kind—but did you know they believe owls are vessels that carry souls back and forth between the land of the living and the land of the dead?"

"Are they coming to take us away?" Graham says in a sober voice.

"No," Justin says. "Of course not. I was just saying. . . ." He cannot look his son in the face so he focuses on his feet instead, where a soda can reflects the orange shimmering light of the fire. "Drink your Pepsi, okay?"

Graham nods and takes a sip and uses his knuckles to rub some wakefulness and good feelings into his eyes.

And then comes night. Stars blink to life and Justin studies them. When he was a child, his father frequently pointed out the constellations, their names so strange, like code words that might open a secret door. He tries to remember one of them now, fancying the idea that a great black door would open and they might all step through it—and into his kitchen, where sunlight would stream through the window, warming his skin. The coffeemaker would be burbling on the counter. Bacon would be frying on the stove. NPR would be playing from the faux-antique radio.

But he is still sitting here, staring into the fire. "You're so stupid," he nearly says, "look what you've done," but doesn't.

Instead he says, "What should we do?"

"What should we do?" Graham says. His face tightens into an ugly expression, revealing someone Justin doesn't know. He hurls his Pepsi and it thuds and fizzes somewhere off in the darkness. "You're the dad. You're supposed to know." And then his face melts, becomes soft again. He closes his eyes, his eyelids paper-thin. "I'm scared," he says. "I wish Grandpa were here."

The comment doesn't wound him, but it gives him a shove and his vision shifts, abruptly, laterally. His father is not here. It is up to Justin to make a decision. He feels something inside him growing to fill the space where there was nothing. He tells his son not to worry. He looks around and his mind muscles its way around a plan. He explains it as it comes to him. He will climb up a tree, a tall tree, and see if he can get cell coverage. "And then," he says, "if I can't get a signal, we are going to hike out of here." They aren't going to try. They are going to do it. There is no sense sitting here, he says, like a couple of sitting ducks.

As he carries on in a resolute voice about how they are going to do this and that, he hears a familiar gruffness, passed on from father to son like a baseball glove that doesn't quite fit but carries in its leather the certainty of experience. "Does that sound like a plan?" he says and Graham nods eagerly.

Justin can't decide whether he is being brave or stupid. He unlocks the safety on his rifle and moves out of the firelight, and as he does, he feels as you do when stepping off the sidewalk and into a busy street with cars barreling toward you, their silver grills like gleaming mouths. The clouds open up and the moon takes the sky, brightening his way, but also making him feel exposed. Looking up at it, he remembers the corpse's glass eye and imagines it in the moon's place, floating there and observing him with an uncanny sight that sees clean into his marrow and understands his fear and enjoys it.

All the trees here are amazingly fat and tall—old growths—so far saved from the fires and the loggers, never to be razed—until tomorrow. He walks hurriedly to the tallest, closest one he can find, a ponderosa with an X spray painted on it. Around its roots spreads a carpet of browned needles that crunch beneath his weight. He freezes like an intruder who has disturbed a creaky floorboard. He stands there, listening hard, but the silence hangs unbroken around him.

Before he begins to climb, he briefly concentrates on the X and thinks about how it would feel to be devoured by a saw and smoothed by sandpaper and then hammered into something somewhere, freshly lacquered and etched with pretty designs, renewed, given a second life—yes, he will keep that image, tuck it in his pocket and carry it with him as he tries to make it through this night.

The lowest branch hangs fifteen feet above the ground. He will have to shimmy his way up to it. He shoulders his rifle so that it hangs diagonally across his back. He then essentially leaps onto the tree, wrapping his legs and arms around it in a hug. The bark scrapes against his cheek and his palms, the insides of his wrists. The rifle digs painfully into his spine and he curses, knowing he should have loosened the strap. The only smell is the tang of sap and pine needles. There are small recesses between the scales of bark and he works his fingertips into them, using whatever purchase he can to keep from slipping. He then brings his legs around to the sides of the tree and presses upward until they have straightened out.

His legs and arms are already quivering, their muscles not yet ready to give out, but close. He continues his slow crawl up the trunk, gripping and sliding and grunting and bleeding and sweating until at last the branch appears within reach, only a foot from his head. It is a risk, throwing his arm out to seize it. If his palm is too slippery or if his muscles give out, he will fall to the ground, where he might break an ankle or impotently stare upward, unable to gather the will to climb again.

He tightens his legs around the trunk. His hand rises—trembling—from its place on the trunk and ties his fingers around the branch in a grip so tight his knuckles pop. He feels something crawl over the back of his hand, a spider. His grip almost loosens out of instinct, but he somehow maintains his hold and clenches his bicep, drawing himself upward until he pitches his other arm around the branch. His legs come loose from the trunk and hang dangling in the black air. The muzzle of the rifle nudges the back of his head and he realizes he has forgotten to engage the safety. The possibility of a bullet cutting through his skull makes him freeze for a moment, drawing in a deep breath.

Then he pulls, every muscle in his body straining, until he heaves himself onto the branch, so that his torso hangs on one side, his legs on the other. His shirt has come up and the bark scuffs away his belly hair, leaves the skin there abraded. He tries to breathe, but the breaths will only come in tiny gasps because of the pressure on his stomach. The branches are now clustered thickly all around him. He grabs for one of them and misjudges the distance and almost loses his balance when his hand passes through pine needles and air. The ground seems to swell and shrink beneath him as he teeters on the branch. He stretches out his arm again, this time more carefully, and gets hold of a firm branch and uses it as leverage to pull himself up, bracing his body between the branches in a kind of seated position. The rifle clatters against the tree trunk and with some difficulty he pulls it off and clicks on the safety and then pats the stock as he would a companion who has shared an upsetting experience.

He waits for a minute, waiting for the breath to calm in his chest and the burn to subside in his muscles, and then he peers over at the campfire. Graham is standing up; he is staring in Justin's direction. Justin waves even as he knows Graham probably can't see him. Then he fits the rifle over his shoulder again and begins to climb. Above him the tree seems to rise endlessly. He snakes his way through the branches, constantly pausing to readjust his grip, his footing, anticipating the next rung of his ascent and considering the best path. The moonlight filters through the branches in needlework patterns.

Beneath the canopy there is no wind—the air, motionless—but as he climbs and moves above the darkness of the forest, below the darkness of the sky, the wind gusts, drying and watering his eyes, swaying the tree, carrying the faraway smell of a skunk, or something like it, its odor both sweet and sickening.

Above the treetops, the sky swells around him, incalculably huge and black.

In the distance, the gates of the canyon open up into the desert. There he can see the silhouettes of the Cascades, so small in the distance, their jagged corners and glaciers glowing with moonlight, but otherwise dark. The sight of them brings the same sort of oriented relief a traveler in a strange city experiences when he glances up at the familiar face of the moon.

Below the mountains, he spots tiny universes of light—Bend and Redmond and Prineville—with John Day the closest of them. He clings to the trunk with one hand and pulls off his rifle with the other and carefully arranges himself in a perch to peer through his scope at the silent wilderness of houses, its blocks and buildings lit up and surrounding patches of blackness. He thinks he can discern, in a glimmering shudder of light, headlights moving along the streets and highways, some filing into garages and parking lots, some spreading out into the countryside. There, so far away, so safe and tranquil, is the little world in which he has been living so securely. And there, way off in the distance, he spots a cell phone tower blinking its red warning against low-flying aircraft. But when he pulls his phone out of his pocket and punches it on, the green glow of its screen reads "Searching System." When a minute passes and it still hasn't found a signal, he feels a sick sense of panic. He is off the grid completely—it is as if he has fallen out of time.

From this vantage, the trees seem solid enough to walk on and for a few seconds he seriously considers running across their canopy, journeying away from here in any way he can. He only wants to return to Bend. Things have always been fine and safe in Bend. They will laugh about all of this in Bend.

He nearly falls and then catches himself against a branch, suffering from a terrible case of vertigo, so that he hardly knows where he is, with civilization seeming so close and so far away.

BRIAN

At the time the CSH-Baghdad was the only hospital that could handle level 1 trauma. Seventy-seven beds, three operating rooms, six general surgeons, three orthopedists, two neurosurgeons, two emergency medicine physicians, a vascular surgeon, a radiologist, a psychologist, a neurologist. A cluster of anesthesiologists and nurses. They worked on everyone—from U.S./coalition soldiers to Iraqi soldiers, civilians, and detainees—and they worked on everything—from toothaches to mass casualty events that ripped a body in half or tapped a hole in a skull, as it was with Brian.

Even once he got used to the shock of having a hole in his head, it remained a strange feeling, compounded by the strangeness of his surroundings, a white bed in a white room full of white beds on which lay soldiers blanketed in white bandages. At first, after waking from the red haze of surgery, he wanted to scream, to shut his eyes and refuse to accept his circumstances. That lasted for a few minutes, after which time he was still there and the whiteness and the blood soaking through the whiteness and the pain throbbing in his skull had not disappeared and in the end he just accepted it all because he was lying there and the doctors and the nurses were speaking to him—"Can you tell me what year it is? Can you tell me who the president is? Can you spell the word *dog*?"—and what else could he do except believe this was almost reality?

He was there for two weeks. During this time many men moved in and out of the beds surrounding him, but he remembered one in particular, a Private Mars from Louisiana who had lost his hand when the troop carrier he was riding atop as a gunner slid off a ravine and flipped on top of him.

They lay there, talking, while clear fluids dripped into them and dark fluids dripped out. They talked a lot—constantly, it felt like—because talking felt safe. Safer than being alone with your thoughts. They talked about how thirsty they were and when the nurse would come around again with Cokes and waters. They talked about their fathers, who had both served in Vietnam and who had opposed them enlisting. They talked about why Jif was the superior brand of peanut butter. They talked about college basketball. They talked about how hot Angelina Jolie was and how with lips like that she must give the most incredible blow jobs in the whole world. They only thing they didn't talk about was their injuries.

Until one day when Mars told Brian a story about his grandfather, a WWII vet who had no legs. He was in the Philippines, on the island of Mindoro, when a land mine detonated beneath him. He was left with little below his knees, flaps of skin, chunks of muscle, broken bits of bone. His platoon had lost its medic in a firefight, so they did the best they could. Three men held him down while another sliced through his knees with a knife. Over a fire they heated a machete until it glowed orange. They used it to cauterize the arteries and then applied ointment and a protective plaster from a first-aid kit. They radioed in his coordinates and left him on a nearby beach and a copter picked him up a day later, feverish and with lines of infection creeping up his thighs.

"When I think of that story, I think I'm lucky." When Mars spoke he gestured with his stump and Brian could almost imagine a ghostly set of fingers waving to the room all around them, a room oozing with blood and moans. "We're lucky."

Maybe for the first time Brian feels this way—he feels lucky—as he hurries through the night. Lucky enough to seek Karen out once more. Lucky enough to ignore the hunters who still wander the forest, looking for him. Though the shadows are thick, he still moves carefully, like a soldier in enemy territory, darting from tree to tree, huddling next to a bush now and then to listen to a faraway gunshot. He wears his hair suit and it makes him feel invisible, powerful.

The memory of her touch lingers—so vivid that her hand might as well hold his, pulling him through the woods, toward her. He does not repel her. This is what he keeps coming back to, to the way his injury brought her closer to him and creased her face with sympathy, warmth. It is as though he has discovered some principle of magnets—he does not repel her, he attracts her—and he rushes now to a point of assembly.

By the time he arrives, it is past midnight and her house is as dark as the forest, the windows offering no lamplight or the trembling, watery glow thrown by a television. He pauses where the trees run up to the lawn, listening for traffic along the road. Hearing nothing, he races across the grass to the garage and peers through the window of the side door, making certain that the husband isn't home. In the gloom he spots only one car and then he heads up the steps and into the house, sliding the key in and out of the lock and pushing his way through the door.

Brian stands for a moment in the entryway. Here is the familiar sight of the shoes lined up by the door, the coats hanging from hooks. Here is the familiar smell of pasta and leather and paper. He knows this place. It is beginning to feel like home.

He takes a step forward, into that transitional space, with the hallway extending before him and archways opening to either side of him into the living room and dinette. Out of the corner of his eye he spots the clock on the VCR blinking—red, red, red, like an alarm—never reset after the storm blew through the other day and briefly knocked out the power.

He moves with such slowness—slowly pulling his feet forward, slowly depressing his weight, making sure he doesn't thud his boot against an end table or scare a creak out of the floorboards—when touring the house. He sits down on the couch. He gently touches the needles of a cactus. He stands below a mounted deer and stares into its wide and glassy eyes and reaches up to tap one of them before running his hand along its neck, the fur dry and rough. He peers into the cold cave of the fridge. He runs his hands along the countertops. He picks up a lipstick-stained glass next to the sink. It has a rose in it that he sets aside before bringing the glass to his mouth, tasting it. He pisses in the toilet, sitting down so as not to make a sound. He smells the toothpaste. The boy's room he peers into but does not enter. In the office he shuffles through a pile of papers, holding them up to the moonlight coming through the window, and then stands curiously at the wooden crib before moving to the master bedroom.

He remembers one occasion when his father repeatedly tried and failed to trap a beaver and finally in a rage kicked his way into their dam and clubbed the animals with a baseball bat while they hissed from their dank den. Now, at her doorway, surrounded by the dark, feeling at once weirdly strong and vulnerable, he imagines himself at once the club and the beaver.

A purple bra hangs from the doorknob. He rubs it between his fingers. He can see her shape beneath the blankets. He can hear the slow rhythm of her breathing. He takes a step into the room and notices a clock seeming to blink from the nightstand—but when he turns toward it, the light scuttles away from him, and then away from him farther when he tries to chase it, always at the corner of his eye, a red flashing.

"Oh no," he says to the room. He brings his hand to his forehead and massages the crater there. The flashing deepens in its color. And now he can feel the first of many painful wires twisting down his cheek, his throat, his arm. The headache has snuck up on him. He didn't notice it, tangled up as he was in the forest and then his thoughts—and now it is here, stretching itself, impatient to grow.

As quietly as he can manage, he retreats to the hallway and finds his legs suddenly heavy. He thuds against the wall and grips the doorway to hold himself up. He staggers down the hallway and tries to remember the way but his headache won't allow it. There is only a pulsing red star, eating up everything with its light. He stumbles back into a room, the boy's room. The ceiling glows with paste-on planets and stars, the constellations wheeling in his sight. He wants only to jump into the bed, to pull the covers over his head, but even now he knows better. He goes to utter darkness. He goes to the closet and drags the door shut behind him.

He grimaces and imagines an ugly black lacework working its way along his neck and arms, the tracery of his veins, as his surprise subsides and the throbbing hurt moves fully through him like an electrical current. Only one of his arms seems to work and he uses it to lift himself into a seated position, his back against the closet wall. Then he closes his eyes and lets the pain take him over.

JUSTIN

It takes him a half hour to climb the tree, but not nearly as much time to descend it. The view from his perch has renewed his energy, reminding him that another world exists outside the canyon. He drops through the branches, almost sliding between them, and when he reaches the lower limbs of the pine, he pauses in a crouch and scans the surrounding forest, peering into the dark doorways between trees.

Nothing moves. A stillness has descended upon the canyon. When he drops from his roost, his hand brushes across the spray-painted X and he feels the hard glob of sap that has bubbled from it. He realizes this is the same tree Graham shot—was that yesterday?—yesterday seeming so long ago.

Thirty yards away, in the circle of light thrown by the fire, Graham stands guard, his rifle ready. Everything seems, for the moment, safe. So Justin hurriedly digs a hole with his hand and sets the dirt aside until the bullet casing from yesterday sits in his open palm, and then Graham's, when Justin returns to the fire pit and hands it to him.

"Still there," Justin says. "Just like he said it would be."

This seems to bring Graham some comfort. He smiles a closed-mouth smile and brings the bullet to his mouth and blows on it. "I wish this was a silver bullet," he says. "And I wish I had a wooden stake. And a rosary. And a bazooka."

"It's easy to be full of wishes when you're in a situation like this."

"Did you call?"

Justin wearily shakes his head even as he smiles against the bad news. "No luck."

Graham is still staring at the shell, his eyes dark-circled and his shoulders resting in a fatigued stoop. "So we're going to leave?"

"We'll wait a little longer. I've got a feeling he'll be here any minute."

"How long? How long will we wait?"

"Not long. Until he comes. Just a little longer."

So they sit there, surveying the woods, waiting in aching inactivity. Graham reaches out to take Justin's hand, and the contact feels good, reassuring, a way to fight the canyon, so deep and cold and dark, its towering walls bearing in as if poised to close around them like a mouth.

Justin snatches up another log and tosses it on the fire, a little too roughly, sending a gnat cloud of sparks into the air. The wood is dry and porous and a few seconds later the flames rise up in a gentle roar, playing orange light across the canyon walls and into the darker corners of the forest. Out of which steps the bear.

One minute it wasn't there and the next minute it is, as if a trapdoor has opened in the ceiling of the night, depositing it at the edge of the clearing, twenty yards away. In the heat waves thrown by the fire, the bear shimmers, like something unreal. Before Justin can register his alarm, the bear begins to lumber toward them in a charge. It moves in a rocking way, its enormous triangular head rising and falling, and with each rock it moves alarmingly closer. Justin registers the grotesque hump rising from between its shoulders. Despite the thick coating of fat, its muscles are evident, shuddering beneath its fur like so many animals trapped in a sack.

Justin remembers what Graham said about a grizzly being able to travel one hundred yards in nine seconds. This seems a low estimate as the distance between them vanishes in an instant. There is a wailing sound next to Justin. He only vaguely recognizes it as a scream. Graham is screaming. Justin knows he ought to, too, but can only watch when the bear approaches the perimeter of logs and rises up on its haunches—becoming a broad brown column of fur.

Justin feels so small, and he shrinks down, pulling Graham into him, under him, waiting for a paw to come slashing down on them. But the grizzly turns at the last minute, falling into a four-legged position once again to circle away. Like a semitrailer, its enormous bulk has shifted the air in its passing and for a moment the fire leans sideways before righting itself.

They stand on the side of the fire opposite the bear. Justin has moved in front of Graham. He snatches his rifle and squares his shoulders against a second charge.

When the bear reaches the edge of the forest it again turns to face them. Here it sinks its head and rumbles low, a growl that sounds like the idling of an engine, the machine of which will be their undoing. When it starts forward again, it does so as a trembling curtain of cinnamon-colored fur. They do not scream. They are too enraptured by the sight of it to scream. In his silence Justin registers the force of its stride, every step like the blow of a rubber mallet, like the fierce beating of a heart with chambers as vast as a ballroom.

When it nears the camp, it lifts its paw—its claws long and yellow—swinging it against the log where Graham was sitting. A splintery gash opens up and the log goes rolling into the fire. They leap back just as the log hits the coals and sends a cloud of sparks swirling all around them. The bear again retreats to its earlier position. When it comes at them the third time, Justin knows it is in earnest as it lets out a growl that seems to suck all the light from the air and smear their faces with charcoal.

Only then does he remember the weight of the rifle in his hands. He gets off three shots, but his aim is wild and the bullets tear off into the night. The noise startles the bear. It slows and thrashes its head from side to side as if to bite the bullets from the air. And then releases a roar so powerful that the air seems to tremble. The bear is close enough for Justin to see the saliva swinging from its chops in long ropes.

He holds his rifle out before him, ejects brass, fumblingly reloads the chamber with a bullet from his pocket, and squeezes off another shot in such a hurry that the scope kicks back into his eye and cuts it open. For a second he sees nothing but white—and then a redness through which the world comes back into focus. The bear spins around wildly and heads off into the woods, struck by the bullet, though Justin doesn't know where. Just before disappearing into a dark cluster of pines, it throws a glance over its shoulder. It seems to be trying to send them a message through its obsidian black eyes.

A thin stream of blood runs down Justin's cheek. He wipes at it with his forearm and it smears away red. Already the skin has begun to swell around his eye so that he can see only half-lidded. He looks at Graham: his mouth is a big black O. Otherwise Justin doesn't think he has moved, seemingly fossilized by what he has witnessed.

"You okay?"

Graham rolls his face toward Justin with his eyebrows knit together in confusion, as if he never really believed in the bear until now. An oily film covers his eyes. His tongue works around in his mouth, working something toward the front of it, a curse: "Fucking shit," is what he says. It is the curse of the boy who feels overwhelmed by the world. He wipes at his eyes and makes the sort of face that normally breaks into crying, but doesn't.

From the forest comes a series of grunts and woofs. The noise of sticks snapping. Noises that could be noises heard on any night, or not. A crack. A rustle. The fingers of firelight can only reach so far, and then the imagination takes over. "We better go now."

"Without Grandpa?" Graham says, and then, more softly, "Without him."

A sound rises up and spreads over them like the groaning of the earth itself. The bear. Fifty yards away, maybe closer, maybe farther. The sound of it like a subtle force pushing Justin back, making him want to fire his gun into the darkness.

"We're leaving without him." There. He has said it. He is not saddened because he is beyond sadness; it can come later. Right now there is only room for the need to keep his son safe. He is trying to steady his breath, trying to keep his face from contorting into a mask of anguish—to remain calm—but the fear, this black-spider-scrabbling-out-from-under-his-pillow fear, has found his blood, is in his blood. "Just come on." When he waves his son forward in irritation, his hand looks like a claw savaging the air.

His fear hurries his heart into a fast beat that matches his feet upon the ground. They begin to run, but in the sluggish way you sometimes dream of running, where the ground clings to your boots and the air tangles around your legs and makes you feel as if you are moving in slow motion.

Above all else he feels the fear and then the stress of stumbling over stones and blundering into trees, as they hurry through the meadow and then follow the blur of the logging road with the big lodgepole pines rising above them, with the river hissing behind them, with the darkness swirling around their legs so they hardly know where to put them. All about them gather invisible threats, shadows.

Justin reaches out a hand for Graham so that their fingers twine and they remain together. It is his job to extract the boy from the canyon and he knows he must to do it swiftly, powerfully. They at first run—and then hike when unable to run anymore. Their boots feel full of lead. They breathe in huge sections of air as they ascend the steep grade of the road with the feeling that something is following them. At their backs, Justin cannot help but imagine, the bear capers along, maybe dancing some old bear dance, experiencing a kind of glee at having them so close at hand and bewildered by the dark.

Before them the trees part and make way, but when he glances over his shoulder the branches seem to knot together like so many fingers, giving them no choice but to proceed, no matter how badly he wants to return to the seeming safety of the fire.

In his chest he feels as if dust has gathered in the shape of a heart. That is how tenuous his courage is, so that a single breath could scatter it through his ribs and upon the wind.

When a great, thick flapping of wings announces itself from a nearby tree—no doubt an owl—he cries out, even as he tries to suppress his terror for the sake of his son.

Frogs drum. Crickets chirp. A small creek spills across the road and the moon makes a milky circle on it that they splash through. At one point his son trips and Justin grabs him and drags him along.

Every now and then he pauses—his head cocked, listening—as does his son. Not looking over his shoulder is impossible. Whenever he can, he shoots a brief glance to the forest, to the road behind, expecting a dark shape hastening toward them. But the woods are too black to tell him anything except run, run, run.

Where he moves, his son follows. They are in the grip of the forest. They lurk and watch and run and hide. Instinct has taken over.

When they finally reach the rim of the canyon, Justin hears a low sharp sound beside him, like someone drawing a blade across wood. He stops and leans into the noise and discovers that it comes from his son. He is bent in half, his hands on his knees, struggling to breathe. The air rasps in and out of him. "Where's your inhaler?" Justin says and pats at Graham's jeans, his pockets, trying to find it, finding only wetness as his son has pissed himself in fear.

"I don't—" Graham pauses for a moment to suck in a few breaths. "I don't have it." He sits down in the middle of the road. He does not seem in charge of his breathing, his chest working according to its own will, wheezing the air in and out of him. He brings his hands to his throat as if trying to choke himself.

Justin looks over his shoulder for what must be the thousandth time that day. Nothing moves in the darkness. The road, he thinks, is empty. To follow it back the way they came seems impossibly far—not to mention insane—but so does pursuing it in the opposite direction, through the Ochocos, such a long distance until it first becomes asphalt and then branches into a highway with semis groaning along it.

It is then that he sees, in the blackened distance, the heavy machinery. A skidder. A bulldozer. A backhoe. A payloader. Two front-end loaders. The moon gleams across their windows and brightly lights their metal blades. He grabs Graham by the hand and they stagger toward them—Justin isn't sure why. Perhaps because they seem, all crowded together, like a fortress they can lock themselves away in—or perhaps because they represent what he seeks so desperately—civilization, the very thing that promises to contain and annihilate whatever wildness pursues them.

They situate their bodies against a payloader. Justin sits on the ground, his back to the big tire, and Graham sits between his legs, his back to Justin's chest. With every breath he makes a little growling noise. When Justin hugs him close, he can feel the growls against his own chest. "It's okay," Justin says. "It's okay." Graham's body begins to shiver and twist in a way that reminds Justin of the snake. Even with a hole in its head, he remembers, it continued to turn over and over and craft itself into so many unusual designs. He prodded it with his boot and even picked it up and felt its hard cold muscle alive and dead in his hand. When five minutes passed and it had not stilled, he remembers feeling bothered and wanting to put it underneath a stone so he wouldn't have to look at it or think about it anymore.

Which isn't so different from the way he feels now, holding Graham and whispering *sh* and petting his hair, even as he glances around, wishing he was anywhere else. He tries to forget about his father, about the darkness and the threat that the darkness holds, as he cradles his son and whispers to him and coaches his lungs until so many minutes later he takes a deep, calm breath and Justin says, "Good. That's good."

He can breathe. And if he can breathe, he can live. That is something. In this instant, several images tumble through his head—his wife curled up on a hospital bed with a sodden pad tucked between her legs, his father positioned by the edge of the canyon with a faulty heart beating its ragged beats. The united losses and gains of the past and present stir up a groundswell of emotion that surges through him. He thinks for a moment it might be more than he can handle.

Then his son turns to look at him and Justin can just see his face, a dim oval shape. "Do you hear something?" he asks in a whisper.

He does not. Not at first. Then he strains to open up his ear to every sound in the forest and nearby hears footsteps that sound, very faintly, like shovels digging.

Both of them stand. Justin takes a deep breath to calm himself and the breath is full of the odor of Graham's urine. He remembers how keen a bear's nose is compared to its eyes—making the sharp, tangy smell equivalent to a trail of bread crumbs.

At that moment the clouds close around the moon. There is a time of bewildering darkness. "I can't see anything," Graham says. Justin holds a hand in front of his eyes and can see it only faintly and only when his fingers wiggle. An unseen shaft of heat passes over him—a breath, he feels certain—that sends him reeling back.

"Dad?" Graham says in a panicked voice and Justin says, "I'm here," and the clouds scud away from the moon and its blue light reveals only their frightened faces and the collection of machinery in a clearing edged by trees.

Justin asks Graham if he is ready to go and he says yes, he is. He stares into Justin's eyes with a mixture of fear, daring, and trust that fills Justin with the desire to hold him forever and keep him from harm. Together they step forward, temporarily renewed—until, at the far end of the clearing, a dimly seen shadow comes alive and moves toward them—growing more and more distinct—the broad triangular head, the wetly spiked fur, and the tumbling bulk of the bear.

They stop and so does it, matching their movements. Its shape seems to waver, almost indistinguishable from the woods, its movement like the movement of leaves in a high wind.

Then Justin takes one step forward, and in either ridicule or contest, it matches him, moving into the moonlight, its broad head rising up into a silver-striped hump. Murky eyes come into view and focus on him, like a dim pair of flashlights deep in a cave. It opens its mouth and grumbles in its throaty language. This time he moves back a step and it moves forward another. He remembers Graham's book and studies its ears. They are horribly small.

Graham makes a whimpering noise and the bear retreats, blurring into the shadows. From behind the tractors Justin hears its labored breathing and the thud of its weight, its footsteps, at measured intervals. He pushes his son against the giant tire of a backhoe and tells him not to move, to keep his eyes and his ears sharp. The wind pauses and an important stillness descends upon the forest. The air seems almost to hum at a frequency he cannot hear but feels.

Then, only ten feet away, a woof announces a shape materializing out of the darkness. The bear has circled around them. Near the edge of the cliff, with the expanse of the canyon behind it, it regards them. The silver stripe along its back glows in the moonlight.

The bear lowers its body a few inches, as if readying to spring. Then comes a whooshing noise as its lungs swell, the breath before the roar. Justin lifts his rifle to his shoulder and squints down the line of it, hesitating at the trigger when the bear takes two shambling steps forward and unhinges its jaw. Thunder comes. Justin feels the air shake, just barely, like when you grip a train track, a trembling.

He suffers from the sense of detachment sometimes experienced in the classroom. He feels as if he is floating away from his body and watching everything from the outside, from someplace remote, separate from the horror of it all. He understands how fragile the whole situation is, how if he moves too fast or shoots too far to the right, the bear will lope toward them and crack open their skulls with its jaws.

Then comes a gunshot that drags him back into reality—the low, flat *crack* shocking him so much he drops his rifle. Because he has not fired. He has not felt the kick, as powerful as a horse's hoof, against his shoulder. The gunshot has come from beside him, from his son, who has stepped away from the backhoe and compressed the trigger of his rifle. Flame seems to jump from the end of its barrel. And in the brief yellow light, while the noise of the gunshot widens around them, the bear staggers. The bullet has zipped past its snarling teeth, over its lolling tongue, and into the shadows of its throat. The bear collapses into a heap, maybe ten feet away, thrashing its head and coughing as though it has swallowed a bee.

Justin does not have time to pick up his rifle. He does not have time to think. He only has time to acknowledge this heart-drumming, bladder-bursting fear as he breaks from his trance and hurries forward to intercept his son.

"Quick," he says when he grabs Graham by the arm and drags him—where?—into the night again. He goes one way, and then another, and then the backhoe is before them, only a few feet away. He pulls himself up by the handrail, and then his son, both of them balanced on the small metal step. He yanks at the glass door of the cab. It swings open. They crawl inside, Justin on the seat, Graham on his lap. They are a few feet off the ground and surrounded by glass. He can only hope that the bear cannot find them here, if they remain still and quiet.

But at that very moment it rouses itself into a four-legged stance to consider them, looking right at them. Its tongue hangs from its mouth and blood drains off it, making what looks like a steadily growing shadow on the ground. The glass of the cab is thin and Justin can hear the growl, the bubbling sound beneath it.

Justin reaches for the ignition and finds it empty. He yanks down the sunshade and the key falls to the floor and he pushes Graham off his lap and reaches around in the dark space between his feet and claws up the key and shoves it into the ignition and looks out the window to see the bear lumbering toward them.

He cranks the ignition and the engine comes to life with a roar. He has operated heavy equipment before, working for his father. The light is dim and the controls somewhat different from what he's used to, but he figures out the boom, the dipper, the bucket. He disengages the safety locks and jams down the stick and the backhoe comes to life, rotating, swinging the boom, the bucket, like a scorpion's tail.

Something has come loose inside him. Rage. He is in a trance of rage. He feels it expand inside his body, filling him up, pushing against his joints, his skin. It finds an exit through a scream so feral it seems to belong to someone else, separate from what he is capable of, powerful. There is a kind of joy that joins his craze, a heightened thrill.

The grizzly rises up on its haunches just as the bucket hits it—the backhoe shuddering—the bear staggering back and teetering at the edge of the cliff, grappling with the dark air, swinging its arms madly in a vain attempt to find some purchase. And then it is gone.

He imagines the wind roaring in its ears. He imagines its enormous body turning over and over again in the air, as the bear plummets toward the bottom of the canyon, so that the moon in the sky is visible one moment and the moon reflected in the fast-approaching river the next.

He imagines all of that soft fur seeming suddenly to gather into a fist and the great snap of its spine breaking against the water. He imagines the water carrying it away, a great shape vanishing into nothingness.

Maybe a minute passes before he cancels the ignition and pulls his son again into his lap and wraps his arms around him in a crushing hug. They remain there for a long time. They remain there—in and out of sleep—until the darkness, like a curtain, slowly lifts and the sun washes away the stars and colors the canyon red, a color that to his agonized imagination looks like blood.

BRIAN

Brian wakes to a high-pitched murmur—a voice, he realizes, a voice at the edge of panic. Not from a television or radio, and not from some pissed-off Sunni throwing up his arms and yanking at his beard and hurling a shoe—though foggily he considers all these possibilities—but from the woman, Karen. In the dark, he is sitting upright, his knees tucked against his chest and his arms hugged around his legs, a ball. Who am I? he thinks. No, not who—that's not the word. *Where* is what he means. His mind is so far gone he cannot find the right words. Where am I?

For some time his eyes have been open, but it isn't until her voice rises in volume—"Are you listening to me? Do you hear the words that are coming out of my mouth?"—that he blinks away the last of his dreams and notices the clothes hanging dimly all around him and understands where he is and feels a wretched panic. He startles forward, through the vine-like tangle of pant legs, toward the bars of light leaking through the closet doors. The sudden movement brings with it dizziness and a starfish-shaped throbbing in his forehead that tentacles its way into his teeth and down his arm into his fingers. He mouth tastes like metal. His tongue is like a dried-up slug. His skin, enveloped so long in fur, feels gluey and raw. His crotch is sopping wet and he can smell piss—he has pissed himself. He takes a deep breath and waits for the pain to pass before pressing his eyes to an open slat and peering into the bedroom.

Sunlight is filtering in the window. The room is empty. The migraine knocked him out all night, he realizes. Sometimes this happens; hours will pass in a fog of pain. And now she is awake and maybe the husband and the boy are home. And now he is trapped.

His eyes go to the open doorway, where he hears and feels the thud of footsteps. Karen walks by, and then walks by again, pacing. She is wearing sweatpants and a white T-shirt. Her hair is pulled back in a ponytail and a phone is pressed to her ear. "I know they're all right—you already said that—but I want to talk to them. Why can't I talk to them?" Her free arm cuts the air as if she is trying to stab something with it. She is gone for a few seconds and then flashes by the doorway again. "When will they be released? When can they come home?" She sighs heavily on her way to the kitchen. She continues to talk but her words are distant and garbled, lost to him.

He studies the room. The bed across from him has a Star Wars comforter. The dresser in the corner has action figures marching across it. The bookshelf is crowded with fantasy and sci-fi novels. It looks a little like his room, he sadly realizes. When he shifts his position, he hears the squelch of his piss-soaked pants and the sound makes his face scrunch up, makes him want to weep at his pathetic condition. He is pathetic. He feels revulsion for himself.

He can dream all he wants about making someone his but in truth he does not know how to. He has only slept with a handful of women and all of them turned him away after a few days. There was always a good-bye for him and in some deep part of his mind he has already realized that this is good-bye.

His hidden nature has been suddenly revealed, as it is with those 3-D books he owned as a child, pages full of seemingly random patterns that disguised a picture—a skull, a train, a flock of birds frozen in flight—exposed once you let your eyes go out of focus. He is a beast. That is what he is. Just look at him. He holds out his arms as evidence. He is like some beastly toy passed down through a family, handled roughly, ripped apart and sewn back together over and over again, finally ending up in the back of some closet, forgotten and collecting dust.

The engine of hunger that brought him here quits. He puts his hands to his eyes and hides in the darkness he creates. He wants to leave, wants to leave right now, but what else waits for him? Where will he go and what will he look forward to there? He wishes he could crawl into the wall, behind the Sheetrock, among the studs, where he could shove puffs of insulation into his eyes and ears, where he could disappear for the rest of time.

In a blank state of mind, no longer thinking about all the things he might have done or all the things he might do, thinking only about what he sees with his eyes open or shut—the color black—he waits until he hears water running—she has started the shower—and then drags himself from the closet.

His headache still tolls against the side of his skull when he pauses in the hallway. To his right waits the front door—to his left, the master bedroom, the master bath, the shower, her. He goes one way and then changes his mind and goes the other, laying his feet down as softly as he can, testing the hardwood before depressing his weight on it, one deliberate step after another, making his soundless trail down the hallway.

Her clothes are scattered across the floor of the room, a trail that leads to the open doorway of the bathroom. Steam escapes from it, white tendrils of steam that grope the air and beckon him forward. Straight ahead, through the clear plastic curtain, he sees her—her nakedness fogged over, indistinct, like something out of a dream.

For a moment he stands there and as he lingers imagines that if he just stays long enough, if he studies her body hard enough, if he wishes desperately enough for his hair in the drain and his magazines by the toilet and his blue-handled toothbrush at the sink, then that life might take form.

There is a small blinking blackness at the corner of his eye, like the pulse of a cursor on a computer screen. He turns his head to look for it and finds only the emptiness of the hallway stretching to the front door. He remembers how not long ago he hunched on the other side of it and picked at the lock, picked his way into her life. He walks toward it now, and then through it, into the painful brightness of the day, with the knowledge that looking inside yourself is a little like looking inside a lock—you find darkness and a maze of confusion.

Away. That is where he wants to go. Deep into the woods, far from the glow of streetlamps and television sets, the gaze of human eyes. Imagining the spaciousness of the forest makes him feel calmer, more certain of himself, his ability to live.

When he sets off into the trees, when he lurches forward, staying low to the ground, using his hands as well as his feet to guide him, away from his house, away from Bend, he becomes the woods, which means he doesn't have to be anything else, invisible, gone.

EPILOGUE

Today Echo Canyon hosts a party to celebrate its opening, nearly two years after they broke ground. Justin has traded in his Subaru for an F-10 pickup and he drives it there, along the winding road through the Ochocos, so familiar except for the black crosses of telephone poles that stagger their way into the canyon with low-slung wires hanging between them. In the passenger seat sits his father.

They never found the bear, but they found him. A mile downriver. Soaked, hypothermic, sprawled out in the mud of the bank. A stroke. It had laid him to waste, made him into a thing only half alive.

A part of Justin can't stand to think of his father as he is now, limp and doughy, with a bit of drool sliding from his mouth, one of his eyes lazy and always rolling away white as if to investigate something in his skull.

And another part of him feels serene, relieved, maybe even a little triumphant.

An ironwork gate—its metal cut into silhouettes of quail and moose and trees—hangs at the front entrance, and when he passes through it, the luxury cabins begin, each set back from the road on a one-acre wooded lot.

"Here we are," Justin says and in response his father says nothing, has said nothing for more than two years except to moan or smack his tongue around wetly. His body, strapped in place by the seat belt, leans with every turn of the road. His face is like one appearing on a milk carton: lost.

The freshly paved road dips down into the canyon whose floor has been swept clean of trees and carpeted with fairways and putting greens, their green an unnatural shade, like something sold in a bottle. Nylon flags flutter in the breeze, their tips pointing downwind, pointing the way past so many sand bunkers and water hazards rimmed by cattails, until he finally reaches the first tee, and rising up next to it, the lodge.

It is four stories and stretches the length of a football field, a veritable castle of iron and timber that took hundreds of men and days to complete. Since the stroke, his father's company has dissolved, along with its contract with Bobby Fremont. Justin wonders how the lodge would have looked if his father had built it. Likely wilder, more splintery and rough-hewn.

Smoke curls from a river-rock chimney and then the wind flattens it out and spreads it into a hazy gray layer. He parks in a lot full of cars. From the back of the pickup he pulls a wheelchair and locks its brakes and opens the passenger door and unbuckles his father and says, "Okay, Dad. Down we go."

His father breathes with a sort of wounded rasp. One of his eyes is closed and his mouth is open and Justin hugs him gently, as if afraid he might break, and then lifts him out of the truck. In his arms his father feels like nothing, like sticks wrapped in soft parchment. He lowers him into the wheelchair and buckles him in and touches his hair, neatening it. His father's good eye regards him severely—an ember in a dying fire. Justin smiles at him. It's a curious smile, at once comforting and contemptuous.

They follow a shale pathway that leads through a wildflower garden that runs up against a vast lava-rock patio busy with Adirondack chairs.

At the entryway of the lodge, oaken double doors reach ten feet in height and carry etchings of mountains and forests and an eagle backlit by the sun. They open up into the reception area, where the ceiling rises to the full height of the lodge. Here a wall of segmented windows looks out onto the nearby river, the South Fork, its waters humming along cold and black and streaked yellow from the setting sun. A wooden walking bridge makes an arch over it. You can enjoy the view from one of many Navajo-patterned couches with potted plants set between them. Everything here is costly, the thousand little touches to make it perfect, from the curved wooden staircases that glow like honey, to the ironwork railings, to the carved hutch in the corner that features pottery by Native artists, and so on. There is a pro shop to his left, and to his right, a massive fireplace that crackles as he pushes his father past it, into the reception hall.

Two dozen long walnut tables are staggered across its length. The tables have been set for dinner and the plates are thin and silver and will soon carry steaks and roasted asparagus and mashed potatoes drowned in white gravy. Elk-horn chandeliers hang over each of them, their light revealing the many dozens of fancily dressed men and women milling about with wine goblets and ale mugs in their hands. A jazz band plays on a temporary stage erected at the far side of the hall.

It isn't hard to spot Bobby Fremont. A flurry of movement surrounds him wherever he goes, shaking hands and clapping people on the back and laughing at their jokes and his own. Justin watches him approach a big man with a face like a dried creek bed, Tom Bear Claws.

He is wearing cowboy boots polished to a shine, blue jeans with a crease ironed into them, and a blazer over a white collared shirt. His plaited braid reaches halfway down his back. His rings and his gold tooth catch the light. He shakes hands with Fremont. He smiles broadly. As he should. For years he has been pushing the construction of, and a consortium of lenders for, an off-reservation casino. A few months ago, the *Bend Bulletin* reported that the Cascade Locks is at last under construction, with plans to open by the new year. Fremont provided a good chunk of financing, which will have a projected 40 percent return every year. For the first time in Oregon history, with governor approval, there will be an off-rez casino. Justin remembers clearly the grotto full of rock art; it is clear now why the Indians gave up Echo Canyon with only the pretense of a fight.

A minute later Fremont moves on to chat with another gaggle of donors, abandoning Bear Claws, whose eyes meet Justin's across the room. Bear Claws's gaze drops to Justin's father and his smile fades. He gives a nod and Justin returns the gesture. They have not spoken, they have not even been in a room together, as far as Justin can recall, since that time at City Hall when Bear Claws and his father grappled with each other. A waiter walks by carrying aloft a tray of champagne. Justin grabs one and brings it to his lips like an antidote to the gathering dusk outside.

He tries to imagine his father out of his wheelchair, standing among all these suits, shaking hands and making small talk, and can't. He wouldn't want to be here; Justin won't hold him hostage. He pushes his father from the hall to the foyer, where Justin runs his hands across the polished wood of the front desk. On it sits a cut-glass vase from which lilies lean palely. And on the wall behind it hangs an oil painting of bears. There are a half dozen of them lumbering along a browned hillside. The air above them is an October gray, a parking-garage gray, anticipating the onset of winter. At first glance the scene appears serene. Then he looks closer. An aspen in the foreground seems to throw up its arms in terror. The undersides of its leaves glimmer with a murky light and rattle as the wind passes through them. And the bears, their fur seems to be moving, shimmering like windblown wheat. Their eyes are wild and they look like they are going to crawl out of the frame and into the room and eat Justin to fatten themselves up for the cold months ahead.

He leaves the lodge, pushing his father, whose body and wheelchair shudder along a cinder path that takes them to the first tee. The wheels of the chair whisper on the grass when he shoves his father up the rise and pauses there. The breeze plays across his face and carries a different smell to it, as if the earth has been tilled and turned. Above him the sky is darkening and clouds glimmer like pearls in the purple distance.

He gives a pretend swing of a club and then follows his invisible ball down the blue-green softness of the fairway, maybe fifty yards, and then pauses. This is where the tree was, he thinks. With his toe he traces an X in the grass to match the X spray painted on the tree near where he last spent time with his father before he was rendered mute and lame. A place that had once been so dark and strange and wild to him is now a place of friendly sunsets and fresh-cut grass and jazz bands and gold watches.

From behind him comes a voice. "There's a monster in those woods," it says.

Justin turns to find Bobby walking toward him. He is smiling and pointing with the flute of champagne he carries. "Just a bear, I'm sure. People have been talking about it. It hides in the trees, just off the ninth hole. Hairy. Some say Sasquatch." He laughs at this. "When people park their golf carts, when they pull out their putters to putt, sometimes the thing sneaks over and steals whatever food or beer they have on them. Can you believe that shit?" Beneath his white-toothed smile and gym-built shoulders is a terrible dog-like presence, oily and rank, pressing up against you, always hungry and wanting to either hump your leg or bite your neck.

"I hate bears," Justin says.

"Yeah," he says. "Yeah, I imagine you do." He lets loose a sigh that smells like Dentyne and alcohol. And then his gaze drops to Paul, who is breathing heavily through his nose and observing Bobby with his one good eye.

"Can you hear me, Paul?" Bobby says and his tongue plays his gum from one side of his mouth to the other. "Pauly boy?" His voice louder now, almost yelling. "You like what we did with the place, Paul?" He sweeps his hand across the length of the canyon as if speaking of a re-decorated bathroom. "We sure could have used your help." As always his smile has a way of lingering several beats too long. He looks at Justin when he says, "Can he even hear me?"

"Yeah."

"He can understand me?"

"I think so. Other people aren't so sure, but I think so."

"Huh." He cocks his head and studies Paul a moment longer. "Shame." Then he drains his glass and says, "Anyway. How's Karen?"

"Karen?" Justin is surprised he even knows her name. "She's pretty good. We're pretty good actually."

"Is that right?"

"Yeah. We're doing really good." And they are. There are bad days. But there are more good days, when they stare across the pillows at each other and run their hands across each other's faces, tracing the line of a nose, the curve of a chin, as if they forgot the shape of love and are trying, carefully, to remember.

"That's good."

"It is."

"Good," Bobby says, with seemingly nothing in his voice, not enthusiasm, nor questioning, just volume to carry the words. He pats Justin on the shoulder and lets his hand rest there. "Okay then. Just wanted to say hello. Now it's time for me to disappear." He massages Justin's shoulder. "Always nice seeing you. Come inside, join the party."

"In a little bit."

A band of crows flies by, gabbing as they pass over Justin to roost in the high branches of a tree. Before vanishing, their shadows play across the wide expanse of green grass and he thinks about the innumerable hands and nails and trees that have built this human reef and of the forest that has been peeled away to make room for it. He thinks about how the canyon was once alive and powerful, no longer. That part of it has been chopped down and dug up and seeded and fertilized and mowed, all the wildness conquered and gone, so that men—the biggest animal—might live and play.

About this he feels mixed up. He knows the beauty of the development comes from the ruins of the wilderness, but in those ruins, as in the ruins of his father, he finds some peculiar satisfaction. He still wakes up sometimes believing he is back in the woods: his heap of laundry is a boulder, his cedar chest a stump, his closet a cave that hides some creature hungry for him. He calms his racing pulse—he feels a little bigger, stronger—by imagining the trees sawed down to stumps to make room for sunlight and green grass.

With his sleeve he wipes the drool from his father's mouth. "What do you think, Dad?" he says and takes in the basalt walls, the way the rock lifts and arcs around him. His father stiffens and moans and swings an arm clumsily before going still again, his eye trained on the sky, where the light is fading. Justin says, "Time to go home," but before he grabs the handles of the wheelchair, before he turns them back to the lodge, he takes one final look at the forest that borders the fairway as if searching for something among the trees, the wild remains of his father, maybe all three of them, still out there somewhere, huddled around a campfire or loping along a darkened trail.

ACKNOWLEDGMENTS

Thanks—a million times over—to Graywolf. This novel went though the editorial wringer—and its evolution from first to final draft was truly a collaborative process. Thanks for your patience, your thoughtfulness, and your support. I'm so damn lucky to be part of the pack.

Thanks to Katherine Fausset, my first reader, my first line of defense, my pal, and my advocate.

Thanks so much to Alison Granucci and Ofer Ziv at Blue Flower Arts.

Thanks to the Whiting Foundation for the generous support that helped me complete this manuscript. Thanks also to the Center for Excellence in the Arts and Humanities and the mini-grant program at Iowa State University.

Thanks to Dean Bakopoulos, my boozing buddy, my cross-eyed colleague, my partner in crime. We'll always have Murfreesboro. To Bret Anthony Johnston and Paul Yoon and Laura van den Berg and Josh Weil. To Helen Schulman and Peter Straub. Thanks to James Ponsoldt for his friendship and passion and our storytelling alliance. Thanks to Danica Novgorodoff for her extraordinary artwork and collaboration.

Thanks to Debra Marquart, Steve Pett, Mary Swander, David Zimmerman, Barbara Hass, Charlie Kostelnick, Dave Roberts, Linda Shenk, and all of my colleagues at Iowa State for their support and for hiring me despite my ugliness and crabbiness and half-baked talent. Thanks also to Shelley Washburn and my colleagues at the low-residency program at Pacific University. And thanks to all of my students, too, for their hunger and eagerness and inspiring talent.

Thanks to Nat Rich and Philip Gourevitch at the *Paris Review*—and thanks to Tyler Cabot and Tom Chiarella and David Granger at *Esquire*—

and Kevin Larimer at *Poets & Writers*—for their continued support of my work. Thanks to *Amazing Stories* and *American Short Fiction*—in which sections of this novel appeared in different forms.

Thanks to Dan Levine for his friendship and his early comments on the manuscript. And for jumping out of a plane with me. Thanks to Abi and Jeremy Solin, Jeremy Chamberlin, Ron Mitchell, Dan Wickett, Steve Gillis, Matt Bell, Alan Heathcock, Oliver Tatom, Jim Boggs, Becky Broderick, Ellen Waterston. Thanks to Michael Collier and the staff at the Bread Loaf Writers' Conference.

Thanks to my parents, Peter and Susan, and my sister, Jen, for their love and support. To my uncle Dave and aunt Cynthia. To my in-laws, Lynn and Dave, and all the rest of the Dummer and Spielman clans.

The biggest thanks of all goes to my beautiful wife, Lisa, who told me—so many years ago—"You should be a writer." To which I replied, "Okay." That's why this book, why all the books, are dedicated to you, Chief.

A GRAYWOLF PRESS READING GROUP GUIDE

THE WILDING

A Novel by

Benjamin Percy

An Interview with Benjamin Percy

A longer version of following interview originally appeared on Powells.com. Reprinted and edited with permission. Read the entire interview at www.powells.com/reader/interviews.

Jill Owens is the marketing coordinator at Powell's Books in Portland, Oregon.

Jill Owens: As I was reading *The Wilding,* I remembered that it grew to some extent out of the story "The Woods" in *Refresh, Refresh.* But I didn't realize until I went back to reread *Refresh, Refresh* how almost all of the stories lent elements to it in one way or another. How did *The Wilding* evolve in that way?

Benjamin Percy: My father once said to me that the problem with my stories was they were too short. That began to make sense years later when "The Woods" became stuck in my maw. I couldn't let it go. It felt as though the story wasn't complete yet, so I started to turn it over and over in my head, polishing it like a stone, and eventually figured out a way to make it into a novel.

That novel came first as a single-track, first-person narrative, which my publisher, Graywolf, liked. They bought it, but with some concessions. They said that it wasn't yet a novel—it was a "shnovel," sort of like a long short story.

Fiona McCrae, my editor, said that I should switch it from first person to third person, and in doing so, with the freedom of four different characters, create five interlocking plot lines. I set to work, and it took me a strenuous year to put forward that next draft. Fiona read it and said, "Great. Fantastic. But two of these plot lines aren't really working for us, and we want a female perspective."

I went back to work again, and that's the draft that went to the printer. It's been a long revisionary process, that collaborative process. I'm very grateful to Graywolf for helping me figure out how to write a novel, because I had been for so long in short-story mode. I had punched out four failed novels prior to this one, and the failure often came from structure, from me not understanding the structural causality that has to go into a novel, and the thematic sweep that needs to inform it.

For the first time, it clicked, and it took somebody else to shove me in that direction. And now, bizarrely, all I do is think in novelistic terms. It's hard for me to write a short story.

Jill: I also didn't realize until I went back and reread *Refresh, Refresh,* that "wilding" was a term coined during a particularly bad time in Central Park when several brutal rapes took place. How did you think about the title of the new novel?

Ben: Well, the novel is in so many ways about animalistic impulses. Every character is struggling with this inner wilding, and in some cases it boils over. It manifests itself most obviously in the character of Brian, who in donning this hair suit becomes almost lycanthropic. Then there are more subtle examples such as with Karen, where she's stepping outside the boundaries of marriage and wrestling with sexual impulses that might lead her away from her family.

This is an idea that parallels some of what we see in James Dickey's *Deliverance.* This year marks the fortieth anniversary of that novel, and it's one of the most important books in my library. I modeled *The Wilding* in many ways after it. If you look at *Deliverance,* it's one of the central themes that Dickey is trying to explore as well.

I didn't set out to write about animal instinct. I didn't set out to write about the clash between wilderness and civilization. I never set out with a theme in my mind. I begin with images in mind, with characters in mind, and the themes rise up organically. It's at first an instinctual process for me, and then it becomes more intellectual as I go through draft after draft. Dickey's *Deliverance* and its furry, toothy core became kind of a model for this work.

Jill: That's a great phrase. I love the scene where Justin and his father are literally throwing deer organs at each other during their mock fight. That's about as animalistic, in a way, as you can get.

Ben: That's one of the few scenes of levity, where hopefully you can crack a smile even though the circumstances are a little bit disgusting.

Jill: Yes, definitely, and in some ways, as a reader you need to at that point. The relationships between Justin and his father and his son are the meat of the book, in many ways. So the book brought up a lot of questions in my mind about what role genetics and then culture plays, and what is determined by some other innate force. How much do you think their differences are generational versus based in personality?

Ben: That's something I've thought about a lot, even just with my own family. My grandfather was an incredibly powerful personality, someone who physically and emotionally dominated every room he was in.

My father, too, is a powerful personality, although he has almost no words. He's one of the most intelligent people I've ever met, and he has no words. He's silent—he's almost Vulcan—and incredibly logical and not driven by emotion in the way my grandfather was. It's almost as though he's trying to model himself apart from the man who tried so desperately to control him, to mold him.

Then I look at myself, and at my son, and I wonder about behavioral patterns and the way that they're passed along from generation to generation.

One of the things that scares me about my family is the way that we're all alone. It's a Percy male trait that you end up in a kind of hermetic existence. You end up not getting close to too many people. My father and my grandfather didn't really have friends. I've made a concerted effort to try to fight against that.

I think you see some of these things at work in the novel, some of these things I'm struggling with myself, the way that there's this Darwinian line-up between Graham, Justin, and Paul—the grandson, father, and grandfather.

Paul, the grandfather, is a menace, and he is constantly bullying his son, and pitting his grandson against his son due to his disappointment in how Justin has turned out. Justin's physically slight. He is a teacher. He doesn't use his hands for a living. He doesn't find himself out in the woods often unless Paul is responsible for dragging him along. So Paul is trying to make another son for himself in Graham.

These issues are especially interesting to me now that I'm a father, and I'm trying to take care as often as I can in the way that I present myself to my son and the way I try to control his behavioral patterns—because some things are obviously inherited, from big ears to bad tempers. But other things, I know, are ingrained through training.

Jill: The Iraq wars are a focus in this new book obviously, and also in a lot of your stories. What's your experience been with those wars?

Ben: Well, I have friends and family who are in the service, but the initial interest came from reading so many articles about the war, watching so many news programs. In 2005, when I wrote *Refresh, Refresh,* I had read no fiction about the wars yet.

So I sat down with the express purpose of trying to tackle what was going on over there. But I knew that I couldn't necessarily, with any credibility, write about the streets of Baghdad. So I chose to write about the battleground at home. Even when the war doesn't play a central role in the story, as it does in "Refresh, Refresh" and "Somebody Is Going to Have to Pay for This" and "Meltdown" and *The Wilding,* even when the war is only at the margins of the story, I think that it comes back to something that Barry Lopez once said to me: writers are servants of memory. If you're writing about characters that live in this present world, it seems to me that in some capacity you have to acknowledge the war, even if it's only the state of fearfulness and anxiety that we live in.

Part of writing about the war has to do with the zeitgeist. But another part has to do with the fact that you can pick up a newspaper and see on the front page articles about Paris Hilton and Britney Spears, but you see nothing about the war until you flip to page seven. And there it is, in a sidebar column that is overwhelmed by the Younkers underwear ad alongside it.

So I think it's important also to remind people of what's going on, to force them to engage with it. But not in a really overt way, not in a way that says, "Here's how you should feel about the war in Iraq." I'm never trying to write an editorial. I'm never trying to write something with an Afterschool Special message attached to it. I've always distrusted that kind of partisan fiction. I'm not trying to say war is good or war is bad, but *here is war.* Here's its effect on us.

Jill: There are elements of horror in some of your stories, and definitely in *The Wilding,* too. How do you think about those elements in your work?

Ben: I've always been obsessed with horror. I can remember distinctly when I was in first grade, in the corner of the elementary school's library I pulled off a shelf *The Universal Book of Horror,* or *The Universal Book of Monsters.* I was looking through it and stopped on the page that had the shaggy, snarling face of the wolf man on it. I was completely terrified and stayed up most of that night crying.

But, then next day, I went to school again and took the book off the shelf once more, and that defines my relationship with horror: from a very young age I've been addicted to the genre. And I was reading Stephen King in third grade, sneaking books off my parents' shelf.

Jill: I did that exact same thing.

Ben: I think that everybody begins with genre. We fall in love with reading because we are obsessed with books that have dragons on the cover, or cowboys, or spies in overcoats, or whatever. I mean I went through a period where I was reading sci-fi novels. I went through another period where I was reading Tony Hillerman mysteries. I went through another period where I was reading Zane Grey novels.

Then I went to school and ended up in creative-writing workshops where genre was forbidden, so I fell away from it for a while. But then I encountered this book by Michael Chabon called *Thrilling Tales* that McSweeney's Books put out. In the introduction to *Thrilling Tales,* Chabon talks about how literary fiction is a genre of its own, and it always ends sparkling with epiphanic dew, nothing ever happens in it, etc. And he says that, ideally, what if we straddled the two worlds?

What if we took what's best about literary fiction—the gorgeous sentences, the gorgeous metaphors, the three-dimensional characters—and blended that together with what's best about genre, which is the propulsive quality that it has because it concerns itself primarily with what happens next?

When you take literary fiction and you blend it together with plotted fiction, you have a beautiful thing. You have the work of Margaret Atwood. You have the work of Jonathan Lethem, of Dan Simmons, of Dennis Lehane, and I'm very interested in this sort of hybrid writing.

It's nothing new. I've been reading for years the work of Steven Millhauser, Peter Straub, people who care about craft as much as they do a rip-roaring plot. But it's only recently that it really clicked for me, and I really began to pursue it in a concerted way. Justin Cronin, I think, really paved the way for what I'm hoping to do.

Jill: I noticed at least twice in the stories in *Refresh, Refresh* that you use an image of reaching through something that seems solid otherwise. One time you're describing Portland and its moisture, and you say something like, it seems as though you could just reach through the sidewalk or the sky and pull out a handful of wriggling worms. It occurred to me that a lot of your work could be said to deal with breaking through the surface of things, beneath this veneer of solidity or civility as though some more real, frequently darker, version of the world is underneath.

Ben: Yes, you certainly see that in the "Caves of Oregon," where a door opens up and a staircase descends, and that's where the relationship between these two people plays out. You see that again with characters like the ones in "Somebody Is Going to Have to Pay for This." After night falls, they take on a much more foreboding stance as they creep along the streets and peer in windows.

I think that one of the central ideas of *The Wilding* also comes out of this. There's the face we put on when we're around others, our outside face. And then there's our inside face, the one beneath the masks we wear. If you boil it down to a thesis, it's the idea that when you push back, when you push past the veneer, as you say, we're all hairy on the inside.

Jill: I love the treatment of animals in your work, too, just in general, but especially in *The Wilding*. There are so many. There are snakes and bats and owls and bears and deer and wolves, to name just a few. I find it interesting that you give animals almost as much pride of place in some of your work as people.

Percy: I'm also very interested in the way that these intersections occur between civilization and wilderness, if you think of the environmental sensibility of the novel. You have this wilderness area that's going to be torn up, and a golf course community built over it.

If you look at the beginning of *The Wilding,* you have a bear tangled up in a barbed wire fence. If you look at the neighborhoods of Boulder, Colorado, you have cougars lurking about and carrying off toddlers into the trees.

As we continue to develop, as we continue to expand, as we raze forests and lay down concrete, there's going to be a kind of confusion of boundaries that occurs. That's one of the central concerns of the novel. It's no surprise then that you have animals rising up and sharing the stage with humans, and their characteristics aren't too different.

Jill: I have to ask—do you have a real life bear story?

Percy: I worked in Glacier National Park one summer. I worked sometimes as a waiter, but my primary job there was gardener, which seems like a really bizarre gig, to be a gardener at Many Glacier Lodge. I was not doing a lot during that time: mowing the lawn, watering the geraniums, and otherwise hiding in the gardener's shed, reading or napping.

The rest of the time I spent hitting the trails and camping in the backcountry. That park is crawling with grizzly bears, and I lived in constant fear of being consumed by one of them. When I first got there, when I got off the train at Glacier, I was told that one of my colleagues, one of the other people hired on for summer work, had just been eaten. And they found his boots with his feet still in them, and a long strip of his vertebrae.

It was a mother with her cubs. Supposedly she now had no fear and even had a taste for human flesh. Later on my roommate was on a hike, and that same bear and her cubs bluff charged my friend for ten miles.

Can you imagine how terrifying that would be? Ten miles of being chased by grizzlies, chased and paced by them. Those grizzlies were later hunted down and killed. But I would be mowing the lawn, and I would look up at the hillside surrounding the lodge and I could spot sometimes fourteen grizzlies, moving among the huckleberry thickets.

I was crossing the parking lot one night moving from the bar to the dormitory, and then this black shape crossed in front of me. I was hiking down trails and a grizzly would shoot across twenty yards ahead of me, moving from one thicket to another. I would be camping, asleep in my tent, when all of a sudden I heard heavy footsteps thudding around my tent. That summer brought out the terror. I had a lot of close calls, and you'll see that emotion on the page.

Jill: How do you think about writing on the paragraph level or the sentence level?

Ben: I pay a lot of attention to the line by line. I think of writing as a kind of music, and I read aloud everything that I write. I think I have an ear for just the orchestration of it, and I'm trying to always make the style match the content. In moments where maybe the character is in a fragmented state of mind, I'm trying to have a series of choppy sentences. I'm trying in a moment that is maybe swelling in its power to have a series of long, lyrical sentences.

I'm trying to constantly expand and contract the length of sentences to create a kind of rolling rhythm. This is something that doesn't happen in the first draft. It's something that happens as I continuously run sandpaper over the burrs of an initial rush of writing. It's hard for me to say anything more than that, except that as a teacher, I'm intensely concerned with craft. I don't think ideas can be taught.

I don't think that passion can be taught. I don't think that vision be taught.

But I know that you can help people understand how to employ the arsenal of tools available to a writer. I've spent a lot of time reading books like *Rhetorical Grammar* by Martha Kolln, where she talks about grammatical choices and rhetorical effects. I've spent a lot of time outlining the paragraphs and the pages of Denis Johnson, and Tim O'Brien, and Flannery O'Connor, trying to figure out how their work ticks. I'm very strategic and very mathematical in the way that I put together every element of a line, which adds up to every component of the story.

Book Notes

This essay first appeared on the blog Largehearted Boy. Reprinted with permission.

I write in silence, but I revise to music. There is something about the zone—that coma-like place I visit when writing first drafts—that requires no distraction, no noise at all except the insectile buzz of my desk lamp. I am gone, completely checked out of this world, my mouth slack, my eyes glazed, and sometimes I rise up from the ether after several hours with five pages in front of me that I haven't written so much as I have dreamed.

But revision is careful carpentry. Revision is where I sand away all the splinters, caulk the cracks, tighten the screws. And I'm in a much different mindset, no longer following my heart but my head. I pace around. I do pushups. I chew on pens. And I listen to music to put me in the mood of a scene.

Here are some of the songs I was tapping my boots to when tapping my fingers across the keyboard.

"Dueling Banjos"—Arthur "Guitar Boogie" Smith

This is the fortieth anniversary of James Dickey's novel [*Deliverance*]. It is one of the most important books in my library and its themes—about development, the jarring intersections of society and wilderness, the latent animalism within us all—are explored again in my novel, set in the vanishing West and seen through the lens of myriad point of view characters. When writing, I could not help but think of Dickey's ghost perched on my shoulder, and when I wrote a scene in which a wilderness map is laid out on a table, held down by Starbucks cups (a direct nod to the novel), I heard the distant tremble of banjos.

"In the Air Tonight"—Phil Collins

My first memory of this song, which is one of my unapologetic favorites, comes from a short-lived series on Fox—in the late 80s—called *Werewolf.* I recorded the pilot and watched it dozens of times. There is a moment when the hero—who does not yet know he is a werewolf—is wandering through a nightclub. As the song plays, he shoulders his way through a dancing throb of people, so many of them eyeing him suspiciously. There is something wrong with him, they know. He ends up stumbling out of the club and holding up his palm, which bleeds in the shape of a pentagram. And then he sprouts fur and fangs and eats some people. There is a character in *The Wilding*—named Brian—who has come back from Iraq with a hole punched through his skull, the result of an IED. The damage to his frontal lobe has left him emotionally damaged. He does not feel so much as he hungers. He has trouble interacting with people, his company best suited for the woods. He begins to trap animals and sews their hides together into a hair suit that he wears at night. It feels to him like armor—and when he moves through the shadow-soaked woods, negotiating the periphery of Bend, Oregon—he feels so alive, experiencing an almost lycanthropic transformation. During these scenes, I often had this song playing through the caves of my mind, taking me back to that time, so many years ago, when I watched *Werewolf* over and over, obsessed with the show for the supernatural element, yeah, but more so the story of the outsider.

"*Braveheart* Main Title Score"—James Horner, performed by the London Symphony Orchestra

Do not mock me. This movie makes my heart swell (so long as I forget about Mel Gibson's recent descent into freakdom). For whatever reason, maybe the time I spent backpacking in Scotland, I associate misty woods, the mucky roll of the moors, sweeping shots of nature, with the noise of bagpipes. A good chunk of my novel takes place in a wilderness area—called Echo Canyon—in the weekend before construction will begin on a golf course community. As the men zigzag their way up hillsides, wade across rivers, tramp through piney forests, I found myself listening to the *Braveheart* score, which sent my author's gaze taking in the shadowy expanse of this canyon.

"Big Man with a Gun"—Nine Inch Nails

A grandson, a father, a grandfather. Graham, Justin, and Paul. They are a kind of Darwinian lineup. The grandson so delicate, his eyes studying constantly a book or a video game—the grandfather so enormous and hairy and wild, dominating every conversation, his hands crushing a grip around a fishing rod, a boning knife, a rifle stock. Caught in the middle is Justin, who—as a teacher who now lives a very domestic life—finds himself torn between the two extremes, his son pitted against him by a grandfather trying to mold a new son more in his own image. The dark, sharp-edged lyrics compellingly wrestle with the violence and the rooster-chested challenges that edge their way between the pained, difficult love existing between these men.

"I and Love and You"—The Avett Brothers
One of my favorite songs from one of my favorite bands. My ears never tire of their rusty voices, their rambling lyrics. They sing here about a pained love—"my hands they shake, my head it spins"—that has lost its course, that is trying to find its way. "Three words that became hard to say—I and love and you." This poignant longing is at the center of my novel, seen the perspectives of three different men, all of them in love and lust with the same woman who eventually settles back into a marriage she at first wanted nothing more than to escape.

"Hurt"—Johnny Cash (cover of Nine Inch Nails)
One of my central characters—Brian—is a wounded soldier home from Iraq. An IED detonated beneath his Humvee, and a piece of metal, driven through the air, excised part of his skull and left a spider-shaped lesion on his frontal lobe. He can't feel the way he once did: he acts on animalistic impulse. And he is plagued by migraines that blind him and turn him into a thing half-alive. He is the very definition of hurt.

"I Love the Dead"—Alice Cooper
There is a moment, later in the novel, when Justin realizes he may not make it out of the canyon. His father is missing. His truck is destroyed. Night is falling. And the great shambling presence of a bear lurks at the edges of his vision. He finds himself temporarily unable to act—paralyzed—the walls of the canyon rising all around him and I imagine the steadily darkening woods as a sound-chamber for the wail of this banshee song, mocking his indecision.

Recommended Reading

Wilderness Adventure Novels

Deliverance by James Dickey
The Call of the Wild by Jack London
Blood Meridian by Cormac McCarthy
Lonesome Dove by Larry McMurtry
McTeague by Frank Norris
The Terror by Dan Simmons
Angle of Repose by Wallace Stegner

Environmental Texts

Why I Came West by Rick Bass
Silent Spring by Rachel Carson
Hole in the Sky by William Kittredge
A Sand County Almanac by Aldo Leopold
Coop by Michael Perry
Where the Bluebird Sings to the Lemonade Springs by Wallace Stegner
Refuge by Terry Tempest Williams

BENJAMIN PERCY is the author of *The Language of Elk* and *Refresh, Refresh.* His honors include the Plimpton Prize, a Pushcart Prize, a Whiting Writers' Award, and inclusion in *Best American Short Stories.* His fiction and nonfiction have been published by *Esquire, Men's Journal,* the *Paris Review,* and *Orion.* He teaches in the MFA program in creative writing and environment at Iowa State University.

Book design by Rachel Holscher. Composition by BookMobile Design and Publishing Services, Minneapolis, Minnesota. Manufactured by Versa Press on acid-free 30 percent postconsumer wastepaper.